My Fat

To Neil,

Enjoy this of M.C.

Cheers,

Philip

Philip R. Jordan

My Father's Letters

Copyright © 2008 Philip R. Jordan

The moral right of the author has been asserted.

Apart from any fair dealing for the purposes of research or private study, or criticism or review, as permitted under the Copyright, Designs and Patents Act 1988, this publication may only be reproduced, stored or transmitted, in any form or by any means, with the prior permission in writing of the publishers, or in the case of reprographic reproduction in accordance with the terms of licences issued by the Copyright Licensing Agency. Enquiries concerning reproduction outside those terms should be sent to the publishers.

Matador
9 De Montfort Mews
Leicester LE1 7FW, UK
Tel: (+44) 116 255 9311 / 9312
Email: books@troubador.co.uk
Web: www.troubador.co.uk/matador

ISBN 978-1906221-607

Typeset in 11pt Bembo by Troubador Publishing Ltd, Leicester, UK
Printed by Cromwell Press Ltd, Trowbridge, Wiltshire, UK

Matador is an imprint of Troubador Publishing Ltd

To Dawn

Prologue

Prague, 1999

The footsteps echoing loudly behind me suddenly stopped. Glancing over my shoulder all three men had disappeared and I stumbled into a doorway panting. After two large gulps of night air I zipped up my jacket, grasping the large envelope concealed inside. My hotel meant security; I had to get there. I was certainly no native to Prague but I recalled a narrow street just ahead could be a short cut to my goal.

I stepped out quickly from the doorway; my body hunched forward looking neither left nor right. The alley way was only fifty meters and I turned into it, relieved. In the daytime puppet and gift shops intermingled with cafes and bars, now everything was locked and boarded up and the street looked empty and menacing. The alley narrowed after a hundred meters and I became disorientated. I stopped, and fumbled for my street map.

I never saw the owner of the fist that struck hard on my upper jaw. My knees buckled and cracked onto the hard damp cobbles. The thick, sweet metallic flavour of blood engulfed my taste buds. One arm instinctively clutched my precious packet whilst the other lashed out at my attacker, hitting only the cool damp air.

A snarled laugh was followed by a kick in the middle of my back; the resulting scream stifled by lack of air. My body crumbled further onto the floor despite my brain demanding action. The brain was right; another kick connected with my kidneys causing my body to jack knife. Still no air to scream. In a blur I saw a foot draw back and I rolled myself into a ball. The kick never came.

Strong hands grabbed my arms and forced me onto my back. My jacket was ripped open and the envelope extracted. At first I didn't dare open my eyes in case it antagonised them.

'Danke, mein Herr,' was spat at me in a mock German accent.

I finally looked up to be face to face with a man I had only briefly seen twice in my life, his distinctive tattoos confirming I had not mistaken his identity. This time he had won. He let go and I saw the other man stand drawing back his leg; his intentions clear. I put my arms around my head and cursed.

'No,' came a deep, well spoken voice from the shadows. 'We have what we want. Leave the poor wretch.' Shouts came from the main street. I recognised the tall man with long grey hair as he stepped forward. 'Well young Pinner, it seems luck is on your side again,' he said glancing behind him. He took the envelope from one of the other men. 'I'll be in touch again after I have read all these,' he said starting towards me.

I drew my knees up putting my arms around my head and closed my eyes, waiting for another beating. I heard my tormentor's footsteps fading into the distant hum of a city. I rolled onto my back and tried to get up, but the pain caused me to wince and I slumped back onto the cold ground.

Hurt, but relieved at being alive, I lay still in disbelief at the recent chain of events. 'Thanks Dad,' I whispered to the night sky. 'You always said I needed a good hiding. If you're looking after me from your heavenly haunt then you have a strange way of doing it.'

More commotion came from the main street and I saw some figures calling out and approaching a little warily. I did make out the word "Police", or something similar, and relief cascaded through my body. Several people arrived and fussed around me talking quickly in a language where not a single word was comprehendible. They gently helped me to my feet and I shuffled to a nearby bench. I could hear the sound of a siren getting louder.

I shook my head slowly reliving the last few moments. My life had changed since I had found and started to read; *My Father's Letters* …

Chapter 1

MISSION TO POLAND

September 1944

The Mk111 Wellington Bomber, affectionately known as a Whimey, struggled with the thin air at 15,000 feet heading East by South East for Poland. Unseen pockets of turbulence would catch the twin engined bomber and buffer the aircraft as if a light toy in the night sky. Flight Lieutenant Paul Pinner checked his instruments and altered the trim, staring into the dark abyss below. The smell of cordite from the gun tests was slowly being taken over by the scent of aviation fuel, wood and leather. Flashes of light to the south illuminated the sky and sent eerie shadows into the cockpit highlighting his co-pilot who was scribbling on his thigh pad.

Pinner lent forward to take a further look at the flashes over Northern Germany. 'It looks like another big raid tonight.'

His co-pilot Peter Wilkinson glanced up and shrugged. 'Serves them right,' he said returning back to his pad.

'It must be strange to unleash such fury on an unseen enemy,' continued Pinner, glad to have never been on a night bombing raid. The moonlight highlighted the dust particles floating inside the cockpit.

'Well I'm glad we aren't over there in this old tub,' said the navigator, George Tomkins, over the intercom.

Wilkinson switch his radio to just his skipper. 'When are you going to tell them?' he asked already knowing the answer.

'When I have to, you know that.' Pinner looked forward trying to make out the coastline far below him.

'I hope it will be worth it. Bloody risky business in broad day light, if you ask me,' said Wilkinson admiring his handy work on the pad.

'Well nobody is asking you,' Pinner said glancing sideways at his co-pilot. Their eyes met for a second. 'You know the rules Wilkie, so let's drop it.'

'Sorry skip, I'll shut up. It is just sometimes I wished I knew more.'

'Trust me you don't,' said Pinner straining to look at his co-pilot's thigh pad. 'Anyway what is that you are writing? In all the two years I have known you I have never seen you write anything, and how you can manage with all this turbulence is beyond me.'

'Well I'm not writing, but drawing a plan,' said Wilkie tearing off the top sheet and handing it to his skipper. Pinner tried to make the drawing out, turning it around and raising his eyebrows to Wilkinson in an enquiring manner. 'Well, I'm sick of this war,' continued the co-pilot, 'and afterwards I have decided to become an architect in the hope of rebuilding the mess we've made.'

'It is not over yet, Wilkie,' said Pinner glancing at his instruments. 'I am still hoping that Operation Scorpion, I told you about, will work.' Pinner was almost whispering into his oxygen mask and wanted to tell his friend everything. 'If not, I think the Nazis will fight to the last man, but then we will be faced with a new neighbour. A neighbour whose culture and politics are so diverse from our own, it will only result in more conflict and …'

'So tell me,' interrupted Wilkie, 'why are we flying into Russian held territory, delivering sensitive equipment to help *their* war effort?'

The memory of a small room off Piccadilly, flashed back into Pinner's mind, this is where he had been told about Operation Scorpion and how he would be required to assist, as and when necessary. He recalled the plans for his next mission to Poland, especially the return route; his body made an involuntary shudder. This operation would only mean more war, where allies would become foe and enemies our friends. He shook his head lightly to rid himself of the memory of that day.

'I could see you as an architect,' he said ignoring Wilkie's outburst and leaning to his right he threw a playful punch at his co-pilot. 'It is about time you started thinking about your future and not just beer and girls.'

'It's alright for you. Public school, Cambridge, beautiful and wealthy girlfriend. You don't have to think too hard if you make it through the war,' said Wilkie smiling at him through his oxygen mask.

Pinner frowned and turned away. He hadn't heard from Marie for weeks. The American base not far from his home town had had mixed reaction from the locals. The young women seemed to approve, or so his mother had told him in a recent letter. Pinner sat silently and sensed Wilkie occasionally looking at him. After a short time dawn was starting to dispel the darkness, and the navigator broke the silence.

'Turn five degrees to starboard, Skip.' Tomkins may not have wanted to be in the bomber command but he was a superb navigator, "lost" was not in his vocabulary. 'I estimate you should see the airfield in 20 minutes.'

'Ruddy hell, we're early aren't we?'

'Tail wind all the way, but we will be fighting it on the return,' said Tomkins woefully. Fuel was always a concern on these missions.

Pinner started to descend but could not make anything out in the gloom below. Eventually he saw the control tower and two large hangers. The radio crackled into life and a message was barked to them in a foreign tongue.

'The wind is from the East at 12 knots,' translated Polanski, the front gunner. Polanski had acquired this name when he first joined up. His eyes were dark and sad as the first rays of light revealed his shattered and scarred homeland.

Pinner made two circuits over the airfield to get his bearings and to allow the sunlight a little more chance to break the gloom.

He headed west, banked for his final approach, engaged the flaps and de-throttling he dropped the under-carriage. The radio crackled another command.

Polanski translated again. 'We are to follow a truck once we have landed and await instructions.'

'Usual friendly style,' muttered Wilkinson.

Pinner added some rudder to compensate for a light side wind and touched down for a near perfect landing. An old grey truck waited for them at the end of the runway and Pinner followed him with the plane bouncing on the hard uneven surface to one of the hangers. Wilkinson shut down the engines and finally the vibrating stopped. No one stirred. A Russian grease monkey came out of the hanger wiping his hands on a dirty cloth and waved at the bomber. He turned and shouted to someone inside.

'Come on everyone, we have a job to do. Our Russian friends have to unload the cargo,' instructed Pinner.

Slowly the crew exited from the front hatch way and Pinner opened the bomb doors. He disembarked the aircraft to be greeted by two fighters coming into land.

'Christ, they're Hurricanes,' said David Stewart, the rear gunner. 'How come they've got those?'

'Well you're young enough to still believe in Father Christmas,' said Wilkinson watching the fighters taxi to the other side of the airfield. 'They are supposed to be to help their war effort against the Nazis.'

'What do you mean, suppose to be ...?'

'Hello, yar!' came a shout from the hanger. Out strode their usual contact, his overalls stained with oil. 'I have prepared some good English breakfast, yar.' He ushered the men towards a small hut. 'Sorry, but no pig, it has come out.'

Pinner winced at the Russian's English. Fortunately this man seemed eager to please rather than calculating and professional. Pinner suspected he had ambitions to come West after the war, and thankfully rarely checked his aircraft. Today was no exception and after an awkward conversation over breakfast Pinner pressed to leave. To his surprise a fuel truck was already at the aircraft, its exhaust fumes engulfing most of the bomber in black smoke.

Pinner climbed the ladder into the bomber and met a uniformed Russian who was examining the navigator's table. Pinner coughed loudly, with more than a hint of anger and the Russian recoiled from Tomkins' position. The intruder said something quickly in Russian and scrambled out of the hatch. Pinner waited a few moments and started to check that the cameras and the package were still in their concealed places. Wilkinson entered the aircraft and called to his Captain.

'All in order and would you believe they have given us some fuel...' Wilkinson spotted Pinner checking the hidden compartments. 'What's up?'

'Let's get out of here, I'll tell you when we are airborne.'

Wilkinson shouted to the rest of the crew to get ready. A few minutes later and after the checks had been completed, Pinner gunned the Hercules engines and slid away from the hanger. Their contact waved to them from the hanger door and mouthed good luck. The radio came to life but Pinner didn't need to have it translated that they were clear for take-off and he opened the throttles before Polanski could come on the intercom.

The plane hurtled down the runway passing the two Hurricanes and as Pinner pulled back the controls the plane growled in protest due to the strain being put upon it. He banked westward.

'What was that all about earlier?' asked the co-pilot.

'I found one of them snooping around the aircraft.'

Wilkinson turned to his captain. 'Oh hell, do they suspect anything?'

Pinner shrugged his shoulders. He clicked his intercom switch. 'Right, first part of our task over with, but as usual we have to take some photographs of the local scenery,' said Pinner to the whole crew, trying to sound matter of fact. He looked towards his co-pilot. 'Oh, and we will be making a small detour over northern Holland. We have a package to deliver at low altitude, a sort of person-to-person service.'

No one responded. A lone bomber in broad daylight, at low altitude, close to the Western front was not a prospect to be relished. Pinner suspected the men had thought he had gone crazy; they may not be wrong.

'Take the controls Wilkie,' said Pinner unclipping his mask. He went to the navigator's position and opened his orders. 'Tomkins,' he said, 'we have to go to Torun on the Wista River. There is a railway line heading to Warsaw, and in a siding nearby are several cargo trucks we need to see.'

'I'll get straight onto it, Sir.'

Pinner pulled out an envelope from his inside pocket and took out a sheet of paper. 'Then make for these coordinates,' he said stooping over a chart. 'It is an island called Ameland. On the South Eastern coast there is a small bay which will have a large field to its north where four crosses will be marked out on the ground. You have to drop the parcel in the middle.'

'Right Skip, I can't see a problem with the navigation, but …'

'That's all Tomkins, leave the thinking to me.'

'Sir.'

Pinner went back to his seat. 'Right everyone, be very vigilant,' he said into the intercom. 'Tomkins when you have the courses let me know and could you check every so often in the navigation dome for aircraft.'

'Right Skipper. Turn 15 degrees to port for Torun. We should see the river in fifteen minutes.'

'You had better get ready,' said Pinner to his co-pilot. 'Stewart could you come forward and help Wilkinson.'

The co-pilot started to unscrew the hidden compartment beneath the control panel. Slowly he handed the pieces of camera to the young rear-gunner, who had just arrived onto the flight deck. They went down to bombardier's position and assembled the equipment. When all was ready Wilkie indicated for the rear-gunner to return to his position.

'Tomkins come up here and help me spot anything around the railway line,' said Pinner searching the ground in front of him.

The landscape was littered with the remnants of war. Burnt out bridges, black scorched scars, empty roofless buildings and a thin veil of smoke seemed to be desperate to shroud man's destruction.

'I can't make out anything, I'll go down a bit,' said Pinner almost to himself. Tomkins flashed him a frown. Pinner ignored it and put the nose down de-throttling at the same time.

'There, just to right of that big church,' cried Wilkinson. 'My God, there must be hundreds of freight trucks.'

'Ack-ack battery to the north,' shouted the Pole.

'No lower skipper,' screamed Wilkinson.

'You take the ruddy photographs,' bellowed Pinner.

Two flashes of orange and brown burst in front of them.

'Ruddy hell,' hissed Pinner. 'Get back to your position Tomkins!'

Pinner banked round increasing the revs and pulling the nose of the bomber up. Two more explosions below them sent a vibration through the aircraft. Several more this time further away and Pinner willed the bomber on.

The ack-ack stopped but no one spoke or moved for several minutes. Wilkinson eventually came back to his position giving his skipper a concerned look.

'Take a course 280 degrees skipper,' said the navigator over the intercom.

'Still going for the drop?' said Wilkinson.

'Yes.'

'I thought you might have had enough excitement for one day,' said Wilkinson trying to lighten the atmosphere.

'This is not a ruddy outing Wilkie.' Pinner levelled the aircraft at 15,000 feet and set the trim. 'I don't know what is in this packet, but I am pretty sure it is important for Scorpion.'

Wilkinson nodded at his captain and indicated he had the controls. Pinner lent back and rubbed his sore eyes. 'Did you get any photographs?'

'Yes. As you banked round I had a perfect angle on the whole sidings yard,' said Wilkinson adjusting the controls. 'There were some very strange looking shapes down there.'

Pinner lent down and extracted a thick metal tube from under his seat. He went to the rear of the plane and spoke to Tomkins and the young rear-gunner, giving them their instructions. Three hours later Tomkins indicated they were close. Pinner could make out Ameland clearly and started a slow decent. He wanted only one run at it. He crossed over the coast at 4,000 feet.

Pinner felt the aircraft yaw to the port just as the rear-gunner screamed the warning of an ack-ack battery below them. The bomber shuddered violently making Wilkinson hold onto the controls as if his life depended on it. Pinner also instinctively grabbed the controls at first to help, but he then yelled for Wilkinson to go and check the damage. The co-pilot ran aft to where the young rear-gunner was shouting and pointing to the Starboard tailplane and rudder. Wilkinson squeezed into the gun position and a few seconds later could see enough to access the damage. He rushed back to his position.

'Christ there is no record of that ack-ack battery,' he said to his skipper watching him fighting with the controls. 'We need altitude, Sir.'

Pinner pressed the intercom. 'Tomkins, Stewart, you know what to do.'

Wilkinson looked at his captain aghast.

'Look ahead we are right on line for the drop,' said Pinner still struggling with the controls. 'Tomkins I'm stable at 3,000 feet.'

Wilkinson strapped himself in and saw the four white crosses just off a beach ahead of them.

'How bad is it Wilkie?'

'Difficult to tell, but there are bits of wood hanging out of the starboard tail wing and the rudder is flapping.'

'I know I can feel it.' Pinner stared ahead and decided to bank rather than use any rudder. 'Tomkins are we on it?'

'Keep this course and level,' he replied. 'Open the bomb doors.'

Pinner's mouth was dry but the sweat from the palms of his hands had made his gloves moist.

'Now Stewart, *now*,' screamed the navigator. Pinner turned round to see the rear-gunner throw the metal tube through the bomb doors. He nodded at Wilkinson to close the doors.

'Altitude I think you said,' croaked Pinner his throat tight and dry, pushing the throttles and bringing the nose up.

Slowly the aircraft ascended making the Altimeter turn slowly clockwise; Ameland disappeared beneath them. A high pitch whine was followed by a metallic grinding. Pinner turned desperately looking at his port engine from where the noise had originated. His heart sank as he saw a thin, wispy trail of smoke from the spluttering engine. He shot a glance at his co-pilot and, in unison, they both looked ahead. The English coast was still nearly 200 miles away.

AIRMAIL / PAR AVION

180450 F/L Paul Pinner
September 1944

Dear Mother,

I have so much to tell you, and so little time or even space to write. However, as usual, I hope you will fully understand I cannot give any details of my location for operational reasons. First, how are Dad, James and your good self? I cannot wait to see you all again, it seems an age since I was home. Thank you for your last letter, and do not let things pray on your mind so much. How many times have you told me not to worry, and that life has a habit of sorting itself out. Dad will be alright, but please make sure he sees a doctor; those dizzy spells do seem to be very odd.

Have you noticed my 'deliberate mistake'? Well, it is not a mistake; I have been promoted to Flight Lieutenant. I will get another 5s per day! Naturally I will send some home to help, especially with Dad being ill.

We celebrated my promotion at a flight dinner, which are always great affairs. These dinners include all from the C.O., to lowly cadets. We all sit around a long table with the C.O. (known as the 'old man') at the head, and go through the usual procedure of soup, hors-d'oeuvre, main, sweet, and finally we drink the King's health. After dinner we clear the decks, strip off to the waist and do a bit of in-door rugger. Another game is to stand in two lines facing one another and cross arms. The senior officers then take it in turn to jump on the crossed arms and be pitched into the air as they are flung down the line, even the prim and proper, dignified C.O. takes his turn. F/O Ross hit an electric light and broke it. It is difficult to believe that these fellows are the disciplinarians of the day – but they are all great sports.

The same night Ross did his aerial act, the C.G.I. (Squadron Leader Cummings) was hiding in his office. A chorus of "we want the C.G.I.!" went up in the mess. It took twelve heavily built cadets and F/Os to drag him out. Was he tough? He laid out three of them in the fight and bruised many others, and broke two windows to boot. We were flying the next day and you can imagine the state we were in.

I am thinking of you all a lot, but I have not heard much from Marie. Mother, I have to say your concerns about the amount of Americans being around has given me some jitters. Could you please ask her to write, or check she has the right address; I need to know what she is up to!

I flew back home the other day and England looked so green and lush. It was difficult to believe there was a war on. The fields were full of workers. Even from the air the villages seemed to be bustling. The only sign of war was my own plane which had suffered some anti-aircraft fire. Don't worry we made it safely home; the Wellingtons are tough old planes and take some knocking out of the sky.

Then suddenly, we saw a burnt out plane, I was furious that they had not moved it. It was definitely one of ours, and I could clearly see the remains of a fuselage. It is hard enough to keep morale high without having to contend with such sights. I have to confess to looking forward to the end of the war. My fear is the Germans will fight to the bitter end but then we will be faced by a new challenge. Can we really trust the Russians?

I have changed billets recently, due to the promotion, and I have to admit I like the new system. I share a Batman, who is very helpful, but he has a wicked wit, and a very pronounced Liverpool accent. At first I was not sure how to take him, and was prepared to tear a strip off him. However, it is just his way and I am now used to him. The only problem I have is he manages to obtain lots of cigarettes, which I am sure are from the black market. He also seems to be friendly with every young female for miles around.

The man is very brash and to demonstrate this he heard the C.G.I. was looking for a present for his young boy. Out of nowhere there came a train set, and an admirable looking one at that. He sold it to the C.G.I., who eyed him with much suspicion, but could not resist such an opportunity to spoil his son. Incidentally, he was found to have it out in his quarters a few days later. Nobody dared tease him after his performance the night we dragged him out of his quarters!

Leave is proving frustrating, as the maximum, at the moment, is 48 hours and I cannot make it home in time. I would love to write more but I have to go now. When I come home remember to ask me about the recent guest night we had. The place was littered with girls, and we had to behave ourselves, as if we would do anything else? Don't mention this to Marie, or maybe you should!

All my love,

Paul
xx

Chapter 2

London, June 1999

Max Lilley rolled onto his left side causing his long grey hair to fall over his eyes. Pushing the hair back he watched the contours of the sheet which matched the womanly shape underneath. He put his hand on the nape of her neck and stroked downwards pushing the sheet aside slowly revealing his lover's back. The early morning sun emphasised the highlights in her hair and he could just make out the change in skin colour at the bikini line on the top of her buttocks. He moved his hand under the sheet stroking her firm bottom and then his fingers probed gently between her legs. She turned onto her back making a fake protest groan, but outstretched her arms around his neck and pulled him towards her. Feeling his manhood she wrapped her legs around his and raised her body against him. They embraced for a while and Lilley felt his ardour start to increase, his heart rate causing a thumping sound in his chest cavity. He moved his hips back to adjust himself for further intimacy when the phone made a shrill metallic ring.

'Damn,' he said in a deep voice, leaning over her to stop the unbearable noise.

'Good morning Mr. Lilley, your wake up call,' came a voice from the phone.

'Thank you,' he said hoarsely slamming the phone down and rolling back over the woman onto his back. His manhood already lying limp and still on his groin.

'Max, you hurt me you heavy lump,' said Alison gently rubbing her left breast.

'Stop whinging Ali; it was you that wanted to be up early this morning,' said Lilley checking his watch.

'I remember the time when you would have ignored the bloody fire alarm to finish what you had begun with me,' she said still massaging her ample bosom.

'Yes well, that was when I was younger,' said Lilley stretching his torso. 'Christ I'm seventy three and you still expect me to shag like a thirty year old. Do you realise one night with you takes me weeks to get over.'

'So that's why you hardly ever call me,' she said leaning over and cradling his testicles in her hand. 'I was starting to think you only called me when you wanted information, or does my new husband frighten you?'

Lilley swung quickly out of bed and walked to the bathroom. He searched for a bathrobe which he found hanging behind the door. He struggled to disentangle the tightly knotted waist cord.

'Why do they tie these things so damn tight?' he shouted back into the bedroom. He caught a glimpse of her naked body; the sheet draped partly over one leg. He considered going back to her but he was exhausted from lack of sleep, too much wine and a physical night of passion.

'Alison, could you call room service and order my usual.'

'Yes, sir,' she answered in a submissive voice. 'So I do have my uses in the morning after all.'

Lilley shaved and tried to ignore the sagging jaw line and bags under his eyes. He continually had to keep pushing back his hair. She was right, he thought, twenty years ago nothing would have curtailed their passion. He stopped and looked into the bedroom. She was lying on her back her legs twisted to one side and her arms behind her head. He gaped at her in awe remembering when he had taken her for the first time. What a catch, if anyone had known they would have been jealous, that's for sure. He had only loved one other woman, and even this beauty laid out naked in front of him, many years his junior, would never be able to match her. It was at times like this that he felt a loneliness creep from the recesses of his mind to ambush his enjoyment. At least he still saw Alison a few times a year; not perfect but it was something.

Lilley put on the shower. 'May need some help scrubbing my back,' he said putting his head back into the bedroom. Alison slid smoothly out of the bed and sauntered provocatively towards him, her long hair dropping over her shoulders. Age had thickened her figure but as she moved towards him, Lilley was memorised by her swaying body. She slowly pushed him backwards into the shower and started to lather his body; pleased with his reaction which she could clearly see. When she was finished she handed him the soap.

'Your turn,' she said watching the suds flow down his body. 'I don't care what you say about your age you certainly look after yourself, Max.'

'And you my girl are all woman,' said Max rubbing the soap over her breasts and down her belly.

The door bell sounded at least three times before Lilley could pull himself away. Dripping wet, towel around his midriff, he let the waiter in and found some change to tip him, leaving wet foot prints on the carpet. Alison had finished the shower and was also having trouble untying her bathrobe.

'You're losing your timing Max old boy,' she said grabbing a croissant as she re-entered the bedroom.

They started to get ready totally at ease with each other. Twenty years of an illicit affair had brought a degree of familiarity. Max splashed copious amounts of aftershave over his reddening face.

'My God Max what is that?' said his lover curling up her nose. 'Smells stronger than your usual.' Max just pulled a tongue at her and continued dressing. She brushed her hair looking at herself in the mirror. A pang of guilt stung her as she looked at her half naked body and the blurred image of her lover behind her. No wonder her marriages didn't work she thought. She would kill her husband if she even suspected he was unfaithful. She, however, had cheated on her third husband already and after only two months. She put her hair up fighting back some tears. She stopped and looked at her lover in the mirror again. If only Lilley hadn't been such a moody bastard, she thought, she may well have tried to make a go with him. She recalled the night he had lost his temper and hit her. It was not only the physical humiliation, but the feeling of betrayal she had felt, that finally made up her mind to keep a certain distance from him. But when it came to sex she was like a moth attracted to a light. He had been the best by far, no one else had come close and despite her attempts to break from him she had always come meekly back asking for more.

Lilley came up behind her and kissed on the top of her head.

'Thanks for getting me the information on Paul Pinner; I hope I repaid you amply,' he said, looking at her swaying breasts in the mirror.

'Yeah, last night was OK, but you lost it this morning.'

Lilley gave her a two handed prod in her kidneys.

'Oh, Max that hurts,' she howled trying to catch one of his legs with her hair brush. 'Anyway what's up between you and this Pinner guy anyway? He left MI6 absolutely ages ago.'

Lilley sat on the bed and put on his shoes. 'Well there's nothing between us now; he's dead. May his soul rot in hell.'

'Yes, there was …' she started to speak, but stopped. Lilley saw her hesitation and strode towards her grabbing her arm pulling her from her stool and swinging her round. Her hair came loose and fell down and Lilley couldn't help and watch her breasts joggle helplessly in front of him. He enjoyed the sight.

'Max, you're hurting me,' she said trying to release his grip on the top of her arm. 'I told you if you hurt me ever again…' she said continuing to struggle. Lilley glowered at her squeezing even harder. 'Max, the last time you hit me *that* was to do with this guy if I remember or one of his girlfriends. Max, let go …'

Alison felt she had no choice and twisting her body she slapped him across the face.

'Christ, you bitch,' he said releasing his hold on her arm and rubbing his face; she backed away stumbling into the dressing table.

'Ali, look I'm sorry. It is just Pinner has always caused me ...'

'Max, you have got to do something with your temper,' she said examining her arm and starting to sob. 'At times you frighten me and I can't, well I can't trust you.'

Lilley backed off and sat on the bed. He watched out of the corner of his eye as she quickly dressed; an awkward silence filled the room.

'Ali, I'll make it up to you.'

'No let's just forget it.'

Alison started to put her makeup on as quickly as she could, her hair getting in the way.

'Alison I need to know what you were about to say. It is very important to me. This man might be dead but I suspect he still could do me harm, even now. Anyway I recently found out he has something of mine,' Lilley said approaching his lover again. He laid his hands on her shoulders and gently massaged her. Alison normally loved this but she felt a menace.

'Max, I'm breaking every rule in the book by just being here. *You* know that.'

His hands stopped massaging her shoulders and made a slight movement towards her neck. Alison froze and she tried to look into his face but her hair was over her eyes.

'Max, please don't make me do this.'

'We have many secrets you and I. Come on Ali, I promise it won't go any further.' Lilley's hands moved again. Alison stayed rigid, her mouth dry and she swallowed heavily. Blinded by her own hair she could not see the look in Lilley's eyes. This man could show such affection one moment but in a trice could yield frightening brutality.

'There is a separate top-secret file on you, as well as Pinner. You are also both cross-referenced, not only with each other, but an operation called Scorpion, plus an incident in 1954, which involved a serious allegation of ...'

Lilley's grip went around her throat. She slowly raised her hand and pushed her hair back. She gave a gasp as she saw his dark brooding eyes staring at her, but they were not in focus.

'I thought so; there was something that bastard had done. Go on,' he said from deep in his throat. He pushed his thumbs up her neck either side of the spine.

'That's all really. There is a letter from a Sir Richard someone. Max please you're frightening me.' She prayed he wouldn't ask her anymore. If she told him everything she knew he would lose his temper and she feared his reaction. She desperately wanted to run to her husband, but of course she couldn't.

Lilley brought his hands down onto her shoulders and started massaging again.

'That is the last we will ever mention Paul bloody Pinner,' he said trying to smile at her in the mirror. 'I am sure your bosses wouldn't want to know you have been telling me confidential stuff.'

'*What!*' She stood up and turned towards him. 'You bastard. I have put a lot on the line for you and you think you can just …'

Lilley grabbed her with both arms and shook her then threw her on the bed.

'You're nothing but a cheap whore, now get out.'

Alison got up and, although terrified, her anger fuelled her courage. 'Whore! How dare you call me that.' She avoided eye contact and with her hands shaking she stuffed her belongings into her suitcase and made for the door.

'Ali! Listen I'm sorry,' said Lilley putting his head in his hands his long greyish hair spilling through his fingers. 'I will explain everything in a few weeks time. It's a bit complicated.'

'What you just did to me is totally, I repeat, totally unacceptable Max.' She stopped at the door. She took off a ring on her right hand and threw it at him then pulled the handle down and took several long breaths. 'I am in my early forties, and I am not a whore. I have loved most of our time together. You are probably the reason I have ruined so many promising relationships. Well you are not wrecking this one. It's over Max, and if you ever try and contact me again I am, for once in my life, going to come clean and tell all.' Lilley started to stand, glaring at her. 'Oh don't worry you old fool, I am not stupid. You keep away from me and the whole sordid affair is forgotten.'

'Alison, last night you said I could have the picture back ...'

'You should have thought about that before you started ...'

She began to leave but checked and looked at him from the safety of the other side of the door. 'Would you have really strangled me Max?' she said as softly as she could.

'Wouldn't you like to know? Maybe if you were naked ...'

The door slammed and Lilley heard her footsteps running down the corridor.

Lilley cursed and finished packing before he opened his phone book and wrote down a number. He picked up his mobile and called it. Joey Habbul answered the phone.

'Joe, usual place at nine o'clock, OK?' said Lilley. 'Make sure your brother comes as well. I need a few words with him.'

'Fine, see you there Gov,' came the reply.

Lilley clicked off the phone, left the room and checked-out.

He walked with no real pace down Park Lane and into the walkway coming up behind Buckingham Palace. The early June sun soothed his mood. Would that be the last time he would see Alison? They had rowed before and she had always come back but this time he felt uneasy. He briefly thought how he could get the picture back but decided to deal with Paul Pinner first.

When he reached Victoria Station he made his way to a café on the Vauxhall Bridge Road. He stopped and examined some umbrellas in a shop window checking for any signs of someone following him. Lilley stared blankly at the window. His gut wrenched as he recalled the day when the only woman he had ever really loved opened a door to him. Barely dressed and expecting to be faced by her new lover he remembered the horror in her eyes as he dragged her inside only to be met by the sight of a love nest warmed by a roaring fire. That was fifty years ago but the pain still filled him with hate for her and the man who had taken her from him. Time for some retribution, he thought.

Lilley checked around him again, and then crossed over to the café and straight to the back of the room where the two men were waiting. He sat down opposite them at the table and nodded. The men had a Mediterranean look about them despite their near shaven heads.

'How are you Mr. Lilley? It's been a while since we have seen you about in the manor,' said the older, but smaller, brother.

'Retired now, well I have been for years officially. But still do a bit of private work.' Lilley tried not to make eye contact with the younger brother who towered over him. His white T-shirt revealing his tattoos. Lilley could never understand people who wore tattoos and especially such grotesque ones; bands of barbwire, dripping with blood, entwined his neck and biceps.

'You look a bit tired Max,' said the younger man.

'Mr. Lilley to you,' snapped the older brother. 'Sorry Mr. Lilley, but Nicoli isn't much cop with protocol. Coffee?' Joey motioned to the man behind the counter and ordered three coffees.

'OK, let's get to business.' Lilley didn't want to hang around for long. He extracted a piece of paper from his jacket. 'This is an address of a man who has just died in Knutsford, Cheshire.' The younger brother went to take the paper, but his brother snatched it from him. 'The funeral is on Thursday and then I have established most of the family will be leaving within a few days. I still have some contacts in the old firm.' Lilley smiled as the coffees arrived and started to sip his steaming mug cautiously. 'His widow is going to Canada and the only possibly person who maybe around is the son, a bit of a pathetic wretch, I believe. You should be able to hit the place around Sunday.' Lilley turned to Nicoli. 'You can give him a bit of a pasting but nothing permanent, understood? Any sibling of Paul Pinner is no friend of mine, but I don't want too much of a fuss from the old Bill.'

'What exactly do you want us to do Gov?' said Joey checking the address.

'I want you to search for any paper work, letters or diaries from 1944 till after 1954. Anything from documents to official letters. You've done this sort of thing before so you know what to look for.' Lilley glanced around the café as casually as possible. 'However this time I want you to make it look like a burglary, so gentlemen help yourself. Some nice bits of stuff worth pilfering I suspect. Oh, and if you see a small picture,' said Lilley showing them a sketch, 'then I would like this returned to me.' The younger brother smiled at Lilley, but remained silent.

'OK,' said Joey. 'Do you have any info on the house? Is it alarmed?'

'Sorry chaps, but I am not privy to that sort of thing anymore.'

'What about the dosh? Are you privy to that,' said the bigger man barely hiding his dislike for the old man in front of him.

'Shut up Nici, I am sure Mr. Lilley will be generous.'

Lilley pulled a long white envelope from his jacket.

'A grand now and four more when you bring me any letters or documents.'

'But what if there isn't anything?' said Joey.

'I am sure you will bring me proof you've done your best. Don't try anything on with me Joey, you know better than that.' Lilley gave the older brother a long stare making the larger man straighten up. Lilley stood up and left, throwing a few coins on the table for the coffees.

'Don't call me. I'll call *you* after the weekend. Understand?' Lilley turned and walked out of the café into the sunshine.

'Little shit. Who does he think he …?'

'Shut up Nici.' Joey looked inside the envelope. 'We don't get many jobs as easy as this every day.'

'Yeah, might get myself a few nice pieces of antiques while we are at it,' said Nici picking up Lilley's coins.

'Not on your nelly,' said the older man.

'What? You heard what he said, we could help ourselves; he told us we could.'

'The one thing you never do is accept a free gift from Maxwell Lilley.' The smaller man looked into his coffee cup. 'We ain't taking anything that could be traced back to us.' The older man put up his hand to stop the protestations of his younger sibling.

AIRMAIL / PAR AVION

Officers' Mess,
R.A.F. Vienna,

180450 F/L Paul Pinner
June 1945

My dearest cherub, Marie,

What a relief, off duty at last, but not for long unfortunately, I have a terrible schedule as I am flying nearly everyday, especially difficult, as you can imagine. I know I have been very amiss in not writing more often, but I've just been indulging in one of my daily habits, namely thinking of you.

You have expressed the opinion that all the girls wherever I am will be having some sort of effect on me. (It is I who should be worried about all the Americans around your home, but I understand they have all left now. Thank heavens!). Now although I take that with a pinch of salt, knowing that teasing one another seems to be our favourite pastime lately, it simply is not true. I am sure that you do not realise what a large part you play in my life. I would like to take the opportunity to change a few things between us, and explain how I feel towards you, so here goes.

I feel a little sad sitting down to write you this sort of letter – it brings me very close to you, and when I stop writing and "come to", and realise where I am, a feeling of intense loneliness envelopes me. Oh, how I wish I didn't have to write. If only I could walk across the room and just put my arms around your waist and kiss you on the lips – this would say more than a thousand letters ever could.

On my bedside cabinet I have two snaps of you, one in the bathing costume and the other when we walked up Green Gable. I hope I can find the negatives, as I want them enlarged. I have a friend with a dark room and equipment, who could help. I think the one of you in your swimsuit is sweet, you look positively angelic – Lord, how the camera lies. There I go teasing again. Wilkinson cannot take his eyes off your legs, and I must admit they are coming on Marie, very nice and smooth. Marie-Anne you've got a smashing figure and why wasn't I allowed to see it before in all its glory.

Well Sweetheart, are you alone in your room? For the next few minutes just lie on your bed – read this letter – relax and think of me. The theme of this letter is my love for you and why it has taken so long to manifest itself in my mind. I think you are the loveliest and most beautiful girl in the world. I want to try and put into words what physical and mental effect you have upon me. Perhaps the best way of describing what being in love with you means to me is you are continually in my thoughts every day. I just can't stop thinking about you. I hope I have chosen my words carefully and been as discreet and delicate as I can, but there are things I must describe frankly – they are meant as a true expression of love for you, so don't take offence.

The trouble with me is I still have difficulty in believing my good fortune in having won you for my girlfriend. When I look back at our first attempts at courtship, and how I used to agonise whether you would ever bear my name, I realise just how you have been the all-important thing in my life since we first met. Do you remember the first time I took you to the Regal – you were wearing a green nipped-in-at-the-waist coat? I just turned over and over inside and I don't think I saw a bit of the film for looking at your wonderful profile. Do you remember we just said good night and I didn't try and kiss you, I went home on air – utterly and completely head-over-heels in love. You were so young then but I'd fallen for you so hard in just one evening – the crash must have been heard for miles.

I have spent my war years with a huge shadow over me, not about my own fate, but whether you would still be my girlfriend at the end. At last the war is over and I am hoping that I can return to my studies as quickly as possible. You know my sweet, that feeling for you which is in my heart, and which I cannot describe, surges up many times during the course of the week. I feel a need for you that almost makes me feel faint. This war has separated us against our will, and I am so glad it is finished. I am frustrated on two accounts; the first is I must fulfill my duty here until I am de-mobbed. I know you have some idea of my current role from your father, but I must implore you never to ask me too much about the last two years. It is better forgotten, and I want to look forward to my life with you. The second is my desire to have you near me, really near me.

I promised to be discreet but also frank. Marie, I want to come home and start our life together where we left off. I have been too frightened and shy to be so bold, but I cannot hold my emotions in any longer. I know I have several years studying to undertake first, but at least I want to build the relationship where I can be totally intimate with you, as only a man and woman can be. I am sure you understand my meaning.

Perhaps I am being too open and giving away my "trade secrets", but I don't care any more. I want you to know how I feel and I will walk to the end of the earth to please you. When I come home I want to go away with you to a small hotel with a sea view. Naturally we would have to have two rooms, but I hope that would be to satisfy the landlady and your parents. What do you think my pet, does this send a shudder of passion through that beautifully shaped body of yours?

My Precious, I end this letter with my heart pounding and a strong urge to come home to Cumbria, R.A.F. or no R.A.F.! I would cite you as the reason for my desertion, and they would be gunning for you – but of course you'd love that wouldn't you Marie. (Oops, I've done it again, more teasing. I actually don't apologise, for I make no secret I want humour as well as love in our lives.) Your photographs are on my bedside table, and I would do anything to have the real thing here tonight. I would honour and respect you my darling Marie-Anne, but most of all love you.

Thinking of you always,

Paul
xxx

Chapter 3

THE FUNERAL OF PAUL THOMAS PINNER

Cheshire, June 1999

I have not been to many funerals, and for that I am thankful, but those I have attended the weather has always been cold and damp. Today was no exception. A cool mist shrouded the whole village and the unseasonal chill was intensified by gusts which tore at the young leaves on the trees. I turned and looked through the front door of my parents' home. The close family members mingled and busied themselves in the large beamed hallway. My young son, Jason, played with cousins he rarely saw now that he was living abroad with his mother.

My Uncle James came up to me and put his arm across my shoulders. He was my father's younger brother and one of the few relations I had a close understanding with.

'Marie, oh sorry, your mother will be ready soon,' he said in a hushed voice. He looked at me trying to smile but he too was feeling the pain. 'So how's the job going in London?' he asked trying to take my mind off the coming event.

'I don't know how many millions there are of us in London, but it is the most god awful loneliest place on earth,' I replied keeping my eye on the gates, awaiting my father's hearse. 'Since Erica and Jason left I don't seem to have the stomach for it.'

'Well they're looking for a new deputy head at the King's School up the road,' he said, his eyes full of hope.

'Really? I'll bare that in mind,' I said turning towards him; my mind immediately considering the option. 'I've been given dispensation for extended leave for several months, so I'll have plenty of time to think about it.'

A soft crunch of gravel made me turn as the black hearse glided gracefully through the gates. It would be the last time my father would come to his beloved Elm Farm. I quickly went inside.

'OK everyone,' I called in a loud, but at the same time, subdued voice. The faint chatter ceased. 'The cortege is here, can we make our way outside please.'

My mother and sister appeared at the top of the stairs. A fixed frozen smile etched onto my mother's face could not conceal her grief. Jason grabbed my hand and pulled me outside. His face was serious and puzzled as he pointed at the coffin.

'Papa?' Jason muttered. He could never say granddad when he was young.

'Yes, it's Papa.' I said stooping down beside him. 'He is asleep and with Jesus now.' The boy remained still and wide eyed, uncertain what to do.

My mother came outside and seeing the hearse made a small gasp. She put her hand out to steady herself. I took hold of her and helped her get into the lead car with my sister, bundling my son, who was still memorised by the coffin, in beside them. The journey to St. Oswald's church was not a long one and as we pulled off the main road, the funeral director jumped out of the hearse, and led the procession on the cobbled drive up to the church car park. We passed the pub I had spent so many happy hours in; mostly with my father. He had always treated me as an equal, even when I didn't deserve it.

A sombre single bell tolled. The pall bearers placed the coffin on a trolley and we followed him into the old half timbered church. The service went so quickly I felt cheated. I followed the coffin to the graveside, and watched in disbelief as my father was lowered from sight. Jason was now clearly upset and my concern for him managed to keep me strong. My sister held tightly onto my mother as she let some soil slip through her fingers hitting the coffin and making a sound like a rifle shot. My mother took out a small white flower from her lapel, kissed it and threw it into the grave turning quickly and leaving the only man she had ever loved. I looked up to be caught by a gaze of a tall woman. She was immaculately dressed in a three-quarter length fur lined black coat and knee length matching boots. Long blonde hair cascaded down past her shoulders and out of view. She had a concerned countenance, and she eventually broke her stare and looked down into the grave. She sent a shudder of fear through me. I had no idea why, or did I?

I took my son's hand and followed my mother back to the car park. People, most I had never met before, muttered their condolences, and I in turn made sure they were invited back to the house. I actually felt a sense of relief the funeral was over. I went over to my mother who was also showing signs that the tension had also subsided as she laughed with a group of guests.

'Mum could you take Jason, I err, well just want to say goodbye privately,' I whispered to her.

'Of course dear. I'll send a car back for you.'

'No, no it's all right I'll walk.'

'OK dear, anything you say,' she said and squeezed my hand. More people came over and she was soon involved in another conversation. I waited until most the cars had gone and wandered over to the grave on the far side of the cemetery. The gravediggers had already started to make their way towards the gaping hole, but catching sight of me they slunk away behind some trees.

I wanted to say something but felt a little foolish especially as the gravediggers were possibly listening. I closed my eyes and tried to imagine him, which proved very difficult. I never normally prayed but today I did; not only for my father but my mother. Her life would never be the same. They had spent their entire lives together; neither had ever had another partner.

I heard a faint footstep close to me. I opened my eyes to see the long black coat and mass of blonde hair. She was standing on the opposite side of the grave. Her eyes were closed. I had no idea what to do, so I waited. A murmur of voices from the trees indicated the diggers were becoming impatient. The blonde heard it too.

'I apologise for disturbing your privacy,' she said opening her eyes. She had a faint Germanic accent. She studied me; her eyes highlighted by the mascara seemed like two search-lights boring into me. We both went to the head of the grave. I was speechless, and the sense of fear I had felt before returned.

'My name is Michaela Von Berckendorff.' She held out her hand. I took it noticing how large it was for a woman. 'Are you David?'

'Yes, I am sorry, but you see ...' I stammered.

'No, it is I that should be sorry. It was very inconsiderate of me to interrupt, but ...'

A cough from behind us made us both turn to be greeted by two men with shovels. Their patience and manners had run out.

'Yes sorry, of course,' I muttered, and gently steered the woman towards the car park. The men did not wait and the thud of the first shovel of earth hitting my father's coffin seemed to echo around the graveyard. An involuntary shiver engulfed me. The woman sensed it and took my arm. I felt uncomfortable being so close to her.

'Err; are you coming back to the house?'

'No, well ...' she hesitated.

'It is an old custom in England, that we throw quite a party at a funeral,' I said; not sure if I really wanted her back at my parent's home. 'I believe we got it from the Irish. Any excuse for a shindig.'

'Shindig?'

'Oh, a party, a knees up,' I said my face flushing.

'It is the same in Austria.' A pregnant pause allowed me to hear the birds singing. The mist was starting to lift.

'You speak English very well,' I said awkwardly.

'Paul, your father, taught me initially when I was just a little girl,' she said tossing her hair back across her shoulder. 'He was friendly with my mother, err parents.'

I sensed it as soon as the words came out of her mouth. She had not wanted to say the last sentence. She made a polite cough as if to clear her throat.

'I was in London and my parents asked me to come and pay their respects.'

'Austria, you say,' I said. 'My grandmother was Austrian, and if I am not mistaken dad spent some time in Vienna after the war.'

'Yes, that is where they met.'

We stood in the car park both feeling each others uneasiness.

'Well, I'll see you back at the house then,' I said starting to turn away. She was looking around the car park where only one vehicle remained.

'Where is your car?' She had her keys in her hand and pressed a button. The car a few yards away responded by blinking its indicators.

'I was going to walk actually,' I said taking a few short paces.

'Can I give you a lift? It would also help me find your father's house.'

'Well it is very easy. First go down this drive and then …'

She was looking at me with her eyebrows raised, her head slightly on one side and a puzzled smile.

'David … ?' she said motioning towards the car.

'Yes, sorry, stupid of me.' We sat in the car in silence bar my brief and clipped directions. She parked close to the gates. I started to get out but she put her hand on my shoulder.

'David I am staying at the George Hotel in Knutsford,' she raised her hand as I tried to interrupt. 'Are you sorting out Paul's estate?'

The sense of fear now turned to panic.

'Yes, but I fail to see why that is any concern of yours, and …' I stopped talking and forced her hand off my shoulder. Dad said he preferred blondes, I thought, I had started to consider the possibility she could be an ex-mistress. My mother must not know.

'Yes, The George. Right, why don't we meet there later, or better still tomorrow,' I said devising a plan in my mind. 'The atmosphere may possibly be a bit stuffy in there.' I motioned towards the house. 'I suspect you're tired …'

'David,' she took my hand. 'David, I am not here to take anything. Quite the reverse,' her voice had dropped to a whisper.

'The reverse?'

'Yes, there are some things that need to go *into* his estate,' she said releasing my hand and getting out of the car. I followed her. 'I *am* tired but I am also hungry and thirsty. I would so love to see Paul's house.'

'Quite, I am so sorry. It is the funeral and everything,' I spluttered still convinced she spelt trouble.

'Will you stop saying sorry,' she said taking my arm and striding out towards the house. 'Call me at The George when things quieten down; we do need to have a talk.'

I went into the house to be greeted by a very angry scowl from my younger sibling. I introduced my new acquaintance to several groups, forgetting her name every time, and fled to the kitchen. I spotted my sister following me there.

'Who is that?' she demanded snatching the beer I had just opened for myself.

'*That* is apparently the daughter of some old friend of dad's,' I answered wrestling the beer back. My sister glowered at me.

'You're not telling me everything, are you?'

'Look I've already made a bit of a fool of myself with her …'

'You didn't? David, how could you, today of all days.'

'No!' I shouted. All the catering staff stopped and looked at me for a moment. 'Julie will you listen.' I hesitated. I couldn't tell her I thought she could be dad's mistress. 'She interrupted me when I went back to the grave. I was a bit rude, but she still kindly gave me a lift, and then to top it all I kept forgetting her name when I was introducing her.'

'You clod!'

'God you sound like mum,' and I turned to raid the canapés.

'David, get yourself into dad's study. There is a group of his old RAF chums who are asking after you.'

'Great, thanks,' I said crumbs falling from my full mouth. My sister sighed and started to turn away in disgust.

'Oh bugger, I forgot the toast. I promised Dad,' I said devouring another canapé and grabbing my beer, disappearing into the crowd.

'Toast, what toast?' said my younger sister shaking her head watching me cross the hallway trying to avoid conversation.

I bustled into the study to be greeted by a room full of men, mainly congregated around the bookshelves. I went to the desk and held up my hands.

'Excuse me everyone. Could I have your attention please?' The talking stopped. 'Right, it was one of my father's last requests that I got together any remaining members from his crew of the Wellington Bomber of 1944.'

I hadn't noticed him when I first came in as he was sitting in the old Parker Knoll facing the fire. The slim but obviously tall man had one of the photo albums, my mother had left out, on his lap. He had long greying hair and bags under his eyes but looked very fit and well for a man of his age. His withering stare at me over his reading glasses was so disdainful I could swear his top lip was curled. He had put me totally off my stride. Two men had left the main group and came towards me.

'Peter Wilkinson,' said the first man holding out his hand. 'I was your Father's co-pilot. And this is the navigator, George Tomkins.' I shook both of their hands trying to force myself not to look at the seated man, but I did make a quick glance. Wilkinson followed my look.

'Great, I am so glad you could come.' I noticed Peter Wilkinson was still looking at the seated man. 'Dad said he would like you all to make a toast to David Stewart.'

I busied myself finding some fine old Cognac he had insisted I used. Feeling a little embarrassed if I excluded the other men, I placed enough glasses on the desk to allow everyone to join in. I poured out the remains of the bottle and motioned to the group to help themselves. The seated man was still thumbing through the album with an uninterested air about him.

'Excuse me,' I said to him. 'Would you like a glass?'

He slowly looked up and in a deep voice said. 'Not on your life.'

I flushed and took a small step backwards in astonishment at his rudeness. I saw Peter Wilkinson frown.

'Thank you David,' started Wilkinson. 'First I suppose you all want to know who David Stewart was.' A murmur trickled around the room. 'David Stewart, who I suspect you are named after,' he said nodding at me, 'was the rear gunner. He died in an unfortunate incident over Russian held Poland in late 1944. Paul was devastated by his death and blamed himself, but it was nobody's fault really. That's war.' The seated man got up and mumbled something, plainly unpleasant, and left the room closing the door too hard. Wilkinson cleared his throat.

'A toast gentlemen, to David …'

The door flew open. Julie stood there, mouth half open ready to speak. Her face was full of astonishment as she tried to take in why several men were all facing me around her Father's desk with brandy glasses raised. I couldn't resist a smile. She looked towards me, raised an eyebrow, sighed and left closing the door gently behind her.

'As I was saying,' continued Wilkinson. 'A toast to David Stewart.'

'David Stewart.' Reverberated in a deep tone around the room.

I noticed Wilkinson quickly assessing everyone's glasses.

'I think it would be right for another toast.' He raised his glass. 'Paul Pinner.'

'Paul Pinner,' came a reply from all.

I could never bring myself to call my father by his first name and whispered, 'Dad.'

I went to speak to Wilkinson to thank him, but he was

staring, his eyes wide in astonishment, out of the window. I turned to see the long black coat and the locks of blonde hair flowing as she strode purposefully towards her car.

'Bugger, excuse me I must go,' I said to him.

I left as quickly as I could opening the door only to be met by Julie.

'What in heaven's name was all that about?' she demanded.

I heard a car start up.

'Not now Julie …' I ran out of the front door to see the blonde's car speed through the gates.

'Damn, damn, damn and bugger,' I hissed under my breath.

I turned to see Julie standing just behind me.

'Just the daughter of some old friend of Dad's, hey?' She had crossed her arms under her bust. I tried to speak but she waved me away. 'Actually I am more interested to know what the hell was going on in there,' she said jabbing her thumb towards the study window. A face in the window caught my eye. It was Peter Wilkinson looking at me with a troubled frown. 'I suggest David you check to see if Mum is alright.'

I followed Julie into the house. Making polite conversation I manoeuvred myself towards the kitchen. The cognac was starting to burn my stomach. I took a handful of snacks and a fresh beer and went to find my mother. A weak sun was finally trying to break through the clouds as I entered the garden. She was standing by a water feature talking to a group of people who I vaguely recognised. I joined and she put her arm around my waist. After a few moments I made our excuses.

'Are you OK Mum,' I said softly.

'Yes dear, but more to the point, are you? Julie's worried about you.'

'Yes, I know. The whole day seems almost surreal.' My mother nodded and we sat down on a bench on the main lawn. 'Mum,' I said turning to face her. 'I felt a strange sense of relief after the funeral.'

'That's why we do it,' she said her eyes moist. 'It's painful, it's sad, but there has to be a goodbye. Me next!' I put my arm over her shoulders and for a few moments let the strengthening sun warm us.

'Are you looking forward to Canada?'

'Yes, I really am. It has been so long since I have seen Seb.' Her focus came back and she straightened up. 'Could you clear your Father's things while I am away, dear?'

'If you want me to, but don't you want to be there at least?'

'No, I don't think I could bear it.' I gave her a little squeeze with my arm.

'I'll start the probate and sort out his papers as well.'

'There isn't much. You'll find all you need in his green metal document box.'

'What happened to his old trunk and all those papers and pictures?' I said, quite looking forward to finally opening up his RAF trunk. We had been banned from ever going near it as children.

'Oh, you know how he was after the stoke. I found him one day burning everything on the bonfire.' She nodded at the back of the garden shed. 'I wouldn't bother searching for it, he seemed determined to get rid of everything.' I felt a huge pang of disappointment. 'I know he has left all his affairs in order, so probate shouldn't be a problem.'

'Mum, he was quite ill how could he have left everything in order?'

'He may have been ill when it came to doing anything around the house, but I'm telling you the finances and all that kind of stuff, he had to a T.' Uncle James and a few others ambled towards us. My mother took a deep breath. 'Come on David, the show must go on.' In a few moments she had taken her guests into the house. I lent back and let the sun bask my face.

'David,' shouted my mother from the door. 'A very nice lady asked me to tell you that she had to go, but would be in touch.' I sat bolt upright blinking in the sunlight at her. 'Quite tall, with very long blonde hair. Foreign I think, but a very expensive coat and I loved her matching boots.'

'Mum,' I called, but she had gone back inside. Had she come to see her lover's home out of curiosity? No. Dad wasn't the sort, I knew him too well; so who was she?

I ambled inside to see most of the guests had left. I was a touch shocked and felt guilty at not being more sociable as I went through to the hallway. I started to look for my son and noticed Peter Wilkinson had his coat on and was scanning the room. He came across as soon as he saw me, and ushered me into the empty dining room.

'I am sorry to be so forward but I must speak with you,' he said. I nodded.

'Peter, where are you?' came a woman's voice from the hall.

'Just coming,' he shouted back. 'Sorry my taxi has arrived.' He seemed to be in deep thought and struggling over what he was about to say. 'The man sitting down in the study; the rude one,' he whispered. I nodded again. 'Do you know who he is?'

'No, I'll be honest I don't know half the people here,' I replied. His frown returned.

'*Peter.*' Came an agitated voice from the hallway.

'I *am* coming. Just a minute,' he bellowed back. She continued to shout something but he ignored it.

'That woman with the black fur lined coat, very long blonde hair and tall. Do you know her?'

'No, we met by the grave when I went back; she gave me a lift to the house. She did say …'

'What, what did she say, David.'

'Well she wanted to talk, that's all.'

'Was her name Michaela Von Berckendorff?'

'Yes, something like that …'

'*Peter!* The taxi is going, *now.*'

Wilkinson rummaged in his pocket and handed me a small calling card.

'Be very, very careful and call me. Whatever you do, don't let your mother know any of this.'

'Any of what?' He turned into the hallway to receive a

scolding from his wife, and then he kissed my mother and glanced back at me before leaving.

'Any of what?' I muttered to myself.

Sandy Grange
Penrith
June 1945

My Darling Paul,

Until today I have had no news from you. Yesterday morning I was in despair as not even a note from you for over two weeks. The Postman thinks I am "half-baked" cos' whenever he shows his face in the road he finds me either swinging on one of the gate posts or rushing out of the front door to greet him. He has recently started to just throw me a look of pity and shakes his head for he knows your handwriting and usually waves it about if it's from you.

I would rather like to be a Postman watching people's faces lighting up at the sight of a letter, you would be able to follow people's lives, rather interesting, don't you think?

Darling, thank you a thousand times for that magnificent letter I received today. It was the most moving and intimate one that you have ever written – the effect on me was remarkable. I've read it over many times, and each time it works me almost into a frenzy. Mummy knows something is up as I disappeared for ages when it came and now I feel as if I am walking on air. I suddenly gave her a big hug before and she gave me that knowing smile. She asked how you were, as if she couldn't already tell! In a way it was a little unfair of you to make such a wonderful exposition of your love when I am unable to answer it. The only way that a letter of such depth can be answered is by being alone with you. Then I can show you my true feelings; you know I am not such a good writer and find it hard to put my feelings down on paper.

I wish you would hurry up back Darling. I feel the sooner you do, the sooner you will be home for good, and I am missing you so very much, all day and every day, that I feel terribly lonely at times. It will be really wonderful when you are home for good My Pet, no more long goodbyes, no misunderstandings as in the past, and I promise to stop the teasing, but only if you do as well. What is this about Americans? We have hardly seen any in the town.

I do love you My Precious, you do know that now don't you? I know you love me and it makes me so very happy. I do wish some miracle would happen which would make all the wrong, right, and turn this terrible muddle into a peaceful and heavenly dream. Still one day, things are bound to come right and then we can be together forever, and always in our own little home.

Well, I suppose I had better start and tell you it is only a day before the Great Day. I know you are the kindest man I have ever met and that so much is going on in your life it is easy to forget things. Daddy says you are travelling a lot and that is why I don't receive much communication, but to forget your girlfriend's 21st!

Yesterday was hectic. Daddy and I spent most of the afternoon tearing around Penrith collecting my cake, trifles, pastries etc. If only you could have seen my cake Paul, it was wizard, Betty's sister made it and it was just like pre-war. Everyone is coming tomorrow, the list is endless, but there is someone missing from the list who I would forfeit everyone else for; that is you my Darling. Who I am going to cuddle tomorrow as I enter adulthood?

I have a small confession to make. I was going to a Dance with Peter, Keith and John, which incidentally was evening dress. Betty rang up and as she seemed rather depressed after her John was going back to his unit, I persuaded her to come along too. Can't tell you what happened on paper as it would take too long, but if I say I got "pretty" tight and did things I shouldn't 'ave oughta, that will cover everything for the time being. Remind me to tell you some day, because I think it was extremely funny, except of course, the part where I was almost responsible for the car trying its best to shoot skywards via a tree!!!! The problem was when I got home and wrapped myself in the blankets; desperately lonely and cried myself too sleep. I wish I had had your letter the day before, I have felt so wonderful since I have received it. You wait my darling until you get home; your lips will be sore from kissing me so much. I have sent you a piece of cake, I hope you get it but Daddy thinks I am mad. Sorry it was such a small piece, but I had to rescue this from the hoards, it has been so long since we have tasted butter sponge. I do hope it wasn't rotten when you got it!

I have to go now as I want this to get the next post, and I so wish I could be with you when you read this – you will not be disappointed. So many of my friends are getting married, and there seems to be women waddling with huge bellies and babies everywhere. It's all our hot bloodied men returning with burning desires ...

All my Dearest and Fondest Love,
For Ever and Ever,
More love and take care of yourself Darling Mine,
A matured Marie!
XXXXXXXXXXXXXXXXXXXXXXXXXXXXXXXXXXXXX

P.S. I understand that the leatherwear and shoes are famous in Vienna. Just in case you don't know or forget I take size $5^1/_2$, (or 6 If very 'dressy'). You will have a huge conscience about missing my birthday won't you, so you had better make up for it!!

Chapter 4

WHO IS SHE?

Cheshire, 1999

It had not been 48 hours since we buried my father, and the family was back to its usual chaotic state. There never seems enough time to get ready before departing for the airport and this Saturday morning produced a sense of déjà vu. Suitcases and bags lay scattered around the front door. Mayhem had been caused by my alarm clock failing and my mother ignoring hers.

'Jason, where are you?' I bellowed in the hallway. The boy sauntered out of the study. 'Come on I need a bit of help here …'

'David, have you got the tickets. I can't find the tickets.' My mother passed me agitated and tense.

'Mum, I have got everything, now please get in the car,' my voice turned harsh with frustration.

'Julie's, you've got hers as …'

'In the car!' I said pointing towards the drive. 'We'll never make Jason's flight the way we are going.'

She flashed me a smile and skulked off pretending to be on tip toes. 'I am so glad Julie can come with me; she won't shout at me,' she mocked.

The traffic was fairly clear, unlike the weekday where the journey would have taken twice as long. My mother sat on the back seat with my son and they laughed and played together. I checked them in the rear-view mirror occasionally. Guilt nagged at me for not seeing him more often. Then a wave of self pity engulfed me as I recalled him mentioning his new daddy in Italy. Had I lost him to another man?

'I think,' said my mother loudly but still talking to my son. 'That your daddy should come and visit you shortly and take you to Pisa, which is by the sea I believe.'

'Oh, Dad can you?' he shouted scrabbling forward on his seat.

'Yes, I would like that. Let's see what your mother has to say,' I said watching him carefully in the mirror. He slumped back with a sullen face; that told me everything.

Jason was the first to check-in and eventually his child escort arrived; hugs all-round. Walking away holding the woman's hand, he never looked back. In my mind I begged him to, but he went out of sight blissfully unaware of the hurt within me.

'I'm losing him Mum. I can sense it,' I said searching for a last glimpse of him through the departure gate.

'Well get yourself out there and fight for him,' she said wiping a tear from her eye. 'You married too late and to the wrong girl. But you weren't to be told.'

We were walking slowly towards another terminal down a long glass tunnel.

'Mum, I was over thirty; I did have a mind of my own.' My mother ignored the remark.

'Mum, but thanks.' My voice had a serious tone and made my mother take note.

'Thanks? What for?' She stopped and took the opportunity to rest.

'For a great childhood.'

The statement genuinely surprised her.

'You silly clod. We loved it just as much as you did. You're missing out a lot by not being with Jason.' Her eyes glazed over. 'Did you thank your father?'

'Yes, actually I did.' I pulled her case over to the side of the tunnel and put my back against the large hand rail. My mother came and stood beside me. I checked my watch. 'I thanked him twice. The first time when we went walking just before his stroke ...'

'Oh, he did enjoy that weekend walking in the Lakes. Having you and Jason for a few days to himself really thrilled him.' My mother searched for her handkerchief.

'The second time was that afternoon I spent with him in the hospital, just before he died.'

'Yes, it was strange,' interrupted my mother again. 'He became quite perky the day he died. It was odd as if it was a final, a final …oh, you know what I mean.'

The noise increased as a large group came into the tunnel laughing and shouting.

'He said there was an envelope for me. All the papers I would need would be in it. I am assuming it is in the study. He seemed concerned not to burden you with any of the administration of the estate.' My stomach tightened as I was not telling the exact truth.

'I've told you, everything is in that old metal box. It is in the study, in a cupboard under the bookshelves. He showed me everything he had done but would never allow me in the box, and he even had it padlocked …'

We both looked at each other.

'David, I have no idea where the key is. How stupid of me.'

'Well if I can't find it I'll saw it off.' I had to shout as the group of people passed us. My mother winced she didn't care for airports.

'Mum,' I said. Did I dare mention his dying words to her, I thought.

'Yes dear, hadn't we better get going?'

'No it's OK.' I turned and looked at my mother who was dabbing her eyes with her handkerchief. 'Dad told me he still had his RAF trunk …'

'When you were walking in the Lakes?'

'No. On the last day in the hospital.'

'Oh, I don't know dear. As I told you I caught him burning a lot of stuff behind the shed, and I've never seen the trunk since,' she said starting to walk on. 'David, he was very confused in the end. Remember him how he was before the stroke not the last few months.'

I watched my mother turn and walk away. She did not want to make eye contact.

Julie was waiting for us at check-in and completely took over. I was rendered redundant. They checked in and Julie, who insisted in always being first in every queue, was panicking that they only had an hour and half before the gate closed. I took my mother by the shoulders and looked her in the eye.

'Go and have a great time with Uncle Seb.' I said in a deep mock authoritarian voice. 'I will have everything sorted upon your return, oh great one.' We embraced.

'See you big brother,' said Julie struggling with all the hand luggage, walking towards the departure gate. 'Try not and destroy the house, and no wild parties, women, especially leggy blondes …'

'Bye Julie,' I interjected before my mother started asking any questions. 'Look after mum for me.' They went through security and were gone. Now only Uncle James remained at the house, and I had an idea of how to persuade him to leave.

I drove back to Lower Peover quite slowly. My mind drifting to the final conversation I had had with my father. He had become agitated and I had to promise him that my mother never saw what was inside the envelope he had left me. My father had been a quiet man, I thought. Then I thought about Michaela von Berckendorff. What is the saying? "The quiet ones are the worst".

A dark coloured BMW screeched round the corner not far from my parents' house. I had to veer to avoid them. Just behind came my Uncle James's old blue Ford Sierra, black smoke pouring out of the exhaust. I slammed the brakes on to be met with a furious blast of a horn from behind. I pulled over and waved him by, only to be hurtled with abuse.

For a split second I thought of chasing them, but an image of my father's RAF trunk came into my mind. I raced home. I pulled up by the front door leaving a skid mark on the gravel. My key wouldn't work, so I tried the door; it was open. I flung it ajar and instinctively called out. 'Hello!'

I checked the back door. Open. I went into the rooms one by one. By the French window in the dining room; glass littered the floor. One of the small panes on the Georgian windows had been smashed. I then saw a glint on the lawn a few feet away and could just see a crowbar. The sound of gravel on the driveway made me rush back to the front door. Uncle James's car spluttered next to mine. The smell of hot oil and brakes filled the late morning air.

'Why didn't you follow them?' He was out of breath and clearly annoyed.

'Follow who?'

'The thugs in the BMW. They were trying to break in,' he said pulling in some long breaths and trying to calm down. 'I was hoping you would take over the chase.'

'Sorry Uncle, my instinct was to get back to the house. What happened?'

'There I was, in the kitchen tidying up,' he said escorting me to the dining room. 'Then I heard the sound of glass smashing. I picked up that large cleaver your mother has hanging up by the chopping board and came in here.' He pointed towards the French windows. 'Two guys with a crowbar were trying to get in. Really thick bastards they were.'

'What makes you think they were thick?'

'Obvious! Both the front and back doors were open!' We both let out a small laugh. 'Well, actually it's no laughing matter, David.'

'No, sorry. What did you do?'

'Well I brandished the cleaver at them.' Uncle James was clearly enjoying himself. 'Then I did something really clever.' His eyes were twinkling. 'I shouted back towards the kitchen for you and Jason to come and help me. One of them was a really big guy with a horrible tattoo around his neck, so I thought that if they think I am not alone …' He finished with a knowing, slightly superior expression.

'Did they just scarper?' I said quite impressed with Uncle James's guile.

'Vanished. Then I heard them running down the drive and saw their car on the apron, so I gave chase.' We walked through the front door. 'I think I have knackered my car. Just smell it.'

We went round to the French window and I found the crowbar they had used. They had made a deep gouge in the doors where they butted together.

'We'd better get hold of your mother before she goes,' he said looking at his watch.

'No, please Uncle James I'll sort it. She desperately needs this break …'

'Mmm, yes well you may have a point, and it would only worry her. I think we should add some extra locks.' He went inside and I heard him pick up the phone. I chased after him.

'Uncle James what are you doing?'

'Calling the police of course.'

'Did you get the registration number?'

'Damn, how bloody stupid. I completely forgot. You daft old fool,' he shouted at himself.

'They're probably in Manchester by now, and to be quite frank Uncle James I would like some peace and quiet. Police pouring over the place taking finger prints is not what *I* need right now.' I took the phone off him and placed it back on the cradle.

'No point.'

'No point in what?' I asked him.

'They had those gloves on you get in hospitals,' he said moving towards the kitchen. 'As I said they were ugly bastards, the big one had tattoos like blood stained barbwire around his neck. Horrible! They were shaven but both had a good tan. That's how I noticed the gloves.'

'Using gloves doesn't sound like petty thieves to me,' I said growing concerned.

'No, it's the norm nowadays. It's very common for houses to be targeted when weddings and funerals are going on. They can almost predict when the best time is to strike,' said Uncle James removing a brush and pan from the utility room. 'I saw it on The Bill once.' He stopped and looked towards me. 'You want some privacy don't you?'

'Yes please. I hope you don't think I am being rude …'

'Not at all. I sort of know how you feel.' He went into the dining room and brushed up the glass. I didn't move and watched him come back into the kitchen. 'But before I go I insist on putting some extra locks and bolts on all doors and windows. Your dad was *my* big brother and he would expect that at least.'

'You're a star Uncle James, a real star. I'll go and get some lunch.'

★ ★ ★

Joey hit the corner too fast nearly colliding with an oncoming car, which just veered away in time. He checked the rear mirror, accelerating and quickly left the old Ford behind.

'I think that car will fuckin' explode before it catches us,' he said pulling the car around another bend.

'Nice one bro. "The house will be empty." "Let's get it over with." "Strike while the family is away". Only good thing is Lilley was right; some nice stuff back there.'

'Shut up Nici. Call Patrick for me; we need to get the car off the road. They must have the reg number.'

'Patrick lives in bleedin' Leeds. That's miles away.'

'Just do it, and don't take any calls in case it's Lilley. He'll kill us. We'll try again in a few days. This time we'll wait till just the son is there; alone. You can keep him busy and earn your keep while I look for them letters Lilley wants.'

'I could have taken care of three of them. Have some faith in me Joey.'

'You just don't get it do you Nici,' said Joey entering the motorway and speeding towards Yorkshire.

★ ★ ★

Uncle James worked hard all afternoon fixing extra bolts and locks. He also replaced the window pane. I offered for him to stay the night but he would not hear of it. He left at 5.00 pm, leaving me alone in the old rambling house. I slowly wandered around building up strength for the task ahead.

I called Peter Wilkinson, but was greeted by an answering machine. I left a brief message. Then I called The George Hotel, but Michaela was also out for the day. Another message. I entered my father's study and finding the metal box extracted it from the cupboard. A large robust copper and chrome coloured padlock rocked on the catch, mocking me. I pulled at it examining its size. This would need a serious saw. I decided it would be easier to break the catch.

The phone rang and Uncle James's voice sounded weary. He was home safe and sound and he implored me to keep everything locked; even when I was in the house.

My next job; search for the RAF trunk. I went to the rear of the garden shed, taking a rake on the way. The bonfire area looked dark and bleak. A smell of damp charcoal and rotting compost greeted me. It was a far cry from when I used to frequent this patch when dad burnt all the garden rubbish. He loved to do this on a Sunday afternoon, making himself not too popular with the neighbours. I raked the whole area but only found garden remains. No tell-tell signs of bits of paper, a charred front cover of a book or the metal handles of my father's trunk.

The search went inside and I pulled down the loft ladder. I entered the attic to be surprised how neat and tidy it was. There was only a small layer of dust which also surprised me. Mum was right the trunk wasn't in its usual place. Several gable end loft spaces seemed clear but I hadn't got a torch to make sure. The phone rang downstairs. I rushed only to hear Peter Wilkinson leaving a message. I snatched up the receiver.

'Mr Wilkinson, sorry about that I was in the attic,' I puffed.

'That's OK. How is your mother?'

'She is fine she went off to Canada today, I'm expecting a call any moment.'

'So that's why you're in the attic.'

'No, no I was ...' I couldn't think of a suitable lie.

'Sorry David it's none of my business. By the way please call me Peter.' There was a pause and I was still at a complete loss at to what to say next. 'You called me this afternoon,' he continued. 'I was out shopping. One of the curses of retirement,' he said laughing lightly. 'Have you spoken to anyone?'

'No, not yet. It has been manic here. And then today with the break-in ...' I knew I shouldn't have mentioned it.

'Break-in? What happened? I'll come round immediately.'

'*No*! Sorry Mr err, Peter. I just want a bit of space, some time to myself, can you understand?'

'Yes, I most certainly do, but I must speak with you David.' Another awkward pause. 'Was anything taken?'

'No, Uncle James chased them off. They just broke a window that's all.'

'Good. Are you up for a light lunch at The Bells tomorrow?'

'Yes, I never turn down a Sunday lunchtime drink.'

'Great I'll pick you up at 12 o'clock. See you then. Bye'

A clink and then the dialling tone.

'Now where was I?' I said to the empty house. I went into the kitchen found a heavy duty torch and grabbed a beer. Thirsty work in an attic. I re-entered the loft and saw the faint imprints of my shoes in the dust. The gable over the guest wing was lower than the rest. I scrambled in but within six feet I hit a wooden stud wall. I frowned. The wall had been placed on a rafter and was not to dad's usual high standard of carpentry. I could not see over or around it. Half way down a plank of wood a large knot seeped with resin. Several minutes later I had extracted it; my fingers now sticking together. I wedged the torch in a small gap right by the roofing felt and peeked through the hole. The diffused light of the torch showed me enough to know dad hadn't burnt his trunk.

'There you are,' I said quite elated, only to be answered by a ringing tone.

'Bugger that phone.'

I ran down stairs tripping and falling onto the landing. I lay still and heard Michaela leave a message. I decided not to speak to her until after lunch with Peter Wilkinson. Michaela's message clicked off. I remained there praying hard Dad hadn't burnt the trunk's contents.

It was becoming late so I opened a bottle of wine took last night's left overs from the fridge and picked through them. Cooking wasn't my forte. I retired to the study deciding to have one of dad's cigars and a brandy. I poured a good measure of alcohol, opened the humidor to be greeted by several Monte Cristo No.4s. I picked up one and there in the box was a bright metal key. I looked at the padlock still holding on tight to the metal box. A smile emerged slowly across my face. Two successes in less than an hour and I raised my eyes to the heavens.

'Thanks Dad,' I said reverently. 'I know you're behind me on this, somehow.'

A few minutes later the entire contents of the metal box lay across my father's desk. Numerous files, envelopes to mum and Julie and finally a large document wallet addressed to me. I opened it and more files and papers fell out. I shook the wallet and a small parcel wrapped in sticky tape spun off the desk onto the floor. I retrieved it and placed it on the blotting pad.

I suddenly felt tired, almost listless and decided to return to the finer things in life. A file labelled "The Will and Last Testament of Paul Thomas Pinner" caught my eye. I wavered but curiosity overcame my fatigue. I opened the file and extracted the Will. I flicked through quickly trying to read the legal jargon, but clipped separately onto the back was a codicil. It changed one of the clauses where the definition of 'Any Issue of Paul T Pinner' to be changed to 'Any Issue of Paul T Pinner and Marie-Anne Pinner (Nee Ryder)'.

The implication was blatantly obvious, but I didn't or wouldn't accept the consequences at first. I poured more brandy not realising I hadn't touched the first. Clipping the end off the cigar I warmed it with a long Dunhill match. I lit the Monte Christo inhaling into my mouth and then slowly breathing out.

The smoke lingered over the desk and I took a pen and started to write:

Learnt English from Dad when she was a girl

Met her mother (corrected to parents?) in Vienna after the war

Bringing something to Dad's estate

Will changed to only the issue of Mum and Dad – (Thank heavens)

I then looked at the fire place. It was 1971 when I saw my Father burn something in that very fire during the summer. He also went to great lengths to leave nothing in the grate and I saw he had crushed all the ash to dust. I added:

1971

I then racked my brain to remember her name, and wrote:

Michaela Von Berckendorff

I put a line through part of it and added a name:

Michaela ~~Von Berckendorff~~ Pinner

The evidence seemed pretty convincing. I had met an unknown sister at my own Father's funeral. I gulped at the brandy causing me to choke. I cleared my throat and softly said, 'Bugger me, Dad this is a really bloody awful thing to do. Wait till you die before letting us know what you've been up to? I never took you as a coward.'

I finished the brandy hoping it would wash away the growing sense of confusion and deep concern at the consequences of my discovery that was creeping into my mind.

Elm Tree Farm
Lower Peover,
Knutsford
 Cheshire

11th May 1999

Dear Grete,

I hope I find you well (it took ages to find your address), and I cannot believe it is nearly 30 years since we last communicated. I apologies for this, and also the typing, but I am afraid I have had a stroke and my writing is now illegible. You will find attached a bank book made out to you and Michaela. You both need to sign it for validation. If there are any problems I have left details of the solicitor in London who arranged matters. The money is untraceable, so don't worry.

As I type, one finger only, I can hear you ask the question: Why after so long?

I could never really accept that Michaela was mine; I ignored all the evidence and, to be honest, my own conscience. Grete I had to. Marie was my life and I had already started a family with her. I know your marriage with Albert was a convenience, and a disaster, and my behaviour at letting you live such a life was unspeakably callous. I prayed you would find another love. As I sit here now, knowing my end is near (the doctors say I could go on for years, but I know better), I have reflected upon our story. We should have left our love on that first night and we should certainly not have re-kindled the flame in 1971. I know it broke both of our hearts, and poor Michaela's as well. Did you ever tell her who she is?

Time is not the great healer they claim, and not a day goes by without thinking of you. I still love you, but more accurately lust for you. Love manifests itself in many forms and I have been lucky to have really loved twice in my life.

Dear Grete, I never wanted to hurt you, but I know I have in so many ways; trust me I had to turn away. I still believe if I had gone with you I would have ended up hating you for taking me away from Marie. However I have made a decision: I will try and rectify the situation; a little. I know you will probably want to hand this money to Michaela; she probably has children of her own, so feel free to do as you please. I have tried to tell Marie but couldn't in the end; I just didn't have the courage. Fortunately she does not suspect anything. My estate will be finalised by my eldest son, David, and I have left some papers with him where he will deduce the truth. I feel duty bound to come clean. I am not a Catholic like you but I now understand the need to confess one's sins. Yes Grete, it was a sin. How can such love be a sin?

I would have so loved so see you and Michaela once more. I was hoping if I was strong enough to have told my family and I could have visited you openly. I dread to think how Maria and my daughter would react. They would spit and dance on my grave: I don't want that. David my eldest is more pragmatic and I know he will understand. He has had his own problems of the heart and I have had a great relationship and understanding with him.

Thank you for loving me, and I hope God looks upon our souls with a generous heart when Judgement

Day comes upon us.
 All my thoughts,

 Love,

 Paul.
 XX

 PS: If you are thinking of replying, please send any correspondence to the solicitor's address in London.

Chapter 5

THE FIRST LETTER

I browsed aimlessly around the house all morning the effects of beer, wine and the copious amounts of brandy taking a heavy toll on my energy levels. I kept going into the attic to look at the stud wall, taking the newly acquired crowbar, but any attempt to start extracting my father's trunk caused a banging inside my cranium. I wanted Wilkinson to come and put me out of this misery.

I made a coffee and sat at my father's desk. The notes I had written last night lay there seemingly content with prolonging my utter shock at what I believed I had discovered. I was hoping Wilkinson would disprove my assumptions, but I doubted it. I sat back in the chair and swivelled to face the wall. A picture of my father scrabbling off a Hurricane fighter's wing faced me.

'Dad, what the hell am I suppose to do now?' My voice seemed to evaporate into the room.

Below him was a picture of Jason taken on the walking holiday just before my father's stroke. I put my head in my hands and recalled my wife's shattered look when I had told her I had being having an affair. Her eyes filled with disbelief, which changed to despair knowing the trust was gone forever and then a few minutes later; hatred. The hatred took over and our love was gone. My own honesty had destroyed my family. I never understood why I had done it for I never really felt anything for the other woman.

My eyes drifted between my father and Jason. What if my father had told mum about his affair? It would have ruined my childhood; destroyed a fantastic family life.

'OK,' I said getting up and walking around the study. 'So maybe there is a time when you bury your past, but …' I stopped at a small picture frame where a tiny Edelweiss had been pressed: the flower of Austria. I had always assumed it had come from my Grandmother. I looked back towards my father's picture.

'Alright, I am not going to judge you, for now,' I was pointing my finger at him in the picture, 'but I need to find the reasons for why you did what you did, or so help me, or I *am* going to let Mum know.' I looked up to see Peter Wilkinson trying to see through the window. The sun was in his eyes and I hoped he hadn't seen me talking to myself. I grabbed my notes from the desk, then some keys and went to the front door.

Wilkinson wanted to come in and see the damage of the break-in but I persuaded him to go straight to the pub. We spent a while talking about England's cricket performance, or lack of it, New Labour, even the weather. I became fidgety.

'Peter, how well did you know my father?' The change in subject strangely relaxed the atmosphere.

'We flew together for two years,' he said sipping his drink. 'Our relationship during the war and immediately afterwards was about as close you can get in those situations.' Wilkinson put his drink down and looked me hard in the eye. 'We were together when we were brought down over occupied Poland. David, it seems to me almost like a dream, or someone I had read about. Your father suffered an intense interrogation, and …' Wilkinson stopped and to my horror his eyes were filled with tears.

'Look Peter, tell me another day when, well when it is less painful.'

Wilkinson nodded and composed himself and continued. 'We were more reserved in those days, but my friendship with your father was one the closest of my life even when we didn't see each other regularly.' He sat back and seemed to be studying me. 'He really loved you and I know for a fact he sacrificed a lot for you, and of course Julie.'

'Sacrificed?' I pulled out of my pocket the piece of paper

from the previous night. 'What sort of sacrifice?' I held the paper in my hand. I wasn't sure what to do. My anger at my assumptions was being tinged with guilt. Wilkinson glanced at it but didn't comment. Within two days of my Father's funeral I was discovering a very different man than the one I thought I had known. A silence descended between us.

'That woman we talked about at the funeral, Michaela. Have you spoken to her yet?' Wilkinson eventually asked, still eyeing the piece of paper in my hand.

'No.'

'Do you intend to?'

'Yes. I intend to call her this afternoon. Why?'

'Do you, err fancy her in any way, as …'

I opened the sheet of paper and pushed it towards him. 'I may look like a scatty scholar but incest is not my bag.'

Wilkinson eyes narrowed as he looked at me while he took the paper and I saw his reaction. Damn I was right, I thought.

'Peter,' I continued. 'May I ask for your full co-operation in trying to unravel this somewhat perplexing and potentially damaging situation? I am stunned quite frankly, but my greatest fear is my mother finding out. It would shatter her …'

'I agree, your mother must never know. I think you understand what this would do to a woman in her highly emotional state of mind.' I noticed his hand was shaking as he read the paper.

'Exactly, so will you help me?' I asked him directly again.

'Of course, but I can only tell you what I know, and I suspect this is not the whole story.' Our lunch arrived and Wilkinson went to replenish the drinks. He had put the paper in his jacket. A move I was not comfortable with. Could I trust this man?

He returned and for a few moments we ate in silence.

'David, how do you feel about all this?'

'What, that my father has a love child? Who turns up at his funeral? I am right aren't I?' Wilkinson nodded watching me, and looking to see if anyone was in ear shot. I continued, 'I have to go through probate keeping my mother and sister in the dark and I am assuming I am going to have to deal with this woman …'

'I am glad you said she was a love child for that is exactly what she is.' I had almost finished my lunch but Wilkinson was still chewing slowly.

'Bastard doesn't seem to ring too well when a female is involved,' I was starting to get the feeling Wilkinson was supporting Dad. 'Please don't start to wash over this as being justified in the name of love. I not sure I will sit here and take it.' I said feeling a little unkind after I had said it. Wilkinson continued to eat and the tension between us returned. Finally he finished, took a large gulp of his wine, wiped his mouth with his serviette and sat back.

'Are you going to listen or not. My only concern was that you and Michaela knew exactly who each other are; just in case … well you know.' He said making himself comfortable. His tone had a hint of anger. 'You don't know the situation and I would prefer if you had a bit more of an open mind. Your father has carried a great burden all his life in order to make sure you had a stable home life. The affairs of the heart are not easy; I believe you have your own experience of that.'

I flushed and nodded. 'Quite, OK I have an open mind. Peter, don't get the wrong idea I want to believe he had a good reason. I loved my Dad more than anything; it is just finding out he has kept such a secret until after his death; it feels almost like a slap in the face. I feel cheated on; could you imagine how Mum would feel. It would kill her.'

'Then she must never find out.' He looked at me enquiringly, watching me carefully. 'When we were in the RAF together your father was always Mr. Goody-Two-Shoes. Professional, courageous, hard working he was the ideal officer. He never bothered with the girls except to be ultra pleasant and polite; while I would chase everything.' He closed his eyes for a moment and continued. 'Then one evening in Vienna we went to an opera. It was there he met a certain beautiful woman. I am not going to recount the whole situation, suffice to say he had completely fallen for her. I had never seen him so besotted.

'He agonised about what to do for years. He loved Marie, but this woman had got under his skin. I think I was the only person who knew about the affair. Strangely enough at the time I was having woman problems myself, so we confided in each other. Finally, when you arrived, he ended the affair, or so I thought.'

I sat transfixed on Wilkinson. I just couldn't see my father as a love sick young man.

'There was however another complication. You are aware your father was affiliated with the British Intelligence?' Wilkinson whispered the last phrase, leaning forward.

'Well sort of. It was never as such mentioned but Mum had hinted as much and we were never to ask Dad anything.'

'As I said we had been involved in a secret operation in 1944, but that is all water under the bridge.' His pace quickened.

'What sort of operation,' I asked also leaning forward. He waved at the air. 'Forget all that,' he said irritated I had interrupted him.

'In late 1944 and 1945 he met and had to work with a Max Lilley.' Mentioning his name seemed to make Wilkinson take another large sip of wine. 'I was there when they first met. I have never seen such animosity between two men. It was totally unlike your father. Well they continued to work together, which always surprised me, for nearly ten years. The relationship became so strained I couldn't understand why his bosses permitted it. Then something happened in 1954; they were working together on an assignment in Prague. Your Dad never told me exactly what happened, except he said it was the worst thing that he had ever experienced. I believe he withdrew from MI6 after this.'

'MI6, you're kidding,' I blurted out

Wilkinson's eyes flashed angrily at me.

'Sorry, bugger me. Dad was a spy?' This time I whispered.

'The question still remains; why did Lilley go to the funeral?' Wilkinson almost said this to himself. 'I would love to know all that had gone on between those two.'

'This man was at the funeral?' I was taken aback that a man who had been Dad's enemy would come to his funeral.

'Yes, that rude man in the study. Do you remember?' Wilkinson pushed his plate away eyeing me cautiously.

'Yes, bloody cheek,' I said trying to recall what he looked like. 'Did they see each other after 1954?'

'Not that I am aware of, but the incident in 1954 changed Paul. He became a little more distant and, as I said, he never told me what happened. We drifted apart and only really started to see each other again in the last year or so. Shame I always liked Paul; great fun at a party.' He laughed. I could tell he wanted to reminisce, but fortunately he refrained.

'Peter, what do I do with Michaela?'

He mused for a few moments playing with his glass. 'Better see what she wants,' he mumbled also deep in thought. 'My heaven's she is like her mother. Much longer hair, but her looks ... It's quite uncanny.' He turned to me with a twinkle in his eye. 'She has your Father's nose.' I couldn't help but laugh.

Wilkinson finished his drink and slowly his expression glazed over. I could see he was back in another time zone. I coughed politely.

'She may well contest the will,' he said still deep in thought. 'I wonder if Grete is still alive?'

'Grete?'

'Oh, that was her name. Grete Semmler, but she married Albert von Berckendorff. Paul told me she had never loved her husband, and that he knew the child could be his.' He checked his watch. 'Heavens I must go, David I am sorry.'

I managed to pay for lunch despite Wilkinson protestations and I persuaded him to let me walk home via the grave. The walk home happened in a daze and as I came to my parents' front door I heard the sound of the telephone. I just managed to hear Michaela leave another message as I struggled to open the door and turn the alarm off. I called her back and we agreed she would come round to the house as soon as she was able. I checked the freezer and found some frozen lamb chops. She could help me rustle up something, I thought.

The lunch time drinks had made my headache subside so I decided to go and release my father's trunk. I went into the study to get some old papers and noticed the packet with the tape all around it. It took an age to cut through the tape without damaging the contents. Inside was a large brass key and a small envelope addressed, in terrible scribble, to me. I checked a few cupboards to see if I could match a lock, but nothing fitted. I put the envelope down and eyed it nervously. Curiosity was demanding to open it but I was sure it would be a painful read. I looked at Dad's picture and he seemed to be looking right back at me. I could have sworn I heard him say, 'open it.'

I went to the kitchen opened a bottle of wine and taking the letter sat in the Parker Knoll.

15th May 1999

Dear David,

You know my writing is now illegible so I am typing this with one finger. I enclose a key which is to my RAF trunk in the attic. I now give you permission to go in it! I am leaving all the contents to you: Only you. There are all my uniforms, my few medals and your Grandfather's WW1 medals. You will find my Flying Logs; one day you might find them interesting, but I doubt it.

My eyes filled with tears and I could not read for a while, for as I read the letter I could almost hear his voice.

Inside you will also find many letters and photographs. I should have burnt them all a long time ago, but I just couldn't bring myself to do it. I once burnt a letter in 1971 and regretted it ever since. That is why you must open the trunk on your own, and please make sure your Mother or Julie DO NOT find any of these letters. David, this is very important; I am trusting you on this.

David, what you will read will be more than a bit surprising, and I know you will discover some things about me that I have had to bear on my own for most of my adult life. So why do I burden you with them now? I feel that the truth will come out anyway, and I would rather you find out from me, even if it is in the written form. In the letters you will find one I wrote to Grete Von Berckendorff and her daughter on 11th May this year. Michaela von Berckendorff is of my issue. I have protected both you and Julie with a codicil in my will; however I have sent some money to them. It is the least I could do. The letter explains everything, and I suggest you contact the solicitor named.

I took a large mouthful of wine and slowly swished it around my mouth to let the flavours flow over my taste buds.

A creak upstairs made me freeze, but it was just the old house settling. I know I should have checked but the letter had almost a paralysing effect on me.

You will also see I was involved with British Intelligence. I always intended to share some of the events that befell me, especially after fifty years had gone by. But as you will see there are too many emotions and memories that I felt it best to leave the past alone. So I can hear you ask, why bring it to light now?

The reason is hard to explain in a note like this. My finger does not work as quickly as my mind, even in its current, confused state. In short there was a man I met in 1944 who plagued me most of my early life. To say we hated each other was an understatement. This man is called Maxwell Lilley and if you ever meet him, or he contacts you, walk away. Do not enter into any dialogue with him; he is wily and very devious. I believe if he survives me he may come and ask you for the document I have. He is tall, charming, doesn't look a day over sixty, never mind seventy, and has longish greying hair. He is a viper; his hatred for me knows no boundaries.

Suddenly my father's voice seemed to disappear. It didn't sound like dad anymore. Wilkinson had been right my father was a very popular man and I just couldn't imagine him having such a feud. He seemed to spend his life resolving conflicts not manifesting one. Another gulp of wine, and I ignored more creaking from upstairs and in the hallway.

When I tell you he is a viper, I mean it. For years he threatened me with blackmail. The most terrible thing is the only way to counter him was to blackmail him back. Yes, me threatening another? Unthinkable, but true. What weighted more heavily on my mind is that, despite my efforts, he went unpunished for what I knew he had done. He was a traitor. I should have tried harder to stop him but I now know the fear of him telling your Mother about Grete, and of course Michaela, was too distressing to contemplate. It would have destroyed your Mother, me and the family. This affair that, Dear David, began well before I married and ceased before you were born, well almost. I will make no excuses or justification, but the letters will allow you to make up your own mind.

I have made huge mistakes, you will see that. I have tried to do what was right, for my family but I fear I left a terrible legacy; a woman who suffered all of her life because of me. I accept my relapse in 1971 was idiotic and could have hurt so many people who were so dear to me; I am truly ashamed of myself. How could I have acted so stupidly?

My greatest regret is that I could never sit down and tell you face to face. I had the opportunity many times, none so better than our last walking holiday together. I wish I could have told you then – and all the other tales I would have liked to have shared with you. I wasn't all bad you know!

I also wanted to really find out what had happened between you and Erica. Her love for you was unquestioning. What did happen? I suspect I know; have you repeated my mistakes?

Riveted to the letter at first I thought a draught had moved the door. A creak of the floorboard and I knew I was not alone.

I looked around for a weapon; the poker by the fire. I got up just as I saw a shaven headed man look around the door. I bolted upright, stuffing the letter down the side of the chair.

'Nici, get him,' came a shout. I lunged for the poker hearing the crashing footsteps coming across the room behind me. I turned waving the poker threateningly. My confidence and bravado melted as I saw the huge man rushing at me. The barbwire tattoos seemed to hypnotise me. His hand grabbed my wrist and with alarming ease he bent my arm back making me drop the poker. I noticed he had surgical gloves on.

'Now then,' said the other man. 'Let's be civilised about this. Nici, bring him over here.'

I tried to struggle but the beast holding me took full advantage of his strength and twisted my arm right round. I let out a scream.

'Oh, Nici. Don't hurt poor Mr. Pinner,' said the first man, his London twang thick and aggressive.

As the man with the tattoos dragged me over to the desk. I caught the fleeting glimpse of Michaela's long blonde hair going through the front door. I started to shout, but realising she must have seen what was going on, I hoped she would call the police; I feigned more pain.

'Now Mr. Pinner, let's 'ave a little chat,' said the smaller man. His looks and accent made it difficult to define his origins. I glared at him and decided to remain silent.

'Don't be tardy with my brother, nancy boy,' slobbered the man still holding my arm up my back, and holding his other arm around my throat. 'One more twitch and I'll break your fuckin' arm.' He demonstrated by a small movement of my arm. He was nearly right my arm felt as if was going to snap. I tried to speak.

'Lighten up on him Nici, you might hurt the poor chap,' said the other walking over to my glass and taking a large swig. 'Nice stuff, Mr. Pinner. Raiding your Dad's cellar? I suppose he has a cellar in a house as posh as this.' I shook my head as far as I could. The grip tightened and I made an attempt to take a breath. I could feel my pulse racing and face flushing. My eyes felt as if they were bulging from their sockets.

'Nici, Nici, give him some air. Sorry about my brother but he gets very upset when someone comes at him with a poker,' the smaller man said finding his own humour amusing. 'Now if you help us get what we want then Nici, here,' he gestured at his brother 'won't need to trash the place. We're looking for some documents your father may have left …'

'Don't forget the picture. That little one that Max …'

'*Nici!* Shut up for Christ sake,' screamed the older man. The screeching alarm bells wiped the smile from his face to be replaced by an angry sneer.

'What in the name of God is that?' The grip tightened around my neck and nausea filled me as the larger man jammed my arm further up my back. I felt it had to break soon.

'Are you wired to the Police,' screamed the brute from behind me. I could only manage a faint nod.

'Little fuckin' bastard. What shall I do Joey,' he said, but released me as he saw his brother making a hasty exit.

He pushed my head hard onto the desk; fortunately the discarded sticky tape from the small packet softened the blow. I heard shouts and doors being slammed above the din of the alarm. A few moments later the study door moved and I checked to see where the poker was.

'David, are you all right?' The door opened slowly to reveal Michaela nervously scanning the room. I let out a long low groan and collapsed back into the chair.

Officer's Mess,
R.A.F. Vienna,

October 1945

My Dearest Adorable Grete,

Oh, what a night! I will never be able to forget last night for the rest of my life. I know we are probably ships passing in the night, but what an encounter; I was truly memorised by your charms and beauty. I want to tell you all about your luscious lips, your full bosom, your sleek figure and that oh so full behind, you are certainly a woman of many talents. But you know all this don't you.

I know you're blushing now, and I also know you are reading this in private, so I can say almost anything I like. I knew the moment we met that there was an electric field between us, so strong that a hurricane could not part us last night. When I returned to my room, I found a lone carnation; I think the maid must have left it. I have pressed it and wrapped it in some tissue paper, and I enclose it. The smell has gone, but you can keep it as a reminder of our first, and hopefully not our last passionate encounter together. I know it is not much, but they say in England it is the thought that counts. Talking of England, I have to return there soon. Will I see you before I go? Whether I return is not certain, but I have been totally honest with you my dearest, and you know I will probably marry another; that does not mean my desire for you is undiminished. I have known Marie since school, and although we are not engaged I know it is probably my destiny. That was before I met you and I have this desire that I want to hold you near to me forever. You did something to me last night that is tearing me apart.

Girls like you will marry wealthy men, not my kind, and I will soon be just a distant memory; a little plaything you enjoyed. You, however, will always be in my thoughts. I will never forget the way you undressed me last night. My arousement was so great I now know what a volcano feels like before it erupts. I believe you could tell!

I will lie in bed at night and think about you constantly, for the rest of my life. I know this is wrong as I must return home to my world, but I swear I can still smell your perfume on me. I cannot remember what shade of lipstick you were using or even the colour of your eyes, all I know is I fell into those wide, bright eyes, and I am still falling. Will I hurt myself when I stop falling? Will I hurt you? I doubt it; nearly every man was looking at you. You could have your pick, but you chose me, why? Actually I know why; it is the way we just entwined our naked bodies around each other; totally at ease. I told you I was not very experienced with girls, I have been all but faithful to mine back home, but with you I just seemed to know what to do and how to satisfy you.

Please never change your perfume, or the way we are, especially in bed. How long are your friends away for and can we go back to their house shortly? I have to be a little careful, for being a British Officer I must act responsibly; but I promise not in bed! I really want to write again and again about your body and what we did that night. I have never been so tired, and trying to work today was virtually impossible.

You said I was your first, and I am so glad as I would have hated to be yet another in a long line. I have feelings for you that are confusing me, as I want to be with you, but I also want to go home to Marie. Grete my darling, was our meeting a mistake, or a cruel twist of fate that will confuse my life forever? How can I leave for England with anything except total despair? I have never tasted lovemaking before and now I understand the reason for every love song and poem. I know I cannot walk away, but I must; duty calls, and I must not let my family, my country and Marie down.

I must finish now to ensure you get this letter. Until we meet again …

All my love, Paul
xxxxxxxxx

Chapter 6

WILKINSON INTERVENES

I sat still as Michaela cautiously entered the room.

'It's OK I think they've gone,' I said rubbing my neck.

'Who were they?'

'Oh, just the neighbours,' I said my humiliation turning into anger. She threw me a look and I could see a touch of hurt in her eyes. 'Sorry, sorry I am just shaken up. That was totally uncalled for.'

Michaela turned and left the room.

'Look I am sorry, really,' I called after her.

'I'm calling the police,' she shouted above screeching alarm, picking up the phone in the hall. '999 isn't it?'

'Maybe I should call them?' I continued following her and she handed me the phone and went into the kitchen. 'First things first, I'll stop this racket.' I fiddled with the alarm; entering the code, eventually the noise ceased. Relief. 'Did you see their car?' I shouted towards the kitchen.

'No.' Her tone had not improved.

I eventually got through to the Police, who hadn't yet sent anyone out. Apparently my parents had had too many false alarms recently and were not put down as priority. I explained everything to the duty officer, who seemed to lose interest when I told him that they had taken nothing, nobody was hurt and I didn't have any significant details. Tattoos didn't seem to interest him.

'Someone will be around shortly. Please remain at the premises,' said the disinterested officer. I put the phone down to find Michaela searching in the cupboards.

'Tea, where is the tea?' She said avoiding my eyes.

I took her hand and escorted her to one of the kitchen bar stools. 'I will make it.'

I prepared the tea and not a word was uttered. 'Sugar?' I eventually said and she shook her head. Her eyes were still fiery and glared at me. 'Oh, for Christ sake, I was not angry at you, but at those thugs.' I stopped and sipped my tea. 'How did you know about the alarm?'

'Most alarm systems are the same,' she said looking around my mother's kitchen. 'There is a panic button somewhere, normally by the master bed. I saw the two men and realised what was happening. The door was open so I ran upstairs, found the best looking room and checked beside the bed and voila, there it was.'

'Michaela, thank you. Really, you are a star. I think those two meant business.'

'David you could have been really hurt. They did mean business and David, never speak to me like that again, please.'

'Yes I *am* sorry.'

She started to smile and came over to me. Not sure what to expect I was surprised when she reached forward and ripped a piece of sticky tape still stuck to my forehead. We both collapsed into fits of laughter.

'I'll make dinner as recompense for my rudeness before,' I said going to the fridge.

'Good, because I am an awful cook,' she said still laughing and rolling the sticky tape into a ball.

I suddenly remembered I had left the attic open. Had the thugs been up there?

'Back in a moment.'

I rushed upstairs and entered the loft. The stud wall was untouched. The phone rang downstairs but quickly stopped. I stowed the loft ladders, checking for any marks I may have left. I went and splashed cold water on my face and I noticed my hands were trembling.

Returning to the kitchen I said, 'Right some lamb chops I think …'

'Oh, a Peter Wilkinson just called.'

'You answered the phone?'

'Yes, is that a problem?'

'No, err; I just thought they had rung off.' I said trying to keep my voice flat. How dare she, I thought. 'So what did he say?'

'He was horrified about the two men. He is coming over now …'

'You told him about that? Great.'

I was standing there my arms limp by my side wishing I was alone.

Michaela looked at me warily. 'Look I was out of order answering the phone,' she said coming around the kitchen unit. 'Now it is my turn to be sorry. Shall we start again?' She extended her hand.

I smiled at her and shook it. To get used to a new sibling when you are touching fifty wasn't going to be easy, I thought.

'Look Michaela, you make me feel nervous, because, well it's …'

'What?'

I had to bring the subject up before Wilkinson arrived. I knew he would mention it. I went into the study to get the piece of paper I had written on and remembered Wilkinson had taken it. I passed the Parker Knoll and could see the letter from my father stuffed down the side. I hadn't finished reading it yet so I was reluctant to show her this, yet. Michaela had followed me into the room.

'What a lovely room, so warm and, how do you say, cosy. Is that Paul?' She said pointing at the picture of dad on the fighter wing by his desk. Then she suddenly stopped and turned slowly facing the framed flower. 'My mother has a framed Edelweiss.' I was watching her closely.

'Peter Wilkinson and hopefully the police will be here soon,' I said annoyed at my plan to let her do the talking was being ruined by the circumstances. Damn those thugs, I cursed under my breath. 'I believe that I know who you are.' I blurted out expecting her to show some signs of surprise.

'Oh, you remembered my name,' she said toying with me.

'Yes, I am sorry about that, but seriously …'

'David I have suspected for years, but I only actually found out for sure a few weeks ago,' she said leaving the room. A few moments later she came back with her large handbag extracting a brown envelope from it. 'I found this clasped tightly in my mother's hands. She had suffered a heart attack,' she spoke softly and I could hear a quiver in her voice. She passed it to me watching me carefully. I pulled out a letter and a dark blue bank book. The letter was dated the 11th May and was similar type script as the letter now stuffed down the Parker Knoll.

I slowly read her letter struggling to take in all the contents. Concentration was difficult. I walked towards the Edelweiss picture. Michaela continued to study me. I passed the letter and bank book back to her.

'I don't want it,' she said placing them on the desk. 'There is one thing I will never be,' she said tossing back her long hair, 'and that is bought off.' I went over to the Parker Knoll and carefully pulled out Dad's letter to me.

'I was reading a similar letter from dad when the thugs interrupted. It is about you and your mother.' I smoothed out the letter and cast my eyes over it, rubbing my neck.

'What did he say?'

'Well I had just finished the part about how we all make mistakes …'

'May I read it?'

I hesitated. She had been open with me; why was I being so cagey?

'Yes, but would you mind if I read it quietly first,' I said placing this letter on the desk by hers.

'Of course, I am being very presumptuous.'

'Your English is bloody good,' I said smiling at her. A weak smile returned but I was horrified to see tears welling in her eyes.

I did not know what to do. Do I hug her, like I would Julie? How should I react? She sensed my uncertainty.

'I always wanted a brother,' she said walking towards me and she took my arm just like the first time we met. 'I am so hungry; cook me a feast,' she said gently weeping now. I squeezed her hand and led her to the kitchen and started preparing dinner when Wilkinson turned up. It wasn't long before I became a little irritated with his intense questioning.

'Peter, that is all we know,' I implored. 'Two shaven head thugs, the bigger one with some pretty revolting tattoos. They seem to fit Uncle James' description of the two guys who tried to get in yesterday. Possibly thought we wouldn't be expecting them back so soon.' Wilkinson looked concerned and seemed in deep thought.

'They didn't say anything? No clue as to what they were after?' he continued probing.

'When the big bastard had me trussed up, the other wanted my co-operation or he said he would trash the place. He mentioned the cellar and I suppose he thought there might be a safe or something.' I struggled to concentrate on making the meal as I had invited Wilkinson to join us. He turned to Michaela.

'You saw nothing either,' he asked. 'No car, nothing?'

'I am sorry, I think there was a car parked on the road but I didn't take any notice,' she said a slight flush to her face. 'I ran upstairs to find the panic button. I have a similar system at my apartment. When I heard the alarm go off I waited a few minutes and heard them leave hastily, so I came downstairs.'

Wilkinson sat thoughtfully, chewing a small savoury cocktail nibble.

'David, can you think exactly what they said?'

'No,' I shouted going to the fridge collecting a beer and slamming it in front of him. 'Peter I appreciate your concern, really, but let's leave this to the police.'

'They just asked for your *co-operation*?'

'Yes, they knew what they wanted, that is all …' I said, my

voice slowing down. 'Actually the boss man went on about some letters, oh, and the big fella wanted a picture.'

'Jesus, letters, why the hell didn't you say? Not sure about a picture but the letters … That's it, I'm sure.' He ripped open the beer and took a large mouthful straight from the can.

'That's what?' said Michaela and I in unison, making us giggle a little. The wine was starting to work.

'It has got to be Maxwell Lilley. When he was here he went around the house examining everything especially the stuff your mother had left out in the study; I noticed him.' Wilkinson was now standing looking quite agitated. 'Have you two, err sorted things out.'

'Yes,' we said in unison, this time the laughing increased. 'Good, look this is serious you know.'

'Peter, sit down.' I said gently pushing him towards the stool. 'My father is dead, and finding out about Michaela is quite enough for the moment. Please do not insult my intelligence that someone has sent thugs around to beat me up just because of dad. They would have done that when he was alive. Agreed?'

'Mmm, you do have a point,' he said continuing to drink from the can. 'Maybe I am seeing shadows. Have you ever seen any letters that your Father had?'

'Bugger me Peter; please I want a rest from this …' I didn't want to lie to him. Michaela looked at me; her eyes questioning me.

The doorbell rang and the next hour was filled by keeping two disinterested policemen busy filling in a report. Eventually satisfied with the paper work they informed me it was possibly a gang in the area.

After a poorly cooked dinner Wilkinson finally left, frustrated with my reluctance to talk, and Michaela took the hint and followed a few minutes later. I agreed to meet with her the next day to talk things through. I went and sat at my father's desk after double checking all the doors and windows. I picked up my father's letter to me and finished reading it.

> *David, I have left so many things unfinished. My letter to Grete is not enough, so I must ask you to undertake a small task for me. You will find a small miniature picture in the trunk. It is wrapped in a special cloth. Could you return this to Grete, hopefully she is still alive, or give it Michaela. It was a gift I should never have accepted. Take care how you do this and whatever you do, never let your mother know.*
>
> *I should have done all this and I should also have gone back to Prague to see if Petr and Natalia had survived those terrible times. You will see what I mean in the letters; the last known address is in the trunk. They got married in 1955, or so I was told, and I believe still live in the old part of Prague. (Worth a visit. Excellent beer and cheap.)*
>
> *Finally, I want to say how proud I am of you. It came home to me the day we were walking a few months ago, before this ruddy stroke, when you thanked me for a good childhood. I never judged you, David: I ask you not to judge me.*
>
> *All my love,*
>
> *Dad*

For the first time since his death, my male reserve finally dissolved and I cried uncontrollably.

★ ★ ★

Peter Wilkinson could hardly wait until 9.00 o'clock on Monday morning. He spent the next few hours desperate to speak to Rupert Reeves-Dodd. People in such high echelons of the secret service are not easy to speak to even if you have a direct line. Wilkinson pursued his cause with dogged determination. Finally a call came back and he was on his way down to London. A rendezvous with this man might at least clear the matter of why his old friend's house had been broken into twice in as many days; just after his funeral. Wilkinson knew there was some rather nasty history between Lilley and his old skipper.

They had agreed to meet in a neutral place. The Institute of Directors on Pall Mall, of which he was still a member, had an excellent French Bistro with private compartments. One had been duly booked. The train journey seemed to take forever and he kept thinking of why Pinner had so hated Lilley to an extent that it was totally out of character. He also thought the son was not taking the whole situation seriously enough. He seemed to have almost ignored the fact that two men had roughed him up and he could have been seriously hurt. He was either brave or naive. Wilkinson thought it was the later.

The taxi ride went in a haze and soon Wilkinson signed in at reception, went to the French Bistro and was shown into a cubicle where the Assistant Director of MI6 was sitting awaiting him. He looked nothing like he had expected, a short insignificant, rather dumpy and mild mannered man. First impressions can be deceptive.

'Mr. Wilkinson,' he said standing to welcome his guest, 'I appreciate your time to come and see us.' He motioned towards two tall, wide shouldered men. They seemed a better fit for MI6, thought Wilkinson. They all shook hands.

'No, it is I that am glad you could see me,' said Wilkinson taking a seat opposite Reeves-Dodd. 'I actually hope I may have the wrong end of the stick, but I really feel I should discuss the recent events of an old boy of yours as a matter of urgency.' Wilkinson took a sip of water and without being asked started to recount the entire history. 'Paul Pinner first met Max Lilley in …' Reeves-Dodd wasn't listening and had turned to the man on his right, whispering to him.

'Forgive me, Mr. Wilkinson. Very rude of me, but there is something I must check.' He nodded at the other man. He extracted a strange black gadget from his brief case and held it close to Wilkinson. 'Clean,' is all the other man said.

'I am sorry but there are so many devices nowadays,' he

looked towards the other man who immediately left the cubicle and went and sat on a table just outside. 'Privacy is so hard nowadays, and as you didn't want to visit us ...'

'Well, it was just... I didn't want to become too involved.' Wilkinson felt small and insignificant.

'You are involved, and I am extremely grateful for your efforts, believe me.' Reeves-Dodd said with a knowing smile senior civil servants process.

'I am only trying to help, and I am extremely concerned about some recent events. First ...' Reeves-Dodd was still not listening and had extracted several buff coloured files from his brief case.

'If I may save you a lot of effort,' said the Assistant Director putting on some half moon reading glasses. 'You were Flight Lieutenant Pinner's co-pilot. Flew with him to Poland on several missions. Also assisted in the liaison with Nazi Military High Command in December 1944, code named 'Operation Scorpion.' Wilkinson started and looked around nervously. 'Don't worry most of this is all public knowledge now; not many secrets left,' he said looking at Wilkinson as a headmaster would a reprimanded pupil. 'Spent a few months with Pinner in Vienna; de-mobbed and returned home to civi-street. Ran your own business, I see and had a few problems with the ladies ...'

'Thirty-two.' Wilkinson interrupted starting to dislike this man. Appearances were deceptive.

'Thirty-two?'

'My inside leg measurement.' He felt good at stumping this arrogant sod.

'Oh dear, I believe I have offended you?'

'Well, yes actually you have. I am not sure I like a file on me, and certainly not on my private life. I came here in all good faith ...'

'Wilkie, I know.' Wilkinson recoiled back in his seat at the mention of his nickname. 'Sorry about that but it is all written here,' Reeves-Dodd said patting the file. 'Could I have your mother's maiden name and place of birth, if you wouldn't mind?'

'What? What the hell is this?' said Wilkinson starting to rise. The man sitting next to him put a firm grip on his shoulder. 'Mother's maiden name?' repeated Reeves-Dodd.

'Millward. Halifax, Yorkshire. Happy?'

'Thank you. I had to make sure you are who you say you are. I don't want some reporter getting wind of all this.' Reeves-Dodd thumbed through the file and waited till Wilkinson settled. Wilkinson straightened his tie and wished he hadn't interfered.

'Peter, oh, may I call you Peter?'

'Yes, of course.'

'I'm Rupert by the way.' They nodded at each other.

'MI6 doesn't like its dirty washing out in the open, however trivial,' he picked up the menu. He turned to the man by Wilkinson. 'Get a waiter here would you Platt. The fact is,' he continued, 'I believe there is something not right with this Pinner situation, and thanks to you I think I can nip this one in the bud.' He picked another file and turned the pages rapidly. 'There were two break-ins you say? We only have a report of one.'

'Yes the son didn't report the first one.'

'Do you happen to know why he didn't?'

'No, but I think he genuinely didn't bother as the uncle chased them off and he wanted a bit of peace and quiet. David Pinner, the son, is a touch laid-back.'

'One large man, shaven head with some revolting barbwire tattoos around neck and biceps. The other smaller, also with a shaven head and does all the talking,' said Reeves-Dodd reading from a file.

'Yes, that is how David Pinner described them, and they were ...'

'Brothers. What the Habbul brothers are doing in Cheshire is a little bit of a mystery. I am surprised they could find the place,' said Reeves-Dodd still reading from the files.

The waiter arrived. Food orders were taken; only Wilkinson ordered wine. He tried to retract but Reeves-Dodd would have none of it.

'The son said when they threatened him and they also mentioned some letters. I think that is what they were after. Lilley is behind this I am sure,' said Wilkinson feeling a sense of excitement.

'Mmm, nothing else?'

'No, oh they also wanted a picture.'

'I am not sure what to make of their actions. A little strange to mention it to the son,' Reeves-Dodd said, still engrossed in the files. 'We believe Paul Pinner took a lover in Vienna in 1945.' Wilkinson nodded. 'Not in itself a breach to national security, however we believe he could have fathered a daughter by this woman in 1950. I trust he would have wanted this knowledge to go with him to the grave.'

'She was at the funeral.'

Now Reeves-Dodd was taken aback.

'Well, well, well. I am now becoming very curious,' he lent back and took a long hard look at Wilkinson. 'I am informed an ex-agent has died. Natural causes, with nothing suspicious; we assume the grim reaper at work, usual stuff. A few days later files are issued from our central data department for Paul Pinner, Maxwell Lilley, Operation Scorpion and a certain Frau Grete von Berckendorff, nee Semmler. Oh, I asked for yours after we spoke,' he smiled at Wilkinson. 'Alison Wilson, research assistant in Eastern European intelligence, had requested the files. You can imagine I needed to have a few words with her because she used to work …'

'With Max Lilley.'

'Bravo, Mr Wilkinson, sorry Peter.' The food arrived. 'Ms Wilson had been associated with our Mr. Lilley for many years. They thought no-one else knew about them but walls have ears or should I say eyes.' He smiled as he started to eat his smoked salmon. 'This is too good to eat without wine. Get a bottle of Pouily Fume would you Platt.' Platt scuttled off. 'Peter, tell me about Lilley.'

'I can only say that Paul and he were deadly enemies from the start. In fact it staggered me that you guys seemed to keep putting them together.' Wilkinson wished he could recall more.

'Yes, there is little indication as to what caused this animosity in *these* files. In fact I have to agree with you it all seems to be a bit bizarre.' Platt arrived with a waiter in hot pursuit. The wine was ordered.

'You have more files?'

'Oh, yes, but these may take a little longer to dig out of the system, not everything is on show despite what you may read,' he said approving the wine. He leant forward. 'Is there anything you can recall which might throw some light on the affair?' Wilkinson shook his head slowly, in deep thought. 'Could you at least speculate then?' continued Reeves-Dodd.

'Paul was a very popular man. He was one of those chaps people seemed to like instantly; you know the sort,' Wilkinson acknowledged the wine to Reeves-Dodd and left his glass of house wine. 'Clearly Paul and Grete had fallen for each other and I think Lilley was jealous of him. I will admit I was a little; she was a real beauty.' Wilkinson frowned. 'It doesn't explain why they disliked each other back in December 1944. Maybe these letters the two brothers wanted, have something to do with it, or this picture. Paul never mentioned any picture to me.' Reeves-Dodd was pre-occupied.

'He never mentioned anything else to you, or why he stopped working for MI6?' The conversation stopped as the waiter collected the plates and left.

Wilkinson found himself in a real dilemma. No time to play games, he thought. 'Actually he mentioned that he had a terrible fall out with Lilley, and MI6 for that matter in 1954. He claimed he had been framed by Lilley and it could have cost him everything. He was clearly very, and I mean very, distressed at the time, yet he hardly mentioned it ever again. Was it Lilley?'

'It most certainly was …' Reeves-Dodd picked another file. 'But why try and break into the house now?'

'You are certain Lilley is behind it?' Wilkinson said pleased with his own deductions.

'Ms Wilson finally told us Lilley wanted information on

Pinner; he has a history with the Habbul brothers and then finally he goes to the funeral. I assume un-invited?'

'Shit, I never thought to ask. But why the appearance of the illegitimate daughter?' Wilkinson forced a weak laugh and continued. 'I was worried that she might get off with Pinner's son,' Wilkinson finished his wine. 'I was going to tell him but he had already worked it out for himself.' Reeves-Dodd raised his eyebrows.

'The son knew of her?'

'Well it seems he put two and two together, remarks by this Austrian woman, plus a codicil in his father's will which he had recently found.' Wilkinson produced the paper David Pinner had scribbled on.

The MI6 man read David's notes. 'Bring something to the estate?' Reeves-Dodd looked at Wilkinson who shrugged his shoulders.

'May I,' said Reeves-Dodd putting it into his jacket pocket. 'Peter could we ask you try and keep an eye on the situation. I am calling in one of my men to do some digging. A certain Mr. Charles Carter.' Reeves-Dodd saw Wilkinson's concern. 'No he is not a gun-slinging double-o Bond type character, but actually very diplomatic.' He stopped and stroked his chin. 'Lilley wants something Pinner has.' He quickly retrieved another file spent a few minutes examining it. He suddenly stopped and started to read intensely. Reeves-Dodd pulled out a soft back booklet which Wilkinson only just made out the words "Nazi" and "Works of Art" within a long title. 'I wonder …' said Reeves-Dodd continuing to stroke his chin.

Umslang House,
Vienna

My Darling Precious Paul,

No, I was not blushing when I read your letter, but flushed with desire. I am like the flower: you can press me down anytime and take me with you. It is not a carnation but an Edelweiss, the flower of Austria. I hope our love blooms, but in return I give you a miniature picture. It is the most exquisite thing I own, and I hope shows my love for you. You did say I looked a picture the other night! (Look at the face of the Madonna.)

Marry a wealthy man, me? Why should I when I have you to satisfy my every desire? I am thinking about you constantly, those wide shoulders and strong arms. If you are falling my dear then fall into my arms, and I will always comfort you. You took me as a bud and made me blossom and like you; my only thoughts are of our naked bodies locked together as one. My heart races every time I even think of you, and I am glad I stir your passion, and I cannot wait to see how I arouse you. Next time I will undress for you very slowly to ensure I capture your full desire.

I will save my perfume for you if you promise to save yourself for me. I need you desperately. Do not be the stuffy British Officer with me; be reckless and free, especially in my bed.

My darling, I admire your honesty and your attempt at integrity, it is refreshing in our society at these times. I feel we are not ships passing in the night, and I am hurting already knowing you are going back to England. I cannot bear the thought of you with another, but I could not expect a man like you ever to be lonely. If I have to be your mistress then I must accept my lot. I would rather have a tiny piece of you than nothing at all. I know it will hurt me but next time tell me more about your sweetheart in England, I need to know what I am fighting against.

I do not entirely believe you have little experience with girls, but I would love to believe it. If what you did to me last night was your raw instinct then you truly are a natural lover. Please come and gain more experience from me, I will be only too willing to oblige you. I cannot wait to undress you and cast my eyes over your body, I feel like a harlot, but I cannot hide my feelings and desires for you, and what I want you to do to me.

My hand is shaking whilst writing like this, but it is not with fear or embarrassment but utter desire for you, my love.

Waiting to hear from you,
From your blooming flower,
Grete
Xxxxxxxxxxx

My friend's house is empty for a few weeks ...

Chapter 7

MY FATHER'S LETTERS

Monday morning arrived and I had made my mind up to sort out my father's affairs quickly before my mother's return. I had become anxious that she might get wind of the break-in from Uncle James and suddenly arrive home. My arm was very stiff and I was struggling to bend it. I had some faint bruising around my neck.

Equipped with a large strong coffee I started to sort through the papers. Several hours later all was organised and the two envelopes for Mother and Julie in the top draw of the desk. I longed to know what my Father had said to them.

I then went to the workbench in the garage and selecting some tools I entered the loft. It only took a few minutes to remove several of the planks. Crawling into the space I lay beside the RAF trunk, my Father's name heavily embossed on the top. My heart was pounding but then I noticed the large padlock. I had left the key on the desk. It was then I heard a noise from downstairs. I lay still and the phone rang. 'Damn that bloody phone,' I cursed. The answering machine had come on as I made my way down the stairs, and I heard Michaela leaving a message; asking where I was. I saw her on the drive with her mobile phone walking back towards her car. I opened the door.

'Sorry, Michaela I was in the loft.'

She turned and smiled. 'You had me quite worried for a moment,' she said giving me a continental peck on both cheeks. 'Loft? There are not many words I don't know,' she said striding towards the kitchen.

'Loft is the attic; the roof space. You see you think you can speak the language, but you will never beat a native tongue,' I said preparing a cup of tea.

'Well I think I know your language better than you.'

'Oh, fighting talk. Absolute balderdash.' She frowned again.

'What is the pluperfect of the verb to have?'

'Quite, well I am talking about the spoken word not an English syntax exam.'

She smiled at me with an air of superiority. 'So what's our agenda today?'

I handed her the letter my father had left wrapped in the sticky tape. 'Today we are going to find my Father's Letters.' Michaela sat bolt upright and started to read the letter. I made the tea and handed her a mug; she mumbled a thank you as she read the letter, totally engrossed.

'Have you found the trunk?' she enquired. I nodded. 'He seems to have had a serious feud with this Maxwell Lilley.' She said re-reading the letter.

'When I had lunch with Peter Wilkinson he mentioned that this animosity was instant when they first met in 1944 and went down hill from there.' I sipped the tea watching Michaela read.

'Did you talk about me?' She didn't look up.

'Yes.'

'Well …'

'We didn't know why you had come here. In fact I still don't.' I said eyeing her carefully. She put the letter down, but before she could speak I felt I had to mention my thoughts about my father. 'When I realised who you were I swore at my father, even started to despise him for what he had done. But after reading this letter,' I touched it gently, 'and what Wilkinson had explained; I am starting to see another side to the story. My opinion of my father seems to be changing by the hour.'

Michaela sat still cradling the tea in both hands. 'I came to return the bank book, and …' She stopped and looked away.

'And?' I wasn't going to let her off the hook.

'And I have to admit the curiosity of meeting my real father's family seemed irresistible. However the last thing on my mind is to cause any more grief. David, I *mean* it. My mother and Paul did fall in love, really in love. But I suspect Paul loved your mother more.' I could see her hesitate again, and wanted to continue but something stopped her.

'Let's find those letters and I think we will have a few answers.' I said downing my tea. 'Come on!'

'Do you realise these men are after something Paul left?' she said placing her cup on the draining board. I nodded and shrugged my shoulders. 'David, are you stupid?' She picked up the letter. 'I quote: "When I tell you he is a viper, I mean it." "Blackmail … traitor …" Look at the bruising on your neck. David those guys weren't burglars. I am certain this man Lilley sent them, and they are possibly planning another attempt to get what they want at this very moment.' Michaela eyes were bright but a concern filled her expression.

'OK, so let's say you and Wilkinson are right …'

'And Paul!'

'Quite, and dad. What shall we do? Go to the police?' I stood up and put my hands on the neckline of my shirt imitating a lawyer. 'Yes, M'lord I believe an old enemy of my father is after me. Proof? No, not exactly, but I think he sent two men around to get some old letters of my father's. Oh, I would appreciate you didn't let my mother or sister know anything about this or the break-ins. Ahh, and while we are at it you mustn't know anything that is in the letters, they are more than likely secret.' I finished, facing Michaela, eyebrows raised. 'Then just to rub them up totally I would say nothing had been stolen!'

'I underestimated you David. I thought you were ignoring the obvious, but in fact you've thought this through, haven't you?' Her lips became thin as her face tightened with worry.

'I have done nothing but think about all this since you arrived on the scene on Thursday!' I went and rinsed out the cups. 'I always knew there was something about dad …'

'Your father is not the only one with a mystery about him.' She picked up the letter again. 'Let's see, "I also wanted to really find out what happened between you and Erica ..." Well?' she smiled gently but I just looked away.

'Another day, Miss Marple,' I said making her frown again. 'Miss Marple is a fictional detective character. A real nosy old woman basically.' She flashed me an angry glance but I countered it with a wide smile. 'Let's get going. The sooner we find out what we are dealing with, then the easier it will be to decide what to do.' I started to leave the kitchen but turned to face Michaela. 'Mum mustn't find out about you and all this, please. I know it will break her heart; really.'

Michaela put one hand across her chest and with the other she took one of my hands. 'I know my mother would not want Marie to ever know as well.' She kept hold of my hand and squeezed it a little. 'David, it is *not* going to be easy to keep all this quiet ...'

'You're telling me. If I feel it is going to come out I have already decided I am going to tell mum myself. I have an idea of how to "soften the blow".'

'How?'

'Another day ... come on.' Michaela went to protest, but I pulled her towards the hallway and up to the attic.

Michaela became excited at the sight of the trunk as I pulled it through the opening in the stud wall. A disappointed frown greeted the padlock, but changed to relief when I produced the key. I unlocked the trunk and placed the heavy padlock gently on the floor. Neither of us moved and for a few moments I could just hear our heavy breathing. I opened the catch and lifted the lid. The trunk was full and the stale odour of old paper and leather filled the attic. Uniforms, boots, goggles, a flying jacket covered numerous books, a couple of art portfolio wallets, files and old cigar boxes, full of old coins and medals. Reverently Michaela and I started placing them carefully on the attic floor. Not a word was spoken. I knew she felt like me; fascinated but intrusive somehow.

'I feel awful,' she suddenly said.

I also felt as if I was intruding on my father's privacy. 'I know how you feel but we have to do it. Shall I finish on my own?' I said putting a hand on her shoulder.

'No I'll be alright but it's also the fact I never went near my father's belongings after he died, or should I say my step-father's things. In truth I didn't want to know.' She stood looking blankly into the distance. After a few minutes she took in a deep breath. 'I have a lot to tell you David.'

'My God I think we both have a lot of talking to do; come on back to work.' I really didn't want to go through my father's things all alone, having Michaela there seemed to justify our actions. 'I haven't seen any letters yet,' I said softly.

'They will be there. I know it.'

We were whispering as if we were in a church. The trunk was nearly empty and I lifted out the last few books and magazines. Right at the bottom was a large envelope partly covered in tape. It was not wrapped as much as the smaller one I had found the previous night in the metal box, in fact the tape seemed of a different type and was peeling and turning a brown colour.

'I think we have it,' I whispered. The phone rang making Michaela let out a small screech.

'Oh, I am so sorry, I …' She went silent and took the envelope. 'Downstairs?' she asked and I nodded.

'I think we could both do with a drink and something to eat.' I said getting slowly to my feet brushing off the dust from my knees. It was then that I noticed it under the eaves. A huge ball of discarded sticky tape lay on the ceiling insulation. I went to retrieve it but decided to do this when I was alone. 'Dry white wine and a sandwich?' I asked.

'Perfect,' she replied taking herself slowly down the loft steps holding the envelope as if it were a delicate and priceless object. I followed her into the study, noticing the flashing light on the answer machine, and she placed the envelope on the desk beside her letter from dad and the bank book and his letter to me.

Looking at me she slowly said, 'I have some other letters. I'll go and fetch them.' I gave her a puzzled look. 'Paul wasn't the only one who kept the letters.' She left and I went and made the sandwiches opening the bottle first and taking a large mouthful of the crisp cool wine.

* * *

'You did what?' screamed Maxwell Lilley into the phone. 'Joey, I thought I could rely on you.' He leant forward picking up his whiskey glass, listening to the older Habbul brother spluttering an excuse.

'Joey! I said make it look like a burglary. You were not to torture the guy *and* then tell him what you were looking for. Jesus, what a bloody mess!' Lilley's mind was racing.

'Right you had better lie low, so get back to familiar territory …' He took another sip of whiskey. Then he had an idea. Paul Pinner had too often been one step ahead of him. Maybe Pinner had predicted he would come for the letter after he was dead. What better place to hide it than his son's flat, he thought. His faced formed into a small sneer. 'Yes, get back to London. I would like you to go and visit David Pinner's flat just off Putney Bridge Road, I'll get the full address when you are nearer. This time just trash the place take a few obvious things but search for those bloody letters or the picture, but the letters are the priority. Pinner would be clever, so check carpets, underside of draws, attic, if there is any, and water sistens. You know the score.'

'Certainly Mr. Lilley. This time you *can* rely on us. Oh, we did spend quite a bit of money over the last few days …'

'Wednesday morning 9.00, same place. Oh, and come alone. I might say something to your wooden skulled brother.' Lilley terminated the call. Shaking his head he drained the glass. 'Unbelievable,' he said to himself. 'The question is how much will the police pick up?' He dialled another number. It switched to answer phone immediately causing Lilley to frown. 'Where is that stupid bitch? Women are never there when you really need them.' He turned the phone off and put it in the desk drawer.

★ ★ ★

I had finished making the sandwiches and went back to the study, slightly embarrassed at how much wine I had already consumed. Michaela was standing by the picture of my father on the wing of the Hurricane fighter.

'Sorry it took so long …' I said laying out the lunch on the desk. Michaela had spotted the half full bottle.

'Mmm, seems you were pre-occupied,' she said filling both glasses.

I noticed the bundle of letters on the desk. Several letters were tied together with a dainty light blue ribbon. Michaela saw my interest.

'They are Paul's letters to my Mother, Grete. I found them in her bedside drawer the day she had the heart attack. One thing is for sure; your father could write a beautiful love letter. They were quite breathtaking and not a word of, how do you say, smut.' She picked up a plate, took a sandwich and her wine, and settled into a Parker Knoll. 'I wish some man had written to me like that. For that matter I would have liked any sort of letter.'

'I blame the phone; it is too easy and with this new internet thing the post is redundant.' I chewed my sandwich thoughtfully eyeing the large envelope. I felt a sense of dread, edged with excitement at the prospect of opening the envelope. The phone rang again. Our chewing stopped. 'Bugger that phone,' I said with a mouthful of sandwich. We both broke into laughter. I heard Peter Wilkinson leave a message. Michaela was still laughing, 'Shh,' I said and rushed to the hallway.

'David, it is Peter, Peter Wilkinson again. Could you please contact me at your earliest convenience. David, it is rather important, my numbers are …' I went over and scribbled down three telephone numbers, just in case I had lost his card.

'What did he want,' said Michaela as I entered the room.

'He wants me to call him,' I said picking up my glass.

'You didn't answer it?'

'No, I will call him later when we have sorted all this out,' I said gesturing my arm towards the full desk top. 'The way he reacted last night he probably has been to the police himself.'

'David, I think he has a point.' Michaela stood up and put her plate down. 'They could come back at any time. You know that, don't you?'

'Yes, so more reason to get a move on.'

I went to the desk and taking a few breaths started to cut the tape from the envelope. I opened the end and emptied the contents onto the desk. A small silky but heavy object fell out skidding off the desk. I instinctively caught it. Michaela gave me an impressed look and came and over her eyes widening. The silk purse had a hard object inside. I opened the flap and out slide a miniature picture in a heavily gilt frame.

'Bugger me. What a tiny picture.' I said handing it to Michaela who tenderly took the picture from me. Holding it carefully she examined it closely. Watching her I felt as if she knew something about art, her face was furrowed with concentration.

'What do you think?' I asked.

'Mein Gott.'

'What is it?'

'I am not entirely sure, but I know quality when I see it.' Michaela was examining the back of the picture. 'Do you have a magnifying glass?'

'Yes, somewhere.' I couldn't find it. 'Sorry, it used to be in dad's desk drawer. So what is it?'

'I have rarely seen such exquisite work. The detail is extraordinary. There is a very small mark or initials and the back looks as if this was done in the sixteenth or seventeenth century.' I noticed her hand was trembling. 'David, this is a fine piece of art.' She placed it in the silk cover and gave it back to me. 'That is what your tattooed friend was after I am sure of it.'

'Maybe it is a priceless piece …'

'Don't get carried away. You might be talking a couple of thousand sterling.'

'Oh, is that all,' I said my heart sinking. 'Surely …'

'There were hundreds of reproductions and copies made of the masters about this time.' She still gazed at the silk object in my hand. 'I suspect this is just a copy but if it isn't and more importantly if it is part of a set, then that changes things. It is the Madonna and Child. Miniatures were often portraits and used as we have our loved ones picture in our wallets. Sometimes such miniatures were for travelling monks and priests. I studied art at university.'

'Do you fancy some air?' I asked.

'What a lovely idea.'

We walked into the garden locking all the doors behind us.

'Look Michaela,' I said as we ambled around the garden. 'I think we should get away from here. I would like to find a place we could take some time over reading these letters. I live in London and it is a big place; a lot safer than here.'

'When is your mother coming home?' Michaela asked examining one of the borders in the garden.

'She has an open ticket. Knowing mum I would say she will stick two, possibly three weeks.' I finished my wine and felt the time had come to start reading the letters. 'Come on let's get back to the study.'

The next few hours were some of the most surreal of my life. Michaela and I put the letters in chronological order. One letter, or more accurately, a type of memo or note was a complete mystery to us. It seemed to be a coded message and used the name "Christchurch".

'I am going to put money that these have something to do with Maxwell Lilley.' I said holding it up to the light; no water mark but heavy, poor quality paper. The note has the initials written on "ML", in what could well have been my father's hand, but it was difficult to tell. 'What about us contacting this Lilley chap, and doing a deal?' I said showing them to Michaela. She nodded but I could see she wasn't listening and was engrossed in one of her Mother's love letters.

'She was so in love,' she said her voice stifled by a small sob. 'I have never loved like that. In fact I am not sure I have ever been in love.' She got up and meandered around the study. Spotting a book she went and took it to the desk. Extracting the picture she opened the Miller's Antique Guide, but it was a condensed version and didn't tell her a great deal. 'The letters are an issue, but I think this picture has a part to play.'

'I'm not so sure,' I said carefully putting the letters back in order. 'Anyway I've had enough for today.' Michaela nodded her agreement. 'I feel, reading those letters, as if I am finding out about someone new, not my own father. It feels very strange,' I continued. Michaela looked at me her eyes full of tears.

'Have you read all the love letters?'

'No, not yet. I have concentrated on the MI6 and others. You were hogging them!' I said looking down at the desk top. 'We must also find out what happened in 1954 as that seems to be a pivotal event in all this.' The language used in these letters had, I believed, disguised a very serious incident.

A loud banging came from the back door. We both jumped and instinctively looked at where to hide the letters. I ran towards the kitchen to see our usual window cleaner's van in the backyard area. 'It's OK,' I shouted back to Michaela. 'I paid him some money and told him to return in two weeks.'

'David I am getting very nervous, why don't we go down to your place in London now,' she said placing all the letters in the large brown envelope.

'Maybe, this *is* all becoming just too much. Let's leave first thing in the morning.'

'Not now?'

'No, we have polished off a bottle of wine. Better in the

morning.' I took the envelope placing it in the metal box, locked it and put it back in the cupboard. 'While we are down there we could also find out a bit more about the picture.'

The next morning we waited for the traffic to ease and drove down to London. Michaela had decided to read the letters again on the way.

'So let's see what we have,' she said sifting through them. 'First are several letters in 1944 to Paul's mother, father and general ones to Marie. One to your mother very passionate. Then there is her reply.' Michaela was carefully folding the letters up and ensuring they were not damaged. 'Then there is the letter from Paul to my mother … wow! Then her reply, and the mention of a picture of the Madonna.'

'Must be the miniature,' we said in unison.

'Then a mound of letters between a Sir Richard Ryder, on MI6 paper, to Paul. Have you read these?' she asked.

'Yes, Sir Richard was my Grandfather on my mother's side …'

'Your Grandfather?'

'Yes, all very mysterious, but without dad's original letters it is hard to tell what *he* was saying. It is difficult to decipher. I need to sit down and read them again. This code name "Christchurch" came out several times.'

'Then a letter announcing my arrival,' she said making a mock bow.

'More letters in 1954 and 1955 from MI6 and this Sir Richard Ryder. Ahh and finally in 1971 …' Michaela let her shoulders drop and she looked up. 'I found them, you know.' My concentration was non-existent and the car veered. 'David watch out!' she screamed as I narrowly missed the rear of a truck.

'Sorry about that. You found them, where?'

'In bed.' I could barely hear her.

'You found them in bed. Bloody hell, what did you do?' I had slowed the car right down causing a lorry to flash and blare his horn.

'I had gone to a friend's house for the night. I forgot something and came back. I went upstairs to my room and, well there they were.' Michaela was looking ahead down the motorway; I could tell her mind was back in Vienna nearly thirty years ago.

'So you knew then?' Another wagon was now on my tail and causing me grief.

'No, not that he was my father. It never really crossed my mind. I just thought my mother was having an affair, but …'

'But you suspected?'

'No. It is difficult to explain. I wasn't surprised when mother eventually told me. My parents were never close, in fact almost indifferent to each other. The problem for mother was that *I* knew about the affair; not her own husband. She didn't seem to care if he knew about Paul or not.' She started to read the letter from my father to Grete acknowledging her decision to end their relationship and discussing not to tell Michaela. 'I can't find the letter she must have sent to Paul …'

'In 1971,' I said looking at her as much as I dared while keeping the car in the correct lane. 'That is because he burnt it. I saw him burn a letter in the study in 1971, and then went to huge lengths to ensure all the ash was pulverised to dust.'

The car droned on down the motorway and I tried to drive faster but I visualised my Father in the study back in 1971. 'It is a pity we can't ask your mother about this.'

'You can, but you'll have to come to Vienna …'

'But I thought you said she had had a heart attack?' I was annoyed at having to drive and not concentrate on our conversation.

'She did but she has had several and recovered well each time. This time she is a very sick woman, but she is also very tough.' A hesitation made it clear she felt guilt about leaving her. 'After the heart attack I insisted she stayed at my apartment for a few days to see if I could look after her, but I just couldn't manage.' I sensed the guilt. 'I gave her Paul's letter that she had been clutching when she had the heart attack. David, I was so worried in case it caused her more problems. That is when she told me a little about her life story.

'She told me to fetch her letters. Apparently she used to read them every night. My father, or I should call him Albert, was apparently gay. My mother had found him with one of his friends. She hated him she told me, not for being homosexual, but the deception. However in those days it was viewed differently than nowadays and he needed a wife to get on in business. What better than a desperate girl, pregnant by a man she could never have and who had already left the country? I suppose he never considered the man would come back.'

We both sat in silence for awhile. The pieces of the jigsaw were starting to fit together.

'So how did you find out about dad dying?'

Michaela started to frown. 'My mother insisted in going back to her flat, she has full medical back up there, and then she called me a few days ago saying she had some news. I went over and she gave me the letters and begged me to go over and try and put them in his grave. That's why I went back to the graveside. I never asked how she knew he had died.'

'Oh, now I understand why you were there.'

'My mother made me swear that I gave the money back to you but to try and not let Marie know.' Michaela pulled her hair back. 'I really didn't want to go as I knew it would be almost impossible to give the money back and for it not have any repercussions. Then I saw you walk over to the grave alone and I saw my chance.'

'So it wasn't curiosity.'

'No, it was a promise to my mother, and if you want the truth, a chance for me to say goodbye to a man I had known as a child but only as a family friend. The reality that he was actually my natural father is just sinking in.' Michaela's voice went quiet and deep. 'I found it quite hard if you really want to know.' She then forced a weak smile, 'but curiosity did play a part.'

I reached over and squeezed her hand. Words seemed irrelevant. We crawled through the London traffic and I managed to find a parking space not too far away from my apartment. I saw the police car doubled parked outside but thought nothing of it. Climbing the few steps to the outer front door I found it open. Quickly entering the communal hall I saw my splintered and shattered front door ajar. I sprinted through the door, fists clenched, to be met by a neighbour and two policemen.

'Mr. Pinner?' said one of them. I just stood with my mouth open surveying the scene of complete devastation.

Elm Farm,
Knutsford

July 22nd 1971

Dearest Grete,

I was not totally surprised to receive your last letter, and if the truth be known, I do not disagree with your demands or sentiments. I do however receive it with a heavy heart and it has left me with a void in my life I am not sure I will ever replace.

You are absolutely right that we can and must not let Michaela down. I am so glad you have managed to explain everything to her and avoid telling her the truth of her fraternal parentage. It is your secret and must now, I pray, always remain as such, for to tell a young woman like Michaela could have serious consequences for her, and me.

I promise you that I will never contact you again, and in a fit of utter despair I burnt your last letter. I needed to somehow absolve myself of the past. In a strange way I think it worked. My life with Marie is idyllic and why I should even contemplate more makes me almost despise myself.

I will keep the two gifts you gave me. The Edelweiss is hanging on my study wall. The minature, although hidden, is still very close to me. In return I ask you never to forget our fist night together.

Finally look after Michaela for me. I know one day you may have to tell her the truth, or she may deduce it for herself if she finds out about Albert's sexuality. If you do tell her, I would much appreciate that you let me know as I fear she may want to meet me again. I will take the consequences on my shoulders but I worry they may be grave for me. I couldn't see Marie ever forgiving me. Grete, I hope you take this into consideration before you tell her.

All my thoughts and best regards,

Paul

Chapter 8

THE SECOND PACKAGE

Pinner sat staring into the darkness ahead. The familiar smells acting as a shield of comfort around the uncertainty in his mind. His stomach was tight but he was pleased with himself that he had managed to get back into the bomber at all. The scare on the last mission over the northern coast of Holland had put a fear into him which made him doubt his own courage. He had decided to tell the C.O. that he wasn't sure if he was up to the job. The resulting conversation had put his mind at rest. He couldn't imagine his C.O. vomiting as he waited to be scrambled at the height of the Battle of Britain. The C.O. had told him that he believed those who had fear are the best pilots. They realise the dangers and are not blind optimists who could often be a liability.

Despite his dread of the mission he was in a good mood. The letter from Marie had seen to that. Pinner closed his eyes for a moment and prayed for his return to Cumbria.

'We're still fighting this headwind skipper,' came the navigator's voice over the intercom.

'What's our ETA Tomkins?' asked Pinner.

'At the moment a good hour and a half, but if this head wind continues …'

'Well, think on the bright side, we will have it behind us on the way home,' said Pinner, a settling tone in his voice.

Wilkinson looked at his skipper sensing his conflicting moods. He switched his intercom to his skipper only.

'You seem in a strange mood today, skipper. Quiet, but content?' Wilkinson adjusted his position in his seat.

'Yes, a letter from the fair maiden.'

'Ahh, that's it, but …'

'But …' Pinner leant forward and extracted another package from underneath his seat. Wilkinson stared at it, his eyes at first widening and then narrowed wishing the metal cylinder would disappear. 'We have to do it all again Wilkie.'

'You had better let them know,' said Wilkinson still trying to make himself comfortable. 'I had sensed something was up.'

'Later,' said Pinner stretching. 'They want more photographs as well.' Wilkinson's head span round to face his captain. 'You did too good a job, old boy,' Pinner continued. 'It seems the photographs revealed that our Russian allies had obviously discovered some new type of weapon the Nazis had been developing.'

'Damn, where this time?' Wilkinson's voice not concealing his fear.

'That's the problem. It is further east.' This time Wilkinson's head turned slowly towards his skipper.

'Further east? Are they mad?' his hand smoothed his face.

'That's the problem Wilkie old son,' said Pinner eyeing his co-pilot. 'They possibly are, but they're in charge. They just want to know what the Russians will have when Germany is finally beaten; trust me the war may not end even then.'

'And the package. Same drop zone?' said Wilkie looking pale after Pinner's last observation.

Pinner nodded feeling uncomfortable at lying to his best friend. 'We will fly further north and come in away from that ruddy ack-ack battery.' Pinner's knuckles whitened. The actual drop zone this time would make the last one seem like a breeze.

'Oh, that's alright then,' Wilkie's voice was harsh. 'This is turning into the mission from hell.'

'I can't disagree with you,' Pinner glanced over his left shoulder. He was still nervous about the new port engine. It sounded different. 'Wilkie,' Pinner hesitated for a moment. 'I think the Russians may also suspect something.'

His co-pilot nodded. 'They let loose at us the last time and that is sure to get back to their high command. Especially as we clearly would have seen something we shouldn't have.'

'Exactly,' Pinner looked to his right. 'Do you remember I found one of them snooping around on the last mission?'

'What can we expect?'

'I am really not sure. I don't believe our chaps would send us out here if they felt we would be in real danger, but let's expect the worst and see what happens.' Pinner's voice was strong as he sensed Wilkie's concerns.

'We don't have enough fuel just to turn around and head home after dropping off the cargo, so what is your suggestion?' Wilkinson's voice rose.

'I have been given further orders in the event of us being met with any hostility and we could have fuel shortage,' Pinner said trimming the aircraft.

'What?'

'I'll let you know when …'

'And what if you are injured or …' Wilkinson stopped. Predicting someone's possible fate is something he felt uncomfortable with. Pinner twisted in his seat to face his old friend; he did have a very valid point.

'Head South West and join the allies in Northern Italy. That's all I'll say for the moment. I have the relevant charts in Tomkins drawer.

'Does he know?'

Pinner shook his head. 'I'm sorry Wilkie that's all I can say.'

'We're going back there what ever happens aren't we …'

'Wilkie,' Pinner turned to his co-pilot. 'No more talk on this at the moment.' Silence fell on the cockpit for several minutes.

'This operation you, or should I say we, are involved with. Will it shorten the war?' Wilkinson was watching Pinner carefully. Sensing his friend's look Pinner decided to try and give him some information which wouldn't break any operational procedures.

'No, quite the reverse.' Pinner stopped Wilkinson from speaking by raising his hand. 'I am not going to say anymore Wilkie. But I promise if I have to, I will. Come on you know the rules.'

His old companion nodded and he went about his duties silently.

Dawn broke the darkness sending long strange shadows over the earth below. The bomber shook rhythmically, heading south eastwardly, fighting the continuing head winds. An hour later the landing instructions were received and Pinner circled the airfield and as usual performed an excellent landing. Two Lavochkin La-5s fighters were being made ready at the far end of the airfield.

'Well if things get nasty at least we don't have Hurricanes to contend with,' said Pinner nodding towards the fighters. 'Those things are flying tubs.'

Pinner secured the package in a hidden compartment behind the instruments and watched as their usual contact came across to the bomber from the hanger. Several men followed him but they were not mechanics. No one was smiling. Wilkinson opened the bomb doors for the cargo to be removed. The crew dismounted the bomber and their contact did not attempt to speak English. Pinner and Wilkinson exchanged nervous glances. The plane was to be inspected before the cargo could be offloaded, Polanski translated. Another worried exchange of looks, this time by all the crew. There would be no breakfast and a minimum amount of fuel to ensure their return. Two of the uniformed men accompanying their contact went to the bomber.

'Stay here,' Pinner commanded his crew and strode purposefully after the men.

Pinner reached the first Russian as he started to climb the ladder into the forward hatch. Pinner pointed at the hatch and shook his head. The man shouted at him in Russian and tried to continue up the ladder. Pinner put his hand on his shoulder, meeting the other man's eyes. Pinner slowly shook his head again, making it clear that entry into the bomber would not be allowed. Pinner noticed his crew moving forward.

'*Stay where you are,*' he screamed at them.

Both the Russians turned and squared up to Pinner. Pinner was taller than them and didn't flinch.

'No. Entry not permitted,' he said using sign language to force home his message.

'Very well comrade,' said the first Russian in excellent English. 'I respect your wishes,' he turned and looking back continued, 'for now.' His voice was almost drowned by the two fighters taking-off virtually side by side.

Pinner indicated for the crew to return. They waited by the bomber as the cargo was disgorged and a little fuel was eventually loaded. The crew entered the bomber and Wilkinson waved at their contact. He just stared back making no movement.

'Are we doing the detour east,' asked Wilkinson.

'I know you think I am crazy at times Wilkie,' said Pinner adjusting himself to his seat, 'but I'm not totally barking mad.' Pinner sensed his friend's relief.

'Tomkins, set a course for home, but once we are on the way I'll be giving you a new location.' Wilkinson gave him a long look, but Pinner at first just busied himself; eventually he finally decided to tell his co-pilot. 'The drop is on the Austrian and Yugoslavian border.'

'Dear God. You are barking, do you know that?'

Pinner fired up the two Hercules engines, and with no other aircraft around took off heading east but banked steeply as soon as he could to head west.

'We will not be taking any photographs this time,' Pinner told the crew through the intercom. 'We do however have a different course for home. Take the controls Wilkie.' Pinner went down to the navigator's position and handed him the coordinates and told him where the new charts were. The navigator looked questioningly at his captain, but never spoke.

'Take a course west until I tell you; then give me directions for here,' he said pointing at the silk map. 'I'll let you know where we go from there.'

Pinner returned to his seat feeling his co-pilot's eyes on him. They flew in silence until they reached 10,000 feet. 'Level here,' he said to Wilkinson. 'Tomkins are you ready?'

'Yes, turn port 75 degrees …'

'Fighters!' came a scream from the rear gunner.

'Where,' shouted Pinner.

'Eleven o'clock, port side, coming from above and behind us,' answered Stewart.

'Are they attacking,' Pinner said as calmly as he could twisting in his seat to try and see more clearly over his left shoulder.

'Not sure, but they are coming straight towards us.'

Pinner quickly twisted and stooped down to try and see back up towards the rear of the aircraft.

'Polanski radio to them for Christ sake,' shouted Pinner. He saw his rear-gunner turn his guns on the advancing fighters. 'NO! Stewart, don't move your …'

The thud of cannon hitting the rear of the aircraft made the plane yaw to the left and Pinner saw Wilkinson fighting to keep control. The screech of the first fighter banking away to its left, to avoid the front gunner, filled the cockpit. A brief silence was shattered by more thudding and bullets splintering wood and ripping into steel. The second fighter could not be heard above the screams of the rear gunner.

'All stay in your positions,' ordered Pinner as he searched for the fighters. Looking to the rear of the aircraft Pinner saw the young gunner staring at his shattered body in disbelief. He was desperately trying to stem the flow of blood from his wounds.

'Oh, mum, mum …' he uttered to an unhearing mother.

'They're coming again,' said Wilkinson squinting over his right shoulder. 'Not bad for old tubs, Skipper.'

The front gunner was cursing and Pinner could see his guns moving from side to side. 'Polanski, do not open fire,' bellowed

Pinner. Wilkinson shot him a confused glance as Pinner gestured out of the window as coming along side was one of the Russian fighters. They could see the pilot pointing forwards and then at himself.

'They want you to follow him,' said Wilkie in disbelief. Another Polish curse came over the intercom.

'Polanski, you must not fire. Put your guns forward and exit the gun position,' said Pinner gripping the controls tightly. A murmur was followed by the guns being straightened and Pinner saw him move back into the navigator's section. The Pole looked up at Pinner his eyes dark and broody. He knew they had no chance against two fighters, but he hated the Russians as much as the Nazis. History had taught him that.

'Polanski, get the first aid kit and check Stewy,' called Pinner indicating to Wilkinson he was going aft. When Pinner had reached the rear gun turret, Polanski was ripping open absorbent first aid pads and stuffing them into the gunner's wounds. Pinner took out a capsule of morphine and plunged its needle into the young man's shoulder. The Scot was now going into shock and his body was shaking uncontrollably while Pinner undid his flying jacket and recoiled at the sight of a hole in the man's chest. Shattered bone and ripped flesh were darkened by the burn from the shell. The gunner's leg was twisted unnaturally around the base of his seat. The Pole looked at his skipper and tried to move the leg to extract him, but this caused a weak scream and the Gunner's body went limp.

Pinner checked for a pulse on his neck but wasn't able to find one, however the vibration and his own shaking hands meant he could not be sure if the man was dead or not. Suddenly Stewart's body made a violent convulsion and then went totally still. The expression of pain and horror drained from his fresh face and Pinner now knew he was dead.

Pinner plugged himself into the intercom.

'Where are we going?' he shouted.

'The fighter is high up on the starboard side; our heading is almost due south,' answered his co-pilot.

'We are just passing over Lodz,' added the navigator.

Pinner looked down at the man who would never see his twenty-first birthday. 'Cover him up as much as you can will you,' he said to the Pole. Pinner looked back to see the second fighter well above them and clearly ready to attack if required. Wind was whistling through the shattered glass and holes in the fuselage. Pinner moved forward slowly considering whether to contact his base but what was he to do with the package.

He took a piece of paper from Tomkin's position and wrote on it. Going to his seat he extracted the package. Opening the tube he withdrew a rolled up envelope. Setting it alight he waited until the paper had fully burnt and crushed it with the soul of his boot.

'Wilkie, just open the bomb doors a little and immediately close them,' he said waving the canister at him. Wilkie gave him the thumbs up. Pinner hoped the fighters were too high to see the slight movement of the bomb doors. Tossing the package out as soon as the doors opened a little caused an immediate reaction on the radio. Pinner didn't need it translating. He then handed a paper to Tomkins. The navigator altered the frequency and tapped out in Morse code:

BEEN ATTACKED STOP DESTROYED PACKAGE STOP BEEN ESCORTED STOP UNSURE OF DESTINATION STOP

Pinner returned to his seat just in time to hear the end of a radio message. Polanski translated, 'They want us to follow the lead fighter and land behind him. We are not to open the bomb doors again.'

'We can't be far from the last destination,' said Wilkinson agitated and checking the ground below him. They were too high to make out any detail. 'What do you think they will do?' he looked towards his skipper.

'Wilkie, I have no idea,' lied Pinner. A thorough search of the aircraft and possibly scare them into admitting they had been spying was what he was expecting. Pinner dwelled on the spying issue. Death would be the penalty, he knew that. He must take the responsibility. His mind flashed to Marie and for the second time that day he prayed as hard as he could.

Pinner descended with the lead fighter. The landscape was barren. Hamlets of groups of small houses scattered the countryside. Thin wisps of smoke could be seen drifting upward from a burnt out building as if to escape the horror that must have been. The airfield slowly emerged out of the gloom. Pinner grabbed the controls with both hands and knew with so much fuel on-board the landing was not going to be easy. The lead fighter touched down for a split second and then took off again. Pinner noticed the windsock was blowing from his right. Kicking in a lot of rudder to compensate he hit the runway too hard and bounced. As the airspeed dropped the aircraft plummeted again hitting the ground causing all the crew to exclaim instinctively with the impact.

'Sorry chaps,' yelled Pinner. 'I'll get there this time.' The third attempt he managed to set the aircraft down. Pinner braked and then pulled the aircraft off the runway, relieved. The engines ticked over with the four men awaiting their fate. Pinner was struggling to breathe, as his own thoughts of the consequences of their spying were manifesting themselves in his mind. Several minutes passed and he watched both the fighters land. Pinner took of his gloves and wiped his moist palms on his trousers. 'Come on, do something you ruddy bastards,' he shouted. He didn't look at Wilkie but gazed up towards the control tower.

Eventually an old truck lumbered its way towards them and the driver indicated for them to follow. He taxied a few hundred yards to the remote outskirts of the airfield. The truck stopped and the driver got out indicating to cut the engines and to come with him.

'What do we do?' croaked Wilkinson. 'We can't leave the Whimey here unmanned. And what about Stewy?'

'Polanski, Wilkinson and I will go and have a chat with our friends. You stay …'

Pinner's voice faded as another troop truck, this time with soldiers sitting on the back, started trundling towards them.

'I think that puts another light onto it. Get out everyone,' ordered Pinner.

Polanski earned his pay that morning thought Pinner as all three of them were being driven away, crushed up in the cab with the driver. Apparently they were being taken to the Command post for this area. A coffin was being despatched for Stewart, and Polanski had said they were conciliatory and very apologetic about the whole affair, but beware a friendly Russian he told him. They had been offered more fuel but first they must de-brief the local commander. The officer in charge had posted a guard with the plane and Tomkins had been allowed to stay. Pinner closed his eyes and tried to visualise Marie; he couldn't.

The devastation on the ground was more evident, clearly a major battle had taken place. Pinner stared at the huddled groups of peasant workers trying to salvage anything from the ruins. Winter was starting to strip the land of greenery. The truck passed through a small town. At first Pinner couldn't make out the bundles hanging from lampposts and telegraph poles.

'They helped the Nazis,' muttered the Pole. Pinner looked again and then he noticed the bundles were corpses, all hanging by their necks swaying in the bitter wind. Some of the men had their trousers pulled down and a gapping dark hole was all that was left of their genitals.

'Oh my God,' was all Pinner could muster, his stomach starting to heave.

The driver shouted at the corpses and spat on the floor. Pinner looked ahead he didn't want Wilkinson to see the fear in his eyes.

Not far out of the town they entered the remains of what must have been impressive gates in their heyday. They travelled up a long drive lined with large tree stumps. The old house must have once been a magnificent residence but it was scared by war. Bullet holes blemished the front façade and part of the building at the rear was in ruins. Masonry around the roof and windows was crumbling. The truck stopped and the driver indicated for them to dismount. The troops in the following truck were already shuffling over towards the house. Pinner was disgusted by their appearance and apparent lack of discipline. Wilkie went over to them and offered the tallest, and obviously their commander, a cigarette. The Russian took the packet, laughed and turned to his men ignoring the hapless co-pilot. Pinner watched anxiously. Why so many troops, he fretted. He couldn't help but noticed how these soldiers were eyeing their boots and jackets. The image of the hanging corpses filled his mind. These people had no pity left, he thought.

The door to the house opened and the three British aviators were led in. Already dusk was starting to dispel the daylight. They were taken down two flights of stairs and along a corridor with the occasional skylight high on the wall. The smell of damp and urine tinged their nostrils. Their escort stopped by a large door with a curved top, and unlocked it. Opening it he indicated for the three men to enter. Pinner hesitantly led the way. A small cellar confronted him completely bare except for a long bench underneath a tiny slit of a barred window. A loud bang made Pinner spin round to see that they were alone. They could just make each other in the gloom. Footsteps faded into the distance. The three men stood still not sure if to expect anything else.

Pinner walked around the room and found a pile of threadbare blankets and a rusty metal bucket; the remains inside identifying its purpose. Pinner took the blankets to the bench.

'Right, not exactly the Ritz, but we must take the opportunity to get some sleep,' he said fearing his attempt at optimism could backfire. Both men came and took a blanket each. 'I'll take the floor first, you two should be able to squeeze onto the bench,' he continued. 'Well, let's see what tomorrow brings. It could have been worse ...' Pinner recalled the sight of his rear gunner and decided just to try and sleep. The other two men remained silent and started preparing the bench.

The dark seemed to strangle the air in the cellar and Pinner lay on his back trying to think what he could do. The cold soon penetrated his blankets and clothes and he felt his joints stiffen. The shivering started slowly but soon it was uncontrollable. Pinner could not read his watch and he started to understand the meaning of eternity. He had not slept before he saw the faint signs of dawn. The occasional snore and mutter was relief to him to know his colleagues had been more successful.

A large bang in the distance was followed by footsteps approaching. The door was unlocked and swung open. A torch surveyed the room and rested on Pinner's face.

'Flight Lieutenant Pinner,' shouted one man with a thick Eastern European accent. Pinner raised his hand and tried to get up, but was struggling. Two men came forward and hauled him to his feet dragging him out of the room. The door was pulled shut and locked by the third man and Pinner was half dragged up the corridor his ears ringing with the protests of his two crew members.

Pinner shook with the cold and fear. Finally taking control of his legs he managed to walk with his guards. They entered the hallway and walked across to a pair of large double doors. The lead man knocked and, hearing a shout, entered. An open fire greeted Pinner and the sound of crackling wood felt almost reassuring. It was quickly dispelled as he was roughly manhandled to an old carved tall backed dining chair and his hands tied behind him. He winced as the two soldiers tied the knot as tight as possible. Suddenly the drapes were pulled back and Pinner blinked at the light and he saw three men watching him on the other side to the room. The soldiers left.

'Flight Lieutenant Pinner,' said the shorter of the men advancing towards him with a small glass. He stopped before the chair and placed the glass on Pinner's lips. 'Vodka? Finest in Poland at the moment. Russian of course,' the man said smiling. Pinner could smell the faint whiff of alcohol on his breath. He nodded and the Russian tipped the fluid into Pinner's opening mouth. The fiery liquid made Pinner splutter and as he instinctively tried to move his hands the rope cut into his wrists. The man walked back to a table and charged the glass. No more, Pinner thought.

The other two men watched impassively as the short man approached Pinner again.

'What were you doing over one of our convoys five days ago,' he said putting his face close to Pinner's. The stench from his breath turned Pinner's stomach. Pinner went to answer but the Russian continued.

'What is Scorpion and Christchurch?' This time the man threw the vodka into Pinner's face, making Pinner start and rock back in the heavy chair.

'My name is Paul Pinner, Flight ...'

The Russian threw the glass towards the fire and then struck Pinner's face with the back of his hand. Pinner felt fluid trickle from his nose.

'What is Scorpion and Christchurch?'

'My name ...'

This time the Russian punched Pinner in the solar plexus making him arch forward and the vodka vomited back into his mouth. Pinner struggled for air and spat the acidy fluid out.

'I repeat, Mr Pinner. What is Scorpion and Christchurch?' The Russian was walking back towards the table. He filled a glass, drank it and picked up a riding crop with a horn handle. Pinner started. The Russian approached again and swished the riding crop at Pinner's head. The majority of the blow was taken by the chair and for a brief second Pinner thought this man had mis-judged his aim, but the expression of satisfaction on his tormentor's face showed he was toying with him.

'Scorpion?' said the Russian bring the crop down on Pinner's thigh. Pinner uttered a curse.

'Christchurch?' This time the riding crop hurt and Pinner yelled.

'For Christ sake. We are allies …'

'Scorpion?' Another whip across his upper leg.

'Scorpion,' gasped Pinner, 'is a large predatory insect found in warm …'

The whip caught Pinner on the side of the face and was quickly brought back whipping the other cheek.

'You ruddy little shit …'

'This will continue until you talk.' The Russian turned the crop in his hand and lifted it above Pinner's head the horn handle now visible.

'Did you contact your base?' came a voice from the other side of the room. Slowly the riding crop came down but not towards him. Pinner's mind was scrabbling as to what to say.

'You know I did. It was on the normal hailing frequencies,' he said trying to make out the other two men's faces. They glanced at each other and one of them went to the window.

The man turned towards Pinner and all he could see was his silhouette. 'It is a nice morning, such a shame to spoil it.' The man brought out his cigarettes and proceeded to light one. 'I will give you one more chance to answer my comrade's questions. Believe me Mr. Pinner what I have installed for you will make your current predicament feel almost desirable.' Pinner could just make out a smile in the dark shadow of his face.

'What is Scorpion and Christchurch?' shouted his tormentor and lifted the crop, the handle ready to hand out further punishment.

'Look I have absolutely no idea …' The crop handle cracked his head just above his eye. Pinner cursed, but anger had started to push his fear aside. 'For Christ sake if you let me speak I may be able to explain.' Pinner noticed the man in front of him turning to look at the one by the window.

'The chair is yours, Mr Pinner, if you pardon my humour.' Pinner looked towards the man speaking by the window. The morning sky was bright blue and he longed to get out and feel the sun on his face.

'I really have no idea what you are talking about. Christchurch is a town in southern England plus, I believe, various other locations around the world.' Pinner saw the crop twitch. 'I am totally and utterly serious you can hit me all you ruddy like but I can't tell you what I don't know.'

'So let's forget Christchurch,' said the man turning to look out of the window. 'Scorpion, let's talk about that, or should I say Operation Scorpion.'

Pinner went to talk but stopped, his mouth slightly open. How can they know about this, he thought. How can he get out of this mess; they already must know something.

'Mr. Pinner,' the man by the window exhaled a large plume of smoke. 'I believe your country has the same punishment as ourselves regarding spying. It is a shame your masters, who are safely in London enjoying their luxury, while you are not here to answer the questions. They send pawns like you to do the dirty work. But *you* are here and believe me, very close to your own death. They have deserted you and left you to take all the risks.'

The man crossed the room stopped in front of Pinner and flicked ash into Pinner's face. Pinner didn't react his heart was pounding and his eyes just stared at the Russian. 'All I want Mr. Pinner is to protect my country and I believe Operation Scorpion, of which you are part of or certainly know about, would seriously threaten my mother country.' The man stubbed out his cigarette and lit another one slowly. 'I can understand Churchill's fear of us. We are dedicated unlike the decadent West. Our soviet society is fair to all and does not have a privileged few who take everything. Yes, I can see why Mr. Churchill fears us.'

'If you know so much then why do you need this little *pawn's* input …?'

'You arrogant imperialist, I have had enough of you,' said the larger man hitting Pinner across the face. He turned, opened the door and called in the soldiers. Several orders were barked out and two of them came in and started untying Pinner's bonds. In a few moments Pinner's anger had turned to fear. What if he did tell them all he knew, he thought. Could it do any harm, they seemed to know an awful lot already.

The soldiers took an arm each and he was dragged out into the hallway through the front door and around to the rear of the house. The bitterly cold air took Pinner's breath away and for a brief second he felt the sun on his back. Turning the corner Pinner first caught sight of the soldiers that had been with them yesterday filing onto a square piece of open ground. Pinner glanced in front of him and saw three large wooden stakes in front of a wall. An order was barked out and the soldiers went into two lines. Pinner struggled but his two guards tightened their grip and hauled him to the middle stake. Pinner's legs buckled and his strength seemed to drain away.

'This is madness,' he cried trying to turn round and shout back at the three men in the room. He just caught sight of the man who had tortured him; a broad smile filled his face. Pinner was swung round and slammed against the stake. His arms were brought behind him and tied tightly. A rope then went around his lower chest. Pinner could barely stand as his knees were shaking.

'For God sake, *no*! I don't know anything. London will hear of this.' In the distance Pinner could just make out the shouts of his crew. Did they know what was going on? Another order was shouted and the two ranks of soldiers came to attention. Not a sound for a few moments and in the distance Pinner heard a large engine straining and the distant drone of a plane. Out of the house came the other man who had asked him all the questions. He came forward and stood to Pinner's side. He opened a piece of paper and proceeded to read out what must have been the charges against him in a foreign tongue. The man stopped and looked disdainfully at the British pilot tied to the stake.

'In short Flight Lieutenant Pinner you are to be shot for spying on the Soviet Red Army,' said the man holding up a hood. Pinner shook his head; an instinctive move to show some resilience, but he was ignored and the hood was placed over his head.

Another order and the metallic clatter of guns being primed and loaded. Pinner took a few deep breaths closed his eyes trying hard not to imagine his mother crying when she heard the news of his death. He saw the kitchen at home and his father putting his arm around her, speechless with grief.

Another order and Pinner straightened his back and inhaled a long deep breath.

34 Henderson Avenue,
Livingston,
Scotland

April 1945

Dear F/L Pinner,

Thank you for your kind letter of 28th March last and we fully appreciate the reasons for the delay in your letter.

My wife and I would like to thank you for your kind words about David. We both knew he would conduct himself with the utmost valour and dignity, but his loss has been especially painful as he was our only child. We must confess to being in a state of shock. Our worst fear has now manifested itself and how we are to cope is a little uncertain.

I appreciate the circumstances surrounding his death cannot be revealed for operational reasons and it is therefore especially good of you to ensure at least we knew his death was quick and he did not suffer. We both cried when we heard that his last words in this world were for his mother. Most sons are close to their mother; David was no exception.

Our loss is in part alleviated by knowing he played his part in the ultimate destruction of a most evil regime and a man who led a nation into an aggressive war, which at one stage looked as if he would win. I am so relieved that good has at last, well almost, overcome evil.

Without causing you too much embarrassment; David had written to us often during 1944 and his praise for you and the rest of the crew was almost limitless. I think you knew he was no natural warrior, in fact quite the reverse, and he kept going by his ultimate wish to go to medical school, alas this will never be. I think the world will be the worse for it.

Finally my wife and I cordial invite you to come and visit us if you are ever in Scotland, we would dearly like to meet you.

All out best wishes and prayers go with you.

Cameron and Agnes Stewart

Chapter 9

THE ESCAPE

Pinner held his breath until it hurt but still the shots did not come.

'Fire you ruddy bastards,' Pinner screamed releasing his breath into the hood. The resulting silence was deafening.

'I'll give you one more chance,' said his integrator's voice close to his ear.

The voice made Pinner jump and he bellowed towards the voice, 'You bastards. I'll tell you nothing, never, even if I knew anything.' Pinner turned his head trying to pick up any noise. He heard the faint movement of feet, and the occasional clatter of a gun strap. He shouted again, 'what game is this? I am fighting the Nazis as well. We are meant to be allies.' Still no noise that would enable him to assess what was going on. Fear, pride and confusion jumbled inside him. 'Come on if you're going to,' he screamed again towards the firing squad; then a glimmer of hope overcame him.

The hood came off and Pinner blinked in the bright morning light. No soldiers were there, just his interrogator and the guards.

'You are a lucky man, Mr. Pinner,' said the short Russian untying the ropes. 'Comrade General believes you know nothing. As you say you are a pawn not worth spending anymore time on.' The man turned and went towards the house as Pinner found his body relaxing and his legs started to shake alarmingly. 'You will be taken to the local cemetery where you will bury your dead comrade, and then we will talk again,' he said as he left disappearing around the corner of the house.

Pinner leant back on the stake and lifted his cupped hands to his face taking in a few long breaths. His guards waited patiently; even they knew what he must have been feeling. After a few moments he turned to them and nodded; then he was escorted back to the house and to an upstairs room. He sat alone in what once must have been a bedroom and surveyed the view from the window. Nothing but utter desolation stared back at him. A few moments later Polanski and Wilkinson entered escorted by the guards. A command was shouted out and Polanski answered.

'We are to be given some breakfast,' said the Pole his eyes fixed on his skipper's scarred forehead and face.

'Good, for I am absolutely ravenous,' said Wilkie trying to lighten the atmosphere and smacking his lips. 'Do you realise we haven't eaten since 2 days ago?' He continued studying his skipper's swollen face uneasy as whether to say anything or not.

Pinner nodded but he wasn't hungry. 'How are you two?' he asked stretching his legs. 'Did I hear you shout a while ago?'

'Yes, we thought we heard something going on so we decided to try and get some attention,' Wilkie said. A sound of a door banging in the distance made him look towards their door. 'Paul, what the hell is going on?'

'I'll explain later,' Pinner replied looking towards the Pole who was now also surveying the bleak scenery. 'We are apparently going to bury Stewart.'

'Can't we take him back with us?' murmured Wilkie. 'Surely there is no need for us to bury him here, unless …' Wilkie looked towards the door again. The stark realisation of their possible fate dawning on him. 'We're not getting out of here are we Paul?'

Polanski watched the two men carefully sensing he was not privy to some information. He turned back to the window resigning himself to ending up his days back in his homeland; possibly dead.

'Well, I've just had a real nasty time, believe me.' Pinner went to the door and listened for a few moments. 'We're getting out of here and if it means we get killed in the process then so be it. I'm not going to be shot like a rat in a barrel.' Footsteps came from the stairs outside. Pinner leant forward towards Wilkinson. 'We can't mess with these people. They are animals.'

Wilkie surveyed his skipper's face again. 'Was it bad?'

'Bad enough. I don't want to go through that again …'

The door crashed open and the two guards came in one carrying a tray full of dark bread and some sausage type food. The most welcoming sight was a pot of steaming tea. The guard set the food down and motioned towards it and left. The door closed and for a few seconds none of the men moved. Wilkie was first, 'Sorry chaps but I could eat a horse.'

'You probably will be,' whispered the Pole, a grin forming over his worried expression. The men ate in silence. The food was bland and difficult to chew but it was sustenance.

'I intend to try and get away at the first available opportunity,' Pinner said munching on some dark bread thoughtfully. 'I was accused of spying and then they put me in front of a ruddy firing squad.' Wilkinson's eyes widened.

'Bloody hell, you faced a firing squad,' Wilkie said under his breath. 'That's what all the commotion was about.'

'Yes, but they were playing with me. Suddenly they took of the hood and the soldiers had gone. I really don't know what their game is but I have a gut feeling they are not planning for us to get home.' Pinner cupped his hands around the large earthenware mug. 'I am sorry but I feel the only way out is to wrong foot them.'

'Wrong foot them?' repeated his co-pilot.

'Unless we have a platoon escorting us, we will overcome the guards when we go to Stewy's funeral and get back to the Whimpey.' Pinner took a sip of the hot flavourless fluid and watched the two men in front of him. 'Polanski can you remember the way back to the airfield?' The Pole nodded.

'What if …' started Wilkinson.

'If we are caught, I will take the blame. I think it is me they are concerned about, not you lot.' Pinner finished his tea and gently placed the mug on the table. 'I may be wrong about this, but if we lamely follow their instructions we could have a very ignominious end.'

'You're the skipper,' said Wilkinson starting to stand. The pole nodded again.

'Right, keep your wits about you and be prepared,' said Pinner. 'The problem is we don't know where Tomkins is being kept; hopefully he is still with the Whimpey.'

'Surely they will bring him with Stewy's body,' Wilkie said pacing the room.

'Yes, I was hoping that, but knowing Tomkins he will insist on staying with the bomber. I did give him that order.' Pinner watched his co-pilot pacing to and fro across the room.

'Look Paul, maybe our message got through to London and they will be putting pressure on the Russians as we speak.' Wilkie's legs were shaking.

'Maybe, but I don't believe the wheels of diplomacy move that fast. We have only been missing for twenty four ...' Loud footsteps came from outside.

The door opened and the same driver as the previous day was flanked by the two guards standing in the corridor. He motioned for them to follow and descended the stairs. The three RAF men followed hesitantly.

The battered truck was outside and on the back was a roughly constructed coffin.

Pinner turned to the driver and pointed at the coffin. 'Stewart, is this Stewart?'

The driver shouted back waving his arms. Pinner looked towards Polanski. The Pole was frowning. 'No, it seems Stewart is still at the airfiel,' he said following the driver towards the truck.

'Ask him what's happening, where are we going?' said Pinner catching up with the Pole. Polanski had a brief discussion with the driver and turned to his skipper.

'We are going to the airfield, collecting Stewart and Tomkins and then going to bury him in a church not far away,' said the gunner squeezing into the front seat beside the driver. Pinner and Wilkinson followed suit. The driver turned over the engine and engaged the gears.

'Why don't we take him with us,' demanded Wilkinson.

'Shut up Wilkie,' ordered his skipper.

The two guards turned and went into the old house. Pinner glanced up at the sky and despite the freezing cold it was good flying conditions. Wilkinson saw his skipper's gaze upward.

'Are you thinking about the conversation we just had upstairs, sir,' said Wilkie as formally as possible. The Pole turned towards them. Pinner nodded, and muttered, 'as I said before keep your wits about you; this could be a ruddy mess or an opportunity from heaven.'

The truck went through the town they had passed the previous afternoon. Figures passed uncaringly underneath the corpses swaying in the breeze. Pinner felt his skin crawl. The truck lumbered slowly towards the airfield, and came to the gate where several soldiers peered at them from a small shack. One of them came forward and waved the truck through. They passed some large camouflaged buildings and Pinner saw the bomber off to their left. The truck seemed to be heading towards the control tower.

Polanski turned and talked to the driver. Pinner noticed the Pole's quick glance behind him. The driver started to laugh but then uttered a muted high pitch scream. He coughed blood and the truck veered to the right. The Pole took the wheel straightened the vehicle and slammed his foot on the brake. The driver was still spluttering unsure what was happening to him. Just before the truck stopped the Pole leant across and opened the driver's door. He pushed the Russian out and slid into his seat. Pinner saw the flash of the knife which they had used during breakfast that morning. The Pole revved the engine and turned the truck straight towards the Wellington Bomber.

'Christ Polanski …'

'Look towards the control tower,' shouted the Pole struggling to keep the vehicle in a straight line at such speed and crunching the gears. Pinner turned and could now see soldiers grouped behind the tower. 'You told me to keep my wits about me …'

'Yes, but …' Pinner could not think of anything else to say. He knew the Pole was right. He was shocked and in awe at the Pole's ability to kill in cold blood.

'Oh, my God there are two guards by the bomber,' shouted Wilkinson. 'Try and run them down Polanski.'

'*No*, one of them is Tomkins,' shouted Pinner peering forward and then turning to look behind him to see what was happening at the tower. The turning propellers of the two fighters well to his right caught his eye. 'Ruddy hell, those bloody La-5s are ready for take-off.' The Pole glanced towards them. 'There doesn't seem to be any pilots, maybe they are possibly being kept warm.'

'Watch out,' cried Wilkinson. The guard by the bomber had raised his rifle and aimed it right at them. Pinner saw the blue smoke from the barrel and a large thud crunched into the front of the truck. The engine immediately coughed and the Pole pumped the accelerator. A Polish curse reverberated in the cab. The guard took another aim at the truck but collapsed forward crashing onto the ground sending another puff of smoke out of the barrel.

'Ruddy hell, well done Tomkins,' shouted Pinner as the truck ground to a halt a few yards away from the bomber. 'Polanski could you …'

The Pole was already gone and went to the prostrate guard, picked up the rifle and crashed the butt twice into the Russian's skull. Pinner and Wilkinson were also out of the truck running towards the bomber's hatch. 'Leave him Polanski, for Christ sake leave him,' ordered Pinner.

Pinner climbed into the bomber nervously glancing back at the tower. No sign of anyone chasing them, but he saw a small vehicle being made ready with two men in flying jackets waiting beside it. 'Polanski get in the rear gunner's position and shoot anything that looks remotely hostile especially those La-5s.' The

Pole flashed a frown at his skipper he had never wanted the rear-gunner's position. 'Just do it Polanski!'

Wilkinson was already in his seat and began the starting engine procedure. Tomkins was the last in the plane and kicked away the ladders closing the hatch. Pinner noticed Stewart was not in the plane. 'Right everyone let's just get out of here. Tomkins you should find some charts at the bottom of your drawer of the Adriatic coast of Italy and Yugoslavia. We're going southwest and hopefully get behind our lines in Italy.'

Pinner helped Wilkinson make ready and finally turned over the port engine. The Hercules wheezed for a few seconds but roared into life. Pinner had never heard such a welcome sound. The starboard engine came to life a few seconds later and Pinner immediately released the brake and gunned the engines making the bomber crawl forward. Wilkinson tapped the temperature gauges.

'No time for them to warm Wilkie. Keep the mixture rich and chokes open.'

Pinner increased the revs and trundled towards the runway swinging the bomber round but on full throttle. He entered and started down the runway. The engines sounded different and were straining being at such revs whilst still cold. Pinner saw a vehicle arrive by the two fighters and saw the pilots running towards their planes glancing back at the bomber. Pinner watched his ground speed and just as he passed the two fighters pulled the nose back. Pinner heard the rear guns let off a few rounds and then nothing but Polish cursing over the intercom. Pinner bent down to see the Pole struggling with the bullet belt.

'Sorry skipper they've jammed,' shouted the gunner over the intercom.

'Damn and ruddy damn,' whispered Pinner. 'Now we are a sitting duck.'

'They're taxing to the runway,' continued the Pole looking back at the airfield.

Pinner looked to the south and there was some cumulus

cloud at around 3,000 feet. He bent forward willing the plane upwards and towards the clouds.

'The fighters have taken off,' called Polanski.

'You'd better go to your normal position, Polanski. You might get a chance when they pass us.' Pinner looked at his co-pilot. 'We left Stewart. Do you think they …?'

Wilkie nodded. 'They're not total barbarians, you know.'

Pinner did not have time to brood over his rear gunner.

Tomkins went and looked out of the navigation dome. 'They're gaining altitude rapidly skipper and I think they will be upon us in a couple of minutes.'

'Two thousand feet,' said Wilkinson adjusting the engine mixture. 'We just may make those clouds.'

Pinner increased the revs but it only caused more vibration inside the plane; however it made him feel good.

'Tomkins let me know when the fighters attack and when you estimate they are about fifteen seconds away before opening fire.'

'Sir. They are on our starboard flank, and they …yes they are breaking now.'

'Everyone make sure they are strapped in or and hanging on tight.' Pinner adjusted his grip on the controls. 'Wilkie keep an eye on our air speed and shout when we are near stalling.'

'Stalling? What are you …?'

'Fifteen seconds,' screamed the navigator.

Pinner banked the bomber to the right towards the fighters and brought the nose up steeply. The plane shuddered, slowing alarmingly. Wilkie looked nervously at the airspeed indicator. 'Skipper we're close to the stall.'

They heard the distance chatter of cannon, but no hits. The fighters passed overhead and banked towards their rear.

'Come on you bastards,' shouted the Pole now at the front guns, but he did not have a clear shot. Suddenly the light faded and Pinner could see nothing but greyness.

'Ruddy marvellous,' yelled Pinner. A few moments later they flew out into clear skies. 'Tomkins can you see them?'

'No nothing.'

It never ceased to amaze Pinner how quickly you could lose another aircraft in the vastness of the sky. 'More clouds ahead, but everyone keep their eyes peeled.' Pinner levelled the aircraft and slowly the airspeed built up.

Wilkie pulled off his mask. 'That was a great bit of flying skipper, truly great.'

'Thanks, but I learnt a bit when I trained on fighters so I have a slight advantage, and those La-5s *are* tubs.' Pinner was smiling but he knew they weren't out of danger yet. Another clearing went without incident. 'I don't believe they are going to give up that easily.' The plane shuddered as they entered another bank of clouds.

'I think they will go above the clouds and wait for us to emerge,' continued Pinner. 'Keep at this altitude and make sure you keep her in the clouds Wilkie.' Pinner unstrapped himself and went down to the navigator's position. He tapped Tomkins on the shoulder. 'Tomkins, did you find those charts I mentioned?'

Tomkins nodded and opened them up. 'I think the best route is between Bratislava and Vienna, following the valley south, then hugging the Hungarian mountains from Graz to west of Zagreb,' shouted Tomkins above the roar of the engines. 'Over the coast just south of Rijeka and aim for Ancona. I am certain we secured Ancona a few weeks ago.' Tomkins looked up at his skipper.

'Looks good to me George. Have we enough fuel?'

'My estimate is that with the reserve tank we should have just enough.' Tomkins produced his calculations and Pinner quickly re-did the sums.

'The problem is we will be at low altitude and fuel consumption may be slightly higher, but we have no other options.' Pinner put his hand on Tomkin's shoulder. 'Thanks for hitting the guard before. What did you use? He went down like a sack of spuds.'

Tomkins leant over his table and extracted a very bent naffy tin. 'I think I struck lucky; not the strongest or heaviest of weapons,' said Tomkins smiling at his skipper.

'Well done anyway. Let me know the course when you have done the calculations,' Pinner said climbing back to his seat and shouting back. 'We won't have any weather forecasts, so you'd better take our position on regular intervals.'

A few moments later Tomkins gave the two pilots the courses and the long flight to freedom began. Pinner had calculated they should arrive just around dusk but he hoped the clear night would give some light. The clouds thinned and for a few nervous minutes the crew searched the sky for fighters; all seemed clear. Pinner watched the scenery below and the Alps in the distance looked majestic but serene. Thick forests were broken by the occasional clearing and Pinner decided it was time to increase altitude. Slowly they ascended up and in the far distance the Adriatic coast was just visible with an archipelago disappearing away into the distance. The sea was shimmering in the setting sun and green mountains with a light backdrop of white spread out to Pinner's left. The view from the air never failed to catch his imagination even in the most harrowing of moments. Pinner's stomach rumbled.

'I don't know about anybody else but I am really hungry,' he said over the intercom. He was not alone. Pinner switched his intercom to his co-pilot.

'Do you think I should reprimand Polanski?' he asked his co-pilot.

'Your call skipper. It's not the driver, but the way he caved that guard's head in when he was down, just wasn't cricket,' said Wilkinson pondering the last few hours.

'Mmm, but he does have other reasons to harbour such hatred.' Pinner decided to speak to his gunner and possible leave it at that. 'The fact is Wilkie if he hadn't have done what he did we could be in a little bit of a pickle.' His co-pilot shrugged his shoulders and leant forward surveying the skies above him. The engine coughed and spluttered. Both men looked at the fuel gauges which were in the red. Pinner flicked a switch on the side.

'Tomkins, we are on reserve tank,' said Pinner.

'Already? This is going to be very close,' said the navigator. A short silence ensued.

'How do you feel about leaving Stewart?' asked the co-pilot trying to take his mind off the fuel situation.

'What do you think? I feel absolutely terrible, and I am not quite sure how the hell I am going to explain the whole situation,' said Pinner closing his eyes. The sound of the rear-gunner's screams seemed to ring in his ears. 'I feel as if it was my fault. I should have told him not to turn his guns.'

'Stop being so hard on yourself,' said his friend leaning over and tapping his skipper's shoulder. 'I think they would have attacked anyway.'

'He was such a decent chap,' Pinner felt a lump in his throat. 'I certainly won't forget him.'

The two men sat and watched the coastline slip underneath them. Tomkins kept going into the navigation dome and taking bearings.

'There is an airfield just to the northwest of Ancona,' said the navigator eventually. 'You will possible only have one run at it.' The Italian coastline was becoming clearer and Pinner started a gradual decent. Tomkins came into the cockpit with a pair of binoculars. 'If my calculations are correct you should be aiming right for it.' The port engine started to stutter again.

'I hope you're right Tomkins,' said Wilkie searching for any sign of the airfield. Ancona was clearly visible to Pinner's left and they crossed over the coastline at just over three thousand feet.

'There it is dead ahead,' cried Tomkins. 'Ahh, and there, gentlemen, are DC3s parked up. It seems our American friends are well entrenched.' Tomkins handed the binoculars to his skipper.

'Well done Tomkins, you've done it again …'

The stuttering of the port engine was joined by the starboard one.

'You were right George this is going to be touch and go,' said

Pinner searching for the windsock. Finally he located it. 'There's hardly any wind, so I'm going straight in.'

Pinner banked to his left and then when one of the triangle of runways was in line he banked back and Wilkinson lowered the undercarriage.

'I think we are a little too low,' said Wilkie quietly. The port engine finally ran out of fuel, and Pinner feathered the propeller blades. Pinner could just make out several jeeps and trucks moving towards the runway as dusk drained the light away.

'Come on old girl, you can make it …'

The starboard engine followed its twin and the bomber glided towards the runway.

'Hold on everyone this could be *very* …'

The undercarriage clipped the perimeter fence forcing the nose down for a split second. Pinner pulled back on the controls as the wheels slammed into the rough grass before the runway. The left wheel snagged causing the bomber to veer to the left. Pinner jammed down on the right rudder to compensate and the plane yawed to the right as the plane bounced skywards.

'Oh my God,' screamed Wilkinson.

Pinner felt the plane's speed decreasing as it headed towards the runway like a roller coaster. He went light headed and almost weightless for a brief second as the Wellington descended rapidly; totally out of control. The force of the impact caused the port undercarriage to collapse and the plane spun to the left as the wing cut into the runway. The aircraft continued to pivot on the left wing and finally ground to a halt. The crew sat still for second listening to the creaking of the shattered wing and the distant ticking of the cooling engines.

Pinner opened the hatch above him. He ripped of his mask, 'right everyone let's get out. There may still be a danger of fire.' The four men scrambled down the fuselage and dropped nearly nine feet onto the ground. 'Everyone all right,' asked Pinner. His crew all nodded except Polanski, who was rubbing his ankle. They waited and watched as two jeeps hurtled towards them.

'Boy Mac, that was some landing,' shouted the lead American in a loud New York drawl. 'Didn't you like the look of our runway?'

'Well actually we were out of fuel …'

'Only joking Mac. We heard your engines spluttering away on your final,' the American said slapping Pinner on the shoulder. 'Anyone hurt?'

'Not on landing,' said Pinner. The American looked at the four men.

'I thought these tubs had six on-board?' He went over to the bomber and tried to peer inside.

'Normally yes, but we were only five and unfortunately we lost our rear gunner.' Pinner waited as the main truck pulled up, men jumping from its rear.

'I'll get an orderly to come out and, well you know.' The American had gone round to the back of the aircraft examining the damaged rear gun cone.

'That won't be necessary. He is in Poland …'

'*Poland*? What the hell were you doing there?' The American was coming towards Pinner.

'It is a long and, I'm afraid, classified story,' said Pinner with an apologetic expression. 'However I *can* tell you we haven't eaten properly for three days.'

'Hell, we had better get you something rustled up. Three days you say?'

The American waved the four men onto the two jeeps and barked commands to get the bomber moved rapidly.

'I suspect you guys might want a beer or two,' said the American jumping into the driver's seat and jamming the jeep into gear, making the vehicle lurch forward.

'You have absolutely no idea how well a beer would go down' said Pinner noticing his hands were shaking.

'You limeys have the got the craziest accents …' The wind blew the rest of the American words into the evening air. Pinner closed his eyes and thanked God for his survival.

Chapter 10

OPERATION SCORPION

Pinner watched the bustling aerodrome all morning from a small Nissen hut by the perimeter fence. Poland and the last three days were now becoming a blur. Had he really faced a firing squad? Had the whole episode been one of those realistic dreams you awake up from in a cold sweat? He took in a deep breath and smelt the Italian air. He loved it; it was so different from Cumbria and reminded him of when he trained in Florida. The other three men were snoozing nearby in large lounging chairs as they waited for their orders. The Wellington had been towed to an abandoned area of the airfield. How they had moved such a large aircraft bewildered Pinner. He remembered the feeling of utter exhaustion as their American host showed them to their billet after a huge meal. Pinner just wanted to go home and see Marie; how long had it been now?

Finally a jeep came buzzing up to their hut and he climbed down to meet it.

'Major wants to see you Sir,' said a smartly dressed American serviceman.

Pinner climbed into the jeep and they sped away at great velocity towards the main buildings.

'Great day isn't it,' said the Corporal sliding the jeep around a corner. Pinner just nodded; the young American thought he was another stuck up Limey.

They arrived at the buildings with the young Corporal making sure Pinner knew the jeep's brakes were in working order. Two hours later he was driven back to the others, the same driver continuing his testing of the jeep's primary functions. Wilkinson and Tomkins were there to greet him.

'Everything OK skipper?' asked Wilkie.

'Well I spoke to London and they are delighted we got away,' he said slowly, 'but they seemed astonished about our reception. It seems you and I, Wilkie, are to stay out here for a few weeks but Polanski and Tomkins are to go back to England.'

Tomkins smiled and turned to go and tell the gunner. 'Sorry fellas, but I am not sad about going home.'

Wilkie came and walked slowly along the fence. Pinner followed knowing Wilkie would want to know more.

'Well, what are we to do with no aircraft and now no crew,' he asked turning to Pinner.

'We are to train up on DC3s,' said Pinner.

'Convert up on a transporter, that's a fine thank you for nearly getting …'

Pinner put his hand on his co-pilot's shoulder. 'Operation Scorpion is still going ahead,' whispered Pinner. 'It seems …'

Wilkinson cut across him. 'Paul I don't really know what Operation Scorpion is. Remember you told me not to ask any questions.'

An old trailer lay in some long thin grass thirty yards from the hut. Pinner ambled over and motioned to Wilkinson to take a seat. 'In short we are to fly a few Intelligence chaps into Austria to meet a group of very high brass Nazis.'

'We are to fly into the Third Reich in a transporter with nothing to defend us but our wits.' Wilkie stopped, seeing the frown form on Pinner's face.

'Shut up Wilkie for God's sake. Let me explain.' Pinner straightened his back and waited as a plane took off behind him. 'This will be with the German's blessing and I have already had a lot of hours on a DC2, so it won't take us long to get up to speed. You know I speak fluent German and also with the Austrian dialect, so it seems I am the obvious choice and happened to be in the right place at the right time.' Wilkinson eyed him suspiciously. He never trusted coincidences. Pinner continued. 'There are four of them coming over from London. They should be with us in a few days so we have been prioritised to start flying a DC3.' Pinner pointed over towards several of them parked outside a small hanger on the other side of the airfield. 'One snag is the yanks want us to learn on the job.'

'On the job?'

'Yes, it seems we are to ferry front line troops and other personnel back to Bari. This guy Lilley I spoke to was …' Pinner fell silent.

'They're not happy are they?' Wilkinson got up and came closer to Pinner.

'No, and well, I didn't tell them everything that went on.'

'Paul, why not? You didn't mention the firing squad?' said Wilkie his voice rising.

Pinner shook his head. 'I don't know, he seemed more interested in the ruddy canister and what I did with it, than Stewy or how we were treated. God some of those backroom boys are infuriating. You know it was as if …' Pinner stopped talking again and started to walk towards the hut. Wilkie stayed still and watched him. Pinner stopped, turned and faced his friend. 'It was as if he knew what had happened and he was trying to put words in my mouth. I know I am probably being stupid, but I felt uneasy telling him anything. Call it my sixth sense.' Both men watched a heavily laden Dakota lumber down the runway. 'Come on, the others will wonder what the hell we are talking about.'

The next day Pinner and Wilkinson said their goodbyes to their comrades. There had been so many farewells in their short lives that such occasions were muted and subdued. Emotion was not on show.

Within an hour the two men had been separated and were acting as co-pilots to an experienced American pilot. Two days later they were re-united and given command of a DC3. Their first mission was to fly some Americans to Bari for recuperation and have a little rest themselves for a day or two. The next morning they took off on a fine late autumn morning and the view kept both men quiet as they watched the Italian Adriatic coast stretch out before them. Three hours later they landed at Bari and went their separate ways from the men they had flown down. A truck drove them to an old town of Andria and to a large villa on the outskirts, near Castello Delmonte. They were mainly British servicemen there all suffering from exhaustion, or who were recouping from injury. The majority were army, but there were a few RAF and navy personnel. Most of the staff were Italian except the doctors, matron and a few senior nurses. Wilkinson had immediately made an advance on a young Italian nurse, but fallen foul of matron. The verbal beating he was given left them all in no doubt as to the rules and the consequences of stepping out of line. The Bedford truck, which was used to obtain supplies, was requisitioned by Pinner and he organized a trip down to the sea.

The next day they left early, and picking up supplies they went to Trani and sat on the beach. After swimming Pinner showed the group a case of excellent wine that he had 'acquired'. Twelve bottles of wine were consumed and the group spent the afternoon sleeping off the alcohol. While sitting watching the sea, they noticed a local man on a donkey. He was fast asleep and it was astonishing how he managed to stay on his mount. The donkey was labouring under his owner's weight, some large bundles strapped to his haunches, and seemed to be moving at almost an indiscernible speed. Pinner got up and tip toeing over to the beast he gently steered the donkey 180 degrees. The donkey continued from whence he had come as the whole group tried to stifle their sniggering. Finally the donkey disappeared from sight and they burst into laughter, and speculated on the outcome when the local peasant would wake up back at his starting point. Stories were made of what the wife would say and do. As the group laughed Pinner noticed how much younger he felt compared to a few days ago.

That evening Pinner became restless and he considered the forthcoming visit of the contacts from London. He wandered down to the lounge and sat near a window looking at the beautiful landscape in the moonlight. He had started to write a letter to Marie when a Welsh staff nurse, in her mid-30s, came in. After a short chat she left. A few minutes later she returned and came and sat opposite Pinner.

'I've checked and everything is quiet. I've being watching you since you arrived,' she said coming over to Pinner, standing provocatively in front of him. 'I have always found the quiet ones are the worst,' she said pulling out a condom from her ample cleavage.

In an instant he found himself naked writhing with the nurse on a large rug in front of an old fireplace. It had been the first time he had seen a naked woman, and he could not take his eyes of her pubic area or her large swaying breasts. She was quite plump, and was sweating profusely, sending a scent into the room of perfume and body odour. Pinner's member was large and he tried to put the condom on, but failed miserably. The nurse helped him and clearly enjoyed the experience. Lying on her back, she pulled him towards her telling him to mount her. The condom seemed to kill his ardour and he could not feel himself inside her. The nurse was now really aroused and started to moan loudly, which made Pinner almost panic, and he pleaded with her to stop. Then without warning she came and her body stopped writhing but went limp as she relaxed.

Realising her quarry had not climaxed she rolled Pinner onto his back and pulling off the condom, she started to stroke him, and pressed her breasts against him. Pinner did like her breasts, and she started whispering in his ear words which to him should never have come from a woman. He suddenly arched his back and came with a violent shudder. She watched him, smiling at the sight. Pinner felt embarrassed and tried to get out of her clutches. All he wanted to do was to leave, but the nurse seemed intent on playing with his body and kept her attentions firmly on him.

Pinner sensed this was not an infrequent event for his nurse, and felt almost used. He could not help but brood over not only losing his virginity, but it troubled him in the manner he had lost it. In a strange way he was glad the wait was over.

Fortunately the next morning a jeep arrived and he and Wilkinson were taken to the airport. He never saw his nurse again and he told Wilkinson about the encounter as their orders to fly to Bologna arrived. Wilkie found the story highly amusing.

The hustle and bustle at Bologna was at such a fever pitch that Wilkinson and Pinner were hardly noticed. They were shown to their billet and then Pinner was told he would be collected that evening to meet his brief from London. The two men familiarised themselves with the base's layout. Later on they were taken to the CO where they were shown their new Dakota DC3, in full RAF livery. This plane was virtually new and they were given permission to familiarize themselves with the aircraft.

In the early evening Pinner was summoned and he left Wilkie to fend for himself. Pinner sensed Wilkinson's disappointment at not being included in the briefing; Wilkie never said anything.

Pinner was driven to an old villa on the outskirts of the city. It was almost dark and he struggled to make out the building but followed the driver into the old house. He was led to a large room with stone floors at the rear of the house. The walls were festooned with pictures of all kinds. Heavy furniture filled every corner. A smell of olive oil, herbs and spices prevailed in the house; it was clear dinner was being prepared. Entering a large room Pinner saw four men sitting around a very large old wooden table. Dark stains scarred the table and notches in its side showed the table had been well used.

'Sit down, Pinner,' said a man dressed in a blazer and flannels. Two of the other men were in army uniform while the forth man was in a dark suit, and Pinner couldn't help but notice how young he looked. 'I am sorry about the formality but under the circumstances …'

Pinner nodded and sitting down he surveyed the four men in front of him.

'Due to the nature of this mission we will only be introduced by our surnames and any communication whilst with the enemy will be under a code name. My name is Swindell and my code is Albatross,' said the man in the blazer and held out his hand. Pinner took the firm grip and looked the leader in the eye. 'This is Barker; code name Eton,' he continued. Barker rose shook Pinner's hand and sat back down, 'and this is Pugh, code name Thames.' Pugh stood up and came round the table.

'Nice to meet you, I hope you are a good pilot?'

'He's one of our best Pugh, do stop worrying,' interjected Swindell. 'And last but not least is Lilley, who I believe you have already spoken to.'

'Yes, a few days ago on the phone,' answered Pinner holding out his hand. Lilley looked at him and barely moving forward offered a weak handshake. 'Sorry I didn't catch your code name?' said Pinner.

'Oh yes how stupid off me,' answered Swindell. 'Lilley's code name is Christchurch.' Pinner felt his face flush and his heart missed a beat. Lilley saw his reaction to his code name.

'Have you got a problem Pinner?' he asked watching Pinner closely.

'No, no I used to know a girl from Christchurch,' he lied and quickly continued, 'never been there though.' Lilley looked Pinner up and down and moved his gaze back to the leader of the group.

'You are fully aware about Operation Scorpion?' asked Swindell. Pinner nodded. 'Well Churchill himself holds great store in this Operation's success. Pinner at this moment in time our American friends have not been fully informed. We believe we would have a better chance of persuading them if we had the plan up and running, so as to speak. The assassination attempt on Hitler, nearly a year ago, had resulted in many senior German officers being killed; several of them were key to us.'

One of the uniformed men, Barker, got up and went over to a desk in the corner. 'Drink?' Pinner nodded again, remaining silent. The man poured a glass of wine and picked up some papers he crossed the room to Pinner.

'We have an opportunity in three nights time,' he continued re-taking his seat. 'The Germans have agreed to a "mission of mercy" into Vienna. Long story but it will give us the cover to get in and see our contacts, who we believe will be there.'

'You believe?'

'Yes, we believe, this is a risky mission, not for the faint hearted' said the young suited man with a touch of disdain in his voice. Pinner's instinct about the younger man was that he could not be trusted. But why had his code name been mentioned in Poland, he thought. What was the connection?

'I say Lilley, give him ...' started Barker.

'Yes, that's enough Lilley. We all know your feelings on this matter,' shouted Swindell. Lilley glared at Barker his eyes narrowing.

'You buffoon, we need a trained agent not a ...'

'I said that's enough. Can we get on with it,' commanded the leader of the group.

A pause allowed faint noises from a kitchen to drift into the room.

Pinner broke the silence. 'I am assuming that you do not approve of me as your pilot?'

'You assume correctly,' said Lilley slowly extracting a packet of cigarettes.

Swindell shot Lilley an angry glance.

'Pinner you might as well know that although we fully appreciate your skills; you were not our first choice,' Swindell said going to the desk on the other side of the room and bringing back the bottle of wine. 'However the fact is you are here and you are part of this mission, whether some of us like it or not,' Swindell emphasised the last point towards Lilley. 'Apparently you are now fully familiarized on DC3s. So I am assuming you will be ready in two or three days.' Pinner nodded and picked up his wine.

'You will have priority for continuing your familiarisation on the DC3, and from what I have been told you are a pretty good pilot,' continued Swindell. 'We will also need your language skills not only when flying in but also during the rendezvous. Pinner I am sure you understand the significance of this mission.'

'Yes, I do and I would have preferred to have a situation where I was more comfortable with the plane I was flying,' injected Pinner.

'I told you he wasn't up to it,' started Lilley.

'Listen young man,' spat Pinner. 'I am not saying …'

'Don't young man me,' shouted the tall, suited man. 'You're not that much older …'

'Shut up all of you, for Christ sake what is going on here,' bawled the leader of the group. 'Pinner you will get fully acquainted with the new plane. I understand compared to what you have been flying it will be a piece of cake. In three nights time we will meet again and full flight details will be given then. Is that clear?' Pinner acknowledged. 'Just for once Lilley, can we just get on with a job and not make any political gain.' Lilley gave a nod and forced a smile at Pinner.

'I can assure you Sir, we will be ready in three nights time,' said Pinner avoiding eye contact with the youngest member of the group.

'Good, until then,' said Swindell getting up and holding out his hand. Pinner shook it and gave a small wave at the others as he left the room.

'Why you picked a half German for the job I'll never know,' whispered the tall suited man.

'Oh Max, will you just shut up for once,' hissed Barker. 'He is the best we have and in my mind it was a real stroke of luck he ended up here. Seems quite a nice chap.'

'Luck my backside,' said Lilley looking at Swindell.

Max Lilley went to the desk and opening another bottle of wine, filled his glass. Pinner knew something, he thought. Had Pinner sensed Lilley's true reason for being there, he asked himself watching the other members of the group file out towards the dining room.

Pinner and Wilkinson flew nearly 6 hours a day over the next two days and put in many night hours over the Apennines for practice as the mission would be under the cover of darkness. Pinner did not have the time to think about the young man he had met, as he had to familiarise himself with the charts and the navigation to Vienna. Eventually the evening came and the two pilots waited the arrival of their passengers. Pinner was surprised to see two MPs escorting a German officer into his aircraft.

His puzzled look was answered by one of the MPs.

'In line with Geneva conventions we are returning him. He has gone completely insane, poor sod,' said the MP. Pinner started to protest but a car pulled up and the four men he met a few days ago alighted.

The youngest of the team ignored the two pilots and entered the plane.

Pinner turned to Swindell. 'Look we have a problem; we seem to have three extra passengers.'

'Not a problem,' he replied. 'Two of my best men and the German's situation is genuine; he is absolutely crackers. It is a perfect cover for us.'

'You must know what you're doing,' said Pinner partly under his breath.

'I do Pinner, I do,' said Swindell giving him a stern look.

'Sorry Sir, of course.'

The men were all in uniform and Swindell was the only one with an attaché case. As the night sky turned dark Pinner checked the plane and he and Wilkinson went through the pre-flight checks.

Pinner was given an envelope and inside was his in-bound course, radio frequencies and finally his route home.

After a few moments Pinner started the engines and taxied to the runway. After a quick call to the tower, he throttled the engines and began take-off. The journey did not seem to take long and a clear sky and nearly full moon produced a view of the eastern Alps which was stunning. Pinner made radio contact and was given the location of a remote airfield. Wilkinson started studying the map.

'Hell skip, this is going to be difficult there are mountains all round this one,' said Wilkie pouring over the charts with a small torch. 'I thought you said we were going to Vienna?'

'I did,' said Pinner turning round and motioning towards Swindell.

'Problem?' said the Major-General coming to the flight deck.

'Seems we have a different airfield to go to,' Pinner said watching Wilkinson struggle with the maps.

'Just follow their instructions,' ordered Swindell going back to his seat.

Pinner and Wilkinson planned their route to the airfield trying to avoid some of the taller peaks.

'At least we have some moonlight tonight,' said Wilkinson chewing the end of his pencil. 'I think we are going to need it.'

Pinner followed Wilkinson's instructions and soon the radio came alive as a German voice gave wind speed and direction.

'Get ready for landing,' Pinner shouted to his passengers.

Pinner landed the plane perfectly with hardly a bump; he hoped Lilley would notice.

The airfield was virtually in total darkness but a small canvas covered vehicle came and guided them to a position well away from the main building. A few moments later a truck pulled up and Pinner went to the door. As he opened it and attached the ladders he was met by a German officer in a full-length leather coat. He saluted and waited for Pinner to get down. Soon the four men from Operation Scorpion left the aircraft and eventually the two MPs with their prisoner.

'I understand we are not to use any names,' said the German in perfect English.

Pinner looked confused and as the prisoner was being handed over to another group, Albatross whispered to Pinner not to use his German but listen. Pinner had been told that none in their group could speak German.

'Right come with me,' barked their host indicating to the four men.

'I would like our pilot to come as well, but the co-pilot will stay here,' said Albatross heading towards the truck. The German did not reply and studying Pinner he took the passenger seat. The five men climbed into the back and sat in silence until after 20 minutes they pulled up outside an old wooden house. The five men were then escorted into a room at the rear with low-beamed ceilings. Dark old furniture dominated the room and the walls were festooned with pictures of all shapes and sizes.

Eventually they all sat around a dark heavy table. Two German soldiers stood by the doors staring ahead impassively, as the group waited. The tension mounted as time went on and even their host checked his watch regularly. Everyone was asking the same question in their mind, 'Had something gone wrong?'

Nervous glances were exchanged, but Swindell indicated to them to remain silent and wait. Their host had now left and was nowhere to be seen. Eventually, somewhere in the house, they heard shouting in German. A few moments later a vehicle pulled up outside. The group stirred and Christchurch went to the window to see what was happening. The darkness prevented him seeing anything and he shrugged his shoulders at the group, and he went to examine a group of small pictures near the window.

The door finally burst open and their host went to greet two other men as they entered the room. The two new men were high ranking army officers, one a general and the other the equivalent of a Major-General. They ordered the two guards out. A whispered and rapid conversation ensued between the three Germans and Pinner could hardly make out what they were saying due to the speed and their strong Bavarian dialect. The snippets Pinner did hear confused him. They were talking about the 'pilot' and his journey from Poland. Pinner's eyes met for a moment with Swindell's. He flushed and went to speak but was cut short by their host.

'I am sorry but there are no refreshments. We can not afford to have too many people know of this encounter.' Albatross looked towards the door where the guards had been, and their host read his mind. 'Those two are totally trustworthy; I personally can vouch for them.'

The two German officers now took seats and started to talk to their British counterparts, waiting as their host translated.

'I am afraid to say Gentlemen that your journey has been in vain,' said the officer who had met them. His leather coat was unbuttoned and he was clearly agitated. 'It seems that the Nazi High Command has got wind of this plan. It is a great pity that this operation has come to light, as most of the German senior officers would have adopted the new alliance. However, we have established that the High Command learnt about this plot not only from American sources, but *Russian*.' Pinner was not sure if he was imagining it but the three Germans seemed to look at him when they mentioned the Russians. Pinner blushed and cursed himself for doing so; Albatross was also watching him.

Eton and Thames stood up together and started to protest; Albatross cut them short. 'Well, it is best I think if we leave immediately. On behalf of His Majesty's government I can assure you we had no idea of this development; we certainly would not have come here if we knew the operation had been compromised.'

'That is true Major-General, but may I inform you that I already know many men have been detained and their futures do not look good,' said the German General in excellent English. Pinner nearly choked. Why was he here if they could speak English, he thought? He was to be even more surprised as Albatross went to the Germans and thanked them in perfect German. The British group was escorted to the truck and started their trip home.

Swindell sat by Pinner with the other three opposite them. The noise of the truck allowed him to talk into Pinner's ear, without the others hearing too much. Christchurch was staring at Pinner with dark eyes.

'Did you pick up anything that our friends said back there?' asked Swindell. 'I couldn't make out what they were talking about to each other when they first came into the room.'

Pinner faced Albatross. 'No, they were talking so quickly,' he said but sensed the man next to him did not believe him. He knew he had to tell the truth. He had done nothing wrong, why should he feel so nervous?

'Actually Sir, I did pick something up, which has confused me, well actually quite concerned me.'

'What?'

'They were discussing me and my 'role' in Poland.'

'Yes, I know.' Swindell turned quickly to face Pinner. Christchurch was still staring at him with a lip-curling sneer.

'You don't think I had anything to do with it?' Pinner's voice had gone up two octaves. 'I haven't told you about how they tried to get information out of me, but I swear I didn't. Damn it, I was even prepared to be shot rather than tell anything.' Pinner leant back on the side of the truck. The three men opposite who had heard his outburst were watching him carefully.

Swindell kept his gaze on Pinner. 'Don't flatter yourself Pinner. You're just a pawn.' Pinner started at the analogy identical to the Russian's. He continued, 'and if this operation has been blown it wouldn't have been done by what little you knew. In addition, they must have had wind of this before they interrogated you, wouldn't they?'

A shadow of disappointment veiled Lilley's face as Pinner's heart leapt with relief.

'Thank God for that Sir, I would not have liked to ever come under suspicion for such a treasonable act. Mud sticks doesn't it?' said Pinner his relief making him want to shake Swindell's hand. 'There was another thing that was mentioned …'

'Not now Pinner,' said Swindell making sure he caught Pinner's eyes. 'I have only known you for a few days and I concur with what your file says.'

'File, what file?'

Lilley leant forward. 'We all have files Pinner, even the low lifes like you.'

Pinner also bent forward and matched Lilley's stare. 'Really, well it's the likes of me that do most of the dirty work …'

'Shut up you two,' interjected Swindell. 'Pinner your record is exemplary. As I have already said the reason you are here was firstly a stroke of luck, not just for your language, albeit not being needed too much tonight, but your flying skills. Simple as that, so stop thinking about what has just happened and start concentrating on getting us all out of here.'

They reached the airfield, and with an almost unpleasant haste they were taken to their plane and ordered to leave. Pinner was handed a weather report and finishing his final check, he started up the engines and taxied out; he took off. They climbed slowly and Pinner could see a village below as the first rays of light hit the mountain tops. There was very little sign of military activity. Pinner could make out a city to the east. It had to be Vienna. He had always loved the city since the first visits with his mother, and he seemed to sense it would play a significant role in his life. He made up his mind to apply for a posting there when the fighting had stopped.

The next few months Pinner and his co-pilot settled into mundane flights, ferrying supplies, but neither man complained. The experience in Poland had shaken them both, especially Pinner, for to stare death in the face had given him a different perspective on life. He had become quite moody at times and would have bouts of feeling quite depressed. All he wanted was to get home and start his new life. His thoughts for Marie were growing and he was now writing regularly to her and in some cases quite passionately; he was elated by one of Marie's replies. Operation Scorpion faded from his memory. The battle of the Bulge at the end of 1944 confirmed that the Germans had no intention of surrendering and doing any deal with the Allies. The fight would continue to the bitter end.

As spring came and the war drew to a close, Pinner was told

he would be going home, but first his request for a posting in Vienna was granted. It seemed he was being given the job of a liaison officer, and for his first visit he would go with Wilkinson. He read his papers and stared at the name he had to report to; Maxwell Lilley. Pinner cursed under his breath and decided to write to Swindell. He never did get the chance to tell him about the full story of his interrogation in Poland. He did however manage to discuss the situation with Marie's father; at the end of the day it was his future father-in-law who had recruited him for the Operation Scorpion.

Air Ministry,
Whitehall
May 1945
From: Commodore T.S. Peterson DSO

To: F/L P.T.Pinner

Sir,

SECRET — ADDRESSEE ONLY

I refer to your recent communication with Sir Richard Ryder. I appreciate your comments regarding this matter and the rationale behind your conclusions. I am also fully aware of your concerns regarding your forthcoming posting to Vienna, and the relationship with Mr. M. Lilley must be extremely disconcerting for you.

Please be reassured that the events you have described have been taken to a very high level of investigation and the appropriate personnel have been interviewed. In addition the appropriate Ministry has also undertaken a full investigation into the matter.

It is, therefore, with some relief that I can inform you that no evidence of any inappropriate action has been undertaken by Mr. Lilley; in fact his conduct has been exemplary. I will also like to mention your own level of conduct during this period was of the highest of standard in courage and initiative. I believe you have already been told that due to the nature of your mission, and its high security level, none of the normal acknowledgements will be made.

The reference made to Christchurch we believe was an Operation to be carried out by a small New Zealand unit in late summer 1944. This Operation also had covert operations, of which I am not at liberty to divulge any details, but like Scorpion was of a highly sensitive nature and did also involve the Soviets.

I have copied Sir Richard with this letter and if I may give some advice in that you try and put your concerns behind you and work with Mr. Lilley in the confidence that he is of sound character and intent.

Chapter 11

ESCAPE TO VIENNA

London, June 1999

Charles Carter sat watching two sparrows squabbling over some scraps on the pavement. He stretched and surveyed the scene from his bathroom window. A small side street in west London snaked away with the occasional blank faced pedestrian scurrying past. Cars manoeuvred around the speed humps, accelerating hard between them. He took his razor and started shaving a three day beard. He had started to become used to not working, but then a telephone call from Reeves-Dodd brought him back to reality; the money would be useful though, he thought.

Dressing methodically he decided to keep up appearances, especially for the Assistant Director of MI6, and pulled on one of his best suits. Carter thought about how much money he could earn, but it was no consolation for having his peace disturbed. Leaving the house he walked down towards Edgware Road and, as he was working for the firm again, he would hail a cab. It wasn't far to Park Lane and he could have easily walked it. Pulling up outside the Hilton Hotel he tipped the doorman and went straight to the lifts. Pushing the top most button he was relieved to be alone. What could he tell Reeves-Dodd he had been doing for the past three months, he thought. Best not to let on how he seemed so exhausted all the time.

The lifts opened and he entered the Windows Bar. A table at

the far end of the room was normally where Reeves-Dodd sat and Carter was not disappointed to see the familiar round figure of his ex-boss. Carter walked towards him brushing aside an advancing waiter.

'Charles my dear boy,' said Reeves-Dodd standing when he spotted Carter in a mirror. Carter noticed the MI6 man was dressed casually and cursed under his breath.

'Rupert, how are you?' said Carter taking a seat on the other side of the table. He noticed the familiar buff coloured files on another chair. It was definitely business, but why was he dressed so casually? Reeves-Dodd motioned towards a waiter.

'Same as usual?' asked the MI6 assistant-director.

'A little early isn't it?'

Reeves-Dodd ordered a large Gin and Tonic and raised his eyebrows questioningly at Carter.

'Go on, I'll have my usual,' said Carter already looking forward to an earlier than expected drink. 'So what brings you to call me and, if I may say, in such a casual dress.'

'Oh, sorry about the mufty, but I have an appointment with my daughter later on and she wants me to go shopping with her,' said Reeves-Dodd watching the view across Hyde Park. Only Reeves-Dodd could have an appointment with his own daughter, thought Carter. 'You know what these kids are like nowadays; we mustn't embarrass them must we.'

The drinks arrived and Carter eyed his Bloody Mary with relish. He picked out the celery and crunched into it enjoying the sharp tang of vodka. Reeves-Dodd took two files and handed them to Carter.

'It seems we have a small problem with two old boys,' said Reeves-Dodd stirring his drink. 'I have put a full synopsis of the situation in Max Lilley's file,' he said leaning forward and tapping the file. 'I have also given you the number of a Peter Wilkinson who has been very helpful and is an old friend of Paul Pinner, now deceased.' Reeves-Dodd relaxed back into his chair and let

Carter read the files. Carter read quickly, but carefully, studying the pictures of David Pinner, Michaela von Berckendorff and Maxwell Lilley. He was a little surprised to be involved in what seemed such a petty assignment.

'So what do you want me to do?' Carter finished his drink, his voice unable to hide his clear annoyance at such an insignificant affair.

'Charles, I know you too well not to notice you feel this is beneath you. However there is something else you should know ...' Reeves-Dodd waved at the waiter to re-fill their glasses.

'First I believe there maybe some stolen artefacts involved, of a politically sensitive nature, and more importantly,' Reeves-Dodd waited as the drinks arrived, 'there is a situation with Lilley ...' Reeves-Dodd checked the tables around him and leant forward close to Carter's right ear. A few minutes later the men both sat back in their seats and Carter now realised this was not going to be such an easy assignment as he had first thought. He lifted his drink and stirred it, marvelling at the intrigue that Whitehall could muster.

'OK, I'll take it on,' said Carter. 'I presume I start immediately?' Reeves-Dodd nodded. 'Do you know where Lilley and the son are now?'

'Yes and no, or should I say, no and yes.' Reeves-Dodd gave a small smile. 'It seems the son is now in London as his flat has been burgled or more accurately, ransacked ...'

'The Habbul brothers?'

'Yes, I believe so,' said Reeves-Dodd nodding. 'Lilley has disappeared off the radar screen, and so Charles, I need you to find him and stop any further problems developing. I don't want anyone hurt or any scandal getting to the newspapers. They would have a field day. I feel we owe it to Paul Pinner to let this all go to the grave with him, or at least to make sure the son does not find out anything and if he does suspect anything to keep *his* mouth shut.'

'Does he know anything?' Carter squinted in the bright sunlight.

'Unfortunately he seems to be deducing an awful lot and the combination of him and his new half-sister is worrying me, but Wilkinson can fill you in on this.'

Carter finished his drink. His heart beat had risen. If there was one thing he enjoyed it was to be involved in the tangle of love, hate and intrigue. His weariness had evaporated and he wanted to get started straight away. 'Same back-up as usual,' he asked.

'You are being given Platinum status,' said Reeves-Dodd quietly.

'Wow, you really want this kept quiet.'

Reeves-Dodd studied Carter. 'If this all comes out then a lot of hard work and, more importantly, many agents own personal risk could be for nothing. It is not just about Max Lilley and his hatred for an old enemy; that is almost insignificant. You do understand?'

'Yes, of course. Now I feel I should get started straight away and stop this snow balling,' said Carter stretching out his hand.

'I knew I could rely on you Charles,' said Reeves-Dodd griping Carter's hand firmly. 'Just make sure Lilley backs off without even getting a whiff of what is *actually* going on.' Carter gave a nod and turned towards the lifts He still had the picture of Michaela in his mind. A good looking unattached blonde to stalk; life was looking up.

★ ★ ★

The noise of drawers and doors being banged made me leap out of bed. Recalling the sight that had greeted me yesterday I started for the lounge. A stabbing pain in my head reminded me of my excesses the previous night. I swayed out of my door to be met by the sight of Michaela in jogging shorts and a tight T-shirt. The lounge was virtually completely cleared.

'Voila!' she said duster in hand and she made a twirl around the room.

'Michaela, you are a real star. What time did you get up?'

'Breakfast is nearly ready and then I think we should go for a jog.'

'I don't think you should jog in those, you'll cause a few accidents,' I said laughing. She frowned back at me and put her head slightly on one side.

'Don't you like your sister to look sexy …?'

'There is sexy and obscene,' I said ducking the duster. 'A woman of your age as well …' I was now making my escape from the room.

I showered and went back into the lounge to hear Michaela humming in the kitchen. She had put a tracksuit top on. Laid out on the breakfast bar were croissants, muesli, and various fruit. The smell of coffee was tempting.

'Bugger me Michaela, you really are on form today,' I said smiling at her.

'We, little brother, have a big day; so let's eat and get going.'

Thankfully Michaela went and dressed after breakfast realising I could not be persuaded out for a jog. We took a taxi to Harrods first and after a brief stay we took another to the West End. I showed her a few of the famous stores but she was keen to go to a small art gallery which specialised in a type of art form similar to the miniature we had found in the RAF trunk. After much searching down a few small streets just off Old Crompton Street we found the place she was looking for. A brightly lit show room with a multitude of tiny paintings on the wall greeted us as we entered. A man in a waist coat and bow tie came forward smiling.

I watched as Michaela showed him the picture.

'We found it in our father's belongings,' she explained. 'I'm not sure if it is genuine or not, and I was hoping you could help.' The man was hardly listening but had taken the picture, with some care, over to a desk. A large magnifying glass with an integral light stretched out from the desk on a flexible arm. Slowly the man sat down; his interest in the piece all absorbing.

'Do you know where your father acquired this painting, my dear,' said the art dealer.

'Not for sure but it may be from Austria just after the war,' said my half-sister with a touch of trepidation. We were both uncomfortable about his fascination with the picture.

'Mmm, a very fine piece. Could it be part of a set?'

'I really don't know. You see my father just died and …' I said, determined to be part of the action, but our dealer had risen and was heading for a door at the rear of the room.

'I'll be back in a mo, please make yourself at home,' he said pointing towards a coffee pot on a small dresser. Michaela threw me a concerned look.

'Err just a minute I'd rather one of us came with you.' I was answered by the door shutting. Michaela indicated me to keep quiet and we both crept towards the door. Gentle she pushed it open and I could just make out the dealer sitting at a desk dialling a number on the telephone. Michaela had a better view and turned her head to listen, pushing her head close into the gap. Her expression was impassive at first but slowly a frown furrowed her forehead and then her eyes suddenly widened. She pulled the door shut and indicated for me to follow as she tiptoed towards the exit and once outside she took my hand and began running away.

'Michaela, what is it?'

'Just run and let's get a taxi straight away back to the flat.'

She ran down Old Crompton Street and following her I hailed a taxi. Giving him my address we both slumped back into the rear seat.

'Michaela, what happened?' She lent forward and closed the window between us and the cab driver. She turned and whispered into my ear.

'He was calling the police or certainly some law enforcement agency.'

'Why what did he say …'

'He said that a couple had walked in with a piece of art

which he knew was on the register of stolen Nazi art treasures. When he said we were in his gallery, and he mentioned he would try and keep us there ... that's when I decided we should get away.'

'Oh, my God what is going on here? Look, let's tell the police, we have nothing to hide ...'

'My mother gave Paul that picture, and she was no Nazi, believe me.' Michaela was watching London passing by as tears welled in her eyes. 'Think about it David. If we go to the police will you be able to keep this from your mother? Your father was harbouring Nazi stolen art treasures given to him from his mistress.'

'Oh, bugger, bugger, bugger. This is just getting out of hand. We left the picture there as well!'

'We must get to my mother,' she said ignoring my last remark. 'She may be the key to this or at least tell us a bit more.' Michaela had stopped crying and her jaw line was tight. 'We need to also know why this man Lilley is after you, or should I say the letters, and I want to know what happened in 1954; there are so many unanswered questions.'

'Michaela do you think ...' I said starting to take in the consequences of my next question. 'Are we on the run?'

'Oh David, don't be stupid. We didn't mention names and I don't know about you but I have a clean record, hardly a well known figure on the Police database.' She gave me a quick smile and took my hand. 'Don't forget this guy Lilley can't be well in with the police either; can he?' A worried thought drifted over her expression. 'Let's get to Vienna now.'

'Now, come on Michaela I've still got to clear up my flat ...'

'Bugger the flat.' She twisted towards me. 'We've got to sort this before Marie gets back, remember.'

'Oh dear, you have picked up my bad language. Don't use bugger it sounds terrible from a woman.'

'You use it *all* the time. Anyway that's not important. I think there is a flight to Vienna in the afternoon.'

I trotted after Michaela after paying the taxi, and found her already on the phone.

'How long to Heathrow,' she demanded of me.

'Forty minutes, it depends on the traffic, why?'

'I'll book two tickets, just a minute,' she looked up towards me. 'Go and put a few things together and then get a taxi, we leave in ten minutes.'

'But, can't we just …'

'Just go and do it David. Don't forget your passport!' She started to talk into the phone again giving our names as I rushed towards my bedroom.

★ ★ ★

Carter arrived outside David Pinner's flat. He couldn't see if anyone was in, and then his mobile phone rang. He turned quickly and walked down the street answering the phone.

'Carter it's Platt here, I work with Reeves-Dodd.'

'Yes I know, what do you want, you very nearly compromised me,' said Carter annoyed at himself for not putting the phone to silent.

'Sorry Sir but I would have thought you would have …'

'Yes, yes I know. What do you want?'

'We have just had a call from Scotland Yard that a couple matching the description of Pinner's son and the Austrian woman have been to an art gallery that specialises in sixteenth century miniatures.'

'I'm on my way.' Carter clicked the phone off and ran to the main road hailing a taxi. The traffic was almost solid as the lunchtime rush increased. It was nearly an hour later when he was interviewing the dealer and the sudden realisation he could have made a possible bungle dawned on him.

'They just left, without saying a word, and without the picture?' Carter asked in a disbelieving tone.

'Yes, I went into the back room after I realised what it was, and called my contact at Scotland Yard, but when I came out they were gone.'

'Could they have overheard you?'

'Well only if they had gone over to my office door,' said the dealer pointing towards the inner door. Carter went over and leant slightly against the door which gave way easily and quietly to show the desk and chair. He then noticed a long blonde hair attached to a nick in the door surround. He pulled it out and was surprised by its length.

'Oh dear, she did have very long blonde hair,' said the dealer apologetically getting out the picture from a drawer and gave it to Carter. 'Sorry I was only trying to help.'

'Yes, it isn't you I am cross with. Thanks for your help I will let you know what happens.' Carter left and dialled Platt.

'Listen Platt, I have just been to the dealer's and I wish you had told me they had done a runner otherwise I would have checked the flat first,' Carter was hissing down the phone and trying to find a taxi.

'Well Carter if you hadn't have clicked off straight away I would have told you …'

'Christ sake Platt, Rupert promised me Platinum service not this crap.' Carter hailed a taxi and shouted David Pinner's flat address.

'Carter, will you *listen*,' shouted Platt down the phone. 'They have booked a flight to Vienna. It leaves from Heathrow in forty minutes.'

'Which terminal?'

'It is a BA flight from terminal 1.'

Carter ordered the taxi driver to go to Heathrow and step on it, just as the traffic on the A4 came to a stand still.

'Damn. Platt can you try and hold the flight for me?'

'Already tried. BA aren't having any of it, and we don't want to create any scenes remember.' Platt could hear Carter breathing heavily down the phone.

'When is the next flight?'

'Tomorrow.'

Carter sat half upright willing the taxi on. Stuffing £50 at the driver he ran into the terminal. Pushing his way to a counter he was greeted by an uninterested check-in clerk. The flight had closed over fifteen minutes ago, so Carter wandered up to the observation lounge and watched the flight from Gate 34 pull back. He dialled Platt again.

'How soon can I get to Vienna, I missed this flight,' he said angry with himself more than Platt.

'I've booked you on a flight for 07.15 tomorrow,' Platt said tersely.

'Why couldn't you have done something so I could …?'

'Reeves-Dodd wants to see you before you go chasing after them,' said Platt with an air of superiority.

'Christ Platt, I have to have the freedom to move where I want not to be hauled back to report all the time,' said Carter clicking off the phone angrily. It rang again and reluctantly Carter answered to be told Lilley had been spotted.

★ ★ ★

We were both subdued on the flight, and neither of us had a drink or touched the stale, dry looking sandwich offered to us. Michaela did not appear to be a moody person and her quiet caused me some concern. We landed and collected our cases and took the taxi into Vienna. I had been to Vienna twice with my father and grandmother. My mother had never come. Michaela had an apartment on the Innere Stadt, on Seilerstatte, a couple of hundred meters from Stephansondom, the cathedral in the centre of the city. As we got out of the taxi I looked up at the magnificent old façade and she pointed to a first floor balcony facing south.

'That's mine,' she said punching in a number to the external door security system.

An old lift was available but she decided to walk up the tight circular stairway formed from heavy old wood. Her door was wide and impressive; it indicated what was to come within. Her taste was impeccable, all the colours seemed to blend in and you immediately felt at ease. She showed me to my room and said she would shower and we'd meet in 15 minutes. I quickly unpacked only to find I had forgotten to bring any socks, cursing I showered and went into the lounge. I did not feel as if I was imposing, which surprised me. I made a mental note to ask her about all the photographs dotted around the rooms.

'Do you like my home?' she said walking briskly towards the kitchen.

'Michaela it is fabulous. Very you.'

'You're too kind, but thank you anyway. Drink?'

'Does The Pope have a balcony?'

'Sorry, what do you mean? Do you want to see the balcony …?'

'No, no it is a saying. Yes, I'd love a drink and I would also love to see the balcony.' She stuck her head around the kitchen door and pointed at a pair of tall French windows guarded by heavy drapes, and she disappeared again. After some problems with the catches and numerous locks I finally emerged onto the balcony. Two ornate metal chairs and table nestled in the corner. I put my hands on the balustrade and stretched watching the people below. Opposite were a few very expensive looking shops and some cafés. I was astonished how clean everything seemed. Michaela came out struggling with an earthenware cooler, bottle of wine and two glasses.

'Back in a mo. Is that right; mo?' she asked. I nodded.

'We tend to shorten everything in English; names mostly.'

'Oh, Paul used to call me Mike. Drove my father mad!' She stopped and looked back at me. 'It is so strange. I don't know who to call my father. From now on I am going to call them by their first names, OK?'

'Fine by me.'

She returned several minutes later with some nibbles and a fishy smelling substance on toast. I was hungry so I didn't complain. I had heard her on the phone but decided not to ask who she had called.

'Michaela I have been a bit of a clod, as my mother would call me, I haven't brought any socks.' I sipped a medium dry fruity wine and swished it around my mouth.

'Not a problem, there a lot of menswear shops around here. We can go out in a few minutes. How about a stroll around the city?'

'Mmm, that would be nice. Any decent bars?' I asked her.

'David, you do drink a lot. You should watch it.'

'Don't you start,' I said trying to laugh it off. She did have a point and one of which my estranged wife constantly reminded me. Thinking of Erica brought an idea to me.

'How far is Milan from here?' I enquired.

'Oh, three, possibly four hours. It depends on your speed of course,' she said topping up our glasses. 'Why?'

'Just an idea, but let's get some reading done first.' I watched her as she fiddled with a nibble.

'I called my mother, Grete.'

'Is she alright?'

'Yes thank you, she seems to be recovering well,' she said slowly taking long deep breaths. 'She wants to meet you.'

I sat back and nodded slowly. 'Good, I'm a bit nervous, but it's good isn't it?'

'David I am worried.' Michaela got up and stood looking down on the street. 'I really believe Paul's letter in May caused the heart attack and I don't want her getting ill again.' She turned to face me. 'That is why I have been so quiet. I don't know what to do.'

'Let's do what Grete wants. If we don't do what she wants this could also cause her more distress,' I said standing as well.

'We'll go and see her tomorrow morning, agreed?' She was looking at me with wide eyes.

'Agreed. Michaela, I bet she wants to tell you everything. As it happened, warts and all. I just might be the catalyst she needed to tell all.'

'That is exactly what she has just said. She wants to tell us her story.' Her voice tapered and for a moment we both watched the bustle below us. 'She wants to read all the letters again.' We looked at each other both frowning.

'Come on let's go. We'll buy some socks; I don't want you walking round with smelly feet!'

That evening we strolled leisurely around Vienna, ending up with Michaela taking me to the Bermuda Dreieck, a very lively area of town. Michaela had started to cheer up before we came out but then she listened to her telephone messages. Clearly something was troubling her.

'My ex-husband is coming back tomorrow night,' she suddenly blurted out in the middle of a noisy bar.

'Do you want me out of the way?'

'No well, actually yes. I think it could get a bit horrid.' Michaela stared into her drink. 'He has two children by his mistress now and is desperate for a divorce. I won't give it to him voluntarily.' She looked at me, tears forming in her large eyes.

'Why, you haven't been together for years now,' I asked using the usual male logic.

'I still love the bastard, that's why.'

'Ahh, but will he ever come back?' I thought I was helping.

'Of course not. I couldn't have children and that is why he said he left me.'

'Ohh, sorry I wasn't, well sorry. It maybe best if I disappear for a while.' I said sensing Michaela's anger and hurt. 'Look I have been thinking, if I hire a car I could drive down and see Jason, and do a bit of sorting out of my own life. I think Erica wants a divorce as well. That's saying something from a devote Catholic. What a pair,' I said starting to laugh. To my relief Michaela also started to laugh and we clinked our glass.

'Here's to divorcees!' She took a long hard swallow of her drink. 'We'll go and see my mother tomorrow, book you a car and then I can have a few hours with my husband tomorrow night.'

'Great. Michaela let the bastard go,' I said reaching for her hand.

'Yes, you're probably right.'

The next morning, after Michaela had booked my hire car she drove me to her mother's residence in a very smart VW Golf Sports. Her mother lived in an old peoples' home, a large mansion nestling in the hills to the west of Vienna. Each person had their own apartment but also communal rooms. My stomach tightened as Michaela led the way upstairs. She walked into a large room with a bay window and a fabulous view of the Alps. I literally gasped.

'Wow, what a view,' I said slowly.

'Mother,' shouted Michaela. The door on the other side of the room opened and I could see a bed and dressing table as a woman with short blonde hair and wearing a long house coat came out. Her eyes were fixed on me and she shuffled slowly forward ignoring her daughter. She took both my hands and studied them and then looked up and searched my eyes as if she was looking for something. The hairs on my neck stood on end. None of us moved or spoke for over a minute, but slowly a small tear came out of the side of Grete's eye.

'You have your father's hands and eyes. My God you have his eyes. It is as if, well as if …' she started to sob. Michaela rushed forward and helped the old woman to a chair. She did not let go of my hands and I followed somewhat awkwardly.

'Mother relax don't try and say anything now,' pleaded her daughter. Grete gently brushed Michaela aside, and tugged on my hands. I bent down onto one knee feeling a little clumsy. 'Mother try and rest …'

'Shh, dear. I am alright, get David and yourself a chair,' she said pointing towards some furniture by the bay window. She finally released her grip and I rose pulling up a chair close to the old lady.

'Well,' she started, 'I have told Michaela a lot of what happened but I want to tell you both the full story, everything I know.'

'Well, I am ready Grete. May I call you Grete?' The old lady nodded and beamed at me. 'Before you start, and knowing me I will forget, could you answer one question please?' I was watching her eyes which were bright and sparkling.

'Of course dear.'

'Who told you about Dad's, Paul's death?'

'Maxwell Lilley.'

Both Michaela and I stood up. 'Did you know him and are you still in contact with him?' I almost demanded.

'I knew him, my God I knew him. He is the most evil of men. Bitter through and through and with a temper that he could barely control,' she said as her eyes widened and she made a gasp for air.

'Mother,' cried Michaela. 'Stop this David and get some water.' I rushed towards a small sink area in the corner and found a glass filling it with water and turned to see Michaela helping her mother. I strode over and offered it to Grete. She took the glass produced a pill from her pocket and swallowed it followed by a gulp of water.

'Michaela do stop fussing, please,' she said pushing her daughter gently away.

'I *will* tell my story. I will not wait any longer, Maxwell Lilley or no Maxwell Lilley.' Grete pulled herself more upright and again brushed off the protests of her daughter. She bent forward to us both. 'Maxwell Lilley hated me, and your father, with a passion that was truly frightening. He tried his best to destroy Paul …' Grete gasped for air again and fell back in the chair making Michaela scream.

Vienna Nursing Home,
Vienna
May 1949

Dear Paul,

I am writing with some very good news. Albert and I are proud to announce that we have a baby daughter. We have named her Michaela, and we are delighted that she is healthy and well.

We look forward to seeing you on your next trip to Vienna, and hope you join us for a celebration supper at our house. I am still at the nursing home, but I hope to be out within a few days.

Albert is really besotted with his daughter and I cannot believe we produced such a wonderful thing.

Hope all is well with you and the wedding and your job are going well.

Best regards,

Albert and Grete

***

My Darling Precious Paul,

I have written this separate note so my letter to you will not arouse any suspicion as you can show everyone the 'official' letter.

My love, how I miss you now, but more so when I was giving birth. I was left alone for hours at a time, and they would not let Albert in, not that I wanted him there. I wanted you there, we have experienced so much together I would not have been embarrassed at you seeing the birth.

Dearest Paul, you have the most beautiful baby girl that has ever been. I might be a little biased, but all the nurses agree she is a real 'smasher', as you would say. I wish, oh how I wish you could be here now. Albert is being openly kind in public, and obviously is totally taken with Michaela, who wouldn't be. He has mentioned her fraternity once, but never in public; I am thankful to him for that at least. I think he knows it is yours, but I don't care. I am in need of real love and affection right now, and he seems totally incapable of that towards me. Why? Am I that repulsive?

Paul, I do have some rather bad news as well, which is only just starting to register with me. I had a terrible delivery, and unfortunately they had to operate afterwards. They have told me all the medical terms, which I have forgotten, but it seems it is unlikely that I will ever conceive again. I never experienced so much pain, and they seemed reluctant to help me with drugs, something to do with the complications.

Do you know what Albert said to me when they told me I would not bear anymore children? He said it was my punishment for having conceived out of wedlock, and with a man with whom I had no relationship , except lust. I could not answer or look at him, and he has never even so much as held me once. Oh God, I hate this loneliness, in fact if it wasn't for my new bundle of joy, my life would be a desert.

I have been at the nursing home much longer than any other woman and I am starting to hate the place. It is impossible to get any rest with crying babies and births taking place all the time. How I long for my own bed, and setting Michaela down in her nursery. How I wish you would be there for me when I go home, all I want is a cuddle and some affection.

I cannot wait to show off our daughter to you, please do not shut us out, I know it is a crazy situation, and I swear I will always keep my side of our 'arrangement'.

I just cannot stop loving you. You are in my thoughts every day, but now I have part of you with me all the time, and I promise that this little girl with have everything you would have wanted her to have.

Waiting to hear from you,
Your ever faithfully, and very clever,
Grete
xxxxxxxx
xxxxxxxxxx (from Michaela)

Chapter 12

Vienna, 1945-6

As spring faded into summer Pinner and Wilkinson waited for their final posting to Vienna, but still they were kept busy transporting equipment and troops in Northern Italy. The war had ended and Pinner had regretted requesting the Vienna posting. His longing to get back to Cumbria was becoming an infatuation with him. He would spend hours looking at the two photographs of Marie. Finally their orders came and after a long train journey the two friends disembarked at Vienna Central Station. They were both astonished at the lack of destruction in the city, but just as startled about the amount of Russian presence.

Their role was to monitor the movements and operations of the Russians especially in the East Austrian area which had become effectively partitioned off. Elections were now being planned, and the political tensions were mounting and there was more evidence that the Russians were undertaking a huge asset stripping operation. The centre of Vienna should have been an International Zone but this too was dominated by the Russians and it galled Pinner to see a huge picture of Lenin hanging from the Opera House. One of the other roles his department was charged with was to de-Nazify the country. This was made especially difficult as their French allies were not as keen on this as there had been so many collaborators back in France during their occupation.

The British HQ was in the old Hapsburg dynasty's summer residence, but Pinner had been given an awful room overlooking the back of the building. Lilley had seen to that, but otherwise Pinner had had very little contact him, initially. The times they did meet they could barely be civil to each other and Pinner was inwardly relieved he was not going to have to confront him about Operation Scorpion. His relief ended just after the elections and the poor performance by the communist party effectively ousted the Russians. They intensified their asset stripping policy and Pinner's department was instructed to liaise with the local dignitaries to try and establish the damage caused, and to make proposals for what would be needed to re-build. Lilley walked into Pinner's office one day and slammed a large file on his desk.

'Right it seems you and I have to prepare quite a detailed report on what we have to do to prevent communism spreading in Eastern Austria,' Lilley said looking at the stark view to the rear of the building. 'Great view over the park on the other side of the building,' Lilley was smiling and turned to Pinner. 'Shame you don't have the status to be placed where the real decision makers are.'

'You can think yourself lucky I haven't battered you so hard you wish you were never born,' Pinner's hands started to shake and he slowly rose. Lilley's eyes flashed towards the door. He may have been taller than Pinner but he knew he was no match for Paul's broader physique.

'Fighting talk from a typical grammar school boy.' Lilley edged towards his exit. 'Oh, sorry you did go to St. Bees, but just a sixth form scholarship. Your daddy not up to his responsibilities?'

'Don't you talk to me about responsibilities, Christchurch!'

Lilley now moved towards Pinner his mouth curled.

'You little low life bastard,' he hissed quietly. 'I'll see you will pay for that remark. You have absolutely no idea what goes on and why. You're a nothing Pinner and a pretty obnoxious nothing at that.'

Pinner didn't have time to think. He saw Lilley's head rock back and blood spurt from his mouth. It seemed almost in slow motion as he watch Lilley catapult backwards as another punch caught him right on his jaw. Lilley fell over a chair and lay still on the floor. Pinner looked at his clenched fists and then down at Lilley. 'Oh, ruddy hell,' he murmured.

Wilkie walked in. 'What the hell is going on, I can hardly …' His eyes rested on the crumpled figure splayed out on the floor.

'Paul, for pity sake. What happened?' Wilkie quickly gathered up the chair and lifted the limp body of Lilley onto it. 'Paul, you've done it now striking a superior officer …'

'He is never superior to me Wilkie, never.' Pinner filled a glass of water from a jug and handed it to Wilkie. 'Here this will bring him round.'

Wilkie tried to put the glass to Lilley's mouth.

'No, like this,' shouted Pinner grabbing the glass and tipping it over Lilley's head.

'Paul you bloody fool …' Lilley started to come to blinking his eyes and rubbing his jaw. He looked at Wilkinson and then at Pinner. His eyes were dark but a slow grin formed on his mouth.

'Get out Wilkie,' Lilley said slowly rising from his chair. Wilkinson started to protest but Pinner frowned at him and pointed to the door. Water dripped down Lilley's hair and face spreading onto his jacket.

'I suppose you are going to be a typical public school boy and go running to teacher,' said Pinner, his stomach feeling acidy and bloated.

'That's rich. My school was one of the toughest in the country. Court Martial for you would be too easy.' Lilley pulled out a handkerchief and mopped his forehead. He took a pace towards Pinner. 'What I have in store for you will make *you* wish you had never been born, believe me.' Lilley took another step forward and leaned towards Pinner. 'I promise you that one day you will be begging me for forgiveness.'

Both men grabbed each others lapels.

'I know what you are Lilley and your pathetic threats wouldn't frighten a sparrow.'

'So what do you think I am, grammar boy?'

'The lowest of the low, a traitor …'

Pinner was taken by surprise as Lilley bent slightly and using his knee knocked Pinner's right leg from underneath him. Pinner started to fall, but Lilley swivelled him round sending him crashing onto the desk. Pinner's head cracked the light and for an instance he went faint. Lilley was holding him down.

'If you ever accuse me of that again I will see you in hell!' Lilley shouted into Pinner's face, his spittle splattering him. 'My God Pinner I am going to spend the rest of my life making you regret what you've just said.'

Pinner was short of breath as Lilley leaned on him. 'Your own conscience pricking you Lilley. Hundreds, no thousands, of mens blood is one your hands, and you know it.'

'Pinner, you know nothing. If Scorpion had happened millions would have died …'

'So you admit it …'

'I admit nothing, and certainly not to the likes of you.' Lilley straightened up and stood back to let Pinner rise from the desk. He stood tall over Pinner; both men panting.

'I should have you banged up Pinner, but in your obvious confused state of mind I will give you a chance, albeit I am notifying London of your actions. I think it is time you had some leave.'

'You can't walk away from this Lilley, trust me …'

Pinner was once again taken by surprise. Lilley pulled him up and slammed him against the wall their noses almost touching. 'Leave it Pinner or pay a huge price.'

Something in Lilley's voice had changed; this wasn't an idle threat. Pinner felt the warning tone was from a man who had huge influence, and would use it. Lilley's face softened and he released his grip on Pinner's jacket and touched his mouth where blood was still seeping from his lips. 'I suggest for both of our sakes we leave this here, it seems we could both do each other a lot of harm.'

Lilley turned and left, knocking over a chair and slamming the door behind him. Pinner's legs were weak and his hands started to shake uncontrollably as Wilkie burst into the room.

'Paul, I really don't know what you are playing at but …'

'He won round two, I am afraid to admit.'

'What? What do you mean; what happened?' said Wilkie looking at his friend totally bemused. 'Why do you hate that man so much? He isn't a bad chap actually.'

Pinner went to speak, but stopped. Did Lilley mean he was being sent on leave? He thought of Marie and decided maybe it would be best to let life move on.

'Oh Wilkie, I am not sure. He just gets right under my skin. Pompous ass.'

'Pompous ass or not Paul,' said Wilkie setting the chair back on its legs. 'You don't go around brawling with the likes of Maxwell Lilley, he has got some serious clout, and I mean serious.' Pinner nodded at his old friend and sat down in his chair trying not to show Wilkinson his shaking hands.

'God I need a drink Wilkie,' said Pinner straightening his desk.

'Well you're in luck as I have been invited to an opera and if …'

'*Opera,* you,' Pinner started to laugh. 'Since when have you been interested in opera?' Pinner spotted the look on his co-pilot's face. 'Ahh, who is she then.'

'Well it's not just one, there is a bevy of them,' said Wilkinson his smile broadening and he half shut his eyes recalling the dancing troop and singers he had met the previous night.

'This I have to see. Peter Wilkinson sitting through hours of warbling men and women just so he can grope the dancers afterwards.'

'Paul, you do have a way of debasing everything,' said Wilkinson scowling.

'Come on no more long faces let's go and have some fun.'

The two men went to their rooms, changed and walked out of their building and waited for a tram. They made their way to the Hotel Regina and met some of the girls and Pinner, as usual, was impressed by the way Wilkie could charm them all. Hardly one of them looked at him but he didn't care, he had finally confronted Lilley and must now look at his options; leave it or write to Major-General Swindell. He couldn't let such an act go unreported, however much damage Lilley could cause him.

The opera was not at the main opera house but a smaller one near the canal. It had an old music hall atmosphere, and they were led into a bar at the rear of the theatre for more pre-performance drinks. Wilkinson was actually becoming confused with so many girls around him, he did not know which one to make a play for. Pinner felt content that he did not have to make such a decision and for a few minutes he let Cumbria and a vision of Marie in her swimsuit flow through him. He prayed Lilley meant what he had said that afternoon. It was now two years since he had had any home leave. A desire for female company swelled inside him.

The opera was the *Marriage of Figaro*, and Pinner enjoyed the music and singing much more than he had envisaged. Wilkinson had now narrowed the choice down to two and had one seated each side of him. Pinner shook his head at him when their eyes met at the intermission. After the performance they were again ushered backstage for yet more drinks. Pinner was becoming light headed. He really wanted to return to his room and look at Marie's photographs. He stood talking to a few officials of the theatre when a young woman he had not seen before joined their group.

She had short blonde hair and the largest green eyes Pinner had ever seen. They looked at each other across the group of people and became locked in a hypnotic stare. The woman was quite tall and willowy with perfect posture causing her beautifully proportioned breasts to protrude just noticeably. She wore a long sleeveless black dress which seemed to emphasis her female curves. A man to Pinner's left noticed Pinner's interest and introduced him to Grete Semmler. Pinner seemed to be able to read her thoughts and he felt a wave of desire cascade through his body. He flushed as she turned away and he watched her move to another group her buttocks swinging under the dress.

'Pinner, I say Pinner,' said Wilkie in his ear. Pinner just continued to stare.

'Paul, look I have to get away …' Wilkinson followed Pinner's stare.

'Oh, very nice! Where did she come from?' Wilkinson also couldn't take his eyes off her buttocks moving so seductively. Pinner shrugged his shoulders and swallowed his drink. 'I've made my catch, so I'll leave the field clear for you,' he continued digging a playful punch into Pinner's back.

'Alas, Wilkie old son, I am spoken for …'

'I can tell! What with that nurse in Italy and now this lovely creature, what will Marie think,' said Wilkie turning and collecting a girl on each arm marching out of the room. Pinner couldn't contain a laugh. 'How does he do it,' he muttered to himself.

'How does he do what?' came a voice from behind him. Grete stood there with her hands behind her back and her head slightly on one side.

'I err, he,' Pinner stuttered.

'Do you want another drink,' she said laughing and turning away. Pinner followed. 'I think the beer has finished,' she said looking over to a dumb-waiter in the corner. 'Wine?'

'Yes, that would be great, thank you.' Pinner's throat was tight and he felt a nervousness he had only felt once before. 'So, what is your role here?'

'I run the place, or rather do the work. I don't have any title.' She turned and Pinner couldn't help but let his eyes drift down and take in her curves. 'My father was shot during the war for anti-Nazi behaviour. He owned the place so I took over. For a while I could hardly get performers never mind customers, and now the banks effectively own it, but as you can see things have changed.' She motioned to the busy room.

'Well, I loved tonight's performance,' said Pinner trying to look at her face.

'You're very kind.'

'No really I enjoyed it a lot more than I was expecting. It was Wilkie's idea,' he said pointing towards the door that Wilkie had exited a few minutes ago with a girl on each arm.

'Yes, he is quite a dish and I think the girls will eat him alive if given a chance,' said Grete laughing. 'Not my sort though.'

'So what is your sort?' Pinner noticed how close they were standing, and how she had not taken her eyes from his.

'Actually I rather like Englishmen,' she said tilting her head again.

'Well I match the first criteria,' said Pinner his mind for a second leaping at the thought of being with her. Would it be possible?

'I like pilots especially,' she said making a slight movement towards him. 'Must have blue eyes, not too tall but taller than me, and broad shoulders.' Grete brushed a bit of cotton from the lapel of Pinner's suit jacket. Pinner smelt a hint of soap, mingled with perfume. Her dress tightened slightly as she moved and he saw the curve of her hips up to a narrow waist.

'It just so happens I am a pilot,' said Pinner, his mouth dry despite the wine. 'I know you won't believe it …'

'I know you're a pilot, Mr. Pinner.'

'Oh, right …' Pinner suddenly thought she was playing with him.

They just stood looking at each other, Pinner felt the urge to ask her out or even take her in his arms there and then. Still the silence continued but it wasn't awkward or embarrassing. Pinner felt as if they were talking through their eyes.

'Grete, I know you are possibly going to think me a complete idiot but could we …'

'I am staying at a friend's house tonight,' she interrupted.

'Ahh, that's a shame, maybe we could meet again …'

'I am looking after the house while they're away. There is nobody there except me and a few bottles of wine,' she wrinkled her nose, 'much better than this.'

Pinner opened his mouth but nothing came out. Had he misheard or had she invited him back to a house with just the two of them; alone.

'It's not too far, five minutes,' she put her drink down. 'I haven't brought a coat so you'll have to lend me yours or put your arms around me.' Her eyes, wide and bright, flashed at Pinner. Her smile seemed to fade as she waited for his reply.

'Of course you can have mine.'

'Good, you can't make love when you are cold.'

Pinner choked on his wine as he took the final gulp.

'Yes, of course. Very funny ...' Pinner watched her face carefully.

'I'm serious you can't make love when you're cold.' She shook her head. 'I am sorry I have never said such a thing before ...'

'Well I will have to make sure I keep you warm,' whispered Pinner his heart starting to thump in his chest.

She checked across the room and said, 'go and get your coat and I'll meet you by the entrance, we don't want to be seen leaving together, especially as most of us can see what is on your mind.' She looked down towards Pinner's groin.

Pinner flushed and tried to adjust himself.

Grete smiled and leant forward kissing him on the cheek. 'I'm glad I excite you so much. I can't wait to get you back to the house.' She turned and Pinner watched her disappear into the crowded room. He felt as if everyone was staring at him, so he rushed towards the cloakroom, collected his coat and waited outside by the main doors.

Pinner stood on the pavement wrestling with his own thoughts. The forwardness of this beauty rushed through his mind. Marie would never know he kept saying to himself.

'There you are,' said Grete coming out of the main doors. 'I thought you had run away.' Pinner made a feeble laugh. He took his coat and placed it over Grete's shoulders.

'I have to say your English is very good,' said Pinner walking beside her as she walked off briskly.

'My father was adamant I should speak several languages.' She looked back and seeing they were out of sight she took Pinner's arm pressing firmly against him. 'I am fluent in French as well. The language of love.'

They walked in silence and Pinner was impressed at the pace. They came to an archway and turning into it entered a small courtyard. Two heavy doors faced each other and Grete rooted in her handbag and went to the right hand door. Pushing the heavy old door open she pulled Pinner in, taking off his coat and then entered through another door into a tall open hallway. Pinner could just make out a large wooden staircase off to his left. Grete took Pinner by the hand and gently pushed him backwards towards a heavily carved chair. Pinner sat down and Grete came and sat on his lap. She kissed him sensually on his lips.

'Stay here, please.' Then she was gone through another panelled wooden door to his right. His eyes adjusted to the light and he could make out pictures and several other doors. The floor was wooden with thick piled rugs scattered everywhere. A smell of fresh polish filled the room. He heard several noises from the room to his right. It sounded like a fire grate and then furniture being moved. Then a brief whiff of the magnesium from a match floated by him forcing away the scent of polish. Finally the door opened and the subdued light of a fire and candles escaped into the hallway. He started to rise from the seat, but Grete came over and pushed him back into the seat.

'One more thing to do,' she said whispering into his ear. Her tongue then brushed his earlobe. Pinner froze for a second but something snapped inside him. He grabbed her round the waist and brought her towards him. A struggle ensued with Grete trying to push him off but kissing him at the same time.

'Paul, wait I won't be long.' Grete escaped his clutches and ran up the stairs. At the top she stopped turned and blew him a kiss, and lit a candle on a small table. 'It will be worth the wait I promise you,' she said disappearing out of view.

Paul stood and shuffled in his seat as he adjusted himself; he was now fully aroused and watched the top of the stairs intently. Should he go up? He made a small gasp as the stern stare of a furious looking man caught his eye. He was glad the man was encased in a gilt frame.

A creak from the stairway made Pinner look upwards. Grete was standing in front of the candle at the top of the stairs. She wore a three quarter length white dress. It had buttons all down the front and the candle light filtered through the gown highlighting Grete's contours. Pinner was memorised as she slowly descended the stairs. He could have sworn she was emphasising her hip movement and he devoured the sight of her thin waist and how provocatively her breasts swayed as she stepped down each stair.

'Do you like it?' she said standing at the bottom of the stairs. Pinner stood up and slowly went over to her, his eyes trying to devour her beauty. He went to caress her breasts but she took his hands and led him into the room she had prepared before. The fire crackled in an inglenook, and many candles were scattered around the room sending shadows dancing around them. On the rug in front of the fire she had laid out the cushions from the chairs into a makeshift bed. Pinner was breathing quickly and he could hear his heart drumming its approval in his chest.

Pinner led her to the cushions but Grete turned to him and took of his jacket, undid his tie and opened the buttons of his shirt. She slowly combed her fingers through the hairs on his chest and Pinner watched her nipples harden and show clearly through the dress. He started to undo her buttons but she stopped him putting his hands on her shoulders. She dropped on to her knees and undid his shoes. Pinner lifted his foot as she slipped his shoe and then his sock off; she repeated it for the other foot. Still on her knees she straightened up and unbuckled his belt and slowly unbuttoned his fly. His trousers slid to the floor and he stood out of them kicking them to one side.

Grete pulled him down beside her and laid him on to the cushions. She slowly undid her buttons in front of him, one by one. Occasionally looking up to ensure she had Pinner's full attention. Pinner watched as her naked flesh slowly revealed itself to him; he rested on one elbow, his body tensed with excitement. Her swaying movement occasionally showed some cleavage and he felt the one remaining garment he wore straining under his full manhood. Grete had also seen the extent of his excitement, and lent forward putting Pinner on his back. Taking his arms she raised them over his head. Pinner could feel his surge coming and bit his lip to control himself. She kissed his forehead and then his nose and as her dress fell open he could see right down her torso. Her breasts swung in rhythm to her movements as she descended upon his body kissing him all the way. She pulled down his remaining garment and made a small gasp at his fullness.

'I see you like the dress,' she said just brushing his full erection with her finger tips. Pinner felt as if he was about to explode. He took her dress and slipped it over her shoulders, and twisting round, laid her on her back next to him. Now he placed her hands above her head and she lay still watching him. The candle light flickered over her body and Pinner just studied her nakedness, running his fingertips over her body, exploring her curves. The fire warmed his back and her body warmed his side. He took a deep breath and moved on top of her cupping her head in his hands. Grete let her hands slowly move down to his shoulders and then down to the hollow of his back and onto his firm buttocks. Pinner lifted his head and looked into her eyes and moved his hips back slowly moving himself into position. Her eyes widened and her mouth opened as he gently pushed his pelvis forward and she squeezed his buttocks as their coupling was complete. She writhed rhythmically making a deep contented moan from her throat. Pinner knew at that moment his life would never be the same.

Pinner kept the fire stoked up most of the night and he surprised himself about his sexual appetite always laying down and holding Grete, even when he felt exhausted and spent. They ate some cheese and drank wine, but sleep was not an option either of them wanted. When their ardour cooled they sat and wrapping a blanket around them talked about their lives. A peace and understanding grew between them. Pinner felt a lump grow in his throat as she told the story of how her father died. The fear as the Russians came looking for girls and looting. Her love of a boy killed before he was twenty somewhere on the eastern front. She would never know what happened to him. Pinner told her about Marie, and this did cause Grete to tense and look at him with her large questioning eyes.

Slowly the dawn filtered into the room, and Pinner extracted himself from her embrace. 'I must go,' he said quietly to her. 'Can I see you again?' Grete nodded and watched him dress her eyes still hungry for him.

'Contact me at the theatre and we'll organise something,' she said pulling the white dress over her head. Pinner watched her as the dress fell down her body hiding her full curves and beauty. 'Is there a problem with you seeing me?' she continued starting to button up her dress.

'Well there is supposed to be a restriction on fraternising with the local girls, but certain people seem to ignore that.'

'Your friend Wilkinson for example?'

'Exactly,' said Pinner pulling on his shirt. He could smell Grete's perfume on him. 'I would prefer if we were discreet about this,' he finished.

'Discretion is my middle name, as you English say,' Grete said standing and putting her arms around Pinner's neck. Pinner stooped and kissed her gently letting his hands wander over her body. Another urge swelled into him, but he pulled away. 'I must go, you are a bad influence on me,' he said mock scolding her.

A few moments later Pinner pulled the large door shut behind him and went through the archway checking nobody was around. Turning left he headed back to the main street and tried to remember exactly how he had got here the previous night. His mind had been on other things, he thought.

★ ★ ★

As soon as Pinner had disappeared out of the archway Maxwell Lilley moved out of the shadows at the far end of the courtyard. Walking slowly towards the archway he stopped by the large wooden door and getting out a small notebook he wrote down the address.

Lilley went through the archway to see Pinner turning a corner a couple of hundred yards up the road. He looked back, his throat tight and stomach churning inside him. Hurt pride and shattered ego mingled with jealousy fuelling his hate. He turned back into the courtyard and went to the door Pinner had just exited. He clenched his right fist and started to pound on the wooden door shouting the name of the woman he had fallen in love with and had thought was his.

* * *

Pinner returned to his room. He washed and changed quickly as a meeting had been scheduled to discuss future plans as the Russians were now pulling out of Austria. He noticed Wilkie had not arrived and felt he could hardly reprimand him as he was also late, tired and he even wondered if he could last the day. He gave the orderly a hastily written letter to Grete and told him to deliver it to the theatre as soon as possible.

Opening his office door he was startled to see Lilley waiting for him. Pinner entered the office warily noticing Lilley was unshaven and looked exhausted.

'Morning Max, I thought the meeting was at 10 o'clock.' Pinner put his briefcase down and turned on the desk light. Lilley just watched Pinner, he showed no emotion but black rings circled his dark eyes and he looked deep in thought.

'Good night last night?' he said with a twinge of sarcasm.

'Well actually yes. I went to the opera.' Pinner opened a drawer and searched for a file.

'Opera? Anything else? You look tired.' Pinner looked up to see Lilley looking in a file. He knew instinctively it was his.

'You don't look so bright yourself, Max. What do you want? I thought we agreed to back off each other …'

'That was before you took my girlfriend. You really are a little shit. It was the dirtiest trick you could have played. So …'

'Now wait just a minute. Yes, I am not denying I met a girl last night but I only had a drink with her. I left the opera house on my own, and …'

'You liar,' interrupted Lilley. 'I came to pick Grete up to see you wrap your coat around her and walk her to a house not far away. You had it well planned didn't you?'

'Max were you following me?' Pinner stood up and Lilley reacted the same way.

'Are you denying it?' Lilley picked up the piece of paper with the address on. 'It is nowhere near her home, so I suspect you had …'

'How could I have planned this in such a short space of time, and anyway I had no idea she was seeing you.'

'Oh, really,' said Lilley moving around to the side of the desk.

'Yes, really,' said Pinner starting to shout. Confusion crept into his mind. Something was happening here he didn't understand. Grete had told him he was her first lover, and she had never mentioned another Englishman. Or had she? She did say she liked Englishmen. 'She said the house was a friend of hers that she was looking after. It was late so I …'

'Please spare me the sordid details,' hissed Lilley. 'I saw you leave in the early hours this morning and you certainly had a smile on your face.'

'You were spying on me weren't you?'

'I have my duty to perform,' said Lilley a smile forming on his face and chasing away the tiredness in his features. He reached for the file and took out two pieces of paper. 'Here you are; your leave papers. Three weeks and then you report to London. You leave tomorrow …'

'No, I …' Pinner stopped and took the pass from Lilley.

'Oh, I think you should take the leave,' he said looking at the other piece of paper. 'Marie-Anne Ryder I believe her name is.'

'What? Lilley, what is this you ruddy bastard?'

'It would be a shame if...' Lilley returned to his seat and put the paper back into the file. His smile now broadening to a grin, 'if it were to get back to Marie that you have had been fraternising with girls and making love to them all night long, getting them drunk on two bottles of wine ...'

'How do you know we had two bottles?' Pinner thought about hitting Lilley but realised he was now holding a very powerful hand. How could he have been so stupid, thought Pinner to himself.

'I called and saw your little love nest,' Lilley's eyes hardened. 'I will admit I was disappointed with Grete but when I saw how much wine you had pumped down her she was possibly out of her mind when you groped her.'

Pinner went to speak but decided against it.

'Nothing to say now, well well well.' Lilley slammed the file shut. 'Going about getting girls drunk and taking advantage of them won't go down well in London or with Marie's father, Sir Richard.'

'You ruddy bastard, if you think you can blackmail me ...'

'There you go again accusing me of some terrible deed,' said Lilley taking out a cigarette. 'You should watch what you say. Here I am, trying to prevent the sordid side of your character getting back to the ones you treasure, and you accuse *me* of blackmail.'

'What do you want?'

'I don't want anything from the likes of you Pinner. All I want you to do is stop going around casting aspersions about me, and mentioning codenames.' Lilley held up the file. 'I won't go around spreading muck, if you don't.' Lilley raised his eyebrows questioningly.

Pinner looked at his pass and noticed it didn't start for three days.

'OK, agreed, but I don't leave until Saturday.' Pinner said. Lilley stubbed out his cigarette and snatched the pass. Pinner noticed an envelope poking out of his inside pocket. It was a heavy parchment and of a greyish colour. The last time he had seen paper that colour was on a desk in the house in Poland when he was being interrogated.

'Bloody idiots, well just keep out of my way and,' said Lilley facing Pinner and handing back the pass as he looked him in the eye, 'leave Grete alone. Do you understand?' Lilley's voice faltered and Pinner knew Lilley was hurting.

'I won't pursue Grete, but if she comes to me …'

'I am warning you Pinner.'

Wilkinson ambled through the door. 'Oh Christ, sorry you two. Look this is ridiculous. Why don't you both just bury the hatchet, it's not good for the department.'

'Go away Wilkinson, and mind your own business,' snarled Lilley. Pinner nodded at his friend, who looked remarkably fresh. Wilkinson left muttering to himself. 'I'm going to keep an eye on you Pinner. Believe me you will regret crossing me and seducing my girl. You really are the lowest form of scum.'

'I did not …' Pinner stopped and thought. This fight with Lilley was getting out of control. He could be home in a week and Lilley, Grete and this office just a memory. He held out his hand to Lilley. 'Look I agree let's go our different ways.'

Lilley took Pinner's hand and they shook firmly and slowly. The grips tightened while Lilley kept Pinner in his stare. The handshake ended in silence and Lilley picked up the file and left without another word. Pinner collapsed in his seat as Wilkinson entered the room.

'Paul, you really should back off this,' said Wilkie watching his friend. 'I don't think you realise how much influence he has, and you do seem to bring the worst out in him.'

'Thanks for your support Wilkie. Just what I need at this moment in time.' Pinner got up and left the room to the objections of his closest friend. He walked down the large corridor towards the front of the house, guilt welling inside him as to his last comment to Wilkie, who had always supported him.

He slowed his pace and thought whether he should go straight back to apologise. He stopped outside Lilley's door which was slightly ajar. The outer office, where his orderly sat, was empty and Pinner could see Lilley's desk by a large ornate window. On the desk Pinner could see the file Lilley had just been carrying with him. On the back of the chair was Lilley's jacket. Pinner knocked on the door and waited for a couple of seconds. A few paces later he tapped on the inner door to Lilley's office.

'Lilley?' he said softly. 'Can I have a few moments?' Nothing and Pinner pushed the door open to reveal an empty room. Pinner went quickly back to the corridor. No sign of anyone. He turned and went straight to Lilley's jacket, rummaging in the inside pocket. He extracted the parchment envelope and folding it stuffed it into his trouser pocket. He sped to the outer door and, checking the corridor, he went straight back to his living quarters at the rear of the house.

Bursting into his room he bolted the door behind him. Waiting a few moments forcing himself to listen to any noise close by, he pulled out the envelope. Fumbling with the letter Pinner stood stiff and expectantly as he read the badly and roughly typed note. When he had finished he sank onto his bed.

'This is getting out of hand,' he whispered to the room. He took out his pen and wrote Lilley's initials on the top of the note, he then folded it up and he went to his wardrobe. Carefully unstitching the lining to the inner sleeve of his overcoat, he placed it inside, moulding it to the shape of the cuff. He sewed up the lining and taking the envelope he ripped into several pieces and lighting a match burnt it in the old fire grate. Pinner made his way back to his office and decided that despite all the potential risks he had to tell someone about Lilley; he was duty bound. He also knew the initials referred to in the note were his. A lump formed in his throat.

M L?

CHRISTCHURCH:

Rapid expansion of asset acquisition is now essential after elections.

Do all you can to delay allied response. Vital to have area back to agriculture dependency; more chance of communist counter-revolution.

Try to recruit more people to the cause, locals or allies. Understand French are more open to persuasion. Inform if you need more resources.

Inform if PTP becomes a problem to you, or our plans. He is not a particularly sensitive target, although he does have links to London, but could possibly be liquidated.

Meet usual location and usual time.

Chapter 13

GRETE'S STORY

Michaela helped her mother back to her bed, and taking off her house coat she put a shawl around her shoulders and tucked her into the bed.

'You rest now Mum, please,' said Michaela filling her water glass. I stood in the lounge area watching the scene. Grete was looking at me, and eventually she indicated for me to enter the room.

'No David, we must leave her in peace; another time perhaps,' said Michaela in an angry tone. I stopped at the threshold of the door, but Grete kept gesturing towards me to come closer.

'Michaela,' she started then switched to German. I watched Michaela's reaction and then she pulled up two chairs; I went and sat by her facing Grete.

'Mum, will not be silenced she wants to tell us something,' said Michaela annoyed with her mother's stubbornness.

'I have lived a strange mixed life in many respects,' she started to tell us as she looked out at the mountain view. 'On one hand I have lived a miserable life. My father was shot for being anti-Nazi, and my mother never forgave him for sticking so hard to his principles; it cost our family dearly.' Grete reached and took a sip of water and motioned Michaela away when she tried to help. 'I lost my brother and then my first young love in the war. Just a school girl crush, but it still leaves a scar. When the Russians came it was awful, but not as bad as some parts of Germany, however still a most terrifying experience. I have heard of mass rapes going on for weeks and women drowning themselves in empty desperation; in front of their children! They didn't deserve that, did they?'

Michaela and I didn't move or interrupt, but watched the old woman.

'Then the allies arrived and some normality returned, but we all knew the Russians wanted communism, but they didn't understand us Austrians. Life was so hectic and exciting then. I tried to get the theatre going but I had to borrow a lot of money. My father's past had caused the theatre to be ostracised, but then as time went on he was started to be revered as a man of principle and the theatre became very popular. The Vienna Opera House was dominated by the Russians, who were of course hated, so we did quite well.

'One day a very tall Englishman came in. He took one look at me and tried his best to impress me. He came to the theatre most nights, he bought me gifts, one especially I loved, and even I could tell it was expensive …'

'The miniature picture of the Madonna and child,' interjected Michaela. Grete nodded and put her head right back into her pillow closing her eyes. 'Mum, do you want to rest?'

'Michaela I will tell my story, please be patient.' Michaela got up and left the room and I could hear her making a hot drink. I sat there feeling a little awkward as Grete rested; her eyes closed. Michaela eventually returned with a tray of drinks and a few biscuits. Grete opened her eyes when she heard Michaela enter.

'I feel a bit better now. Where was I?' said Grete.

'The Madonna and Child,' I answered.

'Yes, he gave me so many gifts. He was persistent I grant him that but there was something about him I didn't like; he frightened me.' Grete stopped and looked right at me. 'It was his eyes, I didn't like his eyes.'

'Was this man Maxwell Lilley?' asked Michaela. Her mother nodded.

'Max Lilley continued to shower me with gifts and took me out many times after the performance; mostly he acted properly …'

'Mostly?' interrupted Michaela.

'Well there were a couple of occasions when he just went almost wild with passion,' Grete sipped her coffee. 'He had been so generous I felt almost obliged to repay him. One night we stayed at the theatre and I decided I was going to have a bit of a kissing session with him. Is that what you call it David?' I shook my head.

'It's called necking or snogging.'

'Oh yes, necking. I remember that word. Anyway we were having a nice passionate embrace when suddenly he started to undress me, but quite forcibly. You have to understand I was still a virgin, and pre-marital sex was still frowned upon, although it happened all the time, despite what we say now.' Grete paused and thought for a moment.

'Then he produced a condom. I was horrified and tried to push him away. Don't get me wrong I was almost desperate myself to try sex but not like that. I pleaded with him to be patient and that I didn't want to do it in the theatre. Maxwell was having none of it and told me it was now or he would walk away. I liked him, and didn't want to lose him, so I consented.'

'That is almost paramount to rape, Mum,' said Michaela standing up. 'The bastard, and now he gets thugs to beat up David.' Grete looked at her confused and then to me.

'Max has done what?' she said leaning over and taking my hand.

'Oh, it's a long story. Mum I think you should finish your story first,' answered Michaela.

'Well we made love, or should I say he had sex with me that night,' said Grete her eyes glazing over. 'Actually I hated the experience. It wasn't the enjoyment I had imagined of becoming one with a man. In fact it was physically unpleasant and put me off him. I thought I would love being with a man, heavens it is only natural, but he was only interested in his own pleasure and adding me to his list of conquests, or that's how it felt like to me. The next night he had booked a hotel room and tried to force me back there. He became very angry and if I hadn't managed to calm him down with promising to go with him another night I think he would have been violent. You could feel the anger bubbling inside him.

'I agreed to meet him the following night after the show, but when I came back stage I saw Paul, your father.' Grete squeezed my hand. 'I didn't believe in love at first sight but I stood rigid and just stared at him, and for the first and only time in my life acted in a way that thrilled me. I was going to get this man, not only to get rid of Maxwell but my whole body yearned for him from the moment I saw him. I wanted to have sex the way I had always dreamed of. I quickly asked a few people who he was and walked over and introduced myself,' she said her voice brightening and a smile filled her face. 'I had been asked to look after a friend's house and I took him back there. I was acting like a slut, but I was desperate for him. Nobody would have known where we were; it was perfect. My greatest fear was Paul thinking I was a tart but I didn't need to worry. David, I seduced your father that night. He was so gentle, so sincere; I just fell into him. Huh, and I never came out.'

Michaela took her Mother's cup and sat back down.

'We talked all night as well as made love, real love making. The sort of love making that happens only a few times in one's life time. He told me about his life, his ambitions, even Marie. I told him my miserable life story, except I never mentioned Maxwell. I suspected they could know each other. Just after he left that night you can imagine my delight when there was a banging at the front door and I opened it with glee thinking Paul had come back to me again, but then to be faced by Maxwell Lilley, his eyes seem to burn into my very soul. I seriously thought he was going to do something very awful. I believed rape or murder stared me in the face.'

'Bastard, what did he do?' shouted Michaela.

'That was just it. Virtually nothing.'

'Virtually,' interrupted Michaela again.

'He pushed his way in,' continued Grete, 'and seeing the cushions by the fire he actually spat on them. Then he picked up a glass of wine drank it and turned to me. I was shaking and my legs were so weak I had trouble standing; then I felt nauseous. I only had a thin white dress on with buttons down the front and most of those were undone. He grabbed my arm forcing me onto my tiptoes and towards him. My dress fell open and he stared and snarled at my exposed breasts. Then he just said that we were finished but that I was not to see Paul again. If I did he said he would make life a misery for him, and could even ruin him. He then shook me quite violently with one hand while the other felt my breasts and then down between my legs, and once he had felt me he threw me onto the cushions. Then he called me a whore and stormed out.'

'But you did see my father again, didn't you,' I said quietly.

Grete nodded. 'I most certainly did,' she said leaning over to her daughter and squeezing her arm. 'I only saw Maxwell occasionally mainly from a distance and then I heard he had been posted to Eastern Europe, Prague to be precise. However he did contact me once demanding I returned the picture. I told him I had sold it and he went absolutely berserk. I mean really angry. I was so glad I had nothing to do with him, although I could tell in his eyes he felt something towards me, it was more like an obsession. Paul told me about the hatred between them and I loathed Maxwell for that. Then a couple of weeks ago I got a call from him telling me about Paul's death, and that I had better tell his bastard daughter. I screamed down the phone at him and for some reason I told him I had given his picture to Paul. He was silent but I could hear his breathing on the line, and then it went dead.' Grete looked at her daughter. 'Have you got the letters?' Michaela nodded.

'The day after we first made love, Paul wrote to me and sent me a pressed flower. It was such a beautiful letter but he also told me that one day he would have to go home. Anyway I replied giving him an Edelweiss, and the picture Max had given me. Two nights later we met up after the performance and he told me he was going home in a day or so. Maxwell had organised it. It utterly broke my heart; I can still feel the pain.' Grete took another sip of water and was holding back her tears. 'He was having a hellish time in his role at the British HQ, and his description of how Lilley behaved did not surprise me. My fear was what Maxwell would do with me when Paul had gone.'

'I think Dad knew you had been seeing Lilley,' I interjected.

'Well if he did he never let on to me,' said Grete adjusting her position. 'He was a quiet one your father, but still waters run deep, I believe you say.'

I rose from my chair and went to the window, the midday sunlight highlighting a few remaining snow patches on the top of the mountains. 'But Michaela wasn't born until 1949, so what happened to your relationship with my Father between then and Michaela being born?' I turned to face the two women who were looking at me; their eyes were nearly identical. Michaela turned and looked anxiously at her mother. She also wanted to hear the full story but concern for her mother was etched on her face.

'The next night was Paul's last one before his leave. I missed the performance and took him to my friend's house, but this time I had prepared a bedroom.' Grete blushed and made a nervous laugh. 'I feel like a naughty girl telling you two all this.' Michaela smiled weakly at her mother but we both remained silent.

'We made love. We talked and laughed and I cried. Oh, how I cried as the morning light filtered through the curtains. I had found my man and he was going away ...to another woman. I was so happy and yet so miserable; I had found my wings but I had already been shot down.'

'Did you and Paul ever use ...' Michaela was uneasy asking such a question.

'No we never did. It just felt right the way we did it but I was not regular, you know,' she glanced at me nervously, 'and, quite frankly, I didn't care. I wanted his baby.' Michaela was sitting upright her hands folded in her lap watching her mother intently.

'Paul left but he wrote many times. Such beautiful letters. Most of them were about his life and he would put a small note inside with his love thoughts. The letters were so innocent I showed my mother and friends.' Grete looked at me. 'Your father wrote a superb letter. They seemed to flow, and his love notes weren't bad either,' she said starting to smile.

'Well he had got his place back at Cambridge but before he started he had another posting in Vienna. We saw each other a lot but I could tell Paul was becoming uncomfortable about our relationship, as he had become engaged to Marie. He let me down slowly not wanting to hurt me, and in the end we became almost friends. Well that is how Paul saw it; I was still totally in love with him. I didn't dare put on any pressure for fear of pushing him away all together. Paul did change and become unsettled during the summer as his hatred of Max Lilley seemed to intensify. One day we went up into the hills and he did nothing but rant about Max, so much so *we* had quite an argument. He seemed almost obsessive about him. There was something between those two that ran very deep. Why the British authorities didn't separate them was a mystery to me.'

'Quite, it does beg the question ...' I said slowly.

'David, please let Mum finish,' Michaela said impatiently.

'One night my mother was out and I asked him round for dinner. Our relationship had now become a good friendship and I never thought anything would happen, as Paul never showed any romantic intentions.' Grete turned to me. 'Well your father wrong footed me again. He had managed to get some champagne, which believe me in 1946 Vienna was something. He took me upstairs and made the most perfect and gentle love to me. He told me he would never forget me and that he had always truly loved me; but he had to do the right thing with Marie.' Grete was watching me and she must have noticed my body stiffening as she recounted that night. My mind was struggling with the man I knew and the man Grete was describing.

'Paul went off to university and crammed for eighteen months. By the 1949 he had his degree and was about to get married. Then out of the blue he turns up at our house. He had landed a fantastic job with a British textile chemical company selling into Germany and Austria, plus the Eastern Block, as it had now become known. He looked absolutely fantastic with a very expensive suit and highly polished shoes, brimming with confidence. He was staying at the Hotel Imperial, which was *the* place to be seen, and he asked me for dinner. As he left he whispered in my ear to bring an overnight bag. My mother knew that I still loved him, and although she never interfered she gave me some money and I rushed to the shops and bought a fabulous night gown and evening dress.' A tear slowly rolled down her cheek; Michaela lent forward and brushed it off her face. She knew what her mother was about to say. Grete pulled her daughter towards her.

'That was the night you were conceived. Paul said he had intended to act honourably with me, and to tell me our love must finish as he was getting married in a few weeks. However I looked a million dollars. Hard to imagine now,' she said looking down at her body. 'He told me when he saw me walk into the hotel he just could not resist one more night. I completely gave myself to him and thought to myself better to have a few occasional nights of passion with him than an empty life. Love is a beautiful thing and the power of it crushed my common sense. I was powerless to do anything but be with him. He left a few days later, but I knew even by then that I was carrying you.' She hugged Michaela who was now sobbing softly. 'What was I to do? I was carrying a man's child who was about to get married over a thousand miles away. It was a long way in those days, you know.'

Michaela stood up and kissed her mother's forehead. 'I need a drink,' she said glancing at me with her blood shot eyes and raised her eyebrows at me. I nodded and she left the room. I heard a cork pop and I had turned in my chair to look at the mountains. Grete didn't speak but I could feel her gaze on me.

'What was he like as a father?' she asked. I turned to face her.

'Fantastic. Especially to a son, who let him down all the time,' I said a few tears starting to blur my vision. 'But the last few days I seem to have found out about a man who is so totally different to the father I knew.' Grete smiled weakly at me. Michaela came in the glasses clinking and setting them down on the dressing table.

'Mum?' she said to Grete holding up a glass.

Grete shook her head and turned to me. 'Go on,' she said her voice was a little stern.

'Well Wilkinson, mentioned that Dad had been involved in a nasty incident in Poland around 1944, and they had managed to escape at great danger to themselves, so I know he was a strong and courageous man. He was a spy, or somehow involved with MI6. He had an affair, fathered another child, harboured a grudge or more accurately a hatred that was so intense it nearly ruined his career, or so I believe. Then there is something that happened in 1954 which is a major event in his life, but as yet I can't get to the bottom of it.' Grete started to sit up at my last point. 'So you can see until a week last Thursday my Dad was a reasonably successful business man with no war record as such, married with two kids and, although a bit of a lad from time to time, just a normal typical fella.' My voice had heightened and showed the feelings building up in me. Michaela waited until I had finished and handed me a glass of wine. I took a sip and savoured the fresh, but slightly sweet, German Hock.

'What brought all this on,' asked Michaela looking slightly bemused and sitting down beside me.

'I asked David how Paul was as a father,' Grete said with an apologetic hint. 'What do you know about 1954 in Prague?'

I thought for a moment letting the wine soothe my throat. 'Actually not a lot. In Dad's note to me he suggested I go and visit a couple he knew. He seemed very guilty about something …'

'I wouldn't go there,' said Grete watching me carefully, shaking her head. 'Before you ask I don't know what happened either, but what ever it was ended Lilley and your father's working relationship.'

'Lilley *was* there then. I thought so,' I said, my focus drifting onto my wine.

'David will you let Mum continue.' Michaela was no longer fussing over her mother, and lent towards her. 'You've not finished your story yet. So there you were carrying me and no man on the horizon. How did you meet Albert so quickly?'

'Albert von Berckendorff had been an old bachelor friend of our family for many years. He apparently had helped my mother in the dark years of my father's death and at the end of the war. He was much older than me by nearly twenty years, and in desperation I went to him. I told him my condition and could he help. At first he just looked at me with pity in his eyes, and said he would think of something. I could not believe my luck when a few days later he proposed to me and we were married two weeks later.' Grete looked at her daughter. 'I never loved Albert, and after I found out ...' she glanced at me, 'well you know.'

'Albert was a homosexual, I think I told you,' said Michaela turning to me. Grete raised her hand.

'It was different in those days. It was all kept out of view, and I thought it odd when on our honeymoon we slept in the same bed but he never made love. A few brief kisses but there was no passion there. He told me he didn't want to hurt the baby. That was his excuse.' Grete started to weep and holding her handkerchief to her nose, she continued.

'All seemed fine and little Michaela was born, but I had a terrible delivery. Afterwards they told me it would be impossible for me to have any more children. Albert seemed almost relieved. Finally when I was better I tried to use my womanly charms on him, but still he made excuses.' Grete's voice hardened. 'Then one day I followed him and he went to a house where he met another man. I waited a while and then went into the house to find them in a bedroom, well ...' Michaela sat on the bed and put her arm around her mother. 'I just wish he had told me, I may not have married him. We rowed for weeks after this as he claimed he thought I knew. He then threatened that if I were to say anything then he would tell the world about me and who Michaela really was: the illegitimate daughter of an allied serviceman.

'I didn't want that to happen to you Michaela,' she said holding her daughter tightly. 'I lived a miserable life with only you showing me any happiness and affection. I was so lonely and the rumours abounded about me and Albert and my social life, what little of it there was, disappeared. For years I was alone.'

Michaela went and filled her glass and topped mine up even though I had hardly touched it.

'I still wrote to Paul, and Albert was unhappy about this initially and tried to stop me seeing him. Strangely I could never imagine life without Paul, even the little I did see of him. Then in late 1954 Paul came to my mother's house. I literally ran round at once, but met a man deeply distressed and unhappy. For a moment my heart leapt and thought he had left Marie and come to me.'

Grete turned to her daughter. 'I will have some of that wine,' she said trying to force a smile. 'Well it seems he was visiting relatives but he told me Max Lilley had set him up and their hatred for each other had reached a crescendo. Something nasty had happened in Prague. Paul had a huge lump on the back of his head and bruises over his wrists and ankles. I did try and push myself onto him, but he gently and firmly told me, quite emphatically, that nothing was going to happen. When he told me how happy he was at home and had two fantastic children, my heart nearly stopped beating. His main reason for calling was to see if Michaela was alright, and he wanted to see her. How could I refuse? So for the next few years Paul visited Vienna a lot and even Albert started to like him. He didn't mind me seeing Paul in the end and actually encouraged him to spend a lot of time with Michaela. He was fantastic with you, Michaela. He took you for long walks and soon you were speaking excellent English. I could tell you loved him,' she said holding her daughter tight, 'it was so weird seeing you play with your real father totally unaware of who he was. We never even talked about our past or ever did anything together, except once many, many years later.'

'In 1971, wasn't it,' I blurted out.

'Yes. What a terrible mistake, for because of it, I lost Paul forever. I really enjoyed him just as a friend. Our secret and past love kept me going and just seeing him, even occasionally, was enough light in my life to be bearable.'

'What actually happened, Mum? Why did you do it?' asked Michaela.

'It all started so innocently. He had come around to the house to see us, and you had planned to go and stay with one of your friends. So you had a brief chat with him and left, and Paul and I opened a bottle of gin that he had brought, and started drinking. Paul was going to be fifty the next year and we were joking about a mid-life crisis and for the first time for years we discussed our lives and what we had done together. He started to re-count our first night and I reminded him about our night in the Hotel Imperial.' Grete took a sip of wine and looked away from us. 'The next thing we were undressing each other upstairs in my bedroom. I couldn't help myself and lay back letting him caress me. Then he moved on top of me when I heard the door creak and looked up to see you standing there.' Grete was looking now towards her daughter her face contorted with sobs. 'I'll never forget the look on your face. You went screaming out of the house and by the time we had dressed you had long gone. I told Paul to go and I would write to him, which *I* did and finished with him. He replied agreeing to my wishes. The thing was I was hoping he would plead with me to go back to how it was, but typically Paul was concerned about others and agreed, especially for Michaela's sake. I never saw him again or heard from him until his letter a month or so ago.'

Michaela pulled down the bedclothes a little an adjusted her Mother's position as the temperature in the room was rising as the sunlight moved slowly across the room.

'Then I hoped I would make my peace with him, and that you might meet your natural father knowing who he actually was. It was with that thought I suddenly felt a sharp pain across my chest and the next thing I remember is waking up in hospital with you sitting beside the bed.' Grete took Michaela's hand. 'I so wanted to tell you, but you had inkling didn't you?' Michaela nodded slowly. 'I was building up the courage to tell you and plan a trip when I received the call from Maxwell Lilley.'

Grete closed her eyes and lent back her mouth slightly open. I looked at my half sister and made a questioning shrug of my shoulders. Grete's breathing deepened as she drifted into sleep. We both stood quietly, and collecting the wine, went into the lounge closing the door softly behind us.

'I don't know what to say Michaela, for once I am speechless,' I said eyeing her carefully.

'Look I need to get home soon to meet that bastard husband of mine and his French whore,' she said pouring out the remains of the bottle. 'You need to get your stuff together and go and pick the hire car.'

'Yes, so I don't think we should drink anymore, do you?' I said putting my wine down.

'I suppose you're right,' she said copying me. 'I'll check Mum.' She went into the bedroom and I heard her say good-bye and kiss her mother's forehead. She came back into the lounge and quickly washed the few dishes and glasses we had used.

'Shouldn't we wait until she wakes?' I asked.

'No she could be asleep until the morning now,' she said collecting her things. 'I'll tell the nurse.'

We drove back to Michaela's flat almost in silence, both of us absorbing Grete's story. It was difficult for either of us to comprehend how her life must have been.

'I feel very bad about asking you to go, but it should only be for a couple of nights,' she said pointing at a car rental garage. 'That is the company and only a few hundred meters from my flat. Go and have a good time in Italy and see your son.'

'Yes, don't worry about me. Look, I realise the circumstances and it will be a good chance for me to try and build some bridges.'

Michaela pulled into the private garage under her building and we went up to her apartment. She made a brief snack and I collected my things together as time was getting on and I said a brief goodbye and left. We agreed I would return in three days, so I borrowed a small knapsack rather than take my suitcase. The seed of a plan was manifesting itself in my mind and for a moment I thought about driving to Prague and not Milan. I walked to the car rental company and was just about to enter when I saw two men standing by the counter shouting, with strong cockney accents, at the man behind the desk. The tall one still had the same T-shirt on as when I last saw him that night when he had held me down in my own Father's study. The tattoos were unmistakable.

I backed off quickly and ran up the street checking behind me. Both men had come out of the office and were looking around. I turned the corner and went straight into the courtyard of another car rental company. Fifteen minutes later I was making my way slowly through the Vienna traffic heading for Italy, when my mind suddenly flashed to Michaela, and the two thugs waiting for me at the car rental. A shiver engulfed me and I abruptly pulled over sending the car behind me into a screeching brake, and rummaged for my mobile phone.

* * *

Carter climbed into a taxi at Vienna airport. He kept his wits about him as he scanned everyone near him. Reeves-Dodds had said Lilley and the Habbul brothers had been seen at the Chunnel terminal and it must be assumed that they were following Pinner's son and step-sister to Vienna. Carter alighted at the Stephansondom and checking his street map meandered down to Seilerstatte. It was still only mid-morning and he extracted a piece of paper from his jacket with the address for Michaela von Berckendorff. Although she was still technically married it seemed she had never taken her husband's name. Her apartment was on the first floor and Carter spotted a café just up the street where he could get a good view.

Ordering a coffee he sat on the pavement reading a paper but keeping an eye the windows of the apartment. He then ordered lunch and patiently waited. By two o'clock he paid and paced up and down the street, and then checked behind the building. He was just about to turn back when a dark Golf sports pulled into the alley way and went into the private car park below the building. He could clearly see the two occupants and his heart beat increased as he identified his quarry.

Carter returned to the café and ordered another coffee from a waiter who was now eyeing him suspiciously. Carter watched the flat for a good half hour and then he saw Pinner's son exit with a small knapsack. Carter decided he was probably going to get some groceries and so he made his move. Finishing his coffee he paid and walked slowly towards the outer door of Michaela's apartment. He didn't want to call her in case she wouldn't let him in and warn the son. Carter went to a shop nearby and waited for someone to use the outer door. Nobody seemed to use this building and trying to keep an interested look into the shop window whilst keeping an eye on the door proved difficult. He was worried the son might return, but then he saw the door open. Carter took several large steps and brushed past a man who was leaving the building and, thanking him, entered the hallway.

The door closed behind him, and Carter went up to the first floor. He checked the small name plate pressed the bell to the side of the door putting his finger over the peephole. He heard the door being unlocked and the door swung open.

'I should have known you had forgotten ...' Michaela froze at the sight of Carter and started to slam the door. Carter sprung forward and put his shoulder to the door forcing it and Michaela back into the hallway. Michaela started to scream and Carter grabbed her arm twisting it behind her back and putting his hand across her mouth and forced her back against the wall. The front door slammed shut.

'My name is Charles Carter and I am not here to do you any harm, in fact …'

Carter saw the flash of her knee just before it crunched into his groin. Every nerve ending in his body seemed to explode inside him. He pushed on her and managed to take two paces back bending double with the pain. He saw Michaela reach for an umbrella, and as the pain started to subsided, he kicked at the back of her knee making her collapse on the floor, screaming.

Carter reached into his inside pocket and pulled out some documents. Michaela had started to get up trying to make her escape into the lounge. Carter was still bent forward as another wave of pain from his groin engulfed him making him nauseous again. Carter held out the documents.

'Look for Christ sake read these,' he said his voice horse and unnaturally high pitched. Carter was hurting badly; she had kneed him perfectly.

Michaela snatched the papers and sped into the lounge. 'If you follow me I'll press the alarm,' she shouted moving towards the bedroom. Carter didn't move but lent against the wall taking deep breathes.

'As I said my name is Charles Carter,' he said shouting after her, 'and I am working for the British Government. It is all there in the papers.'

Michaela was reading a letter to her and David from a Reeves-Dodds. Her eyes fell on the words Maxwell Lilley. She slowly returned to the hallway finishing the letter.

'We believe that an old acquaintance of the recently deceased Paul Pinner is after you and David. I *am* here to help.' Carter felt the pain fading and tried to straighten up. 'My God, you caught me right on the button.'

'Why the hell didn't you call me or at least ring the outside doorbell and say who you were,' she said moving towards him to help.

'Would you have opened the door?'

'No, possibly not now you mention it,' she said helping the man into the lounge. 'But I thought it was either David, or my ex-husband who incidentally should be here any minute. When I saw you standing there I thought for a second you were this Lilley man.' Michaela puffed some cushions and helped Carter sit down. 'You did rather hurt me by pushing me back and twisting my arm, so I had no alternative. I still think your behaviour is a little odd so if you don't mind I will call this number,' she said shaking the papers. Carter nodded and tried to adjust his seated position.

'I'd be grateful if you didn't mention my, err, condition.' Carter said smiling weakly at her.

She turned to go to the phone only to hear the buzz of the outer door bell. She went to a wall phone and picked it up and exchanged a few words in German. Carter had risen to his feet and tried some straightening exercises.

'Is that David Pinner?' he asked.

'No that is my husband and his French mistress and their children,' she said storming into the kitchen. 'He's early, the bastard. Anyway David should be out of Vienna by now and on his way to Milan'

'What? When? How is he getting there and why?' stuttered Carter. The doorbell rang and Michaela marched to the door flinging it open and turning straight back towards the lounge. A tall thin man followed her in, then two small children giggling and finally a short plump woman hauling a suitcase. The man stopped and said something to Carter in German.

'This is Charles Carter, and no Leif he is not what you are thinking,' said Michaela moving some ornaments from the coffee table as the two children ran round the room. 'And he was just leaving weren't you Mr. Carter.'

Carter straightened and held out his hand to the tall man.

'Are you all right?' asked Michaela's husband. 'You look in pain …'

The phone rang and Michaela cursed quietly under her breath and waved to the plump woman to take a seat. The change in the French mistress since having two children had shocked Michaela, and made her feel some sympathy towards her.

Michaela picked up the phone. 'David!'

'Who is David?' the tall man asked Carter.

'Oh, he is her half-brother,' said Carter immediately regretting saying it.

'Half-brother? She hasn't got any brothers ...' The tall man followed Carter's gaze towards Michaela who was in a frantic discussion on the phone.

'Mr. Carter,' said Michaela looking up, 'David has just seen those two thugs who tried to beat him up a few days ago.'

'Michaela tell him I am here and to get back at once,' shouted Carter.

'David, get back here ... David? He's gone,' she said slowly to Carter.

'Call him back.'

'You are not going to believe this but I haven't got his mobile number,' said Michaela going to her handbag.

'Great,' said Carter gingerly walking towards the phone. 'Does this phone have a caller identification system?'

The tall man came over and tapped a few buttons on the phone. 'The last number is just coming up; no it just says, international.'

'Blast, of course his mobile is a UK phone,' said Carter slowly.

The two children started to squabble and ignored their mother's interjection. A small table went flying and the tall man now started to shout. Carter turned to Michaela and demanded for her to try and find David Pinner's number. Michaela looked around at the noise and chaos ensuing. She couldn't help herself and put her head in her hands and started to cry.

Chapter 14

LILLEY'S REVENGE

Prague 1954

Pinner's role in Germany and Austria developed with successful deals being concluded on a regular basis. He was travelling a great deal to the Continent and managed to see Grete although he made sure their relationship was strictly plutonic. The shock of finding out she had given birth to his daughter, pulled him two ways. The first instinct was to be responsible and the second to never contact her again. At first he had tried to convince himself that Michaela did have a proper father and for her sake to stay away. But he couldn't. He decided that a friendship with Grete, strictly platonic, would be the best solution for all. Slowly Grete's husband, who Pinner had found most obnoxious, allowed him to spend time with Michaela, and he had started to become fond of the little girl, who idolised him. He made sure though he was never alone with Grete; he was not sure if he could really trust himself, as she still stirred up passions within him.

Over the Christmas of 1952, Pinner told Marie's father about his idea of trading with the Eastern bloc by bartering their finished products for Britain's petrochemicals and other raw materials. Hard currency was their problem. Sir Richard Ryder was impressed with the scheme, and informed London to try and help Pinner and his company as much as possible: within a few months Pinner's responsibilities extended into Eastern Europe. MI6 once again became involved with his life and he was also charged with helping the Prague Embassy in recruiting agents to assist in establishing the whereabouts, or fate, of agents that had been used during the war. After much ground work he teamed up with two Czechs. Their common aim was to rid their country of Soviet rule. Petr Staffanich was a chemist and specialised in dyes and surfactants, while his partner Natalia Graaff had studied languages and was fluent in at least seven. Petr was from the Slovakian Eastern region while Natalia was a Czech. It seemed her Grandfather was French and had settled in Prague after the First World War. He had fought for the Germans and after the armistice fled to the Jewish quarter of Josefov. Pinner was convinced Natalia was Jewish but as the Soviets had anti-Semitic tendencies he understood her reluctance to divulge more of her past.

The only blot on Pinner's life was Maxwell Lilley. He had become his immediate contact at the British Embassy. Although Pinner was a civilian he had to report to Lilley on all his activities regarding the agents and any deals he had procured. Pinner knew the Soviets were watching his every move but because the bartering deals being of great use to them, he was left alone. The intelligence work he was undertaking was of no real interest to them either but even so he knew he had to tread very carefully. Certainly his liaison with Petr and Natalia was being scrutinised. His relationship with Lilley remained strained, but they were civil and professional in public. When alone, cutting remarks and insults were the norm between them. However neither man ever mentioned the incidents in Vienna. A stand off had developed, for a while.

Lilley tried to take control and become the main contact for Petr and Natalia but he could never attain the same trust they had for Pinner. By the summer of 1954 Lilley had become disillusioned with his role and the boredom was only relieved by one of Pinner's visits. A flurry of meetings and deals would be struck, in which he played little part, except to complete the necessary paper work. Lilley sensed Natalia had become besotted with Pinner while she had mainly rejected any advances he had made towards her. Lilley feared she was always waiting for one of Pinner's visits, and when he arrived, they always seemed to be laughing and joking.

Petr was also cool towards him, and Lilley found himself isolated in his position and he considered himself to have quite a menial job considering his huge potential just a few years before. His resentment grew and he once again embraced the Soviets, gaining their trust, he started to feed information to them.

Lilley despised Pinner's life style and his arrogant self-confidence. The loss of Grete was still an open wound, however he informed London that he wanted to work with Pinner. If he was close to him he could effect his revenge and this time he would act before his enemy stole yet another woman away from him. His bachelorhood was starting to depress him and his feelings for Natalia strengthened. Every time he saw her his desire grew, and just occasionally he felt as if she wanted to respond. Lilley began to believe Pinner was the barrier between them.

On one of Pinner's visits all four of them went out for dinner. Lilley sat at the table incensed by her flirtatious behaviour with Pinner; almost it seemed on his behalf. He decided he had to act and slowly in his mind a plan developed for revenge on Pinner and to teach Natalia a lesson she would never forget. He smiled as he watched the three of them laughing; they would all regret the day they had treated him with such derision. For several weeks he prepared his plan.

A few days before Pinner's next visit, Lilley set the trap which he hoped would ruin his old enemy. In doing so he would destroy two young lives but he didn't care. Their sympathies towards the west, which he now started to detest, were reason enough to kill two birds with one stone.

Pinner arrived and after a day preparing at the office Lilley asked him to dinner, alone. Pinner accepted reluctantly. It was over some tough meat and dumplings that Lilley set his plan in action.

'I believe you have never trusted me Pinner, but there is something you should know,' said Liley as Pinner chewed his food scowling at his old adversary. 'I have reason to believe Petr and Natalia are Soviet agents …'

'Don't give me that. You're the turncoat around here,' said Pinner washing down the stodgy food with some beer. 'I'll tell you Lilley I still think you're up to no good, and if I ever get any real proof then our little truce will be over, that's for sure.'

'Really, it would be such a shame if anyone was to know about Grete,' said Lilley smiling at Pinner. Pinner's knuckles whitened as Lilley calmly pulled out a letter from his pocket and handed it to Pinner. Top Secret was stamped across a memo and Pinner read that suspicion had fallen on his two associates and that care must now be taken.

'I have taken the liberty of having them followed and I also know tomorrow they will be de-briefing a Soviet agent near Kolin. Do you want to come along?' Lilley's voice was taunting Pinner.

'A little dangerous isn't, bursting into a secret meeting in the middle of the Soviet bloc?' Pinner watched Lilley but saw expression other than the usual smug face.

'Well of course if you're not up to it, I'll let London know.' Lilley folded up the memo and placed it back in his pocket. Lilley was still smiling at Pinner.

'I am not saying I am not coming, I just think it is a bit fool hardy …'

'So you don't believe they are foreign agents?' said Lilley and ordered some coffee from the waiter ignoring his dining partner. He hoped Pinner would take the bait.

'No, absolutely not. I did a lot of research on those two and in all the time I have spent with them I cannot believe they are Soviet spies, trust me.' He glanced angrily at Lilley as only one coffee arrived. 'They hate the Soviet Union and all it stands for; they have no reason to help them.' Pinner played with his knife and fork and started to run through his mind for any signs of deception he may have missed. Lilley looked deadly serious.

'Well let's see then,' said Lilley getting up, 'I'll meet you outside the embassy at five o'clock tomorrow morning. Thanks for dinner,' said Lilley, leaving Pinner to pay the bill and cursing the day he had first set eyes on Lilley.

The next day Pinner walked to the embassy and Lilley was waiting for him in a car he hadn't seen before. The embassy looked deserted and Pinner climbed into the old vehicle.

'We're not going alone, surely,' he stammered at Lilley.

'Of course we are, do you want us to take the Household Cavalry,' said Lilley shaking his head and starting the car. Lilley gunned the engine impatiently.

'I hope you know what you are doing,' said Pinner his instincts shouting at him to exit the car while he had the chance. 'Really Lilley you shouldn't wear such strong cologne. They'll smell you a mile away.'

'I do not want to reek of body odour like you,' he said reading from a piece of paper. 'Do you know Pinner, you're actually quite a wimp aren't you.' Lilley swung the car out and headed east. After leaving the suburbs of Prague, Lilley drove quickly towards the Kolin continually checking his directions.

'Do you want me to navigate?' asked Pinner a little disturbed by Lilley driving and trying to read at the same time. Lilley just cast him a look and ignored him. They left the road just before Kolin and went up an old track for some distance. Through the trees they could just make out some old buildings. Lilley stopped the car and turned off the engine.

'We'll have to walk the rest of the way,' he said softly. 'My information says they should be here at about ten o'clock, so we have some time.'

'Won't they see the car,' whispered Pinner as they got out.

'Pinner you really take the biscuit,' said Lilley slightly crouching and advancing through the wood. 'I have come round the back of the property; hopefully our friends will use the main drive.'

Pinner heard him mutter some insult under his breath and

they advanced on the buildings as quietly as they could. Pinner's heart jumped as through the undergrowth he thought he saw a man in uniform moving behind one the barns.

'Lilley, this is madness. I am sure I just saw …'

'For Christ sake Pinner,' hissed Lilley. 'Just shut up and follow me.'

Lilley advanced out of the wood into a clearing just before a large barn. The main door stood slightly open. Lilley crossed to the opening, carefully looked around inside, and then coming back out he shook his head at Pinner. 'Nobody in there,' he whispered.

A muffled scream came across the thin morning air. Both men crouched instinctively.

'We're getting out of here,' said Pinner looking back towards the wood.

'As I thought you really have no back bone,' said Lilley looking Pinner up and down. 'Some friend you turned out to be if those two *are* in trouble.'

Pinner hesitated. 'This just isn't right, we need more back-up,' he said searching the woodland. 'Just think about it Lilley …'

'Stop whinging and follow me,' said Lilley standing and going to the end of the barn. Lilley stopped and backed up a pace. 'I think I saw them go into the other barn, come on, Pinner. Don't let me down now.'

'Lilley for God sake, listen to me …'

Lilley had gone round the barn and Pinner went to the end of the wall just catching sight of Lilley tentatively opening the door of the next barn and disappearing through, out of sight.

'The ruddy fool,' muttered Pinner under his breath and followed Lilley. He opened the door and quickly stepped inside waiting a few moments for his eyes to adjust to the gloom. As his pupils dilated what confronted him made him want to turn and run. Two uniformed men stepped out of the shadows and pushed him into the middle of the barn.

Lilley was standing by one of four stables; a few soldiers

slouched around looking nervous. Pinner looked to his left and saw a man with his hands tied above his head and blood oozing from several wounds; it must be Petr, thought Pinner. One of the wall's wooden planks was cracked by the man's head. Pinner heard Petr moan and stir so he started to move towards him. Then another figure, clearly female, tied between two large supporting posts on either side of the last stable, caught his eye.

Lilley sauntered over to the woman, whose arms were splayed open, tied high above her head. She kept struggling to keep her weight off her arms by standing on tiptoe. A thick canvas bag was placed over her head, and her blouse was ripped exposing her bra and a bosom swelled out. She wore a mid-length skirt and Pinner noticed her bare legs and feet. Lilley walked over to some female undergarments and kicked them. Pinner realised they belonged to the woman who he now knew must be Natalia. Pinner started towards the woman but his two escorts stopped his progress. One took his arm and bent it up his back while the other grabbed his other arm and his hair. Pinner started to struggle but Lilley raised his hand. He advanced and lifted the sack off the woman's head. Pinner saw Natalia tightly gagged. Her eyes were wide and she could only manage a faint murmur through the gag as she looked appealingly at Pinner. She then glowered towards Lilley.

Pinner went to speak, but Lilley picked up a long stick lying on the floor and prodded it at Pinner's chest.

'Just shut up Pinner, I think you've already said far too much.' Lilley took a step back and lifted Natalia's skirt revealing her nakedness. Lilley turned to Pinner smiling. 'Quite nice don't you think, but as you have obviously been cavorting with her, I bet this isn't the first time you have seen her in the flesh. I wonder how much wine it took you to seduce this one?' he said letting the skirt drop back down. Natalia shook her head and tried to shout at Lilley; the gag suppressing her pleas. Pinner heard another moan to his left and saw Petr stirring. A merciless blow from a rifle butt silenced him, and made Pinner wince.

'Why, you absolute bastard,' shouted Pinner only to be repaid with his hair tugged back and his arm thrust further up his back. 'Even you can't stoop to this level, you raving lunatic.'

'Language Pinner old boy, ladies present,' he said his eyes drifting to Natalia's bulging breast. 'Well I suppose I had better explain what *will* happen here today.' Lilley extracted a cigarette from the packet in his jacket and lighting it he took a long deep breath. Pinner noticed a shake in his hands and his eyes looked sad as he watched Natalia struggling with her bonds. 'It seems you came here with Natalia, and as you clearly had designs on her you tried your luck.' Natalia started to try and shout at Lilley but tired quickly. Lilley waited till she stopped and turned to Pinner anticipating his protests.

'Lilley you're absolutely mad. Nobody is going to believe this …' A punch in the kidneys drove out Pinner's wind.

'So it seems our hero over there,' said Lilley pointing at Petr, 'came to the rescue, but you hit him over the head. You tied up Natalia and repeatedly raped her, and cool as you like you left them both for dead, or as good as.' Lilley saw Natalia shake her head and start to struggle again. He went forward and placed the sack back over her head. 'Unfortunately for you the farmer finds you and after over-powering you he calls the police. Naturally my friends here,' he pointed at the soldiers, 'will have the pleasure of performing the necessary on your dear Natalia.' Natalia started to mumble and struggle hearing the last sentence. Lilley barked a command at one the soldiers and Pinner's other arm was brought behind his back and his hands tied together with rough cord. Pinner fought and the cord bit into deep into him then he was forced to sit and his feet were bound tightly.

'I thought you might want to see the show,' said Lilley his face taut, and he turned and nodded at the first soldier. He came forward towards Natalia and pulled heavily on her skirt. A button flew off and the skirt fell on the floor. Natalia struggled and Pinner could hear her muffled screams but watched memorised by the horrific sight. Pinner was surprised to see that Lilley seemed agitated and uneasy not seeming to be enjoy the events unfolding either. Maybe he did have a conscience, thought Pinner for a second. The soldier started to unbutton his flies when Pinner saw a movement to his left and the flash of a rifle butt was his last recollection as his skull seemed to explode.

Pinner awoke lying in a bed, the sheets tightly tucked in around him. He was in a small room and the smell of a hospital filled his senses. He could hear the mumble of activity outside his door. A small table and chair were beside the bed and a jug of water rested on a plate. He looked down to see a cone shaped switch attached to a wire. He moved his arm towards it but cried out with pain, and then the throbbing from his head started to filter through to his senses. His vision became impaired as the pain cascaded through his brain. Pinner picked up the switch and his thumb found the button at the end and he just managed to press it. A few seconds later he heard loud clipped footsteps coming down a corridor outside and in walked a large broad shouldered nurse in a dark blue uniform, every bit of her told Pinner he was in a hospital with strict rules.

'Where am I, how did I get here,' he asked. She started to talk to him while she adjusted the sheets, but Pinner couldn't understand a word. The nurse stopped and spoke a few German words which didn't make much sense. She had said he had been rescued by the police after being attacked. 'What about the other two, are they all right?' The woman frowned and shook her head; she didn't know of anyone else. Pinner rested his head back slowly and the nurse helped him with some water. She left the room as Pinner tried to recall exactly what had happened.

Had he imagined Lilley had taken him to an old barn? Then the memories came flooding back. He closed his eyes but he felt his head spinning and so he opened them quickly only to see the door move. One of the Attachés from the British Embassy quietly knocked on the door.

'Oh thank God, am I glad to see you,' said Pinner starting to massage his right shoulder. Pinner noticed the stern countenance of his visitor.

'Stephen Pickering,' he said holding out his hand. Pinner tried to take the man's hand, but couldn't lift his arm. 'Oh, sorry how stupid of me. May I?' he said pointing towards the chair. Pinner nodded very slowly.

'I didn't do it,' he said searching the visitor's expression. 'Look I really don't want to cause offence but I must speak to the ambassador or someone from London. I was set up. I never touched her.'

Pickering looked slightly bemused. 'Take it easy old boy, you have had a terrible blow to your head,' said the man pouring out some water.

Pinner put his hand to his forehead and felt the large bandage swathing his head. It was then he noticed the bruising on his wrists. Taking the water he nodded to the Attaché but regretted it as it felt like a brick had moved within his skull.

'How did you find us?' he asked after he finished the water.

'All a bit confusing really as the police took the others to a prison hospital. We haven't seen anything of them. It also seems the Russian soldiers have been escorted back to their barracks, under strict curfew,' said Pickering extracting a small notepad from his inside pocket.

'Sorry I am so groggy, I am having problems trying to remember what happened,' he said watching his visitor scribble in his notepad. 'So exactly what did happen, remind me.'

'You can't remember driving out to Kolin yesterday morning?'

'Yes, vaguely. I was meant to be meeting Petr and Natalia, I think.'

'Mr. Lilley was furious you had gone out to meet them by yourself with no back up, and when Mr. Lilley and the police found you they were fortunate to have disturbed the soldiers before more damage was done,' he said continuing to write. 'So why did you go to such a remote place on your own knowing the situation with Petr and Natalia?'

'I was with Lilley! He had Petr and Natalia tied …'

'Hello Mr. Lilley,' said the young Attaché standing.

Pinner turned his head to see Max Lilley dressed smartly and holding a bar of chocolate.

'Food is awful in here so you might need this,' said Lilley throwing the chocolate onto the bed. 'How are you Paul? I thought you were a goner when we arrived. My, they were giving you one hell of a beating. However I was furious you had gone on your own, you know. Going to remote places as a civilian was not wise, was it?' Lilley went towards the end of the bed watching Pinner intently.

'Well it was a good job Mr. Lilley came and saved your bacon, isn't it Pinner,' muttered the Attaché getting up and preparing to go. 'I'll have another chat when you are better, if that's alright.' Pinner started to nod but stopped in time and raised his left hand to give a small wave. The Attaché left acknowledging Lilley. Pinner moved his hand to the button in front of him.

'Don't try anything Lilley, bad head or no bad head; nothing will stop me from ripping you apart for what you did.'

'Very dramatic Pinner, but time for a bit of realism; so shut up for once.' Lilley moved over to the window. 'You really do live a charmed life. I had it all worked out. Watching you charged with rape and then all your sordid details of a love child coming out in court. How would have your wife and father-in-law have reacted to that.'

'What? Lilley you really have gone too far. Where are Petr and Natalia and how are they? You filthy bastard, how could you do that to a woman?' Pinner spat out the last few words.

'Oh don't fret; your new precious girl was spared being raped …'

'She was not my girl. I had never had anything to do with her except business. I liked her Lilley as a friend, something you cannot seem to imagine. Women aren't just for rogering you know.' Pinner felt faint as he shouted. 'Anyway, she fancied you, or used to.'

Lilley turned to face Pinner and for an instance their eyes met. The years of hate had meant they rarely looked in each other's eyes. 'She never fancied me,' muttered Lilley his eyes narrowing slightly. He sensed Pinner meant what he had said. 'I had tried, and anyway she also seemed close to that Slovak.'

'You will never understand will you Lilley ...'

The nurse came in and straightened the bed again. Spotting a dark red stain developing on his head bandage, she started to protest to both men. They both stayed motionless waiting for her to depart. Tutting, and muttering under her breath, she eventually left.

'So what went wrong with your little plan?' asked Pinner curious about Lilley's position.

'You Pinner are really one of the luckiest men alive. It seems our farmer friend called the police too early. And just after the over enthusiasm of one of the soldiers on your head, I heard sirens,' Lilley said opening a cigarette packet. 'I had just enough time to put things right and by luck I knew the police chief very well; he owes me more than a favour or two.' Lilley sat down and lit the cigarette, inhaling deeply. 'If you want to keep your marriage and not let your bastard Austrian child be known to all and sundry, then you should consider keeping to my story. Especially for Petr and Natalia if you also want them to have any sort of life. You keep to the official story I have told the police and our people and everything will be alright, do you understand?'

'And what fabrication is that? So you haven't fixed me up for rape then?'

'No, I hadn't the time to organise things properly, and I wanted Petr and Natalia out of the way. The story is it seems my suspicions on Petr and Natalia were correct, and after I warned you about them, you decide to take matters into your hands and go to the barns alone. You caught them red handed with a known soviet agent, but *he* had brought back up and you, and unfortunately the other two, were set upon by soldiers. I realise that you must have gone alone, despite us arranging to go together, but I called up the police. You were being given a good pasting when I and our gallant police chief arrive to save the day.'

'Where are Petr and Natalia?'

'They were arrested for attacking you and are going to go through some re-education, as they call it here. The Soviets seem to believe they were corrupted by you. However if you play ball then I will ensure they will be allowed to live a normal life, well as normal as possible in the circumstances; especially poor Petr.'

'What?'

'Well in the fight it seems he fell and severely damaged his head and neck. Very unfortunate, as you can understand,' said Lilley pulling in a large lung full of smoke. 'He is partly paralysed and if he doesn't get special treatment he will have no life at all.' Lilley looked around for an ashtray. 'It seems they are going to be very reliant on your co-operation, Pinner old boy. If you don't and I have to defend myself then I know the Soviets will ensure they are not available for any investigation or court hearing.'

'You are the most …' Pinner stopped as another wave of faintness enveloped him.

'If you do decide to be pragmatic, then I will play straight with you …'

'You play straight, an impossibility,' shouted Pinner.

'As I said. I can arrange for Petr and Natalia to be married …'

'Lilley their relationship was not like that; it won't work!'

'Oh, yes it will. Their lives are effectively over; Natalia is no fool. She knows it is the only way to get some decent quarters and for Petr to be looked after in any proper way. You see a happy ending after all.' Lilley stood and went towards the door. 'If you don't then poor Petr may even end up in an institution for the disabled, or possibly a mental home, not pleasant places in this part of the world. While Natalia could well find herself in Siberia servicing the camp guards there; if you get my drift. I spared her once, but not again. Think about it. Oh, and don't forget the publicity this would cause. I am sure Sir Richard would be distressed to hear such news of his son-in-law.'

Pinner tried to think of something to counter Lilley. He had been out manoeuvred again. Lilley started to go through the door.

'Wait,' Pinner shouted. 'On one condition.'

'You are not in a position to impose any conditions …'

'I'll do this if you stop wearing that foul smelling cologne,' said Pinner actually forcing a laugh. He knew it was a pathetic gesture to soften his humiliation.

'I don't mind that condition Pinner, as you will never know …'

'Don't try anything,' Pinner hissed his helplessness taunting him.

'Don't worry Pinner old boy,' said Lilley enjoying Pinner's moment of panic. 'You're leaving here and never coming back. Deported for anti-soviet activity.'

'Deported? But I have a job to do …'

'*And* Pinner I hope now we shall never cross paths again.'

Lilley was gone leaving the door open and Pinner slumped onto his pillows. The image of the part naked Natalia tied up and her vulnerability made him shudder. No matter what happened he would never work with Lilley again, at any cost, he decided.

CONFIDENTIAL MEMO

Whitehall,
London,

28th September 1954

Dear ~~Mr. Pinner,~~ Paul

I am writing in response to your letter of the 19th July last and our numerous conversations on the alleged incident at Kolin, Czechoslovakia earlier in the year.

I am extremely concerned that your continuing feud with Mr. M. Lilley is still ongoing despite investigations carried out in 1945 where your aspersions against him were unsubstantiated. Indeed, if it ever transpired that an event did take place, as per your description in June of this year, then Mr. Lilley would be in the most serious trouble. A long jail term would be the most likely consequence so I must ensure all the facts are accurate and collaborated.

However I find myself in the most awkward of situations. I know you extremely well and there is no doubt in my mind that you would never make such claims unless you believed them to be true. Likewise I question why Mr. Lilley would ever perform such a terrible act as he also has an excellent record and a man of good integrity. So why do I have two men of good standing telling me totally different accounts of the same event?

Therefore a further investigation has been made to try and establish the truth. The two agents in question who, although not questioned in person, are now married and I believe have just announced they are expecting their first child. However Petr did suffer very severe head injuries which seem to substantiate your claims. A written statement has been received from them and they have both admitted that they were acting on behalf of the British and have undergone a re-adjustment programme. Both deny that a rape, or even an attempted rape, was carried out and Petr is adamant that he was hit by one of the soldiers and fell, compounding the injury. I am still troubled about the claim that you went to this rendezvous unaccompanied and in the full knowledge that Soviet agents could well have been present. I know you well enough to know that you would never undertake such a foolhardy act and therefore question some of Lilley's account of events.

However I have spoken with the Director-General who after considering the total lack of evidence to substantiate your claims does not wish to take this matter any further. The only exception is that it is agreed that you and Mr. Lilley will never work together again. This now seems quite likely as Mr. Lilley has been promoted to a senior level in Budapest, while you, on the other hand, will not be able to return to the Eastern Bloc for the foreseeable future.

I truly am at a loss to explain why two of our best men have come to such a situation. I can only rationalise this issue by a clash of personalities that has seriously gone out of control. I hope this letter will finally end the entire issue.

I am delighted to hear you have been promoted and will be taking on the African market as well as Germany and Austria. A move I totally approve of and hopefully will enhance your career to a level I know you are capable of. I know Marie and her mother are delighted with your success.

I look forward to seeing you, Marie and the children in a few weekends time. If you wish to discuss this further I will be pleased to do so, but with the utmost discretion!

Yours sincerely,

Richard

Sir Richard Ryder

P.S. Paul, Let's bury this one now and get on with life.

Chapter 15

THE SEARCH FOR PETR AND NATALIA

I shouted into my mobile but it was dead. The battery had been getting weaker due to its age and I had also left the charger back in my flat in London. I cursed and sat there at a loss what to do. Michaela had mentioned that someone from the British Intelligence had suddenly turned up on her door step. The appearance of such auspicious company coupled with my tattooed friends seemed bizarre. I looked over at the knapsack and saw the corner of a large brown envelope containing all my father's letters.

'So Dad,' I said to the car. 'What do I do?'

I lent forward extracted the envelope and pulled out the letters. Maybe it was time to contact Peter Wilkinson I thought, but remembered my defunct phone. Dad's first letter to me slipped out into the passenger well and I picked it up where my eyes fell on the paragraph that urged me to go and find Petr and Natalia in Prague. Despite the letter from my grandfather I still did not know what had happened and decided there and then to find out what caused such a furore in 1954.

I found Peter Wilkinson's number and picking up my mobile phone I took off the battery and rubbed it on my shirt until it was quite warm. Quickly putting it into place I turned it on to be greeted with the start up procedure.

'Come on, come on,' I yelled at the object. Finally a signal was indicated and I punched in Wilkinson's number. I was greeted with a low battery warning beep. The phone rang twice and I heard Wilkinson answer.

'Peter, this is David Pinner,' I yelled down the phone.

'David, at long last ...'

'Listen! I am sorry Peter but my battery is nearly out, please answer my questions. It is important ...'

'Yes but why don't you go to a land line ...'

'Who is a man called Carter, is he *legit,*' I said cutting across Wilkinson.

'Yes, Charles Carter is trying to help and ultimately protect you. He is MI6, and I am sorry David, but I had to get them involved.'

'Why? What the hell for ...'

'David this man Lilley seems to want something your father had. As you know he has two hired thugs, who are not to be meddled with,' said Wilkinson, exasperation in his voice. 'You must get to Carter ...'

'Look Peter, get hold of Michaela and tell her I'll get back to her apartment in a few days. There are a couple of things I must do while I have the chance. I suspect once I am in the clutches of this Carter chap he'll bugger things up for me.' The phone beeped another warning of its ultimate demise.

'No, David. Get back to Carter, please. And more importantly don't go to ...'

'What, Peter what? Don't go to where?' I looked at the phone to see a blank screen. I took the battery out again and rubbed it until almost hot. Ramming it back into the phone I re-dialled the number. 'Come on you stupid thing.' The phone started to load up but went quietly went blank again. 'Bugger, of all the times,' I cursed and threw the phone onto the passenger seat.

I drove on and eventually saw a phone booth. I pulled the car over causing some mild road rage behind me as I jumped out only to finally realise I had to purchase some sort of telephone card. Punching the machine I returned to the car and decided what I would do. Getting out the map book I studied the route to Mortara near Milan. Over 250 miles but I thought I would be in Verona around dinner time and I could find somewhere to stay there. Crunching the gears I started my journey, and was soon speeding westward towards the Italian border.

Alone in the car, the rhythmic hum of the tyres on the autobahn gave my mind time to assimilate the last few days. Twice I shook my head in disbelief. I really wished I could sit down with my father and talk; really talk. I had a lot to ask and to say, I thought. What was bothering me was what could possibly have happened in Prague that clearly had affected my father so badly. Then a wave of reflection made me remember I was fast approaching my half century with not an awful lot to show for it. It was time I had some excitement.

I stayed the night in an awful travel hotel, but did find a decent trattoria to eat in. The next morning I left early and was parked in Mortara outside the apartment that Erica had now moved into. She had until recently lived in the old walled town of Lucca in Tuscany, a much more suitable place to bring up a young boy. It seems her new man was from this small town.

My heart leapt as I saw Jason playing with some other boys on a small patch of wasteland in front of the apartments. Some of the older boys were kicking a duffel bag around. Boys are the same the world over, I mused. Shouting to him he immediately saw me and making a small squeal he ran to me throwing his arms around my neck. Laughing I picked him up and held him in the air. He was now of a size that such a feat was not easy and I quickly placed him back on his feet. He shouted to his friends and then upwards at his apartment. I followed his look to see Erica, standing on a small balcony, watching us; her face impassive.

'Come on let's go and see mummy,' I said.

'Daddy I am waiting for the school bus. School has finished but there is a special trip to the Duomo in Milano. Will you be here tonight?'

'Yes, of course,' I said as I saw the yellow bus come hurtling round the corner at an alarming rate.

'Great you can meet ...' The boy stopped and a frown crossed his face. 'Oh, Giovanni lives with us now.' Uncertainty and confusion tainted his young voice.

'Look you had better go; I'll see you tonight,' I said forcing a smile and watched him rush off, picking up the duffel bag the bigger boys had been kicking. He scrambled onto the bus trying to look back at me and checked the contents of his bag. I saw him waving from the window, his eyes wide and I thought I saw a tear in them. Once again the pain of seeing him leave stabbed into my heart. I continued to stand and watch the bus depart and looked up towards the apartment. Erica pulled her cardigan across herself and left the balcony making no indication towards me.

I went into the building and worked out which apartment she was in. I knocked on the door and a few moments later was faced by my estranged wife.

'Hi, surprise …'

'David, what are you doing here?' she said wearily, her arms crossed under her bust.

'Are you not at least going to invite me in,' I said trying to put on a nonchalant air. She stepped to one side and as I advanced she slammed the door behind me. I followed her into a small kitchen off a lounge cum dinning room.

'Very nice place …'

'No its not, so don't try and be pleasant,' she said clattering a cafetiere around. Her accent was more pronounced than I remembered it.

'Coffee?' She said raising her dark eye brows. I nodded and as she turned her cardigan opened to reveal the full rounded belly of a pregnant woman. She saw my look.

'Look David, I need that divorce and very quickly,' she said gently stroking her tummy.

'Jason never mentioned anything,' I said almost to myself.

'I told him not to,' she said putting the coffee in the cafetiere. 'I would have told you sooner, but you know how much trouble I have had in the past.' I nodded the memories of the pain a miscarriage caused still raw in my mind.

'The main reason for my trip now seems to be superseded,' I said slowly and quietly.

'You didn't really think we would get back together again did you?' she said forcing a short, sharp laugh.

'Well actually, I did …'

'David you are either mad or stupid,' she said putting her hands on her hips. 'I am marrying Giovanni as soon as I can.' She stopped me interrupting her. 'It is good for me, good for Giovanni and more important good for Jasone.'

'*Jasone?*'

'Yes we use the Italian pronunciation now. Giovanni is also fantastic with the boy, and a lot more attentive than you ever were.'

'Now that's not fair,' I felt a sting of anger grow inside me. 'I was working night and day then, for us all.' She was almost ignoring me as she folded up some washing.

'Giovanni will be home for lunch if you wish to meet him, but you won't get a friendly reception. I told him what you did.'

'I thought most Italian men had affairs,' I said now really trying to control my anger.

'Yes that may be the case, but not when their wives are desperately trying to have another of their babies, and are also seriously *ill*.' She turned towards me shouting.

'OK, OK, let's leave it there. I'll speak to my lawyer and get a rapid divorce organised and no dragging of feet, I promise.'

'You will?' I nodded my stomach knotting up. 'David, it is for the best. Jasone loves Giovanni, and he is happy here,' she said coming over to me and putting her hand on my shoulder. 'He doesn't like not having a father. You know what gossip is like in small towns.'

I let out a long sigh and cupped my hands round my face. I could see in my mind Jason looking at me from the bus as it raced away. 'Tell Jason I couldn't stay will you.'

'Of course and when the baby is born and things settle down maybe you can visit then,' she said unconvincingly.

'Yes, maybe,' I replied making towards the door.

'Don't you want a coffee?'

'No, I think it best I leave on a civilised note, you know how you and I can have a row over absolutely nothing, and anyway I really do have to go.' I turned and kissed her on the cheek. 'Good luck with the bump,' I said raising a smile.

'Thanks David, and don't forget the lawyers, please.'

'No, I won't forget,' I said turning and leaving the apartment. I rushed to the car holding back some tears of hurt, anger and desperation.

I kept driving, stopping only for fuel and water. As I approached Vienna the signs for Prague seemed to be beckoning to me. I pulled over onto a service area and rummaged through all my father's letters. I found the relevant papers and decided that as Prague was only a hundred or so miles away the time was right for me to visit.

'Time for some excitement yourself David old chum,' I shouted at the windscreen.

I managed to enter the country with only a cursory glance at my passport and the hire car papers. I drove to Prague and as I had no idea where to go I eventually parked near to what I hoped was the centre. I went to a taxi rank and asked for directions and the man just pointed towards a large square. It seemed I was already near the Old Town Square. I bought a guide book and street map, and quickly booked into Hotel Clemintin, not far away from the car. My eyes itched with tiredness so a few cold beers and an early night seemed the right course of action. Self pity haunted me as I drifted to sleep thinking of Jason and his new father. I kept running over in my mind seeing him playing on the waste ground. Something didn't seem right, and it wasn't just the fact some boys were kicking Jason's bag around, it was the look he gave me as he left in the bus. Was I imagining it, or were his eyes pleading to me for help?

The next day I went to an address my father had left me half way between the old Jewish quarters and Karlin to the east. I was surprised that the building I was looking for was still there and to my surprise I noticed "H. Staffanich" labelled by a button. I rang it for ages but clearly nobody was at home. The initial was wrong but to have the same surname at this address was too much of a coincidence. My heart raced and I scribbled a note stuffing it into the letter box underneath.

I considered buying another mobile phone, but decided it was too extravagant, and would possibly not be operative until too late. I went back to the hotel making detours everywhere. The Charles Bridge enchanted me, as did the astronomical clock. I sat for ages waiting for the hour to strike and took the excuse to purchase a beer, well several actually. I walked down many small crowded streets where puppetry and alchemy were clearly a national occupation.

I got back to the hotel and twice toyed with the idea of calling Michaela but I wanted to find out more about the 1954 affair myself. I was sure she would understand, I said to myself, not very convincingly. It still wasn't two weeks since dad had died and in this short time I had found out nearly everything about my father's secret life. I'd even met his old lover! I gave myself two more days and would go back to Vienna on the Thursday; hopefully with the last piece of the jigsaw in place. I called home and was relieved to be greeted by the answer machine. Hopefully my mother was still out in Canada; however I had better get home soon. There was a lot to do.

I showered and then decided to investigate the bars of Prague. Whilst I was dressing the phone buzzed and a woman introduced herself as Hana Staffanich.

'My name is David Pinner,' I said slowly, emphasising my surname. I had hoped my name wouild cause some reaction. Nothing. 'Well, my father has recently died and he left a request that if I visited Prague I must call on Petr and Natalia Staffanich at your address. I was wondering if you knew anything about them.'

'Well, I should as I am their grandchild.' She made a nervous cough.

'Would it be possible for me to speak to them, or preferably meet them?' I asked.

'Unfortunately my grandfather died many years ago, and my grandmother is away in Israel at the moment.'

'Ahh that's a pity, I was hoping to ask them about something that happened a long time ago. My father knew your grandparents well.' A silence allowed me to hear a ticking clock in the background and I thought I heard someone whispering to her.

'Yes, I know.'

'Oh good, well maybe you can help ...'

'No I don't think so, I am very sorry, goodbye,' she said, and then the phone went dead.

'Hello,' I shouted. 'Bugger!'

I finished dressing quickly and decided to go to the address, hopefully before she went out. I walked as quickly as I could and arrived at the address in the early evening. I had brought my leather jacket as it had started to rain and become quite cool. I took the envelope containing my father's letters and stuffed it inside the jacket. It might make her understand that my line of enquiry was purely innocent and not anything more sinister.

I went to a nearby bar where if a sat in the window I could still just see the door to the building. Night fell and I became comfortable with drinking and watching the door, letting my thoughts wonder. Several people came and went but I was looking for a young woman in her mid to late twenties. The problem was I had no idea what she looked like. I started to lose interest in my quest and considered I should get back to Vienna and then to my parents' house. I had started to make a list of all the jobs I had to do. I hadn't put the RAF trunk away properly which was my main concern. My mother would interrogate me on its contents if she saw it.

Then a woman in a coat with a long scarf stopped at the front door of the building. She rummaged around in her large handbag trying to use the street light to help her. I rushed out of the bar followed by a shout from the barman. I ran down the street towards the woman who now had some keys and was putting them into the lock.

'Wait, Hana please, wait,' I shouted. I nearly slipped on the wet cobbles. 'Look I have brought something about your grandparents.'

She had opened the door and seeing me at first it looked as if she was going to bolt inside. After a moment's hesitation she stopped, extracted the keys, and closed the door. She turned to face me just as I arrived in front of her.

'You're David Pinner?' she said looking quite calm. She didn't smile.

'Yes, look I hope you don't feel I am being a nuisance, but …' Another loud shout from behind me made me turn. The barman was waving his fist from the door of the bar I had just left. 'Look, can I buy you a drink. I had a few beers at that bar,' I pointed at the barman, 'while I was waiting for you, and then rushed out to meet you. Would you mind?'

She gave a sigh and followed me back to the bar as I attempted to make polite conversation. The barman barked a command at me which was clear enough. I reached into my coat and got out my wallet.

'Would you like a drink?' I asked, noticing I had left my envelope on the seat. She turned to the barman and mumbled something while I pointed at my half empty glass and indicated for another. We went and sat at the table I had frequented before.

'Look I really don't want to be a bother but my father …'

'David, I never knew my grandfather, and my grandmother doesn't talk about the old days very much, so there isn't a lot I can help you with,' she said watching the barman bring the drinks to the table.

'Yes quite, but you did say you knew that my father was friendly with your grandparents, and …'

'I am sorry to keep interrupting but I really don't know an awful lot. The only thing I *do* know is gran did mention Paul

Pinner and another man called Maxwell Lilley,' she said looking surprised at my reaction to Lilley's name as I spilled my beer. 'You know Maxwell Lilley?' she asked surprise in her voice.

'Not exactly, but I would sure would like to meet him again,' I said mopping up the beer I had just spilt.

'So would my grandmother,' said Hana making a weak smile at my poor attempt to clear up the beer.

'Have you spoken to your grandmother today?'

'No, it is just that in the past she said she would dearly like to meet the two of them again.'

'Did she mean that in a nice way, or did she want to, let's say settle an old score,' I said feeling this woman knew more than she was letting on.

'I got the impression it was a little of both. She was upset to hear of your father's death ...'

'So you have spoken to her?' I knew I shouldn't have asked as soon as I had said it.

'As I said David I don't know a lot, and I am certainly not going to be questioned by you or anyone else. Now if you excuse me I have a long day tomorrow. I am flying to London, as it happens.'

'Look Hana, I am sorry. I'm not very good at this sort of thing, please let me show you something,' I said flicking through the contents of the envelope. I found the letter my father had written to me just before he died. 'Look at the last few paragraphs,' I said handing her the letter. She started to read it as I continued to rummage through the envelope and found the letter, to my father, from Sir Richard Ryder. I handed it to her and sat back sipping my beer as I watched her read. She finished and raised her eyebrows, shrugging her shoulders.

'I don't know what happened but I really think you should leave it be. I believe you shouldn't rake up the past; too many memories' she said slowly finishing her drink and starting to leave. 'My gran is very ill and I think *this* would not help.'

'I thought you said she was in Israel?'

'She is very ill in Israel, now if you would excuse me.' She stood up and I tried to follow her but this time the barman had spotted me and blocked my way out. I paid him then remembered my envelope and finally managed to leave as she was opening her front door. This time she disappeared inside.

'Damn and bugger,' I cursed to myself. It was dark and three shapes came out of the shadows on the other side of the street heading towards Hana's door. I didn't recognise them at first but as they came under a street lamp I clearly saw all three. The two thugs flanked Maxwell Lilley who looked as suave as when I first saw him at my father's wake. The taller of the henchman had no coat and he seemed to be almost brandishing his revolting tattoos. I gasped at seeing them and dropped the envelope. It made a loud thud and the three turned towards me. As one they all smiled as they recognised me. I stooped and picking up the envelope and ran as fast as I could towards the old part of the city.

The footsteps echoing louder behind me suddenly stopped. Glancing over my shoulder all three men had disappeared and I stumbled into a doorway panting. After two large gulps of night air I zipped up my jacket, grasping the large envelope concealed inside. My hotel meant security; I had to get there. I was certainly no native of Prague but I believed a narrow street just ahead could be a short cut to my goal.

I stepped out quickly from the doorway; my body hunched forward looking neither left nor right. The alley way was only fifty meters and I turned into it, relieved. In the daytime puppet and gift shops intermingled with cafes and bars, now everything was locked and boarded and the street looked empty and menacing. The alley narrowed after a hundred meters and I became disorientated. I stopped at a doorway and fumbled for my street map.

I never saw the owner of the fist that struck hard on my upper jaw. My knees buckled and cracked onto the hard damp cobbles. The thick, sweet metallic flavour of blood engulfed my taste buds. One arm instinctively clutched my precious packet while the other lashed out at my attacker; hitting only the cool damp air.

A snarled laugh was followed by a kick in the middle of my back, the resulting scream stifled by lack of air. My body crumbled onto the floor despite my brain demanding action. The brain was right; another kick connected with my kidneys causing me to jack knife. Still no air to scream. In a blur I saw another foot draw back and I rolled myself into a ball. The kick never came. Strong hands grabbed my arms and forced me onto my back. My jacket was ripped open and the envelope extracted. At first I didn't dare open my eyes in case it antagonised them.

'Danke, mein Herr,' was spat at me in a mock German accent.

I finally looked up to be face to face with a man I had only briefly seen twice in my life. His hideous tattoos made him unmistakeable. This time he had won. They let go and I saw one of my friends with the tattoos stand back to kick me again. I put my arms around my head and cursed.

'No,' came Maxwell Lilley's deep well spoken voice from the shadows. 'We have what we want. Leave the poor wretch.' Shouts came from the main street. A tall man with long grey hair stepped forward. 'Well young Pinner it seems luck is on your side again,' he said glancing behind him. He took the envelope from one of the other men. 'I'll be in touch again after I have read all these,' he said starring at me and coming towards me.

I drew my knees up putting my arms around my head and closed my eyes, waiting for another beating. I heard my tormentor's footsteps fading into the distant hum of a city. I rolled onto my back and tried to get up, but the pain made me wince and I slumped onto the cold ground.

Hurt but relieved at being alive, I lay still in disbelief at the recent chain of events. 'Thanks Dad,' I whispered to the night sky. 'You always said I needed a good hiding. If you're looking after me from your heavenly haunt then you have a strange way of doing it.'

More commotion came from the main street and I saw some

figures calling out and approaching me. I did make out the word "Police", or something similar, and relief cascaded through my body. Several people arrived and fussed around me talking quickly in a language where not a single word was comprehensible. They gently helped me to my feet and I shuffled to a nearby bench. I could hear the sound of a siren getting louder.

The ambulance drive did not take long, but my mind was full of how I could salvage the situation. Michaela would kill me when I told her I had lost the letters, I thought. How could I have been so stupid? Why didn't I get them photocopied, I scolded myself. A few hours later I had given my statement to a policeman and seen a doctor who clearly thought my presence was totally unnecessary. I had to agree with him, I had suffered only bruises and some swelling.

I got back to my hotel and managed to find out whether there was a flight to London the following morning. I had decided to go home to lick my wounds but in the back of my mind was Hanaalso visiting London. It might give me the opportunity to try once more and get any information she may have. I lay back on the bed. No letters and many questions still left to be answered. The biggest one was how had Maxwell Lilley known I was in Prague; more importantly how had he known Hana's address.

The next morning I took the rented car to the airport and after some confusion they found the booking. I had taken the option to leave it at Prague when I had quickly booked the car two days ago. It was then I realised how Lilley might have known I was going to Prague. He must have access to a data base. He would have known then that I would probably go looking for Natalia and Petr. If this was the case then he probably knew I was taking the flight to London, I thought to myself, and I nervously looked around.

I booked in and went to the departure lounge taking a seat in the café close to the main entrance. Hana walked in twenty minutes later. I stood up and beckoned her over. At first I was greeted with an angry stare, which softened as she saw my swollen face and bruises.

'You don't give up do you,' she said approaching me warily.

'Coffee?' I asked. She nodded and took the seat opposite me placing her hand luggage next to mine. 'Oh, I didn't mention I live in London,' I continued standing up and calling over a waiter.

'What happened to you,' she said looking at my wounds. I ordered the coffees and turned to her.

'Well it wasn't a drunken brawl if that's what you think.' I gingerly touched the bridge of my nose and my swollen cheek. 'Actually I was set upon. My letters were stolen and then ...'

'Why would anyone have stolen a few old letters?' She was studying me carefully.

'Well, actually I knew who it was ...'

'Please don't tell me it was this Maxwell Lilley man,' her face stiffened and eyes enlarged.

'Yes, it was and accompanied by his two thugs. I can't believe I was so stupid not to have taken ...' I stopped as Hana seemed transfixed and staring at me.

'Where was this,' she asked her gaze fixed firmly on me.

'Err, last night.'

'I said *where* did this happen?' Hana's colour had drained from her face.

'Actually Hana they spotted me from outside your door,' I said realising I could be putting the fear of God into her.

'What the hell is going on? First you and now this man Lilley in one day. Gran will be devastated.' Hana stirred her coffee slowly but kept her eyes on me.

I started to ask a question, but this time thought better of it. A change of subject was called for, I thought.

'So where are you staying in London?' I asked as brightly as I could.

'UCL. I am doing some joint research with a couple of the senior lecturers there,' she said but her mind was elsewhere. 'Why? Why are you all here?'

'Well I explained to you why I was here …'

'No you didn't actually, not really. Why is Lilley here and why did he take those letters?' She was talking to me but the question was almost to herself. I looked at my watch.

'I'd better check the flight,' I said getting up. I went over to a screen and came back to the table. 'We'd better finish up, we are being called.'

'I need to know David. Why would Lilley be here?'

'I am not sure, let's talk about it on the plane. What seat number are you?' She didn't answer; her look became distant and a frown lined her brow. 'We can also talk about your parents and …'

'Will you please answer my question,' she started to shout. I blushed and sat back down opposite her.

'I really don't know why *he* is here. I am trying to find out myself.' Hana sat back and now looked away. The public address system called our flight.

'I don't have any parents, my Gran brought me up,' she said turning back to me. 'I need to go to the toilet; I'll meet you at the gate.'

She picked up her hand luggage and strode away purposely towards the toilets. I wandered towards the gate to see the last few passengers handing in their boarding passes. I held back a little and waited for Hana. The stewardess pressed a button on a tanoy and I heard Hana's and my name being called. I stepped forward.

'Sorry Miss Staffanich has just gone to the toilet she shouldn't be a minute,' I said to the stewardess. She smiled back politely but also made a gesture of checking her watch. Several minutes passed.

'I am sorry Mr. Pinner you must board now,' said the stewardess becoming a little agitated.

'Could you call her again, please,' I asked. The woman obliged.

The phone rang, and she turned to me. 'The Captain is closing the gate. You must board now or we will take your bags off.'

'Take her bags off,' I shouted back towards her as I turned to run to the departure lounge.

'Mr. Pinner what about yours?' she shouted after me.

I turned and tapped my knapsack. 'I didn't book any in. I travel light.' I didn't hear her reply as I started to sprint towards the exit.

Chapter 16

CARTER AND MICHAELA GIVE CHASE

Michaela stood still her head in her hands sobbing quietly. A wave of remorse and confusion swept threw her and she wanted to just run to her bedroom; her legs seemed frozen. Her estranged husband and Carter stood there not sure what to do. Eventually the young French woman made a pronounced sigh and came over and led Michaela to a chair. She then took her children by the hands and marched them off to a bedroom glancing back at her lover with reprimand in her eyes.

'Look this is a little bit awkward for me,' said Carter to the other man. 'I have only just introduced myself to your wife, and I have some very important business to discuss with her.' Carter adjusted his tie and looked hopefully at the man wishing he would follow his woman and their children.

'Yes, it is a bit strange for me. If I went and consoled Michaela then my girlfriend would not be pleased. Do nothing and that is wrong,' he whispered eyeing Michaela with unease.

'That's women for you,' Carter said trying to lighten the atmosphere. 'Would you mind if I had a few moments alone with her. It is important.'

'No of course not, but you said something about her having a half brother. What is all this about?' The man stepped forward expecting an explanation.

'Well as I said I had only arrived just before you,' Carter said straightening himself; the pain in his groin now turning to a dull ache. 'I have some legal matters to discuss with her regarding her inheritance. I am a lawyer from England and due to client confidentiality I am not allowed to say anymore. In fact I have already said too much.' Carter lied to Michaela's husband with a knowing smile.

'But old man Berckendorff was a raving queer. I am surprised he fathered Michaela never mind another …'

'Oh bugger off Leif. Let me talk to Mr. Carter in the peace of my own home!' Michaela had stood up and was withdrawing a paper handkerchief from a box.

'Yes, well I pay for most of it so …'

'Leif please, I think it best I talk to your wife for a while,' said Carter gently taking the man's elbow and steering him towards the bedroom which emanated screams and thumping of surprising volume. 'I promise I will not be long and if I may suggest, you and Michaela need a long private chat yourselves.' Carter noted Michaela was nodding.

'Right, if we may,' said Carter coming back into the lounge and motioning to Michaela to take a seat. 'It seems we have some talking to do.'

'Yes, but what about David?' Michaela said her eyes red and swollen.

'Where has he gone and how?' demanded the British agent.

'I had Leif coming round to sort out our marriage, or to finish it,' said Michaela still sobbing a little. 'Anyway David is also going through problems with his own marriage and, after we saw my mother this morning, we both thought it best to go our separate ways for a few days. I booked him a car at the Budget place around the corner.'

'When did you book this?'

'Why does that matter?' she said starting to shout at Carter. 'The main thing is to make sure those two thugs don't catch him again.'

'Yes, but think about it. How did Lilley know he was going to be there? Indeed how did Lilley know you had come to Vienna at all?'

Michaela frowned. 'He still has access to the databases that you people use?'

'He must have, but his normal source has been caught. I don't think she will be helping him; if she has any sense.' Carter looked thoughtfully towards the large French windows. 'I'd better let London know and call my colleagues here in Vienna. May I use your phone? My mobile seems to have a poor signal.' Michaela nodded and sat and watched as Carter made several calls. 'Right come on we need to get to the Budget rental place and quickly.'

Michaela went to the guest bedroom to be confronted by her husband, girlfriend and two children sprawled out asleep on the bed. The little girl was wrapped in her father's arms and for a few moments Michaela stood and absorbed the scene. There was a smell and aura about children that caused tears to well in her eyes again. Carter made a polite cough. Quietly closing the door she fetched her coat avoiding eye contact with Carter.

'They have all gone to sleep,' she eventually whispered to him as they walked briskly to the Budget rental forecourt. Carter entered first when they arrived, followed closely by Michaela.

'Do you speak English,' he asked the man behind the desk.

'Of course, can I help you?' The man continued to shuffle papers in front of him.

Carter unfolded a crisp new 50 Euro note and cradled it in his hand. 'Yes, my colleague booked a car from here to be picked up this afternoon. We need to speak to him …'

'Mr. Pinner?' said the man eyeing the note.

'Yes, David Pinner,' interrupted Michaela.

'He is popular man this Mr. Pinner,' said the clerk leaning back and picking up an envelope.

'Popular, why popular?' asked Carter already knowing the answer. He pushed the note towards the man and withdrew his hand.

'A couple of gentlemen were asking for him as well, not so long ago …'

'Did one of them have some rather horrible tattoos on his

neck?' Carter watched him as he took out a key and some paper work from the envelope.

'Yes. You English either dress like a lord, or a football hooligan,' said the man trying to be comical. 'Will you be seeing Mr. Pinner?'

'Yes, why,' replied Michaela switching to German.

'Oh, he hasn't showed but I will have to charge him,' replied the man.

Carter interjected in English. 'Did you say he hasn't showed?'

'Yes and not even a telephone call, so I have to charge him.'

'Thank you,' said Carter watching the man pocket the money. Taking Michaela by the arm they left the booth.

'Right where is he?' said Carter.

'He mentioned he *had* taken a car. Maybe from another rental place not far away,' said Michaela. Carter turned and went back into the booth.

'It looks as though our Mr. Pinner has gone to the wrong car rental company. Is there another close to here?' The man looked hopefully at Carter, his eyes asking for more money. Carter didn't move.

'Yes there is Eurocar, just round the corner to the left.'

'Thank you for your help,' said Carter exiting and, taking Michaela by the arm, marching her down the road. 'Look Michaela it might come better from you in German to ask if David has hired a car, but more importantly where and when is he returning it.'

'Where? Well he will be coming back here, won't he?'

'Mmm, I'm not so sure,' said Carter instinctively eyeing the rump of a tall young woman crossing in front of him.

They entered a small office and had to wait as the two clerks, one male the other female, were on the phone. Eventually the woman finished and looked up and smiled. Michaela asked the question in German. Carter's heart sank as he saw her shake her head. More conversation and Michaela was becoming agitated.

'She says she can't help me; can't give out client details,' said

Michaela throwing an angry glance at the woman. Carter took control.

'Will you give this information to the police?' asked Carter in a very matter of fact way. He noticed the male turning his head, finishing his call and slowly getting up to join his colleague. Carter produced some money and this time unfolded two notes and put the wad back into his pocket; his fingers playing with the cash. 'It is very important we contact this man, and I fully understand that you have to be careful with information; but I must know. I can call the police and we can get the information via them.' Carter left the two notes on the counter.

'He's my brother you see, and there has been a family bereavement. It is vital we find him,' said Michaela with sadness in her eyes. 'I was only hoping to use the police as the last resort,' she said giving Carter a sideways glance.

The man pulled out a printed pad and flicked back a few pages.

'Yes, we rented a car to Mr. Pinner not more than an hour or so ago,' said the man carefully closing the book and retrieving the two notes. 'You are not alone …'

'Two men, one tall with tattoos,' interjected Michaela. She made a small laugh. 'He's my cousin; we're all trying to find Mr. Pinner. A scary chap, I bet you didn't tell him anything.'

The facial expression of the two clerks told Carter that Lilley knew where David Pinner was, and possibly where he was heading. Carter started to ask but Michaela was first. 'When has he planned to bring the car back?' Carter pulled out more money and unfolded two more notes, pushing them towards the woman.

'Three days time,' she answered. 'But it may not be here,' she continued. 'He has taken an option of dropping the car off at Prague International airport. He said he would call us.'

'Thank you, that is very helpful,' said Michaela turning to Carter, her eyes widening.

'Your cousins were also a bit surprised when we told them,' said the man.

Carter closed his eyes and tried to think clearly. 'Could you let me know if he contacts you,' he said handing over a card with his name and a telephone number on it. 'Tell him to call me on these numbers or his sister, urgently please.'

Carter and Michaela walked out onto the street in silence.

'David has gone to find out what happened in 1954 and visit a couple that Paul Pinner knew there,' said Michaela slowly.

'Yes, my worst fears are happening. We must stop him, but more importantly we must stop Lilley from digging up too much.'

Carter started to walk back to Michaela's apartment but noticed she wasn't beside him. He turned and she was standing in the street her head slightly on one side.

'I want to know what the hell is going on Charles, and I want to know now!' Carter realised he might have to break a strict protocol.

★ ★ ★

Hana waited until she saw David Pinner move towards the departure gate. As soon as he was out of sight she slipped through the lounge and after a brief word with a security guard she was in the main terminal. Scanning the crowds nervously she went to arrivals on the next level. She thought she would be safer taking a taxi from there.

Sitting in the taxi, tears started to drop from her eyes. She recalled the nights she had heard the screams of her grandmother in her sleep. She remembered one night when her Gran was so upset she went into her room and tried to comfort her. Her grandmother awoke not sure of why she was in her bedroom, but when Hana told her how she was screaming and crying about a man called Maxwell, the old woman just closed her eyes and cried rocking rhythmically. Hana never found out what happened but she knew something terrible had happened between them. It was never clear to her whether her grandmother ever wanted to see this man again or not. Hana sensed an emotion locked so deep in the old woman that to release it would be painful.

The taxi pulled over a few hundred yards from her house. She wasn't going to take any chances. She slipped down the alleyway that ran behind her building and scaling a brick wall dropped into her back yard. The back door was never locked and she scaled the stairs entering the large bedroom at the rear of the house. Her grandmother sat propped up in a large chair by an old desk. She was reading and was so astonished to see her grandchild that she dropped the book.

'My God, what is the matter, Hana? I thought you were going to London?' Her eyes widened at seeing the distress of the young woman.

'He's here. Gran he's here!'

'Who's here dear, David Pinner?'

'No, the man you used to shout about in your dreams …'

'Maxwell Lilley?' said Natalia starting to rise from her chair. 'No, how do you know? How did he get here? Has this David Pinner brought him?' The old woman's voice was shaking and she picked up a shawl wrapping it around her. She could feel hysteria building up inside her.

'Gran, what happened and why are they here now after Paul Pinner's death. Why is his son here being chased by the Maxwell Lilley man?'

'Being chased, what do you mean? Hana will you please explain yourself, it's important.' The old woman went over and clutched her granddaughter to her breast. 'It'll be alright Hana, just tell me what happened.'

'Well I was in the airport and David Pinner was in the departure lounge. He was on my flight to London,' she said pulling her grandmother towards her. 'He had been in a fight …'

'Fight?'

'Yes, after I left him he started to come towards the house and he saw Lilley and the two thugs who apparently he has tangled with before. They chased him and beat him and took all the letters that I told you about last night.' The two women released their embrace and the young woman helped her grandmother to her seat. 'Gran what *is* going on? What do they want?'

'Hana, I am not sure. I wonder if Lilley knows, but if he did then he wouldn't have …'

'If Lilley knows what?' yelled the young woman.

'Lilley mustn't see me. Hana please get help …'

'Oh Gran, I told him that you said you *did* want to meet Lilley, I'm sorry …'

Both women screamed as the loud thudding on the front door echoed and vibrated through the house.

★ ★ ★

Trying to exit the departure lounge was no easy feat and I was held up for ages at security, trying to explain my situation, which was also difficult when I was fabricating a complete lie. I had decided that as soon as I got to the hotel I would call Michaela and hopefully the British government agent might be able to help. Eventually I left and ran to a waiting taxi. Bellowing the name of the hotel I had just left that morning to the driver, I sat back in the seat to see my tattooed nemesis running towards me.

'Drive, for Christ sake drive,' I screamed at the driver. He muttered and slamming the Mercedes in gear lurched forward and down a service road. I didn't dare look back.

Luckily the hotel was not full so I booked another room much to the surprise of the manageress. We made pleasant conversation but as I started to go to my room she called after me.

'Oh, Mr. Pinner someone was looking for you this morning.'

I stopped and felt my muscles tense and the hairs rise on the back of my neck.

'Three men, one with some noticeable …'

'No, a man and a woman,' she said as I slowly walked back to the desk.

'This man was tall, old and long grey hair?'

'No he was normal height, very English and with a German woman with very long blonde hair and …'

'Long black coat with matching boots.'

'Yes, very nice they were too,' she said with a faint laugh.

'You ladies always check each other's clothes out, don't you,' I said leaning on the reception desk with relief. 'Did they leave any messages or say anything,' I continued as my body relaxed. How on earth could they have found me, I thought?

'Yes, the man left a card and the woman said you had her numbers,' she said looking under the desk. 'Where is that card? Ah yes, here it is. They seemed a little concerned about you,' said the manageress watching me.

'She's my big sister, always fussing,' I replied reading Charles Carter's card.

I thanked her and went to my room. My head was demanding I called them but my heart wanted me to go and find Hana. I had more than an inkling that Natalia was here in Prague. I dearly wanted to sit with her and ask her what had happened. Finding out dad was a spy, had had an affair and a love child didn't seem to satisfy me. I felt I wanted to know everything. I picked up the phone and started to dial, but thought again and slammed it down; pulling on my jacket I left the room. As I passed the reception the manageress came out of a back office.

'Oh, Mr. Pinner your sister is here …'

I turned towards the main door, thinking of making a bolt for it, when Michaela and a man stood in my way.

'David, you have no idea how difficult it has been to track you down,' said my half sister. She introduced me to Charles Carter.

'Well I'll tell you this David, you should consider joining the secret service,' he said giving a firm handshake. 'You're as slippery as an eel.' Carter and Michaela had both noticed my face. 'It seems that you haven't avoided everyone,' said Carter looking at my bruises.

'Yes, our friend Maxwell Lilley, or should I say his two gorillas, managed to catch up with me,' I said stroking my nose. 'It seems that he wants another chat.'

'What do you mean?' asked Carter.

'Well, he was disturbed when they beat me up and took the letters …'

'They took the letters! David you idiot,' said Michaela staring in disbelief at me.

'Just a minute Michaela, I don't need this, if you don't mind …'

'It does seem a little crass to walk around with the letters. No copies I suppose,' said Carter a slight sigh in his voice. I felt myself flush and my jaw tighten.

'Look I was going out to get some aspirin for my face is really hurting, especially my nose. You stay here I'll be back in a minute and I can give you my story,' I said skirting around them. Carter stood still looking at me a little uncertain.

'I'll get them David, you stay here and get to know Carter,' said Michaela standing as well. 'He's quite nice under that rugged exterior,' she said giving him a quick glance.

'No, I'm very fussy about what brand I take,' I said trying not to make it confrontational. 'I'll be back in a tick.' I said as Michaela frowned.

'A tick, what is that?' she asked.

'Ahh, I really am improving your vocabulary. You remember a "mo", well it's the same,' I said laughing weakly and edging towards the door. Carter seemed a bit bemused by the conversation.

'OK,' he said sitting down. 'I'll order some coffees.'

'Great, make mine a cappuccino,' I said opening the door and moving out onto the street. I remembered a chemist was nearby so I walked towards it briskly. Entering I circumnavigated the store and checked down the street back towards the hotel. No sight of Carter or Michaela so I slipped out and walking away from the hotel made my way to Hana's house.

After ten minutes I reached her front door and deciding I

hadn't the time for any subtlety started to hammer on the door. I could hear the thumping resonating through the house. She certainly won't be able to ignore this, I thought to myself.

Chapter 17

NATALIA'S STORY

Carter watched until David Pinner was a short distance down the street.

'Wait here and stay by your mobile,' he said to Michaela moving towards the door.

'What about the coffees?' called Michaela.

'Never mind those, just stay by your phone and be ready to come when I call you,' Carter whispered and disappeared. Michaela threw her hands up in the air and went to the reception to order herself a shot of caffeine.

Carter kept a close observation on David and entered a shop opposite the chemist. David was walking round and constantly checking behind him.

'You're going to do another runner aren't you young Pinner,' Carter whispered to himself. He watched David come out and walk briskly away from the hotel. 'Got you,' said the agent and started after his mark.

Carter was a professional when it came to surveillance and David Pinner would never know he was being trailed. Over ten minutes later he saw David stop outside a door and to his amazement start to hammer his fist on it, quite excessively. Carter drew back out of view and called Michaela. Giving her the address he then called his contacts at the Embassy. He believed back-up would be needed if his assumptions were right.

★ ★ ★

I kept thumping on the door, not even stopping as my hand started to hurt. Several passers-by stopped and stared; one even shouted at me. I ignored them and continued, this time shouting as well.

'Hana, I'm not leaving until I have spoken to you, do you hear me …'

The door opened slightly and Hana peered through a small gap. I could just make out a security chain. 'David, please will you go away, I *will* call the police.'

'Good! Because if you don't I will!'

The door closed a little and I heard the chain being removed, then it opened and Hana beckoned me in. Checking up and down the street I entered, no sign of the tattooed monster, his brother or Lilley. Two pedestrians continued to watch the scene, their eyes hoping for an incident.

'What do you mean you will call the police?' Hana asked slamming the door shut and leading me into a large living room. The house had seen better days and was in need of some repair. Faded paintwork and threadbare carpets gave a sense of gloom.

'Missed your flight?' I said ignoring her question. 'Well I did, thanks to waiting for you at the gate, and then to top it all, my friend with the tattoos saw me at the airport and I suspect he may well be on his way back here, possible with Mr. Lilley. You'd better let your gran know.' I looked around the room and spied some old pictures on a table in the corner. I sauntered over to them feeling Hana's eyes boring into me.

'Look David, I got it all wrong, my grandmother definitely doesn't want to talk to you nor this Maxwell Lilley, so could you please leave, and don't touch those …' she screamed the last phrase as I went to pick up an old and faded photograph.

I tried to hold her back with one arm as I examined the picture.

'Give me that,' she screamed and twisting past my outstretched arm trying to grab the photograph. The struggle disturbed the table scattering a few of the pictures. I stumbled back to see a miniature painting, nearly identical to the one my father had, nestled in an alcove. Hana followed my eyes and made a small gasp and lunged towards the alcove.

'No Hanna, I am not here to take anything; listen to me!'

She pushed past me but we both froze as we heard the click of the catch to the front door. A few faint footsteps seemed to come down the corridor towards us. I instinctively faced the door and stood in front of Hana.

'Whose there?' I shouted. I scanned the room for a weapon and started to shuffle towards the fireplace keeping Hana behind me. The door opened slowly and the tall tattooed brother entered. A smile started to form on his broad face as he saw me looking towards the poker in the fireplace.

'They're in here Joey,' he shouted, half turning his head. 'So Mr. fuckin' Pinner, we meet again. I wouldn't get that poker again, cos' this time Pinner I'll bend it round your bleedin neck.' He crossed the room and yanked Hana out from behind me. 'Nice bit of stuff Mr. Pinner, bit of a baby snatcher aren't you ...?'

'Shut up Nici,' came a deep soft accented voice. I saw the smaller brother and Maxwell Lilley standing either side of the doorway. The older brother was grinning but Lilley's face was impassive. Lilley's trousers were badly stained on one knee and he carried a dark coloured document case.

'So Pinner we meet again, this time I do hope we have the opportunity to have more of a chat,' he said clicking his fingers at the younger brother. 'Put them on the settee Nici, but be careful with Mr. Pinner you know how he bruises so easily,' Lilley said ending with a small laugh.

'How did you get in?' demanded Hana. I admired her pluckiness for the tattoo gorilla tossed her onto the settee as if she was a doll; she immediately tried to get up but he stopped her by a slap to the face. 'How dare you,' she cried out, her eyes flashing at him through her tears.

Nici went to hit her again. 'That's enough Nici. I think they know the score now.' Hana sat still rubbing her face glancing at me, tears cascading down her cheeks. 'It seems you don't bother locking the back door. I unfortunately fell climbing the wall,' said Lilley brushing his trousers.

'I'll go and bolt the doors guv, and I'd better check the house,' said the smaller brother. Lilley nodded and ambled over to where the pictures had been spilled on the table. I watched him as he circled the room.

'What brings you here to this house,' he said turning to face me. 'And where is your bastard half-sister?' Lilley's eyebrows were raised questioningly. 'Lost your tongue or do you want Nici here to loosen it.' He motioned towards the tall man.

'OK, ok what do you want to know,' I said quickly holding up my hands. 'To be honest Mr. Lilley I am here to find out things myself.'

'Mmm, I bet you are,' he said advancing towards me and tossing the document wallet onto a chair. 'But first let's do the introductions. Who is this little lady, as Nici said a bit young for you isn't she?' Lilley stepped forward and pulling Hana's chin round studied her face.

'You don't know who she is, do you,' I said softly. Lilley checked and studied Hana again; a puzzled look filled his eyes. A flicker of recognition danced with his memory. I could see that something in the girl had made him remember something or someone from long ago.

'I'll ask the questions, if you don't mind Pinner. You're certainly a chip of the old block aren't you?' Lilley turned, picked up the document case and went over to the table where the pictures still lay scattered, pushing them to one side. The elder brother came back and shrugged his shoulders at Lilley.

'First I want to know a few things about these letters and then we need to discuss a picture your father, or so I now believe, had in his possession,' he said unzipping the case. 'Are these all the letters? Have you got any correspondence your father sent to Sir Richard …?'

Lilley froze. He lent forward and picked up a black and white photograph of four people; it was the same picture that had caught my eye just before they had burst in. One of the figures was certainly my father many years ago. Lilley was studying it and a silence draped the room. He straightened up and even though he was facing away I could tell he was confused and in deep thought. Then he gave a small gasp as his eyes fell on the small painting in the alcove.

'What is this?' he said turning and in two strides he was besides Hana again. Grabbing her upper arm he pulled her to her feet and swung her round to face him. Hana made a small scream and started to hit him with her free hand. Lilley took the slap without even a flinch and towered over the girl shaking her, his eyes dropping towards her small breasts bouncing loosely inside her shirt; his long grey hair falling forward. 'Who are you?' he said continuing to shake her roughly.

I jumped up, grabbed Hana and tearing her out of Lilley's grasp, pushed her away. I turned to see Nici's fist already coming at me, and ducked. The blast of air from Lilley's mouth meant Nici had hit his boss right in the solar plexus. I took my chance. I punched the tattoo monster with every ounce of effort I could muster, right in his stomach. To my surprise he doubled up taking two small tottering steps backwards, tripping over a low coffee table and crashing on top of it, smashing it to pieces. I grabbed Hana and dragged her towards the door. The older brother actually stepped aside as he watched his brother writhing on the floor and Lilley doubled up. I pulled Hana down the hallway to the front door and pulling the bolts back, started to pull on the catch.

'No. gran is here,' she screamed at me pulling as hard as she could on my arm. I stopped and thought about my father's letters lying on the table.

'Hana, we must go,' I shouted seeing the living room door move.

I freed the catch and the door flew open pushing Hana and I back into the hallway. Two uniformed policemen were on me instantly, one of them turning me around and slamming me against the wall.

'Not them!' came a voice I had only heard for the first time an hour ago. An order was lashed out in a foreign language and several men passed by me following my flaying arm as I tried to point towards the living room door. I saw Joey dart out and down the hall towards the rear of the house. One uniformed man threw himself at him and clawed him down onto the floor, drawing the Londoner's arms back and handcuffing him. A huge scuffle was taking place in the living room and I started to make my way towards the door.

'Huh, and you thought I was trouble. *You're the one whose trouble,*' said Michaela from behind me. 'And who is this?' she said looking towards Hana who was shaking and quietly sobbing by the front door.

'Where is my Gran,' Hana cried quietly, her head buried into her hands.

'Believe me Michaela you not going to believe me,' I said gently squeezing Hana's shoulder and then followed Carter into the living room as the noise had subsided.

I entered the room to see Nici handcuffed and writhing on the floor cursing the large man kneeling on him as he tightened the cuffs. Lilley was seated still gasping for air, shadowed by another officer. Carter turned to a suited man surveying the progress of his men.

'Get them out of here, but I need to speak to *him*,' he said nodding at Lilley who was now watching me as we walked towards him. The two officers in the room grabbed Nici and as he was dragged out he was cursing and swearing at me. The policemen put Nici up on his feet and I called to them. They stopped for a second and as Nici turned to me I slowly raised my middle finger towards him.

'Swivel on this you big ugly bastard …'

I was interrupted by more cursing and he shouted at me stating some startling facts of what he was going to happen to me when he was released.

Carter gave me an angry look and shook his head. 'You really shouldn't have done that,' he said his eyes moving towards the heavens. The front door slammed and peace descended on the hallway. 'I believe in magnanimity in victory, not rubbing his nose in it.' I noticed Michaela was shaking her head at me supporting Carter's view. I blushed a little with embarrassment at my action; I knew it had seemed a little immature, but they hadn't been on the receiving end of that man, I justified to myself.

'So who is she?' Lilley was still wheezing. 'And how come she looks vaguely familiar. More importantly how did she get one of my pictures …?'

Out in the hallway we heard a cry and footsteps on the stairs. Carter started to move towards the door when it slowly opened. Hana was supporting the arm of a woman in her late sixties; her face was drawn and her eyes seemed to have sunk into her skull. Her hair was a dark, almost black and pulled back into a bun; a few strands of her hair had worked loose and were dangling across her face. Her eyes were red and tear stains snaked down her cheeks. As she entered the room she took Hana's hand off her arm and stood up straight.

Lilley slowly stood and stared at the woman. 'Natalia?'

The woman inched forward and looked into Lilley's stare. Carter took a step back to let her past the broken coffee table. Still the woman closed slowly on Lilley. All I could hear was my heart pounding and a clock in the hallway making a methodical tick.

'Natalia?' Lilley said again, confusion in his voice. He pointed towards the picture he had seen. 'It is you, only you could have had that photograph, and my miniature, why didn't you …'

The woman was now standing in front of Lilley. Despite her smaller physique she seemed to tower over him as her presence made him withdraw into himself.

'Natalia I tried to stop them, I swear to you I couldn't control …'

The slap from this woman hit Lilley with such force his head shot back and his knees gave way making him collapse back into his chair. I was astonished that neither Carter nor the suited man moved. I was then completely shocked to see Lilley's shoulders shudder and a tear run down his face.

'I didn't mean you any harm,' he cried. 'It was that little wretch's father,' he pointed at me, 'Pinner, he was the cause of everything.' The woman looked around and pointed at a chair and then at me.

'Bring it to me,' she barked. I responded immediately. Carter, Michaela and the other man stood transfixed by the scene. I brought the chair over and she turned it so she just perched on the arm. She made herself comfortable and looked down on the crumpled figure in front of her.

'Yes, Max. It's me. It *has* been a long time,' she said her tears welling in her eyes. 'Nearly forty five years since we last met I believe.' She let out a long sigh, and I saw pity in her flooded eyes. 'It was you, wasn't it Max?' She continued to watch the man in front of her and then she started to stretch her shaking hand out to touch Lilley but stopped and closed her eyes for a few seconds. Lilley sat there with his head in his hands, his long hair spilling through his fingers, his shoulders moving in time with his sobs.

'Max, I know it was you. Only you could have worn such cologne and we were at very close quarters, weren't we Max. Despite having the hood on I knew it was you.' Natalia seemed calm and her sympathies clearly towards the man in front of her. Lilley pushed his hair back with both hands and looking up at her and nodded.

I glanced towards Carter and raised my eyebrows but he frowned at me and putting his index finger to his lips. Michaela stepped forward and held out her hand to Natalia.

'My name is Michaela von Berckendorff. I am the daughter of Paul Pinner,' she said formally. Lilley had clearly not noticed her and his eyes flashed with anger for a moment. 'May I ask what this man did to you?'

Lilley's eyes surveyed the room widening as he caught sight of Carter. 'Look, just a moment …'

'Shut up Lilley,' interjected Carter. 'I either hear this now or in a court room. Which do prefer?' Lilley nodded and sat back. 'You know who I am, don't you Lilley? I am acting on the specific instructions of Reeves-Dodd' continued Carter. Lilley nodded and he closed his eyes for a moment. 'Please Natalia would you continue,' said Carter taking a seat opposite Lilley. Nobody else moved.

'You are a stupid man Max,' she said. 'Your hatred for Pinner blinded you to anything else …'

'You fancied Pinner as well, so I was surrounded by his …'

'You *are* totally wrong. I didn't fancy Paul. I fancied you! Do you remember the night you gave me the picture,' she said pointing towards the alcove. 'You were so tall and handsome and I made up my mind that I wanted you. But I needed to know if you were serious and I didn't want to be another one night stand. You seemed to have plenty of those, didn't you Max? You were cold as ice at times, but I was determined to catch you by playing hard to get. Paul, on the other hand, used to come and go but *we* were working together. He was a bit too 'nice' for me. All because I liked Paul and I used to love our long debates about politics and ideologies, it didn't mean anything. Why you did such a thing on that day I could never work out. If I had known the depth of your feeling about me, and your hatred for Paul, then I would have done something different, but everyone lost that day; *do you realise that.*' Natalia struggled with her shawl as she searched for a handkerchief. She bent forward. 'Everyone Max, all of us lost that day, and do you know now as I look back; I could see the signs. I could have prevented it but I was actually enjoying the chase,' her eyes narrowed and she lent close to Lilley's face. 'You raped me, Max,' she hissed.

Michaela and Hana made small gasps simultaneously.

'You destroyed me and poor Petr. You destroyed not only our lives and also my son's, as he didn't like seeing me so unhappy. God knows what happened to Paul Pinner and what about yourself. What do I see sitting in front of me? Are you married?

Are you happy? Can you look back on your life with any sense of well being and pride? The answer I suspect is no! A huge *no*'

'I'm sorry to interrupt Natalia, but what happened,' asked Michaela looking down on Lilley with disgust flaring from her eyes.

'Petr and I were recruited by the British Government, through Paul, to help with finding agents who had disappeared during the war. Usual stuff but we also helped Paul with his swap-out deals. Chemicals for finished products; that sort of thing. Of course we fed back any information we had on Soviet activity; they were the enemy.

'Well Petr and I did notice some animosity between Max and Paul, but tried to not get involved. The problem was I had really fallen for Maxwell. He tried to ask me out but as I said I did what most *decent* girls do and tried to be hard to get. It seems I tried a little too hard. It all started I think over nothing really but we all went out together for dinner,' she said standing and going over to the table where the pictures lay scattered around. She picked up the one Lilley and I had both spotted. She came and handed it to Michaela.

'Looking back I made a bit of a fool of myself and flirted a little with Paul. I did it to make Max jealous; I'll admit that. Paul was actually shocked and clearly rejected my advances, but I noticed a look in your eyes Max, that made my blood run cold. That picture was taken that night. Then just before Paul's next visit Maxwell told us to go to some barns near Kolin and we were all to rendezvous there. It was very secretive and he said we would be briefed at the barn.

'We arrived early and then we were set upon by some Russian soldiers. Petr was tied up on a wall and hit with a rifle butt, not once but several times,' Natalia stopped and cleared her eyes. Tears were running down her cheeks and her voice had become a little horse.

'I was tied up and one of the soldiers pulled off my undergarments and I was expecting the worst when I saw Max come into the barn. He seemed furious the men hadn't put the hood over my head. I started to protest but the hood was then put over my head and I was gagged so tightly I could hardly breathe. I heard some more scuffling and then the hood is raised and there is Paul being held by two of the soldiers. Then you lifted my skirt,' she said her voice hardened, 'I'll never forget how you looked at me.'

'Max I saw such hate in your eyes that day. When you started to taunt Paul how he knew about my body, I then I realised how jealous you were. You were in a jealous rage Max,' she said into Lilley's face. Lilley had put his head back and put his hands over his face. 'Max,' she suddenly said softly. Lilley let his hands down and looked at Natalia. 'If you hadn't had me gagged I would have told you how I felt about you. You certainly didn't need to rape me.'

Lilley's eyes widened again and his mouth slightly opened; he wanted to speak but I could tell his whole body was rigid.

'Then I thought I was going to be raped by all those soldiers as one came forwarded and ripped off my skirt, but suddenly, Paul is knocked out and then the hood is put over my head again. I heard a lot of noise but nothing made sense and eventually I am cut down, by which time my arms and back are completely dead with the pain. Then as the barn goes quiet my legs are forced open and a man, well a man, you know takes me. But that man had a very distinctive cologne, Maxwell, very distinctive indeed, it was your cologne, and when you, well when you, *did your task*, I heard your moan.'

'You fancied me?' Lilley said moving forward in his seat and holding out his hand to take hers.

'Don't touch me,' she said to him, uncertainly. 'That was then. Let me tell you what your hatred caused.' Michaela moved and went and sat on the other arm of the chair putting her hand on her shoulder. 'You don't have to do this,' Michaela said softly. Natalia patted her hand.

'I have to, for I want you to know what you did, Maxwell,'

she said. I looked around the room and saw the stern faces. Hana was leaning on the wall by the alcove her head down, and I could see tear drops fall onto the floor. 'The police came and you had managed to squirm your way out of what you did. We were put in prison on some jumped up charges which were eventually dropped; but Petr never recovered. His brain had been damaged and he could barely do menial jobs. I agreed to marry him: I had no choice in order to get somewhere decent to live, but Petr didn't seem to comprehend what was going on; we were never husband and wife. Then my son was born. He was the one good thing in my life. Petr and I loved him, but Petr was getting worse and three years later he died. I brought up Maximillian by myself.'

I noticed even Carter made a small check when he heard the name of Natalia's son.

'Maximillian?' Lilley started to stand up. 'Why call him that?'

'Don't be a fool Max. Petr and I were close friends but there had never been any sexual relationship. We were married as I needed to help him, but we never even slept together; let alone had sex. The father of my son was you.'

Nobody moved. The room seemed full of small sounds, creaking floor boards and heavy breathing, some sobs and the ticking clock. Lilley had risen and was standing his body swaying slightly.

'What happened to him?' He looked towards Natalia his eyes searching hers.

'As far as I know he is alive, but I don't know where.'

Lilley seemed to straighten and he looked puzzled towards Natalia, and then towards Hana, her head still bowed.

'He was a good boy. I loved him and I am proud to say he loved me. He fussed over me when he was small as he could sense my unhappiness, especially after Petr died. It was him that kept me going and encouraged me to open up my little bar. He was tall, very tall, athletic and good at football. He worked hard at school, but always seemed to struggle; he wasn't academic. Then just before he was going to go for an apprenticeship he came home and announced his girlfriend was pregnant. She was a really lovely girl and as my little business was going well I was actually quite pleased, except that they were both so young. Then disaster struck.' Natalia looked towards Hana and waved her to come over to her. Hana did so still keeping her head down. Natalia moved over a little and sat Hana down beside her.

'Maxamillian's girlfriend died during the birth. But her death was not in vain, she gave birth to Hana.' Hana looked up and I could see her eyes swelling with tears. In front of her was her Grandfather but she didn't know whether to hate him for what he had done or to embrace him. 'Maxamillian could not handle the grief and started to drink and not care about poor Hana, so I adopted her. He left when she was no more than three years old, and I haven't seen him since.'

'You haven't seen him, but have you communicated in any way,' I asked.

She turned and looked at me trying to force a smile.

'He writes to me three times a year. Christmas, my birthday and, of course, Hana's.' She looked back towards Lilley.

'You have a son Maxwell. I don't know where because he never sends an address, so I never reply. It is the one thing I struggle to forgive him for. He should know about Hana. He hasn't seen her for over twenty years.' Natalia pulled her granddaughter into her arms. 'But we're OK, aren't we?' she whispered into the young woman's ear.

Lilley slumped back into his seat struggling to take in what he had just been told. He looked up towards Carter. 'Did you know anything about this,' he said to him. Carter shook his head. 'You don't have an idea where the lad is?' he asked Natalia again.

'The last few postmarks have been from Israel, but have they have come from as far as Australia and quite a few from London' she said watching Lilley carefully.

'Max, I have to take you back to see Reeves-Dodd,' said Carter turning towards the man with the suit. 'As long as I can persuade the authorities here not to detain you for a range of offences.'

'Offences what have I done?' said Lilley indignantly.

'In Prague, let's start with mugging,' said Carter nodding his head towards me. 'Breaking and entering as a second and if Natalia wishes, then a rape charge will see you banged up for a very long time.' I noticed Natalia shake her head; Lilley glared at Carter. 'Then back home we have a charge of assault of a woman in a London hotel; a certain Alison Wilson. How's that for a start.'

Lilley closed his eyes. 'The bitch, that's an absolute lie. What's she said Carter?'

Carter ignored him and went to the alcove and took down the miniature painting. 'I already have a similar picture in my possession, and I believe we will find them on a list of stolen art treasures from 1945. It seems the Nazis got the blame for their disappearance, but you took them didn't you? It was when you realised that they were worth a lot more as a set that you started to get back the ones you'd given away to your lovers. Am I right?'

Lilley let out a long breath and lent forward again. 'Looks as if you might as well lock me up and throw away the key,' he whispered to the room. 'Strange you spend your entire life in the service of your country …' Lilley stopped and raised his head looking at Natalia. 'Will you ever forgive me?'

'I already have. I decided the hate I had built up for you was actually consuming *me*,' she said placing a hand on his shoulder. 'Maximillian became my life and I really loved him so much. I re-lived those terrible weeks over and over again in my mind and finally I decided I had a part to play in the consequences.'

'Please Natalia, don't blame yourself,' interjected Michaela. 'He is all to blame for this.' Michaela flashed a withering look at Lilley.

'No Michaela, you're wrong. If I hadn't forgiven him and got on with my life and loving my son then I, well I, wouldn't have survived.' She put her arm around Hana. 'And then along came Hana, and my life was full again. I have simply loved bring her up, and how proud I am. Do you know she is already lecturing at the university?' Hana took her grandmother in her arms.

'If you can forgive, then so can I,' Hana said, standing up in front of Lilley. 'Mr. Lilley, or should I say grandfather, I will try to forgive you, but you must promise me one thing.'

'Anything,' stammered Lilley, disbelief mingled with surprise filling the contours on his face.

'You will do everything in your power to get my father home, and to help gran as much as you can.' Hana picked up one of Lilley's hands and held it tightly. 'Do you promise?'

'I most certainly do but,' he looked towards Carter and the suited policeman, 'I don't have time on my side and I suspect I am not going be around for a long time, am I Carter?'

'The law is the law, but considering all that has been said here, I'll try my best to help you all,' Carter said waving away Michaela's protestations. 'You will however be coming to London with me. There is no getting out of that.'

Natalia stood up and walked towards me. 'How did you find me and why?' she asked.

'My father died a few weeks ago,' I started. Natalia nodded and her eyes dropped; I heard her mutter a quick prayer. 'I found the letters he had left, I think for me, and then there was one he had written just before he died and he asked me to visit you. He hinted that things had not been good, and well as I am going through a bit a difficult patch myself …'

'So *we* were running from Lilley here and his thugs; just in case anybody has forgotten,' interjected Michaela. 'I am not sure why everyone is becoming so coy with this evil man but I …'

'Thank you Michaela, if you don't mind I will sort the situation out, as appropriate,' said Carter nodding at the plain clothes policeman.

'Charles! I would like to know …'

'Not now and not here, please Michaela I have a job to do,' said Carter, taking Lilley's shoulder and leading him out of the room. 'I'll see you back at David's hotel when I've finished.'

'Charles! You're always saying, "I'll tell you later", well this is just not good enough …'

'Michaela would you please shut up.' I noticed Carter's eyes narrow as he spoke to her. 'Later, trust me.'

Lilley was being escorted out of the room when he stopped and turned. 'Natalia, Hana,' he said looking at them in turn. 'I *will* make amends, I give you my word.'

'Huh,' I muttered. 'Leopards don't change their spots.' I saw Michaela nodding with me.

'Pinner,' he said moving his head towards me, his voice clear and surprisingly calm. 'My hatred for your father has brought nothing but grief. A few moments ago I have just seen and heard something that has astonished me.' He turned to Natalia and made a small bow of his head. 'She defeated her hatred by forgiving and loving others; something my life is totally lacking. But I have just been told I have a son. A son who is clearly troubled, or so it seems. I also have a young granddaughter who has good reason to hate me, but has given me a chance. Well this leopard is going to change his spots, you can bank on it.'

I flushed and stepped back. Lilley was led out and Michaela and I sat on the sofa together. Natalia and Hana sat opposite and held each other muttering in their native tongue.

'I don't understand it Michaela. He does all those things, causes all that grief, finds a long lost son *and* then it seems to me Carter is going to go soft on him.' I closed my eyes and recalled Jason's look he gave me from the school bus a few days before. 'My Father's dead and I've lost my son …'

'Oh David, for heaven's sake, you've not lost your son, pull yourself together. Let's get back to the hotel, I want a word with Carter,' she said standing.

'It works you know,' said Natalia. 'Forgiveness is the only way.'

'Well I'm not quite in the mood for that yet,' I said. 'That bastard caused my father nothing but trouble …'

'What do you think he did to me?' asked Natalia quietly.

'Yes, well I am glad you're at peace with yourself,' I said noticing Michaela moving towards the door.

I said my goodbyes to them both and wished them well.

Michaela seemed very distant and in a world of her own. We walked slowly through town watching the bustling crowds.

'She may have a point Michaela,' I eventually said as we stopped to look in a shop window. 'Why go on fighting it.'

'I just hate that liberal pretentious type who can forgive at a whim. It lets the likes of Lilley get away with things. An eye for an eye is what I believe in,' said Michaela bending to examine a handbag in the corner of the window.

'Damn my father's letters, I've left them there,' I said starting to turn around.

'Charles has them.'

'You let him take them,' I said a little aghast.

'Look David, he is actually a really good guy. A bit secretive at the moment but he wants this to be resolved for the best.' Her voice tapered away and she slowly straightened herself a frown developing on her face.

'Are you and he, err you know,' I said watching her straightening up.

'No, but don't rule it out,' a smile pushing away her frown. 'You *are* perceptive.'

'Well it was just you seemed to have sided with him ever since I met you both today.' We continued to amble along and eventually came to the main town square. Michaela ignored most of what was going on around her and her frown had returned. Parties of tourist were being shuffled along by anxious guides towards the Astronomical clock as the top of the hour approached. 'You know Michaela,' I said stopping, 'there is still something not quite right about dad's relationship with Lilley. A blind man on horse back can now see he has been a traitor and raped a woman. What is Carter waiting for, why doesn't he bang the man up?'

'It seems strange, but did you see the look Charles gave me? It was as if it was a plea to keep quiet, for now.' She also stopped and turned to me. 'You *insist* on pressing charges against Lilley for assault. I have got a hunch.'

'Hunch? Your colloquial English is improving being around me. So what's your hunch then?'

Michaela stood in the middle of the square, vendor's stalls and buskers all around. 'Ask yourself this. Why did the British Government seem so sure Lilley was not a spy? Carter didn't seem to be surprised by what Natalia told us, except the bit about Lilley's child.' She paced a little and I followed.

I started, 'I still want to know why Lilley suddenly took it upon himself to come after the letters and of course don't forget the paintings. Natalia had one as well.' We squeezed our way past the crowds trying to get back to our hotel. 'So come on what is your hunch?'

'Lilley isn't what we think he is,' she stopped to face me.

'What?'

'David, think about it. We have been looking at this as if our father was the only one who seemed to think Lilley was a spy, or traitor. What if the British Government ... No it's absurd. Come on I need a drink,' she said linking my arm.

'What if MI6 knew he was a spy, you mean,' I said; the thought coming to me like a punch to my body. Michaela looked at me her eyes questioning.

'Or what if, that *was* his role ...'

'Oh, my God. Then dad could have been blowing his cover all along.'

'Insist that you want to press charges, and let's see what Charles has to say.' Michaela pulled on my arm. 'Come on let's get back to the hotel.'

'I think your man Carter knows a lot more than he's letting on. Do you know, I'm not sure if I want to delve into this anymore?'

'Too late to back out now,' she said excitedly, striding out towards my hotel.

Chapter 18

RETURN TO LONDON

Michaela and I walked to my hotel and waited. We drank coffee; the conversation consisted of trivia as we both absorbed our own thoughts. Carter called her on the mobile after an hour and a brisk, curt conversation followed. Michaela made a few notes, interspersed with the occasional protest.

'Charles, you may as well know that David is going to press charges …' She had been cut short again and I could just make out Carter's distant voice from the mobile. A frown came over her face. She muttered a goodbye and looking at the phone turned it off.

'Charles is flying back direct to London. He wants us to return to Vienna immediately and then fly back to London from there,' she said throwing her mobile into her handbag and flicking her head so her hair tossed over her right shoulder. 'I have never been treated in such a way.'

'Are you in your car?' I asked, rather grateful I would be able to go back to Vienna to collect my things. 'Do we need to book a flight?'

'Yes, I have my car, and no it seems he has organised the flights. He will meet us tomorrow for lunch, in the …' she checked her notes, 'the Window's Bar at the Hilton Hotel on Park Lane.' She looked again at her pad. 'We'd better make a move; the flight is early in the morning.'

I had the embarrassing task of booking out of my room again, but they didn't charge me and thought the whole situation typical of an Englishman. We walked to where Michaela had parked her car and started the journey back. Once on the main road I decided to ask a few questions.

'How is Grete?'

'Oh, she is fine. Naturally she is weak and tired but the doctors say she is quite healthy considering she has had four heart attacks,' she said glancing at me occasionally. 'She really wants to see you again.'

'Yes, that would be nice, I would really like that.'

'We won't have time today, but I *do* hope you come over soon.'

'You can count on it,' I said already looking forward to the trip. 'What happened with your husband?'

'I agreed to a divorce and as quickly as possible,' she said revving the engine and overtaking. 'With all the drama at the time and I now know why he brought his whore and kids. I could hardly object with all that racket going on. Makes me sick how some girls seem to have kids without trying. It was so noisy; I just couldn't think straight. And you?'

'Erica's moved to a town outside Milan. Nowhere near as nice as Lucca. But I had all the right intentions only to be confronted by a rather large belly on her …'

Michaela threw me a quick glance. 'She's pregnant?'

'Yes, and is desperate to marry Giovanni …'

'What about Jason?'

'No it's not Jason, but *Jasone*.' I put my head back on the head rest and closed my eyes. 'Jason seems alright about it, but when he went off on a school trip, the look he gave me made me shiver.'

'What do you mean?'

'I am not sure if I wanted to see something in his eyes, but it looked like a cry for help,' I said recalling him waving at me from the school bus. Michaela turned to look at me. 'Michaela keep your eyes on the road!' My right foot had hit the mat so hard it hurt. 'Some boys were also kicking his bag about.'

'That's typical of children. Leif's kids seemed to be constantly fighting …'

We remained silent, neither of us daring to bring up our conversation about my father and Lilley.

'Well, I am going to make sure we get to the bottom of all this when we get to London,' she suddenly blurted out just after we crossed the Austrian border. 'I am really angry with Charles. I have demanded he tells me what he knows on more than one occasion, and all I get is, "all in good time, my dear".'

'Well I for one want those letters back,' I said my stomach tightening. 'And even if Lilley was part of a larger scheme, what he did to Natalia is inexcusable …' Michaela nodded but she didn't answer.

We arrived in Vienna towards early evening. Michaela parked and we went for a light supper in a café not far away.

'So how did you find me,' I asked her after ordering.

'We found the car-hire company, and they told us you would possibly leave the car in Prague.' She looked towards me with a scolding eye. 'I was really upset you didn't want me with you.'

'Sorry, but I didn't want to kick my heels and with your husband …'

'Anyway, Charles made a lot of phone calls, and the next thing he orders me to drive to Prague. It seems you had been traced. He does have a lot of contacts and wields some impressive influence.' Michaela played with her food. 'Anyway we eventually found your hotel; only to have missed you by a couple of hours. Carter then got a call that you were booked on a flight to London, but you hadn't taken it. We took the chance you'd return to the same hotel,' she put her fork down. 'Then you did another runner, as Charles called it. No excuse this time?'

'If I had turned up with you and Carter in tow, it may have made the situation more complicated. I felt I was getting somewhere, and well, I will admit Michaela, I wanted to do it by myself.' I cleared my plate conscious Michaela had hardly touched her food.

'It was a good job we did catch up with you. David, if we hadn't you would have been given another beating and we could have lost everything,' she said watching me closely. 'Now let's finish this off together.' I nodded in agreement.

'Michaela I have to confess it is worrying me that your hunch about Lilley is right. Did dad get it all wrong? I am almost glad he never found out himself.'

'Even so there is no excuse for what he did to Natalia. Well it won't be long now before we find out, so let's get back and have an early night.' She caught the waiter's eye, signing the air. 'You also need to get home. Your mother will be back any day now, and we didn't put the trunk back.'

I smiled and nodded. 'The first thing I must do is to make sure *my* mother doesn't know what is going on. She would be *devastated.*' We gave each other a nervous laugh. 'I thought I would be able to tell mum, but I am not so sure now. I found out more about my father in two weeks,' I continued, 'than I could ever have imagined. I have a feeling tomorrow will reveal something that I am not sure I want to know. How could you keep all that locked inside you?'

Michaela thought for a moment and whispered, 'and then leave it for us to find after he is gone?'

The next day we collected our tickets from the ticket desk and took the plane to London. I went to my flat first and settled Michaela in. I made a few phone calls especially to establish my mother's and sister's movements. My Uncle James thought they would be home in two days or so. We were both quiet and pensive. We then took a taxi to the Hilton Hotel on Park Lane, and taking the lifts to the top floor stepped out to be confronted by the magnificent panoramic view of London. Michaela gasped and stood transfixed by the scene.

'There's Buckingham Palace,' I said pointing below. 'Big Ben,' I indicated a bit further away.

'What a view …'

'Spectacular isn't it,' said Carter from behind us.

'Oh, Charles you made me start,' said Michaela turning. She kissed him on the cheek. 'I am actually very angry with you …'

'You won't be. Come on,' he said turning and leading us into a virtually empty restaurant and up onto a raised area on the far side. A small rotund man sat at a table by the window, sipping some wine. When he saw us he stood and came around the table.

'Ahh, I am so glad you could come,' he said holding out his hand. I noticed the envelope containing the letters on the table. 'My name is Rupert Reeves-Dodd,' he continued noting my interest in the envelope. He motioned for us to sit down and waved his hand to a waiter standing by the door. 'I have taken the liberty of ordering some Hors d'oeuvres and an excellent Sancerre they keep here.' We both nodded, and watched as he opened his brief case extracting several files.

The waiter brought a huge platter of food and filled our glasses with wine, but Michaela wanted just water. We all took a bit of food and waited as Reeves-Dodd prepared some paper work handing it to Carter.

'I think it best that Charles explains everything,' he said filling his fork with some herring and nodding at Carter.

'First the administration,' said Carter, a little warily. 'If you want to know everything,' he looked directly at Michaela, 'then you have to sign the Official Secrets Act.'

I started to protest, but he cut me short.

'David this is the *only* way, and believe me it is an issue we will not compromise on.'

'We, who exactly is we?' I asked.

'You are dealing with Her Majesty's Government,' interjected Reeves-Dodd. 'I am the Deputy Director of MI6, and I, or we, would like your full co-operation. Believe me larger issues are at stake here. Carter also believes you may have deduced that all is not exactly as it seems.' Michaela and I shot each other a startled glance.

Carter waited until the Deputy Director had finished. Took out his pen and passed me a form. My personal details were already on the paper so all I had to do was sign. I took a deep breath my guts telling me not to sign, but my heart desperate to know everything; I signed. Michaela followed suit. Carter checked the signatures and put them back into the file. He looked at Reeves-Dodd and raised his eyebrows. Reeves-Dodd nodded and taking his wine sat back in his chair.

'I'll quickly run though events as they happened. Most you either already know or certainly suspect,' said Carter picking at a piece a smoked salmon. Taking a sip of wine he lent forward towards Michaela and I, putting his elbows on the table.

'Paul Pinner was recruited by MI6 in early 1943, and his talents meant he was a natural choice for the pilot in any negotiation team in Operation Scorpion. This was a mission to try and persuade the German Military High Command to surrender and join us in the real conflict; communism versus capitalism, in short, fight the Russians. It is a long story but Paul was at the time flying very sensitive equipment to the Russians and, at the same time, carrying out reconnaissance. More importantly he was dropping messages to our German contacts, and on one of his trips he was going to divert and rendezvous with our German counterparts. Then it seems the Russians got wind of the plan and your Father was captured in Poland.

'He was interrogated and as I have mentioned he faced a firing squad. It turned out to be a scare tactic. It worked as it spurred him on, and the crew, to make a most daring escape to Italy. It was during this episode he heard a code name which he thought nothing of at the time, however later on this code was a reference for Lilley.'

'Ahh, now I see …' I started to say but Carter glanced at me annoyed at being interrupted.

'Anyway,' he continued, 'he now found himself in Italy where as luck had it he was in the right place at the right time and actually piloted the Operation Scorpion mission; which regrettably didn't work.'

'Why?' I asked trying to imagine my father facing a firing squad.

'It is another long story, and a complicated one,' interjected

Reeves-Dodd. 'The Americans wanted total surrender, as they had the bigger picture in mind. A weakened Britain after the war meant they would have more influence in the world arena filling the void that was left; it could only be good for them. Churchill, it seems, was the only one that could see this.'

'Well it was during this operation that Paul became suspicious of Lilley. Hatred grew between them, and was fuelled by a woman.' Carter made a weak smile. 'There is always a woman! Lilley met Grete Semmler, later von Berckendorff, in Vienna, and it seems had quite a thing for her. Paul Pinner turns up and takes her affections, as well as making accusations against Lilley. Lilley found out Pinner was virtually engaged back at home to the daughter of Sir Richard Ryder, a very prominent person in Whitehall, and so started to threaten Pinner. This fuelled the feud but didn't stop Pinner from trying to get the authorities to listen to his claims.'

'But why didn't the authorities listen to my father?' I asked.

'Patience David, have some patience,' said Reeves-Dodd with an understanding smile. I sat back feeling Michaela watching me.

'The answer is simple but very sensitive information; hence you signing the Official Secrets Act,' said Carter taking a sip of wine. 'Lilley was a communist sympathiser and had become a KGB spy, or so we suspected. It so happened that a plan was devised to use Lilley, unsuspecting of course, as a plant, not quite a double agent, but as good as.'

'I told you, David,' said Michaela leaning over and taking a sip of my wine.

Carter gave an exasperated look towards Michaela and continued. 'The interesting development was Pinner's aspersions actually played into our hands. The Russians knew of Pinner's suspicions and this cemented Lilley's credibility in their eyes. If something is too squeaky clean in this game it raises more suspicion from the other side.

'Lilley was then used for years. He gave false information to them about agents, our defences and new projects; the list is endless. The best thing is, he never knew. That is what made the plan so perfect, for if you really believe in something you can be very convincing and persuasive. However, even despite the breakdown of the Soviet Union, we are reluctant that Lilley ever finds out about how he has been used. We are not sure how he would react.'

I raised my eyebrows questioningly.

'Well if the Russians got to know the information from Lilley was planted, who knows what they would start digging up. They may have even work out who were genuine agents and who weren't. More importantly there are still some bits of information we would rather they kept on believing. You never know what phoenix may arise from the Soviet ashes.' Carter stopped and observed the two of us. I noticed neither of us had eaten a thing; Michaela had drunk most of my wine.

'Well, actually we had started to come up with this theory ourselves,' said Michaela.

'We thought you might,' said Reeves-Dodd nodding. 'That is why Carter here insisted you were told the truth.

'Thank you Charles, I appreciate it,' said my half-sister.

'You were wearing me down with your constant questions,' he said winking at her.

'But this doesn't explain ...' I started.

'Let me finish David please,' said Carter while Reeves-Dodd topped up the wine.

'Well the Russians knew Pinner was MI6 but his role in negotiating their products for our raw materials was crucial to their economy, as they had little hard currency. So they played along. Of course Petr and Natalia then became involved in Prague as we tried to establish what had happened to a whole network of agents who had worked for us during the Nazi occupation. This was of little consequence to the Russians, in fact they were quite accommodating.

'Then the hatred between the two men bubbled over and you both heard from Natalia herself what happened. However it was decided that we had to pull Pinner out as the situation was slowly getting out of control. We spoke to his company and he was switched to other territories.' Carter stopped to take some food.

'You didn't know about the incident in the barn and the rape?' I asked watching Reeves-Dodd.

'Not exactly, all we knew was that Pinner was out of his depth and we had to believe Lilley's story for us to continue using him. The spy game is a dirty one and has no scruples.'

'So that was why you seemed to protect Lilley in Prague,' said Michaela.

'I had to ensure that he never suspected anything other than what Natalia told him. I didn't want you two blasting out questions which could even hint to him that he had been used …'

'So he does get off scot-free and not only that finds out he has a son,' I said anger starting to fill me.

'Max Lilley played a major role in some of best intelligence scams we played on the Russians. In some respects he laid down the foundation for us making the Russians believe we *would* use our nuclear deterrent, if we were forced to. Let's face it in the 50s and 60s the Russians would have been in Paris quicker than the Germans in 1940!' Carter laughed but realised his attempt at humour had failed.

'But why don't you arrest him for spying and make out you hadn't been feeding him information, and that all he did was genuine,' asked Michaela. 'Then that cements his deception, and he gets his comeuppance.'

'Oh, if only it was that simple,' interjected Reeves-Dodd. 'The simple truth is a court case of this magnitude would only rake up so much stuff. The press will always turn such a trial into a circus and quite frankly we were worried that the real truth may even come out. Trust me the press will probably take his side and he will get the sympathy vote.'

'We decided,' continued Carter, 'that this way would be best for all, and you will have the satisfaction of knowing that you will have played a part in ensuring the deception will continue. One other circumstance of such a court case would be all this becoming public knowledge, especially your father's role …'

'Oh my god, I never thought of that. Won't Lilley think it strange to get off without any repercussions?' I asked. 'And what about those miniature pictures?'

'Ah, yes thanks for reminding me,' said Carter. 'Well it seems Lilley had taken a set of eight pictures from the house he visited during Operation Scorpion. This house had been owned by Jews and they had been taken to one of the death camps. The pictures were listed as missing after the war and that they had been taken by the Nazis. Lilley still has five of them, but he realised that their worth could be multiplied by a huge factor if they were a full set, and he started to try and find the missing three; I now have them.'

Michaela and I both went to ask more, but Carter held up his hands.

'He gave one to Grete, who then in turn gave it to Pinner. Hence why he mentioned it to his two accomplices; I'll come to the letters later. I have that picture from the dealer you went to see in London. Then he gave one to Natalia, and he apparently thought she would have sold it due to her dire financial situation, he was surprised when he saw it in Natalia's house.'

The final one,' interrupted Reeves-Dodd, 'he gave to a young graduate internee working in MI6 twenty years ago and who he had had a long standing affair with. She has recently admitted to providing information to Lilley and she gave me the picture when I interviewed her a few days ago.'

'Don't tell me you gave him the three back so he could get more money,' I almost shouted.

'David, settle down, for God's sake,' said Michaela putting her hand on my shoulder.

'I think you have to stand back and see the whole situation here, David,' said Carter. 'Despite what you think Lilley also did a lot of dirty work on our behalf, he had to or his cover would have been blown. Then, surprise surprise, towards his later life changed his ideologies. Yesterday I sat with Lilley and struck a deal with him. Natalia didn't want to press any charges …'

'The stupid woman,' shouted Michaela. 'Can't you bring the charges against him, he admitted to it in front of us all.' Carter shook his head.

'As I was saying, so for the greater good of all we wanted the whole affair to be resolved quietly and quickly. It is clear to me Lilley is going to spend the rest of his days finding his son and helping Natalia. He gave me the five remaining pictures which are going to be returned to their rightful owners. I told him that we were prepared to forget the whole affair due to his past record. He has agreed to never contact either of you two, or your families. If he does then we told him charges would be pressed by yourself,' he said nodding at me. 'You legally have six years in which you can press charges.'

'So, I *was* right. He will walk away scot-free, and be allowed to go and find his son. Still getting his full pension,' my voice raised again. 'Hiring two thugs to beat me up is allowable for your convenience.'

'As Charles said,' Reeves-Dodd whispered leaning forward. 'There are no scruples in this game, and I won't let years of hard work and people risking their lives to be ruined for the sake of a couple of small incidents with you.' Reeves-Dodd face was stern and his eyes sent a shiver down my spine. 'Your father had the sense to keep his mouth shut about certain aspects of his life I suggest you do the same.'

The atmosphere tightened as Reeves-Dodd patience was running out. 'Lilley will get his pension, and he will be allowed to go and find his son and hopefully help those two poor women in Prague. You,' he looked towards me, 'can have the satisfaction of knowing a lot more about your father than you ever expected.' He reached over picked up the envelope and slid it across the table at me. 'Here are the letters, although I have taken the liberty of extracting a couple of sensitive ones.' He then opened another file, 'and here is a letter from the owner's of the miniature paintings, with the cheque for the reward.'

I took the letter and the cheque. My animosity towards this man growing by the second. 'Reward? If you think I, err we, are going to be bought off …' My eyes dropped back to the cheque. 'Bugger me,' I whispered and handed them to Michaela.

Michaela looked at the cheque and her eyes widened. 'As David said,' she started to stammer, 'we are not going …'

'Well you can do what you like with the money,' said Reeves-Dodd finishing his drink. 'I must remind you of *what* you signed at the beginning of this meeting and if either of you so much as breathes a word then I'll bang you up so quick your feet won't touch the ground. Now I must bid you goodbye, and I hope you both take the pragmatic view on this affair.'

Reeves-Dodd stood and walked away not offering us a handshake and left Michaela and I sat dumbfounded looking at Carter. A few silent moments passed as the bright sunshine sparkled in the wine glasses.

'I do not like that man,' said Michaela leaning forward and grabbing my glass again. 'Sorry David I need a drink.' She gulped all my wine down.

'He does have a job to do,' said Carter watching us.

'You knew he would wield the Official Secrets Act if we didn't play ball, didn't you?' I demanded.

'Look, I think you should also be aware that Lilley did a lot of good work for us. He has a pretty pitiful pension, no family and if we left him to fester he would be more than a nuisance. Locking him up would cause a stink as I have said; so it was the only sensible solution.'

'So why did he want the letters as well?' I asked remembering he had not explained this.

'Quite simply his informant, or lover, had mentioned to him that he had been cross-linked with Pinner and a few other files. This *cross-linking* would have been certainly interpreted by Lilley that something was not right. He believed Pinner's letters would have confirmed or denied this. I believe Lilley just started to consider the possibility he had been used.' Carter fiddled with a piece of celery and cheese. 'My job when I was negotiating with him yesterday was to ensure he didn't get any wind of the amount of damage he had caused the Soviets. He just might have blown the whistle out of sheer spite.' He watched as we sat sullen faced, Michaela playing with her food while I stared into my empty glass.

'I know it is hard to all take it all in and even harder to accept, but you must believe me it is ultimately for the best. I am not joking when I said a court case would have meant *everything* coming out. Your mother would have learnt about the whole affair but possibly from the gutter press. I also didn't want to see such a man as Lilley being allowed to walk free, but all our work would have been compromised,' said Carter filling our glasses with wine. 'I really had to fight with Reeves-Dodd to let you have the letters back.'

'I think we should burn them,' I said turning to Michaela. 'You can take what you want for yourself and Grete, but I *do not* want those letters back anywhere near my mother.'

To my surprise Michaela nodded. 'Let me speak to Grete. I know she read them everyday, but you never know, maybe she wants to let go before she dies.'

'Well I must get back to my parents' house. I spoke to my Uncle James yesterday and my mother is coming home in two days. I have a lot of work to do before she gets back.' I finished my wine and started to leave picking up my envelope and the cheque Reeves-Dodd had given me. 'What are you going to do Michaela?'

'I am not absolutely sure ...'

'Well why don't I show you around London for a few days?' said Charles.

'You can have the full use of my flat,' I offered.

'That would be lovely, thank you both.' A smile started to lighten her troubled brow. 'How are you at shopping Charles?' Charles just put his head in his hands and we all burst out laughing, relieving the tension of the moment.

We went back to my flat and Michaela called her mother straight away. A long conversation ensued in German. Finally it ended and she joined Charles and I in the lounge. We had decided to switch to tea.

'Well she says that she will leave the decision to us,' said Michaela. 'What ever we decide to do she will agree with, on one condition.'

'What?' I said. Carter frowned.

'That you visit her soon, very soon.'

'I agree, in fact let's put something in the diary. I don't start work again until September so we have plenty of time.' I offered Michaela a cup of tea but she declined. 'So what shall we do with them?'

'Let's bury them with Paul …'

'Michaela you can't go digging up graves and plonking stuff in them,' I said slightly exasperated with her logic. 'Let's burn them.'

'All of them? David that's a bit drastic, isn't it,' my half-sister said looking at the envelope.

I took the envelope empting the letters and thumbing through them. 'OK then all the ones relating to Grete and yourself we take back to your mother,' I said studying one of them. 'Any to do with my parents I give to Mum and the rest I'll burn. If there are any left,' I said continuing to examine the letters. 'How many did Reeves-Dodd take Charles?'

'All the MI6 and letters relating to Lilley.'

'Well there is not an awful lot left to burn,' I said picking up the cheque. 'I'll bank the cheque and give you half Michaela.'

'No you will not,' she said looking at me sternly. 'You take the money; I think you have more need being on just a teacher's wage …'

'Hey, I'm not that badly paid!'

'Oh, just take it David. Give it to charity or start a trust for Jason. If you want I will use the money in the Austrian bank accounts. In fact, David, take the all the letters as well, it is time to look forward. I think I will go on a long cruise and hopefully meet a wealthy man who will spoil me.'

I noticed the glance between Michaela and Charles. She was watching his reaction, I thought.

'OK, I've never had so much spare cash, but I will think about what to do with it and let you know before I do anything,' I said looking at the cheque with so many noughts. I'll decide what to do with the letters when everything has settled down.' Michaela nodded.

'When are you going to your parents house?' asked Carter.

'Well I was considering going in the next hour or so,' I said gathering up the letters. 'I had promised mum I would clear out Dad's clothes and stuff before she came home. So as she is with my bossy sister I had better at least make a start.'

I packed a few essentials and had the feeling of being like an unwanted parent with a sibling who had their first lover around and waiting for some privacy.

I drove back to Knutsford without the radio on; the silence giving me the opportunity to assimilate the past two weeks. Trying to imagine how my father had been able to keep all these events bottled up inside him. I kept thinking of how he had faced a firing squad, undertook a daring escape from Poland, a passionate affair with a young woman in post-war Austria. Then the day in the barns outside Prague; surely this must have haunted him. I had only known a fraction of my father; no wonder he was such a private man.

By the time I got near Knutsford I decided to visit the grave; a sense of awe growing inside me. The head stone had not been laid, so I stood by the raised earth, a few flowers still managed a splash of colour on the brown earth. I watched the sun disappear over the church and wished I could have one more evening with him.

Chapter 19

MARIE RETURNS

I drove slowly to my parents' house resisting the temptation of a quick beer at The Bells pub. Pulling into the drive my heart sank as I saw my Uncle James' car. I knew he would have many questions and I would not have the peace and quiet I felt I needed to clear out my Father's things.

'David, thank heavens it's you!'

I looked up to see my uncle coming round from the lengthening shadows at the rear of the house.

'Your mother has been frantic, despite all my reassurances,' he said with a worried smile. 'You know what she's like, especially when she is with Julie. Thinking about it, you should have spoken to her directly, she won't listen to me.'

'Quite. I'd better get my skates on and start clearing dad's stuff,' I said, shaking his hand.

'David, where have you been?' he said eyeing the fading bruises and swelling on my face.

'Uncle James you wouldn't believe it if I told you.'

'Try me,' he said helping me with my bag and opening the front door. 'Your mother will be here in the morning and …'

'Tomorrow? I thought you said she would be back in two days?'

'Yes, well it seems her brother organised an earlier flight in Business Class so she could sleep.' Uncle James started to take my case upstairs. 'Go and put the kettle on, you and I have a lot to do before she gets home,' he shouted back at me as he disappeared up the stairs; I didn't seem to hear him and sauntered into the study. I touched the Edelweiss picture; I couldn't believe it had been less than a week since I had seen Grete. Uncle James came back down and sensing my distraction went into the kitchen. I heard him fill the kettle.

'I suggest we sort out your father's clothes this evening, and I had better go and get some food from the supermarket before it closes. Your mother is organising a lunch for us all for tomorrow; well, I am actually.'

'Tomorrow? She will be absolutely shattered after her flight?' I joined my uncle in the kitchen.

James stopped what he was doing and faced me. 'Something is up David, I know it.' He searched for the tea pot. 'She seems almost desperate to get home all of a sudden and wants to have a 'family discussion' as she called it.' He warmed the pot. 'It seems your disappearance and the break-ins …'

'You told her about those?'

'Oh, David I had to,' he said looking a little sheepish. 'I also had a long chat with a Peter …'

'Wilkinson,' I interrupted. 'I bet he has been chasing me.'

'Very much so, and I also mentioned this to your mother …'

'Oh, bugger. I have an awful feeling I'm not going to keep all this quiet.'

'All what quiet, David what *is* going on?'

'Uncle James we have a lot to do and when the dust settles let's have a beer and a chat, but not now – no more questions, please. It is quite complicated.' My mind flashed back to signing the document Carter had given me yesterday. My uncle started to protest but I cut him short.

'James,' I said still feeling uncomfortable about dropping his title, 'I really can't say anymore at the moment. Believe me.' I had decided in my mind to call Carter and tell him my mother had clearly sensed something was wrong. 'OK, so you go and get all the food. I bet Julie has a list for you.' My uncle produced a piece of paper with over 40 items on it, and we both let out a loud laugh. 'Once she is home there will no chance of any peace,' I finished.

'Fine, but please go and start on your father's things, I think your mother would expect this at least.'

'Do you want anything …?'

'No, absolutely not. I'll help you, but I don't want anything. I am not being funny it's …' His voice faded and he stopped his chores, a memory absorbing his thoughts.

'James, I understand, I feel a bit the same. Am I supposed to keep any of his clothes?' My uncle shook his head and we drank our tea with just the buzz of the fridge breaking the silence.

After James left for the supermarket I slowly ascended the stairs and went into my parents' room. Night had arrived so I turned on all the lights and then taking a deep breath opened my Father's wardrobe doors and his familiar, slightly musty, smell hit me. I took a few steps back and sat on the edge of the bed staring at the neatly hung suits and jackets; shoes regimentally stored at the bottom. Part of me wanted to just put everything into large bin liners and leave the scene as quickly as possible; another part wanted to quietly close the doors. The memories were too fresh.

I sat still and recalled the day we first sailed together, riding the waves as we tried to get away from the beach. Both of us howling with joy and terror as waves flooded the boat. Neither of us would dare admit we were frightened and wanted to turn the boat round. Then the day he bought me a very expensive Cross fountain pen for passing some exams; how proud I was. The moment I had to tell him I had failed to get into sixth form; he still stuck by me and paid for yet more private tuition. His speech at my sister's wedding; the whole room rocking with laughter.

I tried to visualise him as a young man jumping into planes, or wooing a young woman. I just couldn't. My thoughts always came back to him with mum; late Sunday lunches that went on for hours with long debates about life and politics. Friday nights at The Bells pub drinking real ale and looking forward to one of mum's dinners.

'How's it going,' said my uncle putting his head round the door. I jumped up.

'I thought you were going shopping?'

'Been, done and stashed,' he said entering. 'Oh, not had a great amount of success at deciding what to do then,' he said looking at the untouched wardrobe.

'What did you do with *your* father's stuff?'

'Anything not in tip-top condition we binned, the rest we had cleaned and sent to the charity shop. No arguments. Paul turned it into a military exercise; had it done in a morning.'

'Then that's what we will do,' I said taking a pace towards the wardrobe.

'I'll get the bins bags,' James said slapping my shoulder. I had always liked my Uncle James and I now knew why; he understood the moment.

Two hours later my father's wardrobe and his drawers were cleared and piles of labelled bags were tactfully placed out of view in the garage. My uncle had volunteered to take them away the following morning on his way to the airport. I had managed to persuade him to collect my mother and sister as I was keen to make some phone calls before they returned and any chance of privacy would be lost.

My uncle and I enjoyed a few hours together sitting in my father's study reminiscing about the past. James chose his questions carefully only asking after Erica and Jason; he tactfully left it at that.

The next morning as soon as James had left I called Carter.

'Listen Charles my mother is coming home earlier than I had expected and I sense she knows something. What do I do if all this stuff about dad and Lilley comes out? What if mum really suspects something, and what if Michaela and Grete all comes to light?' I asked, hardly taking a breath.

'Wow, wow, slow down and keep calm. Call me on my mobile as soon as you know how much your mother suspects.' There was a pause and I heard him whisper something to Michaela. 'We may have to come up.'

'Don't be stupid! That is about the last …'

'Trust me David, first see how much she knows, and then call me.'

'Well I can hardly just walk off and …'

'David, I repeat, let's see how much she actually does know, and then we will take it from there.'

'OK, but it isn't going to be easy,' I said, frustrated with his cool air of authority.

I paced the house waiting for my mother and sister; my stomach tightening with anticipation. Finally I heard a car pull in and was delighted to see it was Peter Wilkinson's. I rushed out of the front door.

'Thank heavens you're here first,' I said reaching to open his car door. 'I wanted a chat before my mother …'

I looked up to see my uncle pulling into the driveway. I glanced at Wilkinson, shrugged and went over to greet them. The hugs and kisses were warm but an undertone of displeasure was confirmed by a comment that my mother made in that she was surprised I hadn't come to pick them up at the airport. Julie noticed the bruises I was supporting, but didn't comment. I went and prepared coffee as James helped them with their bags. Wilkinson sat around and I could see he felt awkward.

We drank our coffees, the conversation was stunted as we all seemed to labour on trivia and niceties. I wanted my mother to make the first move. She didn't disappoint me. When we finished she stretched and asked us all to follow her to my father's study. As we filed through the hallway I looked up the stairwell and remembered I hadn't put the trunk away. I was furious with myself.

'Oh mum, I have found a letter for both you and Julie that dad left you,' I said sensing some tension mount. 'Do you want them now?'

'No, please sit down all of you,' she said taking the Parker-Knoll by the fireplace. She scanned the faces in front of her as we settled and then looked straight at me. I watched her carefully searching for clues in her body language as to her strange behaviour.

'Before I ask you where the hell you have been or why you have clearly been in a fight,' she said slowly and our eyes locked, 'there is something I think you should see.' I noticed my sister looking at her knees and wringing her hands together. Her face was pensive. 'James could you go and fetch a crow bar or something similar. We are going to the attic.'

I shut my eyes and cursed. Then I recalled the ball of used sticky tape under the eaves. I now realised where that had come from and opened my eyes; looking straight and firmly at my mother. 'That won't be necessary,' I said. Julie's head quickly came up and four pairs of eyes stared at me. 'I have found the trunk and the letters.' My mother's eyes slowly closed and she mumbled something under her breath. She took in a deep breath.

'Have you read them?'

I nodded and stood up taking a pace towards her.

'I was so hoping you wouldn't find out this way,' she said looking up at me. 'Do you know about Michaela?'

'Yes,' I said giving Wilkinson a quick glance.

'David, where have you been in the last two weeks? Vienna?'

I nodded again. 'I also visited Erica and Jason, and then I went to Prague.'

'Prague?' My mother's eyes widened. 'I never did find out what happened there. Have you?'

I started to speak feeling a need to tell my mother everything I had found out. But then I remembered Carter again and his obnoxious colleague. Damn signing that form, I thought to myself.

'And ...' said my sister angrily.

'It seems dad had been involved in some pretty heavy stuff during and after the war. Mum, you knew about this didn't you?' She nodded putting her head down.

'Did you meet Lilley?' she whispered.

'Oh yes, I met up with him,' I said with a mock laugh in my voice.

'He hated that man more than anything or anybody,' said my mother, her voice hardening.

'Love and hate seem to have played a major role in his early life.' I went and leant on the mantle piece. 'Mum, I have signed the Official Secrets Act, and I need to check what I can or can't say.'

'Oh sure. Pull the other one David,' blurted my sister.

'I am afraid it is true,' interrupted Wilkinson. 'You have me to blame for this, as I called in MI6 when I realised that Lilley wasn't fooling around. David had a couple of close encounters with Lilley's henchmen.'

My sister's eyes focused on me and I saw her look soften.

'Well, I am not sure if I want to hear any more,' said my mother her voice faltering. 'Reading those letters was enough. I was so worried about his estate I made him put a codicil in his will.'

'What? Did dad know you had read these letters?' I gasped.

'No he was so confused at the end I had it done and told him just to sign it. He never asked or questioned anything. I have to ask you David, do you admire your father more or less since reading them?' My mother's hands were shaking.

I went and sat on the arm of my mother's chair and put my arm round her shoulders, and looked towards Julie.

'My father was the greatest. He was a fantastic dad,' I said firmly. Julie nodded. 'Wilkinson told me about his exploits in Poland, and from what I understand he did some pretty brave things.' I took a big breath. 'It seems he did have his weaknesses and moments of madness. But on the whole I am in awe of him and what he did.'

'Oh, God I miss him,' cried out my mother burying her head into my jacket. 'I knew he wasn't perfect, but he was a bloody good husband …'

'Mum,' I said softly. 'How do *you* feel about Grete and Michaela?'

She lifted her head back and taking her free arm pulled her hair back from her brow.

'Let those without sin cast the first stone. Nobody's perfect.'

A wave of giddiness came over me. I looked towards Julie who was open mouthed and her eyes stared questioningly at her mother.

'Let those without … What are you saying?' my sister muttered.

'Don't start getting carried away Julie,' she said to her daughter. 'Your father had been gone for years and initially he didn't communicate a lot. I think he was shy, while I had men over me like bees around honey. I was a young beautiful woman for heaven's sake.' Her eyes were glazed over. 'Then his letters became frequent and very passionate and when he did eventually come home, there was no question in my mind. He had been away for so long I had almost forgotten what he looked like. I knew he would have hardly been away for such a long time and been a saint, but I never expected Michaela, not really.'

'Not really!' shouted Julie.

'Just once many years ago something was troubling him …'

'Around 1971,' I interjected.

'Yes, I sensed he was going through a strange time. I just thought it was the mid-life crisis,' she finished with a weak laugh. 'Then after his stroke I found and read the letters …'

Nobody moved or spoke for several minutes.

'So David, what do you want to do?'

'Nothing, except I only wish we could have one more lunch or a dinner together. I want to look at him knowing what I know now. I would love to chat about *all* his life.'

'Oh you clod David, but that is lovely to hear, although your father was far too private for anything like that,' said my mother starting to sob quietly. 'I was worried in case you would hate him.'

'No, far from it, it's strange I feel proud of what he did; the good and the bad. If there is one thing I have learnt in all this is that hatred, or harbouring hatred, causes the individual more harm than the intended victim,' I said slowly.

'My heaven's David. What has hit you,' smiled my sister through moist eyes. 'Next thing is you will be going to church.'

'Maybe I will. I saw something in Prague which has really set me thinking,' I murmured as my sister still looked at me in bewilderment but with a tinge of respect.

'Well that Prague episode is one chapter in your father's life I don't want to hear about. He was like a man possessed for months,' said my mother drying her eyes. 'Come on I am starving. How is lunch going Julie? David you sort out some decent wine and lay the table …'

My mother briskly walked out barking more commands to her daughter and Uncle James. I smiled and knew the subject was now closed. I knew my mother too well. No need to call the all knowing Carter, I thought with relief. My sister started to follow her mother but came over to me.

'I want more than a few words with you big bro,' she whispered in my ear. 'And don't think you can wheedle your way out of it.'

I watched my sister leave the room with my uncle and I looked towards Wilkinson.

'Let those without sin cast the first stone? Who would have believed it,' he said shaking his head.

Epilogue

ONE YEAR LATER

'David,' hissed Michaela as I finished my telephone call and she ushered me out of her apartment as soon as the receiver hit the base. 'I'm worried. She is very ill you know.'

'I am sorry but Jason has just had his exam results; he is doing so well,' I said trotting behind her as we descended the stairs to the car park.

'So how come he is with you now?' she asked opening the car door and throwing in her bag onto the back seat.

'Well it seems Erica's new man lost his job, and with the baby it all became too much. I feel really sorry for her.' Michaela cast me a sideward glance. 'No seriously I am really sorry for her. I know she misses Jason so much.'

'So what happened,' she asked again, as she screeched the car around the tiny garage under the building.

'I was called to my solicitor's office, and there she was with Jason.' My right leg involuntary hit the car floor as Michaela drove out of the car park hardly looking left or right. 'She demanded visiting rights and all sort of other rights and conditions, but I was just so glad to have him back. I had a new job in Cheshire, was living at home and I couldn't believe my luck.'

'So you're living back with your mother. At your age?'

'Yes, a little odd actually,' I said gripping the door handle as Michaela swerved to miss a cyclist. 'Jason has my old room, and he goes to the local Catholic school …'

'I didn't know you were Catholic?'

'I'm not but I promised Erica he would be brought up as one, and I have to say he has settled in extremely well. It's a bloody good school. Nothing wrong with a bit of religious discipline at his age.' My half-sister gave me another sideways glance of disbelief.

'Then Uncle James has taken Julie's old room, not all the time but he helps Mum around the house. I am telling you Michaela, it is a hell of an odd household, but a happy one. The main thing is mum seems content, if I think a little lonely …'

'Lonely … sounds like a mad house to me,' said Michaela accelerating as hard as she could.

'Although at times I find her just sitting and staring into the distance. She has lost some of her zest for life.'

'Do you ever talk about your father and err, well me or Grete?' Michaela braked as a truck pulled out in front of her.

'Not exactly. It is often mentioned in a passing way,' I said seeing the quizzical look on Michaela's face. 'If there is something on television or an article in a paper then mum might say, "Sounds a bit like your father", if it mentions intrigue, affairs or such like. She actually jokes about it.' I looked at Michaela, but she still had a confused expression. 'It's difficult to explain but I think mum knew most of what happened and their generation do seem comfortable to let things lie. I have often wondered how much *her* father told her.'

'What did you do with the letters?' she asked.

'You'll see later,' I replied watching the scenery.

Michaela remained quiet and pulled the Volkswagen Golf sports hard around a corner.

'Michaela, what is the hurry?' I was shocked to see she was nearly in tears.

'Grete is very ill David, and I am frightened we may, well, we may miss her.'

'What's the problem, her heart again?'

'No, she has cancer of the pancreas, and its spread into her liver.'

'Oh, that doesn't sound good,' I said squeezing her forearm gently. 'I am surprised they didn't insist that she went to hospital.'

'There is no way my mother is dying in a hospital bed,' she said turning and looking at me for a second.

'She really wanted to see you again. Why did it take you so long?'

'I don't know; you know how life is. What with my father's probate, selling the flat in London, my new job and then Jason coming home; I just didn't have the time.' I was annoyed at myself as there was a hint of sarcasm in my voice which I hadn't intended. 'Sorry Michaela that was uncalled for. Have you seen Charles recently?' I enquired.

'You know we have, I told you. We are together, although we live hundreds of kilometres apart,' she said revving the car past a heavy wagon.

'Neither of you will move?' I asked and she just shrugged her shoulders, but I could see a little sparkle in her eyes had pushed back the tears for a moment.

We remained silent as the view of the mountains spread out before us and a few kilometres later she pulled into the drive way of her mother's nursing home. Trying to busy herself locking the car I sensed her apprehension of what might greet her when she went to her mother's apartment. A nurse came running up to her as we entered the main doors.

'Frau Von Berckendorff, she is not well, please hurry. The doctor is with her now.'

We ascended the stairs two steps at a time and Michaela rushed to her mother's door and straight through the lounge, passing a nurse seated by the window and into the bedroom. Medical equipment surrounded the bed and Grete lay propped up by several large pillows. The doctor nodded to her, whispered something in Michaela's ear and withdrew from the room giving me a concerned look. The bleeping of a machine and the light from a screen showing Grete's heart rate seemed to illuminate her face. Grete opened her eyes and as soon as she saw us she became alert.

'David, oh David, you came. I am so glad,' she exclaimed.

'Grete I *am* really sorry, but I genuinely have had a lot of things going on and …'

'It doesn't matter you're here now. What happened to the letters? I just want to read them one more time.' Her eyes were wide open expectantly.

'Yes, of course, I am sorry Grete I should have sent them …' I said handing over a small bundle of letters tied with the blue ribbon.

She eagerly undid the knot and sorting the letters started to read them. The monitor had risen and the nurse came in. She tried to make Grete comfortable but she brushed her away still searching for a particular letter.

'Here it is,' she said her eyes seeming to dance over the words on the page. 'He wrote so beautifully, listen: "I fell into those wide bright eyes, and I am still falling." How beautiful, so descriptive.' She let the letter fall and put her head back, as the bleeping from the monitor slowed down.

'Mum, are you alright?' said Michaela rushing forward.

'I am fine Michaela. I am enjoying myself remembering the best night of my life.' She closed her eyes.

'Grete,' I said. 'I have brought you a small gift.'

Her eyes opened, and Michaela also watched me. I pulled a small package from my inside pocket. 'I know Dad would have wanted you to have this,' I said passing her the package. Michaela's head went onto one side as she watched her mother tenderly take off the paper. She finished unwrapping it and smiled as she saw the small framed Edelweiss.

'Oh David, what a lovely thought,' she said a tear rolling down one cheek.

Michaela took my hand and squeezed it hard. 'David that's, well, just so thoughtful. Thank you. I'll go and make some tea. Mum do you want some?'

'No, don't go, just stay for a while would you?' she said closing her eyes again but her fingers gently folding around the framed flower.

We sat in silence for several minutes of either side of the bed. Michaela noticed it before the nurse came in. Grete's blood pressure was weakening and her heart beat had become faint. The nurse whispered in Michaela's ear. Gently withdrawing the drip from Grete's arm she turned and quickly switched off the machines. She touched Michaela's shoulder and left, closing the door behind her. The old woman made a few slow gasps, but then exhaled a long quiet moan. Her face relaxed and a serene smile formed on her face. Her shoulders dropped as the tension left her body. Michaela took her mother's hand and placed her forehead on it.

'She's gone David. Her last thought was that night with Paul. Maybe she's with him now, I do hope she is,' Michaela gently sobbed.

'Do you believe in life after death, Michaela?' I whispered.

'Most certainly; without any doubt. Look at the smile on her face. It's the happiest I have seen her for years. Don't tell me she isn't with Paul.'

'I wish I had that sort of faith.'

'You wouldn't, as it has its down sides.'

'What do you mean?'

'Imagine what will happen when Marie joins them,' she said a watery smile on her face. We started to laugh, quietly at first as not to be heard be the nurse. But the more we tried to suppress our giggles the worse they became. Finally, fighting my laughter, I decided to leave and went round the bed and put my hands on Michaela's shoulders.

'I'll let you say your goodbyes in peace, I'd better go. What the nurse and doctor must think of us laughing in here …'

'Mum would have loved it.'

I turned and left quietly starting to close the door behind me but saw Michaela's laughter turn to tears. She put her head in her hands and I watched her sob uncontrollably. The chapter was finally closed.